Student Bodyguard for Hire

CALLIE JAMES

Copyright © 2014 Callie James

All rights reserved.

ISBN-10: 0990364607
ISBN-13: 9780990364603

This story is a work of fiction and
a creation of the author's imagination.

DEDICATION

For David.
Thank you for your support and love.

CONTENTS

ACKNOWLEDGMENTS

A big thanks to Dr. Marcela Frazier and Maria Gonzalez for their assistance with all Spanish translations. Thanks to Virginia Duke for her assistance with copy editing. Thank you Kristin and Nicole, two wonderful friends who kept me going with cheers of enthusiasm. Thank you Lynn Raye Harris and Christy Reece, two amazing authors who gave me so much advice along the way.

CHAPTER ONE

Peyton

"You've got to be the bravest person I know," Adam said.

I parked Mom's Lexus along the edge of sparse lawn and followed my best friend's gaze to the white, box house where Savanna Guerra had just stepped out from behind a battered screen door. No one would know she was two years my junior. Her constant scowl and badass attitude made her seem older. She fished a lighter from her jeans pocket, lit the cigarette dangling from her lips, and found a seat on the top porch step. Inhaling deeply, her gaze drifted to Adam and me.

"Or the dumbest," I added, as she blew smoke into the September breeze.

He turned to me. "You didn't hear *me* use that word."

"You were thinking it."

"It's scary how well you know me."

Savanna narrowed her eyes as though daring me to step out of the car. I wiped my palms against my jeans. I'd been ready to talk to her brother, Sam, only thirty minutes ago. Now, not so much.

"If Ryan finds out about this," Adam said, "he's gonna freak. You know that, don't you?"

"Right now I'm more concerned about Ryan's face getting bashed into another locker." The thought of the gash above my brother's right eye only fueled my anger. "Face it. Sam Guerra is the most feared guy at school. Even the bullies won't touch him. He's my best shot and I need to do *something* while I still can. Next year I'll be gone and Ryan will be alone."

"I feel so loved."

I dreaded attending college next year without Adam, so much that I kept putting up a mental block about his junior status. "Sorry," I said. "You know what I mean. These guys are built, and you're...well, you're..."

"*Not.*"

Guilt swamped me at his dejected expression. When I eventually noticed his lip twitching, I smacked his leg and he busted up laughing. "Dammit, Adam, this is no time to fool around."

"You fall for the wounded geek act every time." He poked me in the ribs, still laughing. "Aw, c'mon. Smile for me."

I resisted his infectious cackle by acting mad. "This is *so* not funny," I said, pushing his hand away. He grabbed my knee and squeezed with two fingers, a surefire way to make me laugh, and I did until I managed to shove his hand back and scowl again. "Shh. Be *quiet*. What if Savanna can hear us?"

He looked out the passenger window. "She'd think we're mental, and she'd be right."

"I can't care about that now," I said. "We agreed I should do something *big* and this is it. There's no turning back."

"No, *I* agreed *we* should do something big. I never agreed you'd do this alone. And propositioning Sam Guerra...admit it. This is the worst idea you've ever had."

"Or the best. Can I still count on you to have my back?"

He snorted. "For what it's worth."

Adam Cooper had been my best friend since junior high. Standing at six feet, his height remained his only feature that might intimidate Sam Guerra. Otherwise, he looked like the tech geek I'd known for six years—lanky with large feet and a head of blond, wayward layers that made him appear perpetually windblown.

I held out my clenched, clammy hand to him and waited for a fist bump. "Wish me luck."

He grabbed my hand and held it against the console. "Seriously, Peyton. Rethink this. The guy nearly killed his own uncle."

"That was the media exaggerating. We don't know that for sure."

"He *hospitalized* him, Peyton. Over a week. Heart transplant patients spend less time in recovery."

"Yes, and then his uncle pled guilty to two counts of first degree assault," I pointed out. "The guy is serving so much time he may die in prison. Maybe he had it coming."

"Wow." His nose quirked. "That's more detail than I remember. Did you follow the story or something?"

I looked at the carpeted floorboard. "I'm just saying the police would have arrested Sam if he'd done something wrong."

"*Wrong?* Guerra almost beat the guy *to death*. Are you listening to yourself?"

"Yes, and I'm repeating myself, too." I glanced at Savanna, imagining the hard realities she'd experienced growing up in the northeast neighborhood where drug busts and domestic violence arrests happened regularly. Their small, white house looked misplaced with fresh paint and a well cut lawn, nowhere near the same ramshackle shape as the surrounding homes. Sam's black Chevy Impala, waxed to a beautiful shine, sat without a scratch in a section of town where people likely boosted cars daily— yet more evidence that the people in this horrid neighborhood respected him. "Ease up, Adam. Obviously, he hasn't had the easiest life."

"That sounds like your mom talking. Look, at least let me go with you."

"No. It'll go more smoothly if it's just me. You know. A girl. Non-threatening."

"Believe me, I'm no threat to Guerra."

"Give yourself a little credit. You kicked Jason Thompson all over the place, and he used to be Ridgeview High's football god."

He smirked. "*We* kicked Thompson's butt because Jon sucker punched him and I jumped him before he could get up. He never knew what hit him. Besides, blind rage can make a person do amazing feats. Thompson was lucky we didn't drop a car on his head."

I swallowed bile, wishing after three years that the memory of Jason Thompson pinning me against his truck seat wouldn't materialize every time someone asked me out. "Well, you won't have to jump on Sam Guerra."

His gaze slid to mine. "You got that right. I've seen the guy fight. He'd never let anyone get the jump on him. He's much too focused. You know, like a serial killer."

"Serial killer? For all we know, he could be the nicest guy at school."

"Who are you trying to convince?" he said, nodding at my face. "You have sweat on your upper lip."

"Because you're freaking me out," I said, wiping my lip. I glanced in the rearview mirror and pushed a lock of red hair out of my eyes. "Do I look okay?" I turned to him and schooled my features, feeling sweaty all over.

He eyed me suspiciously. "Who exactly are you trying to look okay for?"

"Anyone."

"*Anyone* would think you're gorgeous," he said. "If that's what you want."

I felt my cheeks heat. "Do you think it'll help if he finds me attractive?"

"Do you *want* Sam Guerra to find you attractive?"

Another rush of heat climbed up my neck. "I want him

agreeable. Right now, I'm so desperate I don't care why or how." I reached to the backseat for my book bag out of habit, paused and shook my head. Adam smirked at my nervousness but had the decency not to comment. "Okay, I'm ready. Now remember, only come out if I look at you. That's the signal I'm in trouble." I opened the car door before I could chicken out.

His pale face made his eyes shine bright blue. "I'm so far from okay with this I can't even tell you. Remind me when I wake from my coma that I *did* try to talk you out of this. Several times."

I pursed my lips, trying to stay all business as I stepped onto the road grit lining the patchy lawn, closed the car door, and made my way toward Sam's intimidating little sister. The Portland, Oregon autumn temperatures often fluctuated dramatically. Today it had dropped from eighty to sixty-three degrees, but no one would know it by my sweaty palms. Savanna watched me cross the grass, the sunlight hitting her eyes and transforming those hazel irises to a golden color that nearly glowed. Looking at her jaded scowl, I had difficulty remembering she was a sophomore like my brother.

"Hey." I waved once, feeling awkward. We'd never actually met. Well, I'd said *hello* once in a school bathroom but she'd never acknowledged me.

Like now.

She pulled her fingers through her glossy black hair, which fell over her forehead like a beret. She'd shaved the back and sides to half an inch over the summer, and her multiple piercings helped her pull off the punkish hairstyle beautifully.

"Can I talk to your brother?" I asked, taking a step back when she flicked cigarette ash at my boot.

She quirked the eyebrow adorned with three silver posts and pushed the cigarette between her lips. The cherry burned bright and close to the filter. "I don't know. *Can* you?" Smoke blew through her thinning lips as she glared at my dip-dyed sleeveless top and washed-out jeans.

I looked at her brother's car. "Is he inside?"

"Yeah."

My gaze hooked with hers. "Would you mind getting him?"

She dropped her hand where a large hole split her jeans at the knee and rolled the white, frayed threads between two fingers. "No."

No, she wouldn't mind, or no, she didn't plan to get him?

An engine's loud roar pulled my attention to the road where Eli Jones' red Toyota truck rounded the corner. When he neared the Guerra house, I recognized the two blonde girls next to him. Ashley, his stuck-up, cheerleading girlfriend, sat tucked under his arm, while her best friend, Cassie, hung halfway out the passenger window, gripping what looked like a rock.

"Hey, spick!" She whipped her arm back, ready to chuck the stone. "Come on over. We've got a present for you!"

The screen door slammed open and I pivoted to see Sam Guerra already halfway down the porch steps, the promise of hell in his eyes as he blew past me and stalked toward Eli's truck. Dreading an inevitable fight, my heart pounded harder with each step he took, but by the time he reached the road, Eli had hit the gas and disappeared around the corner.

Relief made my shoulders sag.

I admired Sam's wide shoulders buried beneath a checkered white and green flannel shirt. He always wore faded jeans and a hoodie or a long-sleeved shirt rolled to the elbows. No doubt to cover a bevy of skull-and-crossbones tattoos. This was a guess since his sister already had a flowery tattoo covering her entire throat.

I tried imagining Sam covered in tattoos and couldn't quite wrap my mind around the picture. He was threatening enough without thinking of tattoos and muscles and…

"Sam?" My tongue stuck to the roof of my mouth. "Could I have a moment?"

Hands still clenched, he turned his brooding gaze to me. I stood only five-feet-five-inches to his six-feet-something, which made his glare a little overkill if he was trying to intimidate me. Most days he managed that walking by me in the hall.

"Maybe I should m-mention," I stammered, wringing my hands when he continued to look at me as if I were next on his kill list, "that I didn't come with those guys."

"Peyton Greene," he finally said, his long strides determined as he crossed the grass. "Let me guess. You're lost." He jabbed a thumb over his shoulder. "The mall is that way, *chica guapa.*"

I considered asking what *chica guapa* meant, but that glare of his persuaded me to choose my battles. He seemed to get bigger as he approached, and I ignored my instinct to back into the dead shrubbery. "I'm not here for directions. I want to hire you."

He halted in front of me, tall, menacing and way too close for comfort. "I don't do other people's yard work."

I squinted up at him. "Who said anything about yard work?"

His gaze dropped to my chest. Back up. "Then what?"

The wind blew his dark brown hair, making him look reckless and tough. I swallowed. Sam Guerra scared the hell out of me. His reputation for a bad temper and constant fights had preceded him, and if I were to believe rumor at all, he'd spent last year—his *real* senior year—in juvie. "I need a bodyguard."

A slight smile curled his mouth, which immediately softened those intense eyes, sharp cheekbones and the scar slicing across his right eyebrow. He took a step closer, reached out and pinched my shirt collar. The movement startled me, and I looked down just as his knuckle brushed my skin, the brief contact causing a flurry of goose bumps along my spine. "*Your* bodyguard?" he said softly.

"Um—" My gaze followed his hand as he pulled it back to hold up a ladybug that had hitched a ride on my shirt. Its wings spread and Sam released it to the wind. "It's not for me," I explained, sounding rushed. A section of my hair blew across my eyes and I quickly yanked the stray locks behind my ear and licked my lips. "It's for my brother. You're in his class."

He dropped his hand. "So?"

"So we're barely into the school year and already Carter Delaney and his friends are shoving him around. I want it to stop."

"Let me get this straight. You want me to pick a fight with Delaney *and* his friends. That's four guys." His smirk returned and he glanced at his sister, who only shrugged. He turned back to me. "Nice odds. What makes you think I'm capable of taking on four guys at once?"

"Because people say you're good in a fight." I immediately wanted to reel the words back. "Although…that's not what I'm asking you to do. I don't want anyone fighting. Just say something to scare them."

"People say," he repeated my words, taking another step closer and bringing us toe-to-toe. "What *people*?"

Did he seriously think he needed to intimidate me? He already stood close enough to block the sun. "A-anyone," I said, refusing to move back. "Everyone at school."

"That's a lot of people," he said.

"Well. You know." My throat felt dry as dirt. "You don't talk to anyone and people say you fight because you enjoy…pain, I guess." I seriously could not believe I'd said that. "Everyone is scared of you."

"That's why you're here? Because a bunch of people I've never talked to, who don't know me at all, told you I'm good in a fight." His scathing gaze raked over me. "Forget it. I don't fight for money."

Savanna let out a cackle and Sam turned to her with a glare. She shoved a hand over her mouth, still grinning.

"Oops."

"I…I didn't say I heard you fight for money," I said. "I'm asking you to—"

"Sorry," he said, cutting me off. "Not interested."

My stomach cramped with a heavy sensation, as though I'd swallowed a ten-pound brick. "Why not? I can pay you two hundred. One hundred now and one hundred after. You wouldn't have to fight. You could scowl, like you're doing now. Or say something menacing. Anything from you would intimidate them. I know it."

He looked at his sister with narrowed eyes. She shrugged again, but her smirk and the bitterness in her eyes told me they needed the money. "If you don't do it, Samuel," Savanna murmured, exhaling a stream of smoke from a new cigarette, "then I will."

He ignored his sister's asinine comment, turning back to me. "Ever consider you might be wrong? At four-to-one odds, they're not going to back down because *rumor* has it I'm good in a fight. *I* wouldn't."

Apparently, no one had told him about his terrifying reputation. "I'm not wrong. They'll back down. I know it."

His eyebrows pulled together, twisting the scar into a crescent. "Listen, Sunshine," he said. "Dropping two hundred on a hunch may be nothing to you, but I can't afford to get kicked out of school again. I told you, my answer is *no*."

I loathed violence enough to have a serious, moral problem with what I was asking him to do. But I loved my brother too much to stand around and do nothing. The school administration obviously had no plans to step up their game where rampant bullying was concerned. "I'll do anything. *Please*."

"I told you. Not interested." He pivoted abruptly and walked toward the house, apparently done with negotiations.

Panic flooded and I bolted after him, grabbing his forearm. "Wait—"

He grabbed my hand so quickly that my startled reaction became an awkward stumble when I tried stepping back. "What part of *no* don't you get?" he snapped.

He was trying to intimidate me. I kept telling myself that, finally believing it when I realized his gentle grip belied that hostile tone and hard expression. I should have pulled away, could have at any time, but I didn't. At least when he held my wrist, he wasn't leaving.

"Let me guess," he said softly, his thumb brushing a delicate stroke along my skin when I remained silent. "I'm the first person to say *no* to you. Is that it?"

"You okay, Peyton?"

Adam's voice drifted across the lawn, but I couldn't tear my gaze from the smug smile tugging Sam's mouth. "I wondered," he said, low so only I could hear, "what it would take to get him out of the car. Looks like you're it, Sunshine." He released my wrist and turned to Adam.

The sensation of Sam's warm and callused hand remained on my arm as I pivoted and tried to find a smile for my friend. "I'm fine."

"Don't tell me *he's* your idea of backup," Sam said next to me. "Cooper wouldn't amount to anything more than a witness."

I looked at Sam's hard profile. "Are you threatening me?"

"I'm stating a fact." He never turned his gaze from Adam, proof that my best friend had been right. Sam would never let down his guard. Even around Adam.

I rubbed my wrist, unable to shake the sensation of Sam's fingers as I gave him my full attention again. "Adam lives only three streets over. He came with me because I didn't know where you lived."

"Let's go, Peyton," Adam said as he approached, sounding more determined than I'd ever heard him.

But I refused to go until I changed Sam's mind. "Listen, I'd be willing to make payments."

Sam turned to me then, looking baffled. "Payments?"

"I'm willing to pay more. Whatever it takes. But I'd have to make payments," I said. "Tell me your price. Everyone has a price."

"Come *on*, Peyton," Adam said quietly, yanking my shirt. "Let's go."

Sam's eyes narrowed. "This isn't about payments, Sunshine. And if you had two feet planted in reality, you'd know your brother's little problem will only get worse if he doesn't handle it himself."

Frustration burned a trail up my throat until my eyes watered. "Look, I *get* reality."

"I doubt it," Sam said.

The undeserved insult snapped my last nerve. "Really? So by your logic, you just made things much worse for your sister by going after those knuckleheads in the truck who were—"

"You need to go," Sam said, cutting me off. "*Now*. And take your bodyguard with you. This isn't your neighborhood. There's no telling what might happen to you if you hang around too long."

I stared at him, mouth open. Sam Guerra had managed to snuff out my little plan in less than five minutes. I hadn't expected rejection, and as he'd insinuated, I wasn't used to it. Tears burned the back of my eyes. Everyone feared Delaney and his group. Everyone but Sam Guerra. I'd been so certain he'd agree to my terms. Clearly, I'd overestimated him. Or underestimated him.

I had no idea what I estimated anymore.

Squeezing my eyes shut, I dropped my head and pushed my hand over my mouth and trembling chin. I had no Plan B. No way to stop something horrible from happening to Ryan tomorrow when I couldn't be with him. My stomach twisted until I thought I might be sick.

I heard Sam turn and skip porch steps on his way into the house. Savanna's steps followed and the screen door slammed behind her as warm tears streamed over my lashes.

"Told you this was a bad idea," Adam said, his arm moving around my shoulders as we walked back to the car. "Hey. You tried. Don't worry. You'll come up with another plan. You always do."

CHAPTER TWO

Sam

Sitting in the dimmest section of the locker room—*my* space that nobody messed with—I caught sight of him hovering and I finally looked over.

He stood with two towels wrapped around him, resembling a half-starved, wet cat as he inched past Delaney and his buddies. One would think by those fearful, wide eyes, that he had to cross an ocean to get to his locker instead of a few feet. Yeah, I'd noticed Ryan Greene's skinny, lily-white ass long before his sister had the nerve to offer me money to babysit him. It was impossible *not* to notice him. The kid didn't fit in. At least not in this class.

I rifled through my duffel bag a second time. How the hell could I lose a damn book *during* class?

Hearing the first bell, I knew I wouldn't make it to class before the second, and I already dreaded the next class like a root canal. A class where Peyton Greene would glare at me through the entire forty-some minutes of British Author hell.

She likely blamed me for making her cry yesterday. I rolled my eyes, determined to forget how she'd looked when I left her standing on my lawn. Crocodile tears building. Chin trembling.

I slammed the bag down and stared into my locker, pissed now because I was thinking about her again. I didn't need this nagging memory of her walking away while her friend—limp noodle boy, Adam Cooper—put his arm around her.

Was I supposed to feel guilty because little Miss Perfect Life didn't get something she wanted for once? No.

I also didn't intend to stick around for Delaney's usual bullshit just because I'd lost a book. The harassment he and his friends put underclassmen through tended to get on my nerves, and not in a mildly irritating way. I was bound to kick somebody's ass if I stuck around for it, and I couldn't afford another fight at school, much less a damn locker room brawl where water and steam made every metal and concrete surface slick as hell. A person could get seriously hurt.

Not that Sunshine would give a crap if I slipped and fractured my skull defending her twerp brother.

Sunshine. I'd accidentally said my personal nickname for her aloud, then quickly made it an insult to cover the slip. From the moment I first saw her—God, she would have been a freshman—that's what I thought of when she walked into a room. Summer. Sunshine. A damn mobile sunbeam wherever she went. I used to think it was her hair—a gorgeous red that turned copper during summer, like a shiny, new penny. She'd always worn it long but changed it daily. Straight. Wavy. Curly. I'd never been so preoccupied with a girl's hair before, but something about hers had grabbed my attention and wouldn't let go.

My attraction to her had become a real problem yesterday. Between her perky attitude and entitled smile, she'd immediately gotten under my skin, and I'd done everything I could to unnerve her. I'd stepped into her space. Brushed my fingers against her neck to see what she'd do. I'd even implied I wanted to be *her* bodyguard, hoping to make her uncomfortable in a restraining order kind of way.

She'd blushed deep red and her eyes had darkened blue to green right in front of me. Then those dimples that always followed her amazing smile had left me wondering things I shouldn't be thinking. Wondering if I had a shot at that.

I'd never seriously considered it.

Her comment that everyone had a price had pissed me off. I'd like to think no one could buy me, but maybe I had a price. Maybe I'd risk expulsion if it meant incredible, hot sex with Peyton Greene. Because it would be. I'd heard she had plenty of experience. Yeah, I'd make that trade. Expulsion for an entire night with Miss Perfect Life. It would screw my future, but damn, I'd make every minute count. There'd have to be a few rules. No talking, for one. Her unflinching optimism irritated the hell out of me.

Most of the time.

Maybe that was the sunshine of Peyton Greene. Her chronic cheerfulness and relentless bounce that made people gravitate toward her and want to yack at the same time. No one could be that happy, and if she were, I'd have to hate her.

Delaney and his friends made their way toward Greene's side of the locker. For his sister's sake, I hoped the kid had dressed at marathon speed and taken off while he still could. Why had he signed up for Weight Lifting, anyway? He couldn't weigh more than one hundred-forty pounds. Every jerk in this class weighed one-seventy or more and most did the jock thing after school, which meant Sunshine's shrimp brother had to either contend with these overinflated egos or get the hell out.

"Checking me out, Greene?"

Case in point—*Carter Delaney*. Greene rarely looked up while walking, much less to check out Delaney. Peyton's brother may be gay but that didn't make him desperate. I'd always guessed girls went after Delaney because his parents were loaded. Money *had* to be his appeal, because the guy was easily the most offensive, self-centered prick I'd ever met, and I'd met a few.

Greene said nothing, and when Delaney couldn't taunt a response from him, a loud slam resonated on the other side of the lockers.

Shit.

I'd had a chance to work a few extra hours yesterday and hadn't made it to school. When I noticed the cut above the kid's eye earlier in the weight room, I figured something had gone down yesterday. Probably what set off his sister on her insane quest to my side of town.

From the sounds of it, Delaney planned to finish the job today. I yanked the flannel from my bag and dug through it for my t-shirt. Screw the book. I'd say I lost it— the truth, for once.

A succinct thump sounded against the lockers this time, what sounded like a fist or…forehead. I took a breath as my neck muscles tightened. Fighting Delaney and his buddies would lead to suspension or expulsion and I couldn't afford to screw up my future any more than I already had. And I definitely didn't need to stress out my *mamá*. She'd already been through enough crap for one decade.

Another sickening smack of skin and bone sounded against the lockers, followed by laughter.

"Dude, you're getting blood on the floor," said one of them.

Greene grunted, his voice strained, "Stop it. God…just leave me alone."

"Or what?" Delaney said. "What'll you do, wimp?"

Delaney's friends laughed again and another slam sounded, hard enough to vibrate my locker. The kid slurred something unintelligible.

Well, crap.

I stood and walked the length of the lockers in my bare feet. It shouldn't have shocked me to find three people—

locker room rubberneckers—watching and doing nothing, but it did. I glared, seriously wanting to kick someone's ass. Two of the jokers whispered, shut their lockers and left.

The big guy—a giant who likely played an offensive lineman or defensive back or some other sports position that crushed people—gave me his back and sat on the bench, preoccupied with his shoes.

I finished rounding the lockers to find everything close to how I'd pictured it. Greene hadn't pulled on his pants, though, and stood in his underwear. Delaney had the kid's face pushed against the locker and one arm pulled behind his back. Ryan Greene looked as thin as a communion wafer, his cheeks a blotchy red from embarrassment, pain, or both. When large blue eyes similar to Peyton's pivoted to mine, I noticed the blood running down his face and the fresh cut to his cheek. His eyes widened as if I'd come to join the others.

The notion made me sick. "Let him go," I said without thinking twice. "Now."

Eli Jones, Chris Woodcock, and Tim Nash turned in stark surprise and for good reason. I had a rep for staying out of everyone's business as long as everyone stayed the hell out of mine.

Delaney glanced at me. "Go back to your little corner, Guerra. This ain't your business."

"Yeah, well…you're killing my concentration with this goddamn noise," I said. "So I'm making it my business."

"*Noise?*" Eli asked. "Seriously?"

My eyes pivoted to the short, stocky guy whose girlfriend, among others, had been harassing my sister nonstop since school started simply because she didn't talk when she could avoid it. That she didn't need a fake-and-bake to keep her tan didn't help her stay under the bully radar either. Eli's nervous gaze darted from mine back to Delaney.

"I forgot you're a little slow, Delaney," I said. "You probably need a few seconds to think about it."

"What did you say, you shit bag?" Delaney said, tightening his hold on Greene until the kid grunted and hissed, obviously trying not to cry out.

The jackass had heard me the first time. "Five seconds."

"*Then* what?" Delaney asked.

"Then I knock you out in front of your friends," I said, giving him a visual incentive as I counted quickly. "Five, four—"

"Really, Guerra?" Delaney slammed the kid into the locker once more before releasing him and turning to me. "I always knew you were crazy. I didn't realize you were suicidal."

"We gonna do this?" I said, arching an eyebrow. "Or you plannin' to talk all fucking day?"

Delaney looked at the others. "You think you can take all four of us?"

"One or four. Won't make a difference," I said, keeping my voice low in a pain-promising tone. "I'll still mop the floor with your ass."

Greene backed into his locker as Delaney's mouth twitched. "Nobody could be *that* stupid. I think you're bluffing."

I scanned the locker room briefly, confirmed Coach Reynolds was out, and took a step forward. "You first then."

"Jesus!" Woodcock hissed.

Delaney backed up a step as his gaze dropped to my chest, his eyes widening.

I'd been ready to put his teeth down his throat when everyone's new, sudden fixation on my torso made me pause. It took a second before I remembered I hadn't pulled on a shirt. Wearing nothing more than jeans and a towel around my neck, I'd stepped under the light and given them full view of the two hideous marks that stretched down my chest and through my abdomen. Even Greene stared bug-eyed.

My throat constricted and I had to swallow several times to work past the closing sensation. Most days I couldn't forget my scars. Now I had a full audience, all because of Peyton Greene's kid brother and a damn book I had no intention of reading.

"I ain't never seen scars like that." Nash shut his mouth the second he noticed my glare. I shifted my gaze to Woodcock, the pity in his eyes, and gave him a threatening look that made my neck muscles tighten and my pulse burn. I wanted to hit him, hard and relentless, until his eyes swelled and he couldn't look at me like that.

Shifting and noticeably uncomfortable, he turned away. Nash soon followed, as did the other two. Only Greene continued to stare, looking oblivious to the blood oozing from his cheek through his fingers.

I'd suspected these four jerks had nothing going on, having learned to recognize the bravado type ten seconds into a fight. But Delaney had a short in his circuit board, so I remained ready until he finally took a step back. His friends did a casual back pedal as well, none looking eager to test my reputation.

Sometimes I liked to pretend I'd endured those innumerable beatings years ago for a reason. Maybe this day. For this kid. Maybe something good would come of it. I wanted to believe that, but I knew better. Life was random that way. Some people got everything. The rest of us got shit.

"Whatever, Guerra," Delaney said, running a hand through his spikey, blond hair. "We'll leave you and your boyfriend alone. Give you some quiet time together. Damn faggots."

They left the locker room, loud and boisterous. Greene watched me the entire time, his wide, watery eyes transporting me back to yesterday when his sister had looked at me with an identical expression.

He was trying not to cry.

As siblings go, Ryan's blue eyes and pale skin were his

only similarities to his sister. He had short, dark hair, stood maybe an inch taller than she did, and had a scrawny, underdeveloped body, unlike Peyton, who had curves everywhere.

"Th-thanks," he said, swiping once at the free-flowing blood before looking at his fingers.

"What were you thinking taking this class, anyway?" I snapped.

He grabbed a towel from the bench and pushed it over his cheek to hold it there. "I wanted to increase my muscle mass. I can't take crap forever, you know." His eyebrows bunched as he glared back at me. "What's wrong with that?"

Just looking at him irritated me. He seemed so damned weak standing there all wide-eyed and bleeding into a towel. "Bulking up won't help if you don't know how to defend yourself. And you'd definitely need more than bulk against a group of four."

"Like what?"

The bell rang and I shook my head, remembering class a little too late. Swearing under my breath, I backed away and hurried to my locker, keeping the worst of the scarring—my back—from his view.

Dammit, I'd rather miss class altogether than show up late to British Authors. Ms. Campbell had a weird, obsessive thing about punctuality and could weigh down a person with extra homework like no other teacher I'd had. I already had enough difficulty understanding the class. I didn't need more homework.

I sat on the bench, found my black t-shirt at the bottom of my locker and quickly yanked it over my head, then pulled the flannel over it to cover my arms. Heat stroke was always preferable to gawking stares and stupid questions about my tats.

"Where did you learn to fight?"

I looked over my shoulder to see Greene already dressed, his wet, spiky hair a mess as he held the bloody towel to his face.

"Here and there." I yanked on my socks.

"Where?"

"Look kid," I said, getting tired of small talk. I shoved my feet into my shoes. "Certain people have what it takes to fight. I don't think you're one of them."

A long silence followed until I turned to see if he was still there.

He stared unblinking and looking confused. "How do you know?"

I couldn't stop a smirk from forming. "I can just tell." I finished lacing my shoes, wishing I'd had a different life. That I hadn't messed up so badly. That I'd graduated last year with my class. If I had, I wouldn't be explaining reality to a punk kid, who should probably be a science major, or chess champion or something. He didn't need to waste his time learning to fight when it wouldn't help him anyway.

"*Why?*" he said, sounding defensive. "Because I'm…different?"

God, the kid couldn't even say it aloud. I looked at him. "You mean *gay?*" I may not give a shit about the other students at this school, but that didn't mean I wandered the halls asleep. I'd passed Greene's locker enough times to notice his sidelong glances at Eric Morgan, whose locker was across the hall. The glimpses had lasted only seconds, but anyone who'd ever experienced longing would recognize it for what it was. A crush.

He met my stare, his tightened lower lip daring me to say more. "No," I said, turning back around. "That has nothing to do with it. It's just…you."

"Well that's helpful." He heaved a sigh, sounding exasperated. "Anyway…thanks."

I barely nodded before shutting my locker and pulling my bag over my shoulder.

"Oh, and don't forget your book," he added.

I pivoted to see him looking over my head. I followed

his gaze to see the corner of the book sticking out above my locker, exactly where I'd placed it in my rush to dress down before everyone else arrived for class.

Rolling my eyes, I grabbed it and took off for class, mentally preparing myself for an onslaught of extra homework.

CHAPTER THREE

Sam

I slipped into my seat, trying to look bored—my usual whenever I came in late. The slightest pause in Campbell's lecture told me she'd noticed, even though she hadn't looked my way.

I could only hope she'd let it go this once.

When she didn't say anything, my gaze shifted to Sunshine who sat next to the open window. I settled in to watch the breeze blow her shiny, copper hair across her face. She pushed it behind her ear, only to repeat the movement seconds later. I watched this little ritual daily, mainly because this class sucked the life out of me if I didn't distract myself, and Peyton Greene was a huge distraction. Not because she was pretty, or built, or friendly, which she was—all of those things. It was her smile. She had the most spectacular smile I'd ever seen. That mouth. Perfect, white teeth. And great dimples. It sounded stupid, but my life got a little better the second she smiled.

She'd worn a pink denim miniskirt today and a white, cotton shirt. Her pale skin nearly matched the sleeveless shirt. I loved sleeveless on her, which showed the little indents in her triceps. I had no idea why that slight curve of muscle flipped my switch the way it did, especially given all her other assets.

I let my gaze drop to drift down her thighs, all the way to those small ankles and white tennis shoes. Her foot bounced a tight rhythm, increasing speed when she raised her hand.

"I'd like to hear from someone else," Campbell murmured. "Mr. Guerra, what did you think of the book?"

I looked up at the same time Peyton turned. Our gazes connected, sharp and intense. I couldn't pretend she hadn't caught me staring at her legs, so I held her gaze a second longer to let her know I didn't give a shit. She uncrossed her thighs and pulled down her skirt half an inch.

My focus pivoted to Campbell as everyone watched me—I hate being the center of anything, even when winning a fight—and I slouched, stretching my legs in front of me. "Which book?"

Half the class laughed as though I'd meant to be funny. I frowned and glanced at the book in front of me. *Mansfield Park*. Our weekend assignment.

"Mansfield Park," she said, leveling a glare at me over her glasses.

I guess the stupid routine I'd given her sophomore year was out. The Jane Austen assignment in that class had been *Pride and Prejudice,* and I hadn't finished reading half the book before seriously considering setting it on fire. "I haven't read it," I replied.

"Obviously," she said, her glare unwavering. Campbell kept her silver hair short and military-like, maybe an inch long. Whenever she stared at someone with that unblinking challenge, I couldn't help thinking she would have made a great boot camp instructor. "Read it tonight. You can lead the discussion tomorrow by giving us a summary, which I'm already guessing will be brief. Try to remember when you read the book that I want more detail than *this guy* and *that girl* did *this thing*." The class laughed at her husky impression of a guy's voice—I assumed mine. "And don't forget from your last experience with me…I ask for *your* thoughtful insight and personal opinion. Something Cliffs or SparksNotes won't provide, should you find either online. I'm giving you a second chance here, Mr. Guerra. You know I don't often do that. Please don't let me down this time. Meanwhile, we'll start on the next author."

So, no CliffsNotes. Crap. Campbell had to be psychic. She managed to stay a step ahead of me in every class I'd had with her. Maybe she got her kicks out of failing me.

Campbell continued talking and I glanced at Sunshine, expecting a glare. Instead, she stared at me wide-eyed, looking sweet with that full mouth slightly open. Her lips twisted up in sympathy.

Sympathy. Go figure. Considering what happened yesterday, I had to assume she hated Mansfield Park more than she hated me.

I glanced at the book, trying to care about this shit. God, even the cover was boring. When I felt Peyton's gaze on me, I looked over, expecting her to turn away like other girls did. But her blue eyes sparkled back at me playfully, as if she'd been waiting for me to notice her. I nearly smiled back, too, when I noticed several girls watching us. One snickered and whispered to the other.

Right. They were right. Peyton could have anyone, which meant I had to put this little game down to just that. A game.

Well, brace yourself, Sunshine.

With tunnel vision, I leaned forward, elbow to desk and chin in palm, staring back at her as though I were interested in a hell of a lot more than her legs, because I was. When she licked her lips nervously, I narrowed my eyes, wishing she'd do it again but slower.

Instead, a shy, genuine smile curled her mouth.

I slid back in my seat. Holy shit, was she into me? Not

that it mattered, but what if she was? The thought of hooking up with Peyton Greene even for five minutes was easily more entertaining than listening to Campbell drone on about another dead person. Thinking longer about it, I leaned forward, blatantly looking at Peyton's mouth as I let my imagination fly off the rails.

Her cheeks flushed dark pink.

I couldn't stop a smile as I held her gaze, until she finally glanced away and shifted in her seat to face front. But her peripheral vision remained on me. I felt it, even before that grin formed and those dimples poked deep holes in her cheeks. I couldn't stop grinning as I watched her pretend to listen to Campbell's lecture while knowing through that smile that she was still back here with me.

Was she thinking the same thing as me? I shifted in my seat. Glanced at Campbell. Stalled the few seconds it took me to get my bearings. I had no idea what just happened between Miss Perfect Life and me, but now I was curious to…

Campbell said my name and I glanced around long enough to hear her list three points expected on tomorrow's review when certain people—a.k.a. Mr. Guerra—came to class prepared.

Damn. That was no joke. I needed to get serious and quit screwing around with Peyton as though it might go somewhere. If I failed British Authors again, I failed this *year*, and I wouldn't return for a sixth. I'd also kill myself if I had to get a GED after five years of high school.

Frowning, I opened Mansfield Park to the middle, staring at the print that went on endlessly. Early nineteenth century fiction made me feel dyslexic. How anyone could possibly consider this a great literary work baffled me. Most subjects I got. *Eventually*. But this mind-numbing drivel? I'd already read the first twenty pages twice and still couldn't explain what I'd read.

Jane Austen produced some real crap if you asked me. If I gave a damn about birthright, money, and marriage, I could probably get through these stories without needing half a bottle of aspirin. And God, her characters. They talked forever, never coming up for air and never finding a goddamn point. Someone should have slapped Jane Austen off her writing chair and introduced her to the concept of white space. But no one had the balls to do that, apparently, which meant the rest of us wanting to graduate had to sit around playing guessing games as to what any of this meandering mess meant.

Because it sure as hell wasn't obvious.

After class, I grabbed my bag from my locker and passed Peyton, her brother, and Cooper, in the hall, who all stood engaged in a loud conversation. Ryan's stare followed me as he pulled his sister's hands from his face. My gaze pivoted to the bruising above his eye. The fresh cut on his cheek. She repeated the name *Delaney*.

I whipped around and beelined it for the outer doors.

"Sam!"

Ignoring her shout, I kept going as if I hadn't heard her.

"Sam!"

Pushing open the outer door, I headed for freedom.

"Samuel!"

I'd just made it to the parking lot when she'd shouted my given name. I halted, closing my eyes and loving the sound of her voice when she'd said it. Knowing I could get monumentally stupid over those great legs if she gave me the chance, I stopped smiling and forced a scowl instead, turning to her. She looked beautiful and perky with those dimples and bright smile as she bounced to a cheerful stop in front of me. "You did it!" she said. "You said you wouldn't, but you did!"

I had years of practice playing stupid for anyone who would buy it. "Sorry?"

She reached out and playfully yanked my flannel sleeve while several gawking students passed us. No one at school touched me. Ever. "Don't play dumb," she said as those dimples deepened and blue eyes sparkled. "Will you *please* let me thank you without being a jerk? Come on. Play nice. Just this once."

Play nice? I'd given her my don't-fuck-with-me look countless times yesterday, and I was giving it to her *now*.

Maybe she took medication, because whatever she'd heard about me hadn't made a dent in her positive attitude.

Well, shit. I liked my scary rep. I liked that everyone left me alone because of it. "Delaney's a douchebag," I mumbled. "He was getting on my nerves."

She pushed three fingers into her small, miniskirt pocket and produced a wad of money. "Please take it," she said. "Two hundred. As promised."

I raised an eyebrow. "I thought we went over this already."

She grinned and thrust it at me. "We did."

"You happened to have two hundred on you?"

She lowered her hand and blushed. "What can I say? I had faith you'd come through."

Why? Why would she think that? I'd purposely been a dick to her yesterday. I'd even tried freaking her out by hitting on her. But she'd blushed and smiled, and left me thinking all sorts of crap I had no business thinking. Then today in class…I doubted I'd ever know what that was about.

"You…you paid him?" Ryan walked up, his face turning blotchy red. "What the hell, Peyton. Why?"

She turned to her brother, eyes darting. She obviously hadn't thought about what she'd say if her brother caught her getting into his business.

"I didn't." Her voice trembled as her eyes watered. "Well, I—"

"She didn't pay me for anything," I finally said, bailing her out of her own mess. "And she's not going to."

I'd been engrossed watching Peyton's reaction, when out of nowhere Vanna appeared like a photo bomb, startling all of us when she snatched the two hundred from

Peyton's fingers. "Merci beaucoup," she said, kissing the bills loudly and heading to my car.

I stared after her, embarrassed and kind of proud. Vanna often had that effect on me.

"But you *tried* to pay him," Ryan said. "What the hell were you thinking?"

Peyton's stern expression couldn't frighten a rabbit. She grabbed her brother's hand and shoved her car keys into it. "Take the keys and wait for me. We can talk later."

They were interesting to watch. Nothing like Vanna and me. Vanna and I shouted and cursed—me more than her—and on a few occasions, my sister liked to throw things. These two mimed an entire conversation. He gripped the keys tighter and narrowed his eyes. She glared, blinking several times in sibling Morse code. Finally, he shook his head, pivoted and stalked away.

She turned to me, smiling again. "How can I thank you then?"

I caught a whiff of her subtle perfume and resisted telling her what I really wanted. "Parting with two hundred wasn't enough?"

She looked around me where Vanna stood next to the Impala sorting through the bills. "I get the feeling you won't see it." She pivoted and bounced once. "Come on, we're not even and you know it," she said, her infectious smile broadening. "I hate owing someone. Don't make me beg."

I imagined her begging and not the way she meant. Naked. Breathless. Saying my name. The image struck me vividly and I couldn't answer her right away. "Forget it," I said, quickly turning and heading for the Impala before I embarrassed myself.

"*Mansfield Park*," she said, the two dreaded words halting me after three steps. "I could help you."

I hated admitting I needed the help, especially to her. But I turned anyway, desperate to pass the class. "Help me how?"

Her face lit up. "You have to read it by tomorrow, right?"

"Like that's going to happen."

She grinned. "I have the movie. Well, it's an adaptation."

Chick flicks. Oh, hell no. "So?"

"It follows the major turning points of the book. You could stop by tonight and watch it. Then I'll give you a rundown on the differences between the movie and the book. I've done it for others. It really works. It'll at least give you the details Campbell might ask tomorrow."

I couldn't imagine the father who would allow a *cholo* from the gangbanger side of town to study half the night with his daughter, especially a daughter who looked like that. "I work until eleven."

"You plan to fail the review?"

"No."

"Then maybe you could knock off work early. I have a job, too, but I could probably get home by nine-fifteen. My house sound okay?"

I doubted I'd heard her correctly. Something about having a job. "Don't you have parents?"

She grinned. "They trust me."

I shrugged. "Well I don't know where you live." As if that should nix the whole thing.

"An easy fix. Do you have paper?"

I had a notebook full of it. "No."

She dropped her book bag and rummaged through it until she found a pen. "Give me your hand," she said, stepping so close I could smell her perfume again. She smelled sweet. Nothing familiar I could put my finger on, like flowers or cookies. Just sweet.

When I didn't move, she pulled my free hand from my side, wrapped those soft fingers around my knuckles and flattened my palm to position the pen over it. I held my breath, waiting to feel the pen's smooth tip against my skin. The second Peyton began scrawling her address on my palm—something that should only be erotic by a fourth grader's standards—I couldn't recall a time, even during sex, when I'd been so aware of another person's touch. The feel of her soft fingers curled around mine. Each time they flexed to keep my hand flat when the pen dipped into the lines of my palm. By the time she finished doing her little thing, I'd broken into a sweat.

She blew softly at the ink and lowered our hands to hook her fingers with mine. "So I'll see you around nine?"

If I relaxed my hand even a little, the contact would break. But I kept my fingers barely curled, connected at the fingertips with hers. Studying those large blue eyes, I was tempted to take her up on her offer. I'd heard guys talk about Peyton Greene. If I were to believe the rumors, she was a complete nympho and had already been with most of the guys here. I also wouldn't have to worry about bullshit like feelings and commitment because she never screwed the same guy twice. I'd even heard that she liked it rough. That sometimes she left marks.

Not that I wanted more marks than I already had.

I could easily picture the first part, but the aftermath would blow. I'd become the center of talk. Not that I cared, but I couldn't picture putting Vanna through that again.

Her dimples deepened. "Aw, c'mon. I don't bite."

That's not what I'd heard. But the Ridgeview High rumor mill had done a serious number on me countless times—most of it inaccurate. They might have done the same to Peyton. When a smartass retort to the I-don't-bite comment hovered on my tongue, I remembered that. Besides, looking at those big blue eyes, she didn't cross me as the type. She seemed…sweet.

Not the kind of girl I'd hooked up with in the past.

Besides, I didn't need to mess with my reputation as a loner this late in the game. No one at this school knew me and that was how I wanted to keep it. I'd have to figure out how to pass Campbell's class on my own.

Relaxing my hand, I pulled it away and took a step back. "I'll stop by if I can."

She bit her lip, drawing my attention to that tiny little mole above her chin. "I wrote my cell down, too. Just text if you can't make it. Or call. Whatever." She shifted nervously and turned, grabbed her bag and hurried away. Her brother sat shotgun in her Lexus, fuming in the most epic pout I'd ever seen. Her friends in the backseat, Adam Cooper and Jon Watson, stared at me with open mouths, not bothering to hide their shock.

My gaze pivoted back to her. I couldn't help myself. Even knowing that people gawked, I watched her walk away, checking out the little sway of her hips and perky step, unable to stop myself from wanting her like every other jerk in this school.

CHAPTER FOUR

Peyton

"What are you doing?" Ryan asked, his reflection popping up in the mirror behind me. "It's almost nine-thirty and you're putting on makeup."

"*Refreshing* my makeup," I corrected. He had a point. I'd been preening to watch a movie. But hey, it wasn't a crime to want to look nice. At least my co-workers had understood. They'd even helped me leave an hour early so I could shower and change into something prettier than my black work shirt with Emily's Cake Place printed on the back. "I had cake flour in my hair."

"That explains the shower. But makeup?"

"Maybe I don't want Sam to see the real me." I stepped to the side, blocking his reflection and those piercing blue eyes that often saw way too much.

"Why?" he said, moving to glare at me again. "You've gone out with how many guys before? And not once did I see you give two figs about your appearance. Not like this."

"I don't want to argue with you, Ryan."

"We're not arguing."

"We will be if you don't quit with the overprotective

thing."

"This guy is seriously scary, sis."

I rubbed powder on my nose and brushed away the remnants. "How can you say that after what he did for you today?"

"Because *you* paid him. He didn't do it out of the goodness of his heart."

"That's not true." I stared at his reflection. "Technically, I didn't pay him anything. His sister took the money. Besides, he said *no* to my proposal, numerous times. And then he told me to get off his property. You can ask Adam because he heard him. Maybe he defended you today because he hates Delaney, too. Or maybe he dislikes bullies. You saw for yourself. He didn't want the money."

"I still can't believe you went to his house and asked him to play my bodyguard. I'm humiliated until the end of time."

Ryan could be so dramatic. "I'm sorry you're mad, but don't be. No one else knows."

"Are you kidding? I told two friends in seventh period when they asked about the bloody towel I was holding to my face. Then everyone saw you trying to pay him in the parking lot."

"Not *everyone* saw."

"And when that didn't work, you outright flirted with him. People will figure it out."

"I was being nice."

"You gave him your address and phone number, for petesake. I feel like my sister just sold herself into sexual slavery on my behalf. I'll bet someone had a phone out, too. Probably uploading a picture as we speak. They'll entitle it, *Wimp is a Pimp* or some shit like that."

I laughed.

"You need to get serious." He took a seat on the bathtub corner and shook his head. "You could be linked with Sam Guerra forever on the internet. I'll never live it down."

"Live what down?"

"The way he stared after you."

"He did?"

"Yeah. As if he planned to *tap* that real soon."

"Really?" I couldn't hold back my excitement that this homework assignment might eventually turn into something more. "Do you think he's attracted to me?"

His rounding eyes and horrified expression made me lose the smile. "You're missing the bigger picture here, Peyton."

I looked back to the mirror to see a mottled blush creep into my cheeks. Definitely time to change the subject. "You're in for a long wait if you want me to apologize. Delaney backing off you is a good thing. Every time I look at the bruising on your face, I feel vindicated. And despite what you or your bodyguard say, I think Samuel did it because it was the right thing to do."

"*Samuel?*" he asked. "Since when do you call him *Samuel?*"

I silently debated a cinnamon lipstick. "His sister called him Samuel the other day. I thought he might prefer it."

"Clearly you have no idea what you're getting yourself into." He stood and leaned against the counter, watching me. "Have you ever seen the guy, sis? I mean, under all that flannel?"

Turning pinker, I slapped my mascara comb back into the tube. "No, and please don't tell me you were checking him out."

"He's not my type and you know it."

"Or more like he's not Eric Morgan. Oooh, now I see."

"I'm not letting you flip this conversation to me." He rolled his eyes, but the blush in his cheeks gave him away. "Seriously, I've been wondering why the coach lets Guerra leave earlier than the rest of us to go to the showers. Seeing him shirtless today, I have a good idea why."

"Let me guess. The numerous curse words tattooed

across his chest?"

"No, I think it's because of the scars. Besides, his tats are on his arms."

I stopped pulling stray hairs out of my hairbrush. "*What* scars?"

"On his chest and abdomen."

I had a vivid imagination, and my stomach twisted as several horrible scenarios came to mind. "Scars. Like he was burned in a fire?"

He shook his head. "I was too busy bleeding everywhere and more amazed at the scar severity than the detail. Definitely not burns. More like knife or sword wounds."

"What?"

"Or something equally horrible," he mumbled, shuddering.

I bugged my eyes at him, imagining the size of a sword blade. Surely, he was exaggerating.

"One look at that shit," he said, "and Delaney and his cronies started backing up. Guerra barely had to threaten them."

"So you're saying Carter *and* his friends did this to you?" I recalled what Sam told me about four to one odds. "He took on all four at once?"

"Like it was nothing. The guy didn't blink the entire time. He seriously scares me."

"Why were you scared? He was on your side."

Ryan nodded. "That should tell you how scary he can be. It also didn't hurt that he looks leaner and meaner than anyone our age should. Probably takes steroids."

"What?"

"It's not natural," he said. "His muscles have muscles. He's seriously cut."

Like I needed more encouragement to think of Sam Guerra without his shirt. "Obviously, those jerks prefer picking on smaller students."

"You're totally interested in him, aren't you?"

I tried to look bored and rolled my eyes. "No."

"He's dangerous, Peyton," he said, seeing right through me as usual. "He's dark and moody and not in an interesting way. He talks to no one and he's always pissed. Doesn't that worry you? He could be a serial killer."

"Are you and Adam comparing notes now?" I ran the brush through my hair. "Besides, he talks to *me*. Sort of."

"Of course he talks to you. He wants to get under your skirt. Why does *any* guy talk to you?"

"Thanks."

"You know what I mean. Even dudes who normally wouldn't say two words to me stop me in the john at least once a week to ask for your number."

"That's just gross." I sprayed two pumps of dehumidifying hairspray over my head. Finished. "And don't go trying to convince me again that men and women can't be friends. Guys don't talk to girls *only* for sex. Not always. Besides, Sam and I don't even know each other."

"Like that's ever stopped a guy."

"Adam and Jon are my friends and *they* don't want that from me."

"Oh, they've thought about you that way, believe me. And you know that Adam has loved you since eighth grade."

"Don't bring Adam's feelings into this. He knows how it is between us." I turned to him. "Can I please enjoy this a little without you spitting in my Cheerios?"

"Enjoy what? I thought you weren't interested."

I sighed. "It's homework."

"Fine." He raked a hand through his hair. "Just make sure that's all it is. I couldn't take everyone saying you screwed him, too."

Tears burned my eyes to hear my brother talk about me like that, even though I was well aware of what people said about me. "You realize the people who create those rumors are the same people who say you're gay. Do you think anyone listens to them?"

"*Everyone* listens to them, Peyton. Especially the ones who say they don't. And I *am* gay, so I think your argument just collapsed on itself."

"Well, I refuse to lose any more sleep over what people say about me. The people I care about know the truth."

"It's me, sis, so you can quit with the bullshit. I know you care what people think." He placed a hand over his midsection. "God, I think I'm getting an ulcer."

"Really?"

His frown deepened. "You would too, if you were me. I've noticed you noticing him ever since he came back. I realize the guy's body looks as if he's been doing the P90X fitness routine since second grade but—"

"I wouldn't know."

"Peyton, he has fresh bruises all the time. People say he's in an underground fight club and you *hate* violence." He ran a hand through his hair, making it spiky. "I guess I'd feel better if you'd stop acting so giddy. Like this is a date. How can you have this attraction to him knowing what you know?"

My stomach fluttered to hear him say it aloud. I walked into my room so he wouldn't see my growing smile and tossed myself onto the blue and cream bedspread to stare at the ceiling. Just thinking about Sam made me feel warm. Excited. Even a little terrified.

And…giddy.

Ryan entered my room and plopped down next to me. "Sorry," he said. "You've just never acted like this before. I'm freaked he's going to ask you out and you're going to say yes."

I wobbled my feet at the end of the mattress and grinned. "He won't."

"What if he does?"

"He *won't*. He has too many preconceived notions about me. Rich little white girl and all that."

"Rich?"

I rolled my eyes. "It was news to me, too. What does

chica guapa mean, anyway?"

"No clue."

"Well, he called me that. Right after he directed me to the mall."

"The mall? You hate shopping."

"I know."

"What a dick," he muttered.

"He also accused me of wanting to hire him to mow our lawn."

"Ah. A dick *and* a racist. Or a reverse racist. What exactly do you call a reverse racist anyway? Just a racist?"

"My point is he's not going to ask me out. And I wouldn't get hung up on him if he did."

"I think you already are."

"I'm doing this to pay him back. You know I don't like feeling indebted."

"Only because a would-be rapist once said you owed him," he said sternly. "Get over it, Peyton. You don't owe Sam Guerra anything."

"I *want* to do this. The guy came back to high school a fifth year. What kind of person does that?"

"The kind who's probably never been introduced to a condom. There's no telling where he's been, Peyton."

"Would you quit acting like Sam's coming over for sex?" My cheeks heated. "For petesake, I don't even know him and you're talking about condoms. You're embarrassing me."

"Why? It's only me."

"Because I don't want to talk about condoms. You're grossing me out. Besides, you don't get to be disapproving of a boy who hasn't even asked me out."

"A man," he corrected. "I'm disapproving of a *man* who hasn't asked you out. He's got to be nineteen by now."

"Oooh, a whole year older than me. What a cradle robber. Better call the police," I teased, adding a playful jab to his arm.

"There are laws, you know."

"I'm eighteen, Ryan."

"But you're still a high school student."

"So is he!" I reasoned. "Now stop being ridiculous."

"Fine." He sighed and stared at the ceiling.

I giggled at his disgruntled tone.

"Can I ask you something?" He turned to me. "In the locker room, he said building up my body wouldn't help me if I didn't know how to fight. He said I wasn't the type."

"The type to fight? Sam said that?"

"Yeah. Do you think he's right?"

One glance at Ryan's annoyed expression and I knew Sam Guerra had wounded my little bro's pride with the comment. "Yes."

"Talk about your bullshit stereotyping."

I looked to the ceiling, too aware I still hadn't heard from Sam. "It's not stereotyping. Gay has nothing to do with it. It's…not you. You may be negative and blunt all the time, but you have this caregiver air. You have a gentle nature. Anyone with eyes can see that. I can't envision you in a fistfight, even to protect me. There's a reason why Adam and Jon didn't ask for your help when they beat up Jason three years ago. I think Sam was saying you're better than that."

"Hm." He didn't sound convinced. "So if Sam *seeks* out violence, what does that say about him?"

"Nothing."

"How do you figure?"

"Because he doesn't bully others, and right now, that's all I care about. If he wants to fight in a fight club, I guess that's his business."

"Rumor has it he's in a gang."

I ignored my knotting stomach. "At least pick one rumor and stick with it, Ryan. Besides, why is it I've never seen him fight? Maybe most of that's rumor, too."

"Ask around. Many have seen him fight."

"In his past maybe."

"You need something recent?"

"What if he's using his reputation to keep people out?"

He slid a hand under his head. "Oh God, here we go. Peyton's off to go save someone again. Did Mom and Dad not adopt enough stray kittens and puppies when we were little?"

"I'm telling you, there's more to him than that badass, stone-faced thing he likes to give off."

"Like what?"

"I don't know. There's just something about him. He gives off a...a..."

"Terrible odor?"

"No." I smacked his arm. "Dork."

"Then what?"

"Energy." That was it exactly. "There's a constant energy about him, simmering below the surface. It's exciting, don't you think?"

"Yeah, exciting like a volcano," he said. "One minute, nice little mountain top. The next? Poof. Destruction and carnage. Time to relocate."

"I don't think carnage is the right word here."

"So, you feel that?" he asked, looking at me seriously.

I should have stopped talking ten minutes ago. I hadn't convinced him of anything. "He's different than other guys at school. He makes me nervous but in a nice way. Do I sound crazy?"

"Damn, your hormones are in overdrive with this guy," he said, frowning as he sat upright on the bed. "If you promise me you won't sleep with him, I'll believe you."

I sat up and pushed him so hard he nearly fell off the bed. "Would you quit talking about sex? I'm waiting until I'm in love and you know it. I want it to be important. Not some backseat thing."

"Most guys would tell you they had very important sex in a backseat."

We both paused to hear Mom yell from downstairs,

asking Ryan to take out the garbage and me to unload the dishwasher.

I stood and walked out with him. "You're worried without reason. He didn't even show. I think he blew me off."

"Oh, he'll show," he said. "I told you, the guy is totally going to make a move on you. Mark my words. He'd be an idiot to blow this invite."

I went to bed an hour later, wondering if Sam Guerra was an idiot. Not only did he blow the invite, he didn't text or call to say he wouldn't make it. Not a frowny face or anything. No one had ever stood me up, and I had to admit, it stung.

Maybe Ryan was right. Maybe hormones had influenced my thinking. Maybe I'd been a little too excited to study with a boy I didn't know.

Knowing this didn't stop me from stewing all night, and by morning, the hurt had turned into anger. Then when he didn't show up for school, anger turned to worry. Sam would have to be completely insane to invite Ms. Campbell's wrath after everything she'd said yesterday.

After lunch, I spotted Savanna at her locker and called her name. She looked through me and slammed her locker closed, walking the opposite way. I caught up to her fast stride and walked beside her. "Hey, Savanna." I noticed a shiny emerald on the left side of her nose. Certain people could pull off having multiple piercings without looking like a street person. Savanna was one of them. "Nice nose stud…piercing." I didn't know the technical name. "It's pretty. Is it new?"

Her gaze flicked over me briefly. "Yeah."

Small talk. I sucked at it. "I'm curious…is Sam okay?"

She boosted her already quick pace. "Yeah."

To know Sam hadn't been in a horrific car accident should have relaxed me. "I only ask because he was supposed to come to my house Tuesday night to study, but he never made it." I had a knack for over-explaining when nervous, and her quiet demeanor unnerved me to no end. "He didn't text or phone to let me know, and when he didn't show today, I got worried."

She stopped and turned to me, whipping that shock of black hair from her eyes. "He doesn't have a cell phone and he's fine. Are we done here? Can I go to class now?"

Wow. Abrupt. Got it. "Sure. We're done."

She continued walking to class while I pondered life without a cell phone. They couldn't be *that* poor. Who didn't own a cell phone? I ran to my own locker and next class. Maybe Ryan, Adam, and Jon were right. I must have been out of my mind trying to get to know Sam. Given my reaction to him whenever he walked into a room, I knew dating him would only make me a hot mess like the rest of my friends in serious relationships. I didn't need that. I'd made important plans for my future and I shouldn't let anything get in the way of those plans.

Least of all, Sam Guerra.

CHAPTER FIVE

Peyton

Standing at my locker earlier than usual Thursday morning, I sensed a simmering energy behind me.

"Peyton?" He'd kept his voice low as if someone might overhear us in the empty hall. "Got a minute?"

I braced myself for hormone overload as I turned to see Sam looking tough and gorgeous. He had two fresh marks on his face—a small, black bruise that resembled an ink smudge on the bridge of his nose, and another, much wider bruise along his jaw.

"Hi," he said softly.

"Hi," I replied, feeling small and unworthy of a simple text. I pulled my Calculus book to my chest and slammed my locker closed. "What are you doing here this early?" The buses hadn't even arrived yet.

"I could ask you the same."

His hair looked damp. "Ryan wanted to study for a test and forgot a book. He's in the commons. What's your excuse?"

"To talk to you."

"Really?" I smiled before remembering I was still mad.

"Really." He pressed his palm to the locker next to

mine and leaned over me with that cocky grin I remembered from our staring contest. "Actually, I have something to give you."

I'd never understood the appeal of the bad boys who kept my girlfriends strung along and brokenhearted for months. Until now. I knew Ryan was right. Sam probably wasn't good for me, yet I couldn't make myself care. "I'm almost scared to ask what put a smile on your face this early," I said. "Did you run over a fluffy squirrel on the way to school?"

He smirked and pulled a tight wad of bills from his pocket to hold up between us. "I snagged this from Vanna's coat pocket last night. It's fifty short but I wanted to give it back to you before she notices it's gone."

I frowned. "You know I can't take it. The money is yours. Hers. Whoever you want to have it."

He held the wad an inch from my nose. "That's just it. I want *you* to have it."

I pushed his hand away. "It would be different if I'd helped you study, but...you know. That didn't happen. Please keep it. Give it to Savanna if you don't want it. You care about her, so it's like I'm paying you. Otherwise, I'll still owe you."

He lowered his hand. "I should apologize for the other night."

"Is that what you're doing?"

"Trying to."

"Well, I'm sure you couldn't get away," I said, giving him an excuse like an idiot. I wanted to take it back. To add something snotty about the few seconds needed to call a person, but I kept my peacemaking self in check and leaned against my locker.

"Yeah," he said. "I couldn't get away."

Without thinking, I brushed two fingertips along the bruise at his jaw. "Work looks painful. I hope your co-worker got the worst of it."

His eyes flashed surprise and his hand brushed mine

before I pulled it back. "Listen…Peyton, I don't want to get into—"

"Obviously, you can do what you want," I said. "But if you're going to lie to me, don't apologize. A lie negates the whole thing."

He stared at me for several awkward seconds, looking shocked that I'd called him out. "I didn't lie," he said. "It's complicated. More than I want to explain."

Yet another reason why I shouldn't think twice about him. I doubted I could handle a detailed explanation standing this close to him anyway. "I assume you're planning to wing Ms. Campbell's class today," I said, changing the subject and ducking quickly under his arm to head to first period. "That should be interesting."

He followed me, his long stride easily catching up. "You'd love it, wouldn't you? Probably laugh before anyone else if I did."

I refused to smile. "I try not to laugh at people. Even if they deserve it."

"That dimple in your cheek tells another story. Admit it," he said. "You'd totally laugh."

I wanted to bite the insides of my cheeks to stop the mischievous grin. "Well, my point is, I wouldn't laugh *first*."

We'd reached junior hall when he grabbed my elbow and turned me to look at him. His smile made him appear more relaxed. Even sweet and flirtatious, as he'd been in Campbell's class. I backed up a step.

"I realize this is ballsy," he said, "but I was wondering if you'd still help me."

Another step back had me noticeably and awkwardly pressing against someone's locker. "With what?"

"The review."

I sagged a little. "Are you insane, Sam Guerra? Is that your problem?"

"Possibly." He took two steps into my space and fixed his palm to the locker next to me, leaving me no escape this time. "Of course you don't *have* to help me. But you should know I'm crazy enough to continue stalking you until you take back this two hundred."

"Have you been stalking me, Sam? I didn't notice."

He hovered above me, looking amused as those soft brown eyes pulled me in. "Consider it from my point of view," he said, his gaze dropping to my mouth and back up. "I never agreed to your terms Monday. What I did in the locker room was my decision. I didn't do it because I'd made a *deal* with you." He reached into his pocket and held up the folded bills again, flicking them back and forth in front of my nose. "Take the money, Peyton, and you'll be rid of me. Just take it and I'll go."

"One hundred-fifty," I corrected his earlier slip, glancing at the money. I could take it back, and he'd leave me alone. We'd go back to happenstance glances in the hallway, but I wasn't at all sure I wanted that. "Let me get this straight," I said. "You're saying I don't owe you anything."

"Right."

"And you want me to take back the money."

"Yes."

"*And* you want me to help you with Mansfield Park."

"Yeah."

"Sam, we still wouldn't be even."

"I know."

"*You* would owe *me*," I pointed out.

His mouth twisted into a dangerous grin that made my insides knot. "Sounds much better, doesn't it?"

I wish I had experience beyond kissing. I'd know exactly what he meant. Was he being sweet and flirting, or saying he wanted to have sex and implying he'd be great at it? I couldn't tell. "It's too late."

"No such thing," he said.

"Unless you can add more hours to the day, then yes it is. The second Ms. Campbell sees you she's going to ask you to give the review. You haven't seen her lately. She's put it off twice now. It's a vendetta. There's no way I can get you prepared before then."

"Depends how far you're willing to go."

I stared into his eyes searching mine. Was he still talking about a book review? "How far are you *asking* me to go?"

"Far enough to make it interesting." I arched my eyebrows and he grinned, a full smile this time. He had exceptionally straight teeth for someone in a fight club. "Ditch seventh period with me today," he said.

It was possible we had different definitions of interesting. "Help me understand this. You want me to *skip* British Authors to help you *pass* British Authors?" I looked around, paranoid now that someone might be listening. "You *are* crazy. I'm sure you've heard differently, Sam, but I'm a straight arrow. I'm a straight arrow because I never get away with anything. I'm a terrible liar. We'd get in trouble."

"Claim you're sick and leave early. They'll call your parents and you'll bring a signed note tomorrow. It's as you said—your parents trust you."

True. My parents believed anything I told them because I sucked at lying and rarely did it. Sam obviously had no problem changing that. "Don't you feel bad? I mean, you seem to lie so easily."

He shrugged a shoulder. "I'm not hurting anyone. Think of it as adaptability. So will you?"

"I'm everyone's ride." My last excuse.

"Then give your brother the keys and I'll drive us to your house. He has his license, right?"

Alone in a car with Sam? I swallowed. I doubted he understood what he was asking me to do. I didn't do things like this. Ever. I was an above-board, by-the-rules girl.

"Come on, it'll be fun," he said. "You. Me. Jane Austen. What could go wrong?"

I suspected he could make anything sound tempting.

"Everything. You've never skipped with me." I looked to the floor. "I'll get caught, Sam, which means *you'll* get caught, and then we'll—"

"Listen Sunshine," he said, his finger sliding softly under my chin and pulling my gaze to his. "Don't take this wrong, but you cross me as a first-offense girl. Even if the school or your parents caught you lying, skipping, or whatever, you wouldn't get anything more than a slap on the hand. Trust me."

I bit my lip, staring at his growing smile as his finger did a tap-tap-tap under my chin while he waited for my answer. I didn't want to tell him no. "Fine. Okay."

"Really?" He sounded surprised.

My gaze shifted to the doors. The buses were pulling up to the curb. "Should we meet after sixth period?"

"Yeah."

The doors opened and students piled into the hall, bringing a tornado of noise with them. I straightened, awkward as I tried moving around Sam to go before anyone saw us talking.

He grabbed my waist. "Wait," he said, his face inches from mine as he lifted the money to my nose again. I arched my eyebrows and he grinned, dropping his hand and tugging my skirt pocket, nearly bringing our bodies together as he took his time pushing the money into the small pocket. I could barely draw a breath until he released me.

"Meet me at the north parking lot after sixth period?" he said.

I nodded, staring at the devious grin he gave me before leaving.

The entire day passed similarly, a blur of noise, faces and useless information until seventh period. I should have been thinking twice about skipping class, but my excitement to see Sam overruled. Later, I went to the office, signed out and waited for Ryan by his locker. He frowned when he emerged from Weight Lifting, immediately suspicious to see me.

I handed him the key to Mom's Lexus.

"What's going on?" he said.

"I'm not feeling well and Sam is taking me home." My voice shook slightly.

"*Sam?*" His frown deepened. "Peyton, what are you doing?"

"I may have a fever." I coughed and gave him a quick hug. "I'll see you after school, okay?" I swung my book bag over my shoulder and took off down the hallway, aware of his disapproving stare following me.

Sam was leaning against the Impala when he spotted me racing across the parking lot. His usual scowl became a small smile as he straightened and opened the passenger door for me. I plopped onto the seat, waiting for him to walk around as the lingering scent of aftershave and worn leather drifted from the backseat. I turned to see his old leather jacket stuffed behind his bag.

He sat next to me in the driver's side and soon the Impala roared to life.

"Do you remember where I live?"

He tapped his temple twice as he backed out. "Jotted it down."

"Where did you get this car anyway?"

"Why?"

"Because it's the hottest car on the lot."

He tapped the brakes too hard, making us both jerk forward. "Was it the rust or primer spots that first caught your eye?" he said, not really asking.

His get-real stare made me giggle. "It doesn't have primer spots and you know it." I shrugged. "What can I say? I love the classics."

"No one would know it by the Lexus you drive."

"My mother's Lexus, you mean. I don't have my own car. Besides, I'd still pick this car." My dad had given me a healthy appreciation for the older models that could go head to head with a truck and not break into a thousand pieces. "What year is this?"

"Sixty-seven," he said. "It belonged to my dad." I was curious about the clarification, but he quickly changed the subject to where he worked on weekends—Winchester Auto—and how seldom he saw older models now. He kept the topic going all the way to my house.

Once he parked at the curb, the full magnitude of my stupidity set in. Both my parents were at work and my brother wouldn't get home for almost two hours. I'd be alone with a boy I didn't really know the entire time, and as the memory of Jason Thompson trapping me against his truck seat came rushing back, my heart cramped uncomfortably in my chest, making it difficult to get a full breath.

"You okay?" he asked.

My tongue felt double in size as I nodded.

We strolled up the sidewalk in silence and I unlocked the front door, insisting he cross the threshold first. When my good sense forced me to pause on the doormat, he turned to stare at me, his eyebrow arching with curiosity.

"It's occurred to me I'm way too trusting," I explained, clutching the doorframe and still not moving.

He smiled, shoving his hands into his front pockets. "You just now noticed this?"

I bit my lip, contemplating my options. I could *look* awkward and stupid, or I could *be* stupid and…I didn't want to consider what else I could be. "My brother knows you drove me home," I said, voice trembling as I tried to appear casual. "And my dad owns a .45 Sig Sauer. He taught me how to shoot it. I can clear a mushroom cap off a tree at twenty paces."

"Nice," he said, smiling and taking two steps toward me to lean his shoulder against the doorframe. "I'm impressed. Not many girls believe in the senseless killing of mushroom caps. But I think it's only fair I warn you that in a situation like this, a firearm wouldn't do much good buried in a gun case or kitchen drawer. You could make a run for it, but I've been told I have lightning-quick reflexes."

I noted his large size compared to mine. "I can't believe I let you talk me into this."

He busted up laughing then and reached over, covering my hand with his and prying my frozen fingers gently from the doorframe. "You can trust me, Peyton," he said, holding my hand to pull me from my wooden stance and into the foyer. "But you don't know that right now and I'm glad you're at least aware."

"You are?"

"Yeah." He released my hand. When I didn't move, he shoved his hands back into his pockets—I think to make me feel safer. "Vanna makes me crazy," he admitted, glancing over my head at a picture on the wall before his gaze dropped back to mine. "She never thinks ahead. If she ever had a guy over, for studying or anything else, I'd have to kill him."

He said it so sincerely and nonchalantly I could only stare. "Are you serious? Do you really plan to beat the first poor boy to death who shows interest in your sister? What is wrong with you? Who does that?"

He laughed again, a contagious sound that continued until I smiled with him. "I meant figuratively speaking," he said. "And yes."

Did he make a joke? I couldn't read him for anything.

"Look. Peyton." He grew serious quickly and walked to the door, leaning a shoulder against the frame. "We don't have to do this. I thought it was a good idea at the time, but I forget sometimes what people say about me. What people think." A small line formed between his eyebrows. "Especially when I'm with you. I never meant to scare you."

His softer expression reminded me of earlier today, how his eyes had teased when he leaned over me, his fingertip gently tapping under my chin as he smiled. He'd been just a boy flirting with a girl.

I seriously had to get past this Jason Thompson thing.

Embarrassed, I glanced down. "No, I'm good. We should get started though. It's a long movie." I finally closed the door and awkwardly pointed upstairs. "It's upstairs. Give me a second and I'll be right back."

"Sure." He kept his hands in his pockets.

I hopped up the stairs at lightning speed, rushed into my bedroom, fluffed my hair, and grabbed the movie, hoping Ryan didn't have a stroke when he came home to find me here with Sam Guerra.

Ryan had often accused me of sneaking up on him, so when I emerged on the landing and Sam kept his back to me, I realized he hadn't heard me. He stared unmoving and transfixed at a family picture on the wall. I took the first step, one I knew would creak under my weight. He turned when it did and watched me descend the remaining stairs. The oddest expression crossed his features, as though he'd been expecting someone else. We smiled at each other, but I sensed he had his armor back on. I'd ruined everything with my little dramatic episode back there.

That he hadn't fallen into a resonating snore an hour into the movie meant he could tolerate a girl's movie—literary classic or not—with the right incentive. Maybe he truly wanted to pass the class. "Yesterday, Ms. Campbell gave us a few things to think about," I said, trying to make conversation. "First, to consider if we related to a specific character." He stayed silent. "Do you?"

"Not really."

"What if she makes you choose?"

"I'd choose Edmund."

"Not Mr. Crawford?" I teased.

He looked at me. "I hope you're saying I'm attractive. Otherwise, I think I've been insulted. The guy's a total tool."

"Mr. Crawford is charming and a shameless flirt, but in the book, he's plain as a post." Sam examined my face with interest now, which kept me rambling. "Why did you pick Edmund?"

"Because he doesn't talk much. How long is this movie?"

"Two hours." I expected him to cringe but he didn't. "Think you can stand sitting through another hour?"

"It's not that bad. Beats reading the book. And the company is nice. Who would you pick?"

Wait, was that a compliment about my company? I'd barely said a word. Had been biting my tongue all afternoon. Maybe he liked mutes. A terrible sign since I took after my mother in the chatterbox department, especially when nervous. "Fanny, I guess. If I had to choose."

"Why?"

I shrugged and stared at the young woman playing Fanny Price. "I guess because she knows how to fit in everywhere, but doesn't really belong anywhere."

He didn't say anything but his gaze lingered on my profile.

Fifteen minutes later, Ryan walked through the front door, and I braced myself for his reaction. *Please be cool, little brother.* His footsteps stopped and I twisted to see him standing at the carpet's edge, hands perched on his waist.

"Oh. My. God," he said, his eyes pivoting to the back of Sam's head and narrowing. "You're not sick. You totally skipped class."

Not quite ready to deal with what I'd done yet, I waved Ryan away as Sam watched my reaction. "We're watching a movie for class. I'll talk to you later."

Sam lifted his hand casually in a wave, never turning around. "Hey, Ryan."

"H-hey…Sam." Ryan looked uncertain another few seconds before he sighed loudly and pivoted, stomping through the foyer and up the stairs.

Okay, it had to be weird to come home and find Sam Guerra watching Mansfield Park with me. I had to give my brother props for keeping it together.

"He's protective of you," Sam said, staring at the movie as Ryan's heavy footsteps sounded through the ceiling directly above us.

"Yes," I said, "he is."

"Are you close? You seem like you are."

"Strangely enough."

He turned to me. "Why strange?"

"Our personalities are way different. My mother says I'm the positive to his negative; that combined we equal a normal person. I guess there's some truth to it. I'm the optimist. He's the pessimist. But I'm closer to him than anyone else. We talk about everything. And we look out for each other."

The sudden appearance of his sexy half-smile made my insides flutter. "I figured that out when you showed up at my house with your offer."

I couldn't tell if he was joking or flirting. "Sorry if his hostility makes this uncomfortable."

He looked at the movie. "It doesn't."

"I told him I was sick and we don't lie to each other," I said, over-explaining as always. "I think it shocked him you were here."

"If I were him, I wouldn't want me here either."

"It's not you. I don't know why—" something heavy dropped on the floor upstairs, "—he's still mad."

His gaze paused briefly on my legs, the fourth time I'd seen him do that. "He obviously thinks this is something else."

I pulled my skirt down a little. "I don't know why. I told him you were only interested in help on the review."

His dark eyes flicked over me. "I don't think he believed you. He must think I'm here for other reasons."

Another loud slam sounded upstairs and my cheeks heated. "This is embarrassing."

He shrugged again. "Don't worry about it. If we were friends, I'd tell you to stay the hell away from me, too."

I met his gaze. "You don't think we're becoming friends?"

"You and I could be a lot of things, Peyton, but we could never be friends," he said, turning to the movie. "Feel free to tell your brother you're *more* than safe with me."

As we finished Mansfield Park in silence, I finally admitted to myself that maybe for the first time ever, I wanted more than *safe* with a boy.

CHAPTER SIX

Sam

Once the movie ended, Peyton asked me for my *visceral* response to the story. I looked her right in those pretty blues and told her the literary world might have benefited more had someone invented and introduced Jane Austen to the zombie apocalypse trope. Had zombies overrun Mansfield Park and devoured every one of those irredeemable, selfish bastards she called characters, I would have walked away from this movie so much happier.

But that didn't happen. Instead, Edmond and Fanny got together. Big surprise.

That I'd managed to watch the movie at all was a bigger surprise. Peyton's miniskirt had been a constant distraction. Black and tighter than the pink one, it conformed to her body like a second skin, repeatedly drawing my attention back to those legs.

If I'd been thinking at all this morning, I wouldn't have bothered glancing her way. But I had and one look at her gorgeous backside and I'd immediately regretted standing her up Tuesday night. Luckily, I'd already planned to give her the one hundred-fifty back, which gave me an excuse to talk to her. When she'd turned around so bright-eyed and almost happy to see me, I started to reconsider my earlier decision to leave her alone.

Peyton's constant blushes and easy smiles made me think she wanted more than a flirtatious game that led nowhere. To find out for sure, I'd given her the perfect out—take the money and I'd be gone.

Did she take it? No.

I'd been so damn euphoric at her answer, that I no longer cared if screwing her put me front and center in the Ridgeview gossip column. *If* that happened, Vanna would forgive me for dragging the Guerra name through more mud. *Eventually.*

Setting up the excuse to hook up had been easy. Getting her to agree had been more difficult. But when she finally did, I'd wanted to run my hands over those sculpted arms and peel off her clothes right there.

I'd thought we were both on the same page until we got to her place. Then she did that long delay by the door as if she'd never invited a guy to her house for a little one-on-one action. Given her reputation, I figured she was joking, but a second glance at those wide eyes and trembling chin made me realize she was genuinely scared, if not completely freaked that she'd put herself in a potentially dangerous situation.

That's when I realized she didn't do hookups.

Great. That meant I'd read every signal wrong, I had zero understanding of what was going on, and I needed to get the hell out of there.

She relaxed a little when I suggested I bail, but it wasn't until she'd grabbed the movie and descended the stairs while watching me with those huge, innocent eyes that I finally realized her shy act wasn't an act. Even her smile seemed twitchy and nervous.

I began to wonder if she had any experience at all. Given the rumors about her, it took me a full hour sitting next to her like a mute before I got my arms around the notion that she might be a virgin. It would at least explain her constant blushes when I'd flirted with her at school. Crap. I'd never been anyone's first time. I wasn't sure I wanted to be. She struck me as a serious girl, which meant she'd be a serious *relationship* girl.

Anyone who really knew me knew I wasn't into relationships. Telling her she was safe with me had halted anything before I could talk myself out of doing the right thing. I hadn't always thought of the other person first, but I knew going any further with this girl would have been a mistake.

Papá, God rest his soul, would have been proud.

I should have left then, but I hadn't fully taken doing the right thing seriously. I'd had my heart set on hooking up with this girl and I still wanted to.

When the movie ended, I had a headache and real good idea why I didn't like Jane Austen. What's the word, *vexed?* Yeah, Jane Austen vexed the shit out of me. So did Peyton. Why did she wear short skirts all the time, only to pull the material down repeatedly whenever she caught me looking at her legs? Wasn't that the point? To show off great legs? She also had a chronic blushing problem when I talked to her. Like she was suddenly hyperaware every time she looked at me that I might want to have sex with her. But what was strange about that? Like every other guy wouldn't? Seriously, how could she seem so unaware of her own appeal?

I'd been stuck in that thought, following her and staring at those triceps when she bent to pull a notepad from her book bag.

Yeah, I definitely had to see her again.

But that meant a real date, something I'd always avoided. Seeing Peyton outside this tutoring gig meant we'd have to talk for real, and unlike my sister, I wasn't big on keeping things real. Peyton might even ask personal questions, and as I thought about how I'd get around that, I started getting itchy.

She turned to see me scratching my shoulder like a baboon and I dropped my hand. "Are you hungry?" I asked.

Her eyes rounded and she put a palm to her midsection. "Oh, God. You didn't hear my stomach growling for the last hour did you?"

"No."

"Good." Those dimples deepened. "And yes, I'm starved."

I leaned a shoulder against the wall. "Want to get some food, too? My shift starts at seven and it would save me some time. Would you mind?"

She looked to her notepad and back up. "Could be fun. Although, Mansfield Park and food? That seems social. Almost like friends. I wouldn't want to compromise your man code."

I smiled. Glad to see she had a smartass side after all.

"We could call it a date," she suggested.

Her brother emerged at the top of the stairs, apparently eavesdropping. He glared at me and I dropped my gaze back to Peyton's pretty blues. "Do you *want* it to be a date?"

Ryan began his descent as though he were a heavyweight instead of a flyweight. Never taking my eyes off his sister, Ryan's hostile stare bored into me, and I had to wonder what happened to the frightened kid I'd defended. *This* kid held himself as though he were ready to kick my ass to Texas and back. I was starting to like him.

"Sure," she said.

Ryan avoided the easier path behind Peyton by walking between us. Resisting a laugh, I decided to knock him off his high horse. "Hey, Ryan. Want to go with?"

He twisted around. "On a *date* with you two? Are you kidding?"

"Jeez, man. It's only food." I gave a casual shrug and grinned at her. "How sexy can it get? We'll be talking about Mansfield Park."

She turned to Ryan with those bright eyes and smiled. "You want to come?"

Ryan stared at his sister. "Sure. You know I love Mansfield Park."

The kid had to be the biggest nerd ever to like that shit, but his sister appeared to adore him. It hadn't been my worst idea. If her brother went, she'd have her guard down. I could figure her out quicker, and the next time, we could skip the niceties and jump straight into the action.

I definitely planned for a next time.

Once in the car, Peyton started the comparison between book and movie while Ryan eyed me in the rearview mirror whenever he wasn't texting.

The Japanese restaurant was my favorite, a cafeteria-style place, which kept dining a non-intimate scenario—exactly why I'd chosen it. If I'd wanted intimate, I wouldn't have invited Ryan.

Peyton sat opposite me, writing as if on a mission to transcribe the Divine Word, when her friends, Jon and Adam, showed with two girls from school. Everyone acted surprised to see us, and Peyton bought it. She invited Ryan's troop of reinforcements to sit at the table next to ours.

Ryan gave me a smug look. "Are you going to let her do all the work?"

"Wouldyoushutup?" Peyton said under her breath.

He nodded to her notebook. "All I'm saying," Ryan said, directing his scowl to me, "is I'm not hearing a conversation about the book, which is the point of this dinner date. I'm watching Peyton do all the talking and writing. What are you doing?"

I'd been resting my chin in my palm during his spiel. "Let's see. Taking your shit and showing amazing restraint? Or was that rhetorical?"

The kid's eyes widened, either recalling his wimp status from the locker room or surprised that I knew how to use the word *rhetorical* in the correct context. He probably equated my intelligence to a box of hair. How else could he explain my five-year high school status?

"Sam and I talked earlier," she said, elbowing him. "I'm writing to keep everything straight."

It was practically a lie. *She'd* talked a bit about the book, but *we* hadn't. We'd talked about Vanna's impulsiveness and Peyton's close relationship with her perpetually pissed off sibling. We'd even tried comparing ourselves to two characters that neither of us resembled in any way.

Ryan stared at Peyton's profile until she turned to him. "*What?*" she hissed between teeth.

He shrugged. "I was thinking maybe it's time we adopt another kitten for you."

With the way she moved suddenly and he jumped, I knew she'd kicked him under the table. "I will kill you later," she said. "Stop it."

Peyton turned and smiled at me before writing again.

"Fine," he said to her. "I'm sorry."

Peyton wouldn't acknowledge his apology. Feeling responsible for the tension, I threw her brother a bone. "Your sister and I were debating a point earlier."

Peyton stopped writing and looked at me, her expression curious, probably because we hadn't debated anything. Four stunned faces from the adjacent table stared at me as though I'd learned English in the last fifteen minutes.

"Since you're such a fan," I said, "I thought maybe you could answer this. If Mr. Crawford is as plain as a thumb—" I pushed my empty plate to the side, "—why does Maria want him? She already has money and status in her engagement to Rushworth. Marriage, money and status…isn't that all Austen's female characters care about?"

"Oh my God he did not just say that," the blonde girl next to Jon said.

Ryan contemplated my question. "Her sister, Julia, is supposed to have him. That's why Maria wants him."

The brunette hanging on Cooper's arm looked at me. "Maria always wants what she can't have. She's spoiled. One of Austen's better examples that money, breeding, and education won't necessarily turn out better character."

The blonde leaned past Jon, her eyes narrowing on me. "Jane Austen was easily one of the most amazing writers of all time. Do you know what she did for women?"

"Cindy," Jon said, clearing his throat, "I don't think he meant—"

She held her palm up to his face, halting his next word before turning to me. "I can't believe," she said, "that in one blanket statement you'd reduce *all* of Austen's female characters to fanning little creatures caring about nothing more than marriage, money and status."

"Women *had* to focus on those things," Jon said seriously, pushing his bleached white hair from his eyes. "It was the period. Self-preservation. No shame in that."

When Cooper and his girlfriend joined into the conversation, I turned to the only person at the table who interested me. The entire reason I'd come.

Peyton must have felt my stare because she stopped her pen mid-paragraph, lifting that blue gaze to mine. "Oh, no you don't," she whispered, smiling. "You started this brouhaha. Better get back in there."

I shook my head. "I'm one snide remark away from having a chair thrown at my head. Are you kidding?"

She bit down on her lip, trying not to laugh.

"Elizabeth Bennett," Cindy went on, "is easily the strongest, most complex female protagonist ever written. I challenge anyone to argue that."

"Consider it challenged," Ryan said, chomping his last piece of sushi. "I can name ten heroines more interesting than Elizabeth Bennett."

"Name one," she said.

Unable to take this group thing much longer—even for Peyton—I tuned out the conversation and pulled out my cell to check messages, hoping to disappear into solitaire or mahjong while her friends hashed it out over this stupid ass book.

"You have a phone?"

Frowning that I'd missed a call from my boss, Jonas, I looked up to see Peyton staring at my phone. "Yeeaah. Why?"

"Savanna said you didn't own one."

Wait. What? "When did you talk to my sister?"

She paused, eyes widening as color crept back into her cheeks. "I—" She glanced at the others still talking and back to me. "I'd rather not say."

"Why?"

"It's embarrassing."

Savanna rarely talked to anyone. Ever. Anyone who could get my sister to talk had my full attention. No way could I let this go. "*What's* embarrassing?"

"You're going to think I'm dramatic." She glanced to the other table nervously, leaned forward, and turned back to me. "I was worried about you, so I asked her." She sat back, grabbed a California roll and quickly pushed it into her mouth.

Intrigued, I slid forward on my elbows. "*Worried* about me?" Imagining Peyton worried about me felt...uncomfortable. "Why?"

She chewed quickly, staring at her notes, pen poised.

I leaned closer without leaving my seat. "Peyton?"

Her gaze lifted to mine. "All right. When you didn't text Tuesday night and didn't come to school Wednesday, I worried maybe something had happened to you. She said you didn't text me because you don't have a phone." A crinkle formed between those dark auburn eyebrows. "Why would Savanna tell me that? I mean, she obviously hates me, but that's just *mean* to—"

"She doesn't hate you," I said, interrupting her because I couldn't stand to see the hurt on her face. I also didn't like the idea of Vanna putting it there, inadvertently or otherwise. "She covers for me."

The line deepened between her eyebrows. "Covers for you?"

I lowered my voice so only she could hear. "I worked yesterday."

She took a few seconds to process that. "*Worked? During school?*"

"Yeah. Whenever an employee calls in sick, I ditch to get in a few extra work hours," I said, giving her more information than I should. "But the school can't know. Vanna covers for me whenever anyone asks questions. I don't know why she told you I don't own a phone. She doesn't exactly think quickly on her feet. Your concern probably took her off guard."

Her incredible mouth curled up again. "She must not have your talent for *adapting.*"

That I could lie without apparent conscience wasn't what I wanted Peyton to focus on. "I'm just saying don't take it personally."

She leaned her chin in her palm, eyes shining. "Well that makes this more interesting."

"What's interesting?"

She bit into her lip, giving that gorgeous smile a devious slant. "Do you remember how we agreed you'd owe me for helping you?"

"Yeah." I swallowed.

She rose from her seat, surprising me when she slid her body halfway across the table to stop only a few inches from my face. We both probably smelled of sushi, but I couldn't stop my growing smile. "Would it be possible," she whispered, "to cash in on that favor right now?"

My mouth opened but nothing came out. I cleared my throat, forcing my gaze to stay on her eyes and not drop to her cleavage where her shirt now gaped. "Depends on what you want. In a restaurant. Full of people." I needed to quit talking.

"Just your number," she said softly, her cheeks getting pinker. She put the pen's cap end into her mouth and twirled it once against her teeth. "It's only fair. I gave you mine. You should give me yours."

I watched the tip of her tongue move once against the pen before meeting her gaze. "If I give it to you, are you going to use it?"

She pulled the pen from her mouth. "Do you *want* me to use it?"

With my focus constantly shifting to her mouth, all I *wanted* was to kiss her. I caught that sweet scent of hers and leaned forward, trying to decipher what it was. She leaned in, too, those playful, blue eyes pulling me closer. So close, I could...

"What are you two conspiring about?" Ryan said, loud enough that he startled her into sliding back to her seat.

Staring at each other, we smiled. I couldn't believe I'd almost kissed her. I couldn't believe she'd almost let me.

Ryan cleared his throat and her gaze slid to him, then Cooper. Would she care if either had heard us? She turned her panicked gaze to mine.

Adapt, I mouthed.

She bit her lip, looking miserable. "I was telling Sam how the movie emphasized Fanny's relationship with her younger sister, Susan." Her voice shook. "But in the book, she'd been closest to her older brother, William."

"Why are you upset?" Ryan asked.

"I'm not." She flipped the page to start a third. The sudden strain between Peyton and her brother felt palpable, a pall over the entire table. Jon and his girlfriend stood to make a quick exit.

I pushed my chair back. "I should get going, too."

"Give me a sec." Peyton lifted a finger, not looking up. She continued to scribble out another sentence.

Ryan stood. "Jon, can you give us a ride? Sam's got work."

"Sure. We'll wait outside."

Peyton stood and ripped three sheets from the pad, handing them to me. "That's everything we went over."

I grabbed it, noticing she wouldn't look at me. "Thanks."

She stood a moment longer as though waiting for me to say something else, then quickly left when I didn't. I instantly realized I'd somehow messed up, although I had no idea what I did or didn't do. The remaining girl drifted to the bathroom, leaving Cooper sitting next to me while I punched Peyton's number into my phone, having memorized it the second she'd written it on my palm. "Yes," I texted, certain for once of every damn word I typed. "I want you to use it. Whenever you want to use it. And now you have it." Send.

"You won't hook up with her," Cooper said. "You know that, right?"

I grabbed my receipt off the table, about to ask him what the hell he thought he knew about it, when a feminine squeal pulled our attention to the window. Looking at her phone, Peyton grinned and threw her arms around her brother, doing a quick hop-bounce.

She either had no idea I could see her or she didn't care. "You think so?" I said, unable to hold back a smile as she bounced on the balls of her feet.

Cooper watched her get into Jon's car and looked at me with resentful eyes. "Two dates and you're done."

I kept my expression neutral. "Is that supposed to be a warning?"

"Not at all." He turned to the window. "I'm saying that's her limit. You won't get a third date. Nobody does. She doesn't need the hassle."

On any other day, I wouldn't have stuck around for this bullshit conversation. But I'd seen Peyton too often with this guy. He was important to her. "So…*what?* You're saying she gets bored easily?"

"No," he said calmly, apparently immune to sarcasm. "I'm saying if you believe the rumors about her, prepare yourself for disappointment."

Her reputation as a hot piece of ass had been the

highlight of my afternoon, but not in a good way. I wanted to put it behind me. "Well, I can't speak for anyone else she's dated, but with me it only took one afternoon." I glanced at my receipt and calculated the tip.

"*What* took only one afternoon?"

I'd hit a nerve with the vague comment, exactly as I'd meant to. But proving I could be a bigger dick than a guy only watching out for his friend didn't hold much appeal, even when that *pendejo* was being a judgmental jackass based solely on rumors he'd heard about *me*. The irony of this conversation wasn't lost on me. Still, I didn't want to alienate *everyone* important to her. "It took less than an afternoon to realize the rumors aren't true."

His shoulders sagged.

"So the two-dates thing," I said, trying to sound casual and friendly. I stood and threw the tip onto the table. "For real? She never does a third date?"

"Right."

The third date was usually the putout date. Cooper must think he was cluing me in on something. "Well, it's impressive when you think about it," I said. Pulling my keys from my pocket, I walked toward the back parking lot.

"What's impressive?" His gaze swung back to me.

I stopped and shrugged. "That she can figure out in two dates if someone's worth a third. She doesn't waste time on the wrong people. Guess she knows what she wants. If she'd found it already, she wouldn't be here with me."

The second Cooper's eyes slanted to slits, I knew he wanted more than a friendship with Peyton. "In one day," he said in a calm voice that didn't match his glare, "you've convinced her to skip school and lie repeatedly to the people most important to her. You barely know her, Guerra, and you've already started to corrupt what makes her different from everybody else. Whatever she's searching for...I hope it isn't you."

A dozen asshole remarks hovered on my tongue. I had an impressive ability to make people feel like shit with little thought. I'd acquired this talent through firsthand experience. Cooper likely had the same talent. He lived in my neighborhood, which automatically meant his life hadn't been a party either.

Staring at his brooding eyes and stubborn smirk, a numbing exhaustion settled into my bones. Suddenly, unexpectedly, all this fooling around with Peyton had become more of a problem than I needed.

I wanted out already.

"Doesn't matter," I said. "I don't waste time on the wrong people either." I didn't wait for a reply as I stalked through the back, past the bathrooms and out the door, slamming it behind me.

CHAPTER SEVEN

Sam

I held onto my locker door like a crutch after first period, functioning on fumes and grumpy as hell when a hand touched my shoulder. I must have looked ready to deck someone because the skinny kid standing behind me jumped back a foot when I turned around.

"Sorr-y!" he yelled.

Several students turned and I glared until they looked away. I looked back at the kid and slammed my locker closed. "*What?*"

"This," he said, quickly shoving a small stack of money under my nose.

No. Fucking. Way. I stared at the cash, wondering what the hell happened to my quiet life. Oh, yeah. Peyton Greene. That's who happened. "*And?*" I said, pissed because I was thinking about her again.

He held out a wrinkled, worn paper. The thing looked as though it had been crumpled and thrown away, several times. "Two names. All I ask is you keep them off my ass. If you want more money, I'll pay you when I can get it."

I remembered Peyton standing on my lawn, asking me a similar question with pleading blue eyes. My gaze shifted from the paper to the cash. "Let me guess. Two hundred." There were twenties. Lots of 'em.

His eyebrows arched. "Why? Is it four hundred for two? Because I can get it. It may take me a few weeks, but I'll get it."

Fuck. Just fuck. "Where the hell did you get *this* two hundred?" The kid couldn't be more than fifteen.

"My mom. I told her what you did. She's hoping maybe you'll—"

"Wait." Damn, I'd interrupted him before I fully realized what he'd said. His *mother?* Crap. I shifted into stupid mode, my usual whenever blindsided. "What I did? What did I do?"

He shrugged "Everyone's talking about it. You shut down Delaney for two hundred," he said. "These two should be a cinch compared to him. Well," he glanced at the dirty white tile between us, "a cinch for you."

He stood about five feet four inches tall. Weighed maybe a hundred and five pounds. He also looked terrified of me, which pissed me off. Why? I'd never done anything to him. I grabbed the paper from his hand. "You've listed *three* names here."

"Mine's the top one," he said. "I figured you wouldn't know me."

He'd be right. Scott…I did a double take on his last name. No way. I checked his expression to see if he was shittin' me. He took a deep breath and let it out, probably expecting a smartass comment. "Scott *Semen?*" I asked. He must be tougher than he looked. I couldn't fathom how he'd lived this long. "Seriously guy. That's your real last name?"

He rolled his eyes. "I know. I get crap for it."

No kidding. I read the two names below his. Eli Jones. Tim Nash. I stuffed the paper in my pocket, feeling surrounded by dickheads everywhere. "Any particular period or is it all the time?" I had no idea why I'd decided to get involved, until he looked up at me with that curious expression, as if I were a superhero and he'd figured out my identity. Exactly as Ryan had looked at me after that incident with Delaney.

"Second period." He glanced down, looking humiliated to admit it. I didn't have to delve deep into my past to remember how it felt to have an asshole in control of my life, and the helpless, circling-the-drain feeling that came with the memory. "It's been after school, too," he added, "but mainly around second period."

"Fine," I said. "Let's go."

"Where?"

"To your second period class."

"What are you going to do?"

I shrugged. "Take care of the problem."

He waited but I didn't elaborate. I figured a plan would come to me when we got there. "Don't you want this?" He held up the cash again.

I grabbed it before anyone could see.

"I have Mr. Morrison for American History," he said over his shoulder, leading the way. I didn't need directions, having sat in Morrison's class after school more times than I could count. I'd had two classes with him during the worst semester ever. The worst *year* ever.

We stopped outside the door. "Go in," I said, nodding.

He took a full breath and straightened, walking into class and giving himself a wide berth from the back where the two dickheads sat and talked. I stood at the door and surveyed the classroom, zeroing on the biggest guy there, the bone-crushing Samoan dude from Weight Lifting class.

Cindy whatshername, Jane Austen's biggest fan, sat close to the door. I said her name under my breath, hoping Morrison wouldn't see me.

She'd been writing when her back stiffened. Spotting me over her shoulder, her eyes rounded to huge proportions. Maybe she didn't feel as brave without Jon to run interference. I waved her over. She drifted out of her seat and toward me, eyes cautious as she bit her lip nervously. "What?" she said. "Is this about yesterday?"

"Yesterday? No. I need a favor." I said, ignoring her shocked expression. "See the big guy, second row, third from the front? The guy twice the size of his desk?"

As if there was another student his size, she whipped around, checked the room, and turned back to me. "You mean Maru?"

Maru. His face and name didn't ring a bell, and I doubted I would have forgotten him had I seen him before this semester. He must have moved to Ridgeview last year after I left. "Right. Tell him I'd like to talk to him."

Without asking me to elaborate, she whipped around and crossed the room to his desk. Leaning down, she spoke and he listened, looking over her shoulder a few times to scowl at me. When he stood and headed my way, he moved slowly, as if to tell me he didn't have to move quickly for anybody.

"What?" he asked.

I'd expected a snarl, not a lisp. The guy had an under bite like a bulldog and his size would intimidate anyone. But then he spoke with a soft voice, a lisp, and I immediately equated him to a gentle bear type who planned to buy his mama a new house when the NFL drafted him. "Interested in an easy hundred?" I asked, holding up half the money.

The late bell rang and he grabbed it without hearing my terms. "To do what?"

Morrison glared at us and tapped his watch. Knowing I needed to make this quick, I nodded toward the kid. "The guy by the window. Scott?"

"Blondie boy?" he said, turning back to me. "What about him?"

"You catch Jones or Nash giving him any shit at all, *anywhere*, put a stop to it."

"No prob. That's all you want?"

"Yeah. But be cool. No fighting if you can help it."

"Find a seat, Maru," Morrison said.

"Hey," I said, stopping him before he left, "if it comes to blows, come find me afterward. There's another hundred if you have to fight." I didn't want to encourage him because the guy had bowling balls for arms and could likely do serious damage. Still, asking anyone to fight meant immediate suspension, possible expulsion, regardless of who started the fight. I knew from experience.

His smile widened. "This was the easiest hundred I've ever made. Nice doing business with you, my man." He held out his hand to me, and reluctantly, I grabbed it. He jerked me forward, patting my shoulder in an awkward guy hug.

I felt my face getting hot as Scott watched us, no doubt assuming Maru and I were friends because all the scary people hung out together. Maru turned to the kid and raised a closed fist at the two, oblivious bullies in the back. Scott's wide-eyed gaze followed him back to his seat before looking at me. "No shit?" he mouthed.

I grinned. Yeah, kid. No shit.

A similar experience with a freckle-faced, overweight boy named Lee happened before fourth period, and then a kid named Xu, who looked thin as tracing paper, stopped me in the parking lot at lunch. By sixth period, I'd hit my limit on sad stories.

I had a good idea who was responsible for this phenomenon and intended to talk to Ryan as soon as I saw him. We'd steered clear of each other—not counting sushi yesterday—since Delaney. I didn't want anyone thinking I was his bodyguard, and I doubted he wanted anyone thinking he needed one.

I left Weight Lifting early, per my usual, and headed for sophomore hall, hanging out until most everyone had disappeared to class. When his slow ass finally emerged from the guy's bathroom, I waited for him to open his locker before cornering him. "What the fuck are you telling people?"

He jumped and nearly dove into his locker. "Dammit," he said, recognizing my voice and pushing himself upright to glare at me. "Give a person some warning, why don't you." Turning toward the few people left, his cheeks reddened. He shoved his damp hair from his eyes and looked at me. "What did I tell *who*?"

"People I don't know are coming out of the woodwork to ask me to kick someone's…rather, to keep other people from kicking their asses. I've had more twenties handed to me today than a stripper earns in a week. *Where* are they getting their information?"

"Jeez, let me think," he said. "Maybe it's the damn video of you and my sister on the internet." His face drained of color and he looked back into his locker, grabbed a book and pen, obviously wanting me to go.

I didn't have time for this sulking crap. "*What* video?"

His teeth clenched until a muscle moved in his jaw. "The video named *Student's Body for Hire*," he said, still not looking at me. "Get it? Student body. Student's body. Clever, no? You might want to do a search. Uploaded this morning. You can drool over my sister like everyone else. Oh, wait…you already did that." He slammed his locker shut. "In fact, you know what?" He turned to me, his glare murderous. "If you'd hit me as hard as you could, it would feel better than this. You have no idea how much I fucking hate you right now." He pivoted and stalked away.

Watching his skulking form disappear, I stood there trying to figure out what the hell just happened when the late bell sounded.

Shit. Campbell.

I pivoted and took off down the hall, reaching British Authors and sliding into my seat with a loud thump and jerk of my desk. Several students in the back laughed. Campbell finished writing our next assignment on the board and turned, her gaze settling on me. "You're late, Mr. Guerra."

"Sorry."

"By two days," she added.

"The office has my excuse."

"Well, I don't mind telling you we've all been waiting with bated breath. We're anxious to hear your take on Mansfield Park, aren't we class?" She glanced over her shoulder to the class, who stared back in silence. "I assume you've read it. You had so much more time than the rest of us."

"Yes."

"Then you can explain the premise shortly," she said, "and we'll go from there." She twisted around and rifled through some papers, which gave me a minute to get my shit together.

I took a deep breath, my mind still on the conversation with Ryan. Peyton's gaze drifted to mine, those blue eyes sparkling as a smile formed. Damn. She wouldn't smile at me if she knew about the video. Ryan must not have told her about it.

Knowing her a little better now, it was just a guess that she cared what people thought. That meant when she found out about the video, she'd probably cry, which bothered the hell out of me to think about. Peyton Greene had started to mess with my head and she wasn't even trying. I shouldn't care about this stupid high school crap but I couldn't help it. I hadn't stopped thinking about her all night.

She'd listed thirty-two movie and book inconsistencies during a writing frenzy over sushi, all to keep me from falling on my face today. She'd done all the work, as Ryan had moodily pointed out, and I still hadn't figured out why.

For my phone number? No. She could have just asked. So why?

I also didn't get how she related to the character, Fanny Price. She said she fit in everywhere but didn't belong anywhere. That wasn't Peyton Greene at all. People included her in everything. They wanted her around. She made life look easy and fun. I couldn't recall my life ever being easy, seldom fun, at least since *Papá* had passed. Watching someone else who had it all—watching Peyton in my seventh period class every day—had been the closest I could get to that perfect life.

By the time I'd collapsed into bed at eleven-thirty last night, I'd decided to read the damn book so I could figure out what she'd meant. Even scanning through the endless descriptive sections, I only had an hour left to sleep when I'd finished, and I still came up at a loss. Fanny had been proper, cautious and scared of everything. Peyton didn't seem afraid of anything, including me.

I needed to stop thinking about her.

Campbell turned and nodded at me. Damn. I took a deep breath, dreading the two minutes I'd need to summarize this drivel, and worse, the thirty-minute inquisition that would start once I finished the review.

But once I started talking I didn't stop, having hated the book so much I realized I remembered a great deal of it. Stupid little details I'd noted while reading last night, along with highlights and turning points from Peyton's notes and her comments in the car. I even felt a little smug as Campbell's eyes rounded when she didn't have to prod me through it. For twenty minutes, I gave the class more detail about the characters' vacuous personalities and pointless aspirations than I'd realized existed.

It was the longest I'd ever talked about anything.

Campbell was quiet a long moment after I'd finished before she closed her mouth and cleared her throat. "That was very…thorough, Mr. Guerra. I'd thought you'd disappoint me today but I must say I'm quite pleased."

Everyone else had collapsed into a funeral home quiet, but I'd finally wrapped my head around this subject matter and I intended to get through this stupid review if it killed me. Maybe if I passed Campbell's scrutiny this one time, she'd back the hell off me.

"Tell me your overall impression," she said.

I'd hated it. Even if zombies had ripped their way through the innards of every character, I couldn't have appreciated this stupid story. "I couldn't relate," I said.

"To the characters or the story?"

"Both."

"Why?"

I shrugged.

"You'll need to elaborate," she said.

This damn day would never end. "If I'm going to take the time to read a book, the characters better have more going on than walking the landscape and discussing redecorating or stupid parts in a play."

"You feel the story was pointless?"

"What story? Nothing happened." I needed sleep in the worst way because I hated this story more than I had twenty minutes ago. "The entire book had people talking marriage and money. The characters didn't have jobs. Not real ones. Maybe Fanny, but they handed her the position. The only way Austen could make the reader care about her was to surround her with self-absorbed, classist assholes."

A few people laughed before I figured out why. I'd said the word *assholes*. Christ. I dropped farther into my seat.

Campbell took one look at my disgruntled expression, scowled briefly and let it go. "Well, you are hard on characters, Mr. Guerra, to think Fanny Price had it easy."

"Like I said, I couldn't relate to her…struggle, if you want to call it that. Price wasn't quite the help or family. She didn't feel she belonged. So what."

"You can't relate?"

"Today they call that being a stepchild. More than half this class relates."

Some students laughed as if I were joking. More murmured agreement.

"He's right," said a quiet girl who sat parallel to me but across the room. "Fanny's extended family pulled her from poverty and essentially gave her a job. By today's standards, her relations handed her a middle class position. She never had to work her way up. It's difficult to feel sorry for her."

A few others made similar comments. Some mumbled the word *incest*.

"Interesting," Campbell said, sliding her skinny butt onto her desk. I sensed her peripheral vision on me and wished she'd just tell me what to say. Whenever she did this rapid-fire question thing, she was after something specific. "Nothing resembled your current reality beyond that, Mr. Guerra?"

I refused to blink first. "Only that the world still judges highly or harshly based on money and social status. That much hasn't changed."

She hopped off her desk. "Exactly. Austen's books revolved around money, class and social status. Issues still important today." Campbell needed little encouragement to keep talking, which meant she wouldn't call on me again and I could close my eyes. While everyone readied for a lecture, I buried my face behind a hand, letting my eyes burn. Work would kill me if I went in half-asleep. I couldn't call in sick, even though I felt close to it. The mortgage was due. Maybe Jonas would take one of my sessions and let me crash for an hour.

"Ms. Greene."

Hearing Campbell say Peyton's name snapped me back to reality and I blinked my eyes open. Damn. I'd actually started to doze while sitting up, dreaming of sleeping. I dropped my hand to the desk and looked at Peyton. She was one of those students who read everything and always seemed interested. When Campbell asked her to dig deep and summarize Austen's message, Peyton smiled broadly. "I think it's about following your heart."

I sighed through my nose. Peyton was sweet, and precious, and naïve as hell. If I had been her father, or brother, or a friend, I'd have worried myself into a grave by now thinking about her out there in the big bad world.

She turned and grinned at me, not caring that everyone could see. We stared at each other, her in fairytale land, me half-asleep, and I no longer cared if her brother hated me, if her friends resented me, or that someone had slapped a video of us on the internet. I wanted her. More than I'd wanted anything in a long time.

Campbell called on Josie Buchannon sitting several seats behind me as Peyton and I stared at each other.

"We have to talk," I mouthed.

"After class?" Peyton asked.

I nodded and grinned at how slowly she'd moved her mouth, as if I couldn't read her lips otherwise.

I waited outside the door after class, and when she spotted me, she gave me that shy smile she seemed to reserve just for me. Students swarmed around us like inmates during a prison riot, pushing us together by the wall.

I'd told Vanna I'd give her a ride home today and had to make this quick. I didn't need my sister spotting me talking to Peyton and giving me more shit than she already had.

"We have a problem," I said.

"What?"

Where to start. I pulled three hundred in twenties from my pocket, folded the stack in half, and held it out to her.

Ryan and Cooper approached as she stared at the money, twisting her mouth. "What's that for?"

"Three more people wanting protection from bullies."

"What?" Cooper asked, as if I were talking to him.

"Three people wanting protection," Peyton repeated as she turned to him with wide eyes. They stared at each other, grins forming, before she turned back to me. "You're serious?"

"Unfortunately." I pulled a list from my back pocket. "After the second one, I made a list to keep it straight, in case this went on all day."

"I can't believe you agreed to do it," she said.

"I didn't." Her smile disappeared. "No *one* person could cover this much territory at once. That's why I had to write it down. I listed the person paying, the assholes giving them crap, and the people I paid to take care of it. Each got a hundred, which leaves three hundred in reserves in case they have to fight. I told them there's an extra hundred if they do fight, but to be cool about it." I shrugged. "It was how you originally presented the offer."

"Me?" she said.

"Yeah. This bodyguard thing was your idea. I figured if they would have approached you instead, you wouldn't have told them no. I guess I'm hoping you'll take the money and get me off the hook here. With two jobs, no way do I have time to keep track of something like this."

Cooper pulled the list from my hand and stared at it. "Peeeyton," he said. "Do you know what this means?"

She reluctantly grabbed the money I held out to her and turned to Cooper. "Oh my god, I think this is it," she said, bouncing twice. "Are you thinking what I'm thinking?"

"Already there," he said, familiar with her enough to read her mind, apparently, which irked me. "When can you start? Do you work tonight?"

She shook her head. "Not until Sunday morning. I can start right away."

"Crap, I have to work."

"When do you get off?"

"Nine."

"Come by after," she said. "I'll get started on the database when I get home. Do you want me to call Jon to come over, too? Maybe help put together the webpage?"

"I doubt he will," he said.

A tennis match had less back and forth action. They talked so fast I could barely keep up.

"I'll coerce him with free cookies from the bakery," she said, folding the money into her pocket. "I'll even tell him to bring Cindy."

Cooper looked skeptical. "Jon's not going to agree to *any* of this," he said. "You're right, though. It can't hurt to ask."

I'd intended to ask her what *this* was, but when she turned to me, I no longer cared. Nothing seemed to matter when she looked at me like that.

"We should go, Peyton," Ryan said, scowling.

Cooper smacked her brother's elbow. "Come on. We'll wait by the car, Peyton," he said, leaving with a reluctant Ryan in tow.

Decent of him, given what we last said to each other.

"Are you okay?" she asked me.

"Why wouldn't I be?"

"You didn't want to do this when it was my brother. Now a few days later you have three more, and here you are, collecting money and making lists. You're neck deep in my plan. I figured you'd be mad, like you were when I showed up at your house."

I'd been pissed for several reasons that day. None of which mattered now. I had a bigger problem. I wanted to see her again but I'd never asked anyone out. I couldn't think how to word it.

Movement caught my eye and I spotted Vanna waving at me from the crossroads of junior and senior halls.

Great.

Peyton noticed me looking over her head and turned to wave at Vanna. My sister the socialite barely lifted a hand to wave back before turning on a fast trek to the other end of the hall.

"That's my cue," I said. "I told her I'd give her a ride. She hates the bus."

Peyton turned to me, frowned, and took a step back. "Okay. I'll see you Monday?"

"Yeah." I closed the space she'd put between us, not wanting anyone to hear. "Unless you want to meet me Saturday night."

"More homework?" Her eyebrows arched. "Or are you

asking me out?"

I swallowed. "I'm asking you out."

Her eyes widened as if she'd expected me to say something else. "Sure." She smiled. "What time?"

I guess I'd expected some kind of hard-to-get game. Not her gorgeous smile and eager nod. "Really? Just like that?"

"*Sam,*" she said sternly—sternly for Peyton, anyway. "I owe you for sushi last night, *and* for tolerating my brother's bad mood, *and* for him inviting the entire gang."

Her quick yes had lost its luster. "You want to go out because you think you owe me? What's this owing thing with you, anyway?"

"All I'm saying is I want to buy *you* dinner this time. That's all."

Papá would have killed me had I ever let a girl pay. "You don't owe me. I can't do dinner anyway. I work until seven. We could do a movie though. Wipe this Mansfield Park nightmare off the books?"

"*Or,*" she said, reaching out and brushing her hand across my flannel pocket, her fingertips soft and lingering, "we'll do both. Maybe you'll at least let me buy you coffee."

"You'd better get over this. I'm not letting you pay." Vanna caught my attention again, stretching dramatically and yawning. She dropped to the floor and sprawled flat against the tile, looking like a hobo sleeping on the sidewalk.

Peyton turned to Vanna, her mouth twisting sideways as if stifling a grin.

"She's not known for…subtlety," I said.

Those dimples appeared as she turned and took a small step forward, definitely in my space. Her sweet perfume drifted around me and she gave my shirt a quick yank. "So you're one of *those* guys."

"What guys?"

"The old fashioned type like my granddad, who won't

let girls pay. You open doors, too, don't you? A gentleman."

My *mamá* would have smacked me on the head if I hadn't opened doors. "Let's say I've never typed myself. I don't exactly go on a lot of dates." As in, ever.

Clutching her books tighter, she rotated her upper body back and forth, that restless energy ready to burst. "I feel special. I don't think many guys would admit that."

I grinned, too tired to pretend I asked girls out every day. "I don't think it's that much of a mystery."

She halted, eyes searching mine. "What time did you say? Eight?"

I nodded. "No brother this time."

Dimples now. "Agreed."

"And I'll pick you up."

Hesitation replaced her smile. "Um, it might be better if I meet you. If you stop by the house, you'd have to meet my parents. I wouldn't want to put you through that. Seriously. My dad can be…critical."

If her parents were anything like her brother, I could easily picture how it would go. They wouldn't see *me*. Just another goddamn *Mexicano* living off the government. Never mind I was born in Oregon, as were Vanna and my parents, Spanish was my second language, and no one in my family had ever lived off the government. Not unless one considered a state death benefit *living*.

I wondered what *Papá* would have said in the same situation. "If it's important to you, I'm okay with meeting your parents."

Her hesitant expression slowly turned into a broadening smile. *Sweet.* I'd made serious points. Now if only I could keep my hands off her until I scored a third date.

CHAPTER EIGHT

Peyton

Ryan rolled onto his side, staring at me from the foot of my bed. "Did I say *Fight-or-Flight* already?"

"Yes," Cindy said from her cross-legged position on the floor. "And if you ask me, it doesn't encapsulate the project. It's not as if you can escape these jerks. They're everywhere. In class. The parking lot. Next door."

"Maybe we should start a list," Jon said next to her, sprawling on his back and crossing his legs at the ankles.

I'd been leaning against my headboard and using my laptop as a leg warmer for over an hour. Between four people, we should have been able to think of a decent website name by now. Programming and logic made sense to me. Marketing, not so much. I wished Adam would get here. I wanted to run everything past him before making any final decisions.

"Earth to Peyton." Ryan waved at me.

I looked from my Bleach anime screen saver. "I suck at this, you guys. Why don't I figure out a name later. I don't want to keep you here all night."

"You can't have a website without a name," Cindy said. "It's the first thing you have to decide."

I'd already completed half the database, but mentioning that to Cindy meant risking getting on her bad side tonight. I wasn't up for it.

"I realize I'm repeatin' myself," Jon said, scooting away from Cindy to avoid her punches, "but you're going to take some serious heat. You'll get an A for the Projects class because, well, this idea totally rocks. But this is gonna hit the fan big time."

"Who would have a problem with keeping teenagers safe, other than the bullies threatening them?"

"You might be surprised," he said.

"Here's one," Cindy said, an eyebrow arching. "How about Student Body for Hire?"

Ryan whipped around to look at her.

"Cindy—" Jon said, but she reached over and smacked his shoulder before he could say more.

"I'm serious," she said. "I mean, I know it's a bit soon, but you have to admit the play on words makes sense. Student *body* because you're asking students to play bodyguard to other students. And *student body* because the website is for the entire student body to use, whether they be the guard or guarded. I think it's kinda catchy, don't you?"

"It's too wordy," I said. "No one will remember it." I tapped my laptop to pull it out of sleep mode.

"But it makes sense, right?" she said. "Everyone is searching for that phrase now. Well, something *like* it." She giggled. "It's free advertising. Every time someone searches for the video, they'll pull up a link to your website."

"Will you shut your pie hole for once!" Ryan snapped.

I looked up, shocked by Ryan's outburst. Cindy appeared unfazed as she glanced from Ryan, to me, and back. "Ohmygod. She doesn't know, does she? How is it even possible that Miss Celebrity doesn't know about the video with all of those gossip whores at school?"

My stomach knotted, recalling only one time when I'd

seen Cindy look so eager. She'd worn the same expression three years ago when she'd told me about the slut rumor. The one Jason Thompson had created about me the day after the attack. I pointed to myself. "You don't mean *me*, do you?"

"Of course I mean you." She let out a squeal and leapt onto my bed, grabbing my laptop. "This is hysteeerical. You've got to watch it while I'm here," she said, typing *Student's Body for Hire* in the search field.

Wait. What?

She clicked the top link and pulled up a video. Five hundred thirty-eight hits. Couldn't be too great. Except the person who held the account, *Mondeek*, had only uploaded it this morning. "This is mega hot, by the way," she said, glancing at me. "Even by my standards."

I glanced at Ryan, wishing someone other than Cindy would clue me in on what was happening. My brother shook his head, disgusted, and my gaze flew to Jon, who blushed deep red. Not a good sign. He and Cindy had dated for three years, *seriously* for two of those years, and Cindy had told me more details about their sex life than I'd ever wanted to know. The kinky, experimental stuff no one should ever share. If Cindy said this video was hot, then I was in serious trouble.

I turned back to the laptop and swallowed.

"Cindy," Ryan said, voice shaking, "I totally mean it. I will kill you."

She kicked Ryan's leg to shush him. When he grunted, she shushed him again with another kick and hit play.

The video was grainy and jerky at first. I braced for a flash of skin and the inevitable blue screen of death when this nefarious website infected my laptop with the mother of all viruses. But once the camera did a quick zoom and visually sharpened, I recognized the school parking lot. Another zoom and I recognized Sam. More sharpening and I recognized *me* talking to Sam.

I froze, waiting to hear my voice and our conversation.

Instead, another girl's voice jolted me into sitting straighter. The video culprit hadn't been close enough to record our conversation, thank goodness. Instead, he or she had added audio, a girl's voice that sounded pitchy and giggly, like anime. Rather, anime *porn* because she talked specifically about sex. Okay, the video culprit definitely had to be a guy. They had me propositioning Sam, saying things I would never repeat because I honestly didn't know what most of it meant.

What exactly was a face plant?

What shocked me the most was how perky and wide-eyed I appeared, all while saying the most lewd things I'd ever heard.

"You okay, Peyton?" Jon asked.

I looked at his twitching mouth and bit my upper lip, trying to hold back a smile. When my video counterpart squealed with anime laughter, I contorted my mouth, but video me cooed and I caved in to a fit of giggles.

Jon reluctantly smiled.

"*Watch* this," Cindy said, grabbing my arm.

I looked to the video to see Sam shift uncomfortably at what my character proposed before he said, "*¿Qué?*"

Cindy and I roared with giggles at the sound of Sam's voice, or rather, the voice Mondeek dubbed over Sam's voice. The man sounded old, had a thick Spanish accent and obviously smoked because every time he laughed, he made a hissing, wheezing sound under his breath. The fact that Sam never laughed or even smiled made the scene hysterically funny. The laughter came across as a creepy, pervy laugh in his head. The old man spoke quickly, swapping between English and Spanish. Mondeek had set up the dialogue in such a way that throwing Spanish periodically into his responses made it funnier. Some common Spanish I understood. Others, I didn't, thankfully so, especially when every statement ended with a pervy wheeze laugh.

My character, looking all innocent and bouncy,

responded in that ditzy voice while Cindy and I grabbed each other's arms and squealed with laughter.

Sam's script had him asking for weird scenarios and unique positions. I only knew this because Cindy had been exploring Kama Sutra stuff recently and kept translating in whispers. Our characters spoke back and forth quickly, our mouth movements not meshing at all, and our awkward expressions didn't help.

"Do I always look that…perky? It's as though I'm on springs."

"You *are* pretty chipper," she said. "Well…not usually like *that*. It doesn't matter. You look great. And eager! Girl, check you out. You are *into* him. What did he say to you that made you look at him like that?"

No. He'd said no. A lot.

Ryan let out a moan so I purposely changed the subject. "I can see my bra through my shirt."

"Maybe in the sunlight," Cindy said. "Only a little. No biggie though because you look great."

Ryan stepped into the video, a young, grumpy voice used instead of his. His slumped shoulders and perpetual disapproving expression reminded me of the depressed cartoon character, Charlie Brown. Apparently, Mondeek had cast him my pimp.

"This. Is. Disgusting," Ryan said.

Cindy gave another kick to his shoe.

When my character's dialogue started sounding like Dr. Seuss meets Asian porn, I thought Cindy and I would laugh ourselves into tears.

"I can't believe you two think this is funny," Jon said, grinning then at Sam's old-man pervy laugh.

Savanna showed up in the video and grabbed the money, giving a room number and one-hour time limit.

Cindy wiped her eyes. "That girl will kill somebody for this."

Savanna. Oh, no. *Sam.* I lost my smile, realizing Sam and Savanna would watch this someday, too. That brotherly protectiveness of his would send him into orbit over this.

"Okay," Cindy said, adjusting the laptop. "Here it is. Don't pay attention to the dialogue when you start writing on his hand. Watch Sam's expression."

"Mother of God," Ryan mumbled, hands scrubbing his face.

Video-version me walked to Sam, stood close, and pulled his hand from his side. I watched my fingers slide along his wrist to curl around his palm. I remembered vividly the experience of his rough skin and the thick web of muscle between his thumb and forefinger.

"Are you watching?" she said.

Realizing I'd spaced off into the memory, I quickly squinted my eyes to show her I had my attention on Sam's face, something I hadn't been able to do while writing on his hand. He'd studied my face and his gaze had lowered.

My heart did a weird thwump-thump in my chest to see the desire in his eyes before his demeanor shifted. Like his expression in the foyer when he'd turned to me, that guarded expression back in place.

But why?

Cindy grabbed my forearm. "I know. It gets better."

She couldn't see it. At the time, neither had I. Probably because I hadn't really known him. After spending time with him, I recognized the subtleties. It was plain on his face. He'd never planned to come over Tuesday night.

"You watching?" she asked, squeezing my arm.

I narrowed my eyes again. Sam stared at me walking away, his expression intense, exactly as Ryan had described it. My cheeks burned hot that everyone at school had seen it now, too. By the time the video stopped, my already stuffy bedroom felt as though the temperature had ratcheted up twenty degrees.

"I'd noticed him before," Cindy said. "*Obviously*. He has that tall, dark, and brooding thing going, but when I watched this today…damn. Is he hot or is it just me?" She had a gleam in her eye that made me want to shove her off the bed. "Okay, well, you're right. I take it back. He *would be* hot if he didn't act so antisocial you don't dare look him in the eyes. But *you*." She pushed my shoulder hard. "Can I tell you several people, *including* me, would love to know what he said to you. You both were so into each other." She pulled back. "Wait, you're not seriously into him, are you?"

I looked to Jon, who had passed out on the floor, too wiped out from an all-night study session. Her pointed comments about Sam had been for Jon's benefit. She often noticed other guys aloud to make him jealous. One day her fooling around would cost her the relationship.

Ryan remained unmoving, his forearm thrown over his eyes. "Come on, Ryan," I said. "Don't be mad. It's funny."

"You're avoiding the question," Cindy said, pushing my shoulder.

"*What* question?" I pulled my laptop from her claw-like grip.

"Oh, hon, you're into him." She grinned. "It's almost painful to watch. And that's okay, you know. Hooking up, I mean. You'll want to lose your virginity before college anyway. But you *do* know you can't seriously date him, right? Your social circle would become non-existent within forty-eight hours."

"Sometimes you make me sick, Cindy," Ryan said, pulling his forearm from his face to glare at her. "Please stop hanging out with my sister. I don't want your warped thinking rubbing off on her."

"Not confirming or denying here," I said, "but how could dating Sam affect my social circle? A, I don't have a social circle. B, why would any of my friends care who I date? I don't like everyone my friends date, and I don't say a word." I shot her a pointed look.

"Because Sam Guerra is a freak," she said. "The guy doesn't have any friends. I mean, he's not even low status. He's no status. That's bad. You can't date a no-status guy."

She fluffed her blonde hair back, smiled, and sighed dreamily. "I'll admit I get the attraction. He's a dangerous bad boy. Although, I can't imagine losing it to someone like that. He's probably…well, how can I say it?"

"Maybe you shouldn't," I said.

"He's probably aggressive and rough. Definitely not for you." She smiled in that all-knowing fashion before giving me a frown of sympathy. "Might turn you off to men forever. Especially after that thing with Jason—"

"Shut the hell up, Cindy!" Ryan snapped, startling Jon awake.

"You can go for it if you want to," she continued, ignoring Ryan's icy stare, "but don't think I won't give you a big fat I-told-you-so when he puts the moves on you right out of the gate. I used to date guys like him when I was a freshman. They have certain…expectations. And once they get *that*, they expect it all the time. Pretty soon that's all you're doing is meeting up to have sex."

I looked down at Jon, never surprised by Cindy's oversharing but always shocked when Jon never reacted to it. Luckily, he was out like a light again.

"But if you know that going in and that's all you're after," she said, elbowing me with a wink, "definitely go for it."

"Go for *what*?"

Adam's voice startled us, and we glanced over to see him standing in my bedroom doorway. I reached over and slammed my laptop closed on her hand.

"Ouch!" Cindy pulled her hand away and flexed her fingers.

"No one," I said. "*Nothing*. I meant to say nothing."

"Don't you knock or ring a doorbell anymore?" Cindy asked.

He shrugged, immune to her abrasiveness. "Peyton's mom saw me pull into the driveway and opened the door." His eyes shifted to me. "You should go for *what*?"

"Nothing."

"Sam Guerra," Cindy said.

Adam's mouth flattened into a line and I elbowed Cindy hard. "You must have seen the video," he said.

I put my hands to my hot cheeks. "Did everyone know about this but me?"

"I was going to break the news to you later," Adam said.

"Well I beat you to it. I *just* showed it to her," Cindy announced, sounding bitchy as only she could. She had a self-imposed rivalry with Adam for my affection. Why was a complete mystery because she said as many thoughtless things to me as she did to anyone else. Adam and I only tolerated her because Jon dated her, and we loved him to death. But beyond meeting at a party or laughing over a stupid video, Cindy and I had no chance at a future friendship. We couldn't be more different.

I heard Jon's snore and turned to Cindy. "Adam and I have tons to do if we want to get this online by next week. I'd hate to keep waking Jon up. He's beat, the poor thing. Maybe you should take him home."

She looked at Jon. "He's cute when he sleeps, isn't he?" she said.

Watching her slide off the bed, I turned to Adam, perplexed whenever Cindy said something sweet like that. It was those rare occurrences when I doubted my opinion of her.

Jon and Cindy left and Ryan followed, going to his room and slamming the door. Once alone, Adam turned to me. "Come on, Peyton. You know you can tell me. What's really going on?"

The day I talked seriously to Adam about me and a boy would be the day I'd be so in love I could no longer hide it. I wouldn't hurt Adam for anything less.

I smiled. "You won't believe this, but Cindy just had a good idea."

CHAPTER NINE

Peyton

I pulled on my second heel and positioned the strap, just as I noticed Ryan appear in my bedroom doorway. I straightened, pressing my hand to my stomach and turning away to examine myself in the dresser mirror.

"How do I look?" I asked, glancing at his reflection.

He leaned his shoulder to the doorframe, arms folded over his chest. "Taller."

"I'm serious, Ryan." I dropped my hands to my sides. "*Help.*"

His frown deepened and he sighed. "You look like you give a damn what Sam Guerra thinks about you."

"I *do.*" I smoothed my skirt again. Licked my cinnamon-shimmer lipstick to make sure it wouldn't rub off my lips. "Ryan, please. How do I look? Really."

His smile was brief. "I think you wear giddy well. I swear, Peyton, I never thought I'd see the day when you'd let a guy pick you up at the house again. I may not want you seeing Guerra, but it's nice to see you're getting past that thing Thompson did to you. What I don't get is why *him* of all people?"

"Sam?" I shrugged. "He's wary. It makes me feel safe."

"*Wary* makes you feel safe?"

"I don't think Sam trusts anyone, including me. It wasn't long ago I lived in a similar world." He looked down. "I can't explain why I trust Sam when no one else does, any more than I can explain why I was leery of Jason when everyone else trusted him. And maybe *trust* isn't the right word. It just doesn't seem to me that someone who's worried he could get hurt or used would be actively planning to hurt or use someone else."

His gaze met mine. "Wariness might be part of his act."

"Not everyone has an act."

"Yes they do."

"Really?" I looked at him. "Then what's yours?"

"Pretending to trust."

"Codswallow. I know you too well." I put a hand on my hip at his eye roll. "Ryan, stop. I find him…interesting. That's all. I want to get to know him better." Staring at my reflection, I pulled in a shaky breath.

"Calm down, sis," he said. "Jeez. You're losing it for this guy."

Lost it, actually. I shifted and turned to him. "Is giddy attractive? Or am I going to come off childish?"

He straightened and walked toward me. "It's good. I hope he's worth it."

Sam's Impala rumbled to a stop outside and I rounded my eyes at Ryan. "Oh God, that's him. Quick, go get him before he knocks. And keep him out there. Otherwise, Daddy will get to him first and all hell will break loose. I'll meet you outside."

"You know Dad is going to want to meet him."

"And you know why he can't. If all goes well tonight, I'll introduce him to Daddy another day when Sam doesn't have bruises on his face."

"Repeat that sentence and tell me again why this date is a good idea."

I gave him my pleading look. *"Please?"*

"The things I do for you," he muttered, rolling his eyes.

"All right." My brother was nearly out of the room when he twisted around and pointed a finger at me. "But stop being nervous. I'm about to go intercept a two-time senior for you, and he's probably wearing jeans and a flannel shirt, for God's sake. He's the lucky one here. Don't forget that."

I waved a hand, shooing him out. "Go. Quick. I'll be right down."

I fanned my face after he left. What would I do if Sam kissed me tonight? Keep it together, I hoped. I couldn't imagine. I didn't want to imagine. I just wanted it to happen and I didn't want to be all red and blotchy when it did.

Sam's voice, muffled in the foyer, made me halt all movement.

"Jeez, Dad," Ryan said loudly, giving me a heads-up.

Oh, damn it to hell. Ryan hadn't made it in time. I prayed Sam wasn't standing in the full glare of the porch light. That the bruises weren't visible. Grabbing my small purse, I pushed the thin strap over my shoulder, looked at my reflection and smoothed the olive top and the black and olive floral print skirt that stopped two inches above my knees. No pressure. I'd only been waiting my whole life to feel this excited about someone.

When I reached the top of the stairs, I saw both my parents already standing in the foyer with Ryan, who looked embarrassed by our dad's questioning. I could only imagine. Sam stood on the porch, gorgeous in black pants and a crisp, white shirt rolled up at the elbows. I pressed my fingertips to my chest, unable to stay in denial a second longer. Whether he dressed casual for school or nice to take me out, I was completely attracted. Mom's ardent gaze and unwavering smile told me she agreed.

"Guerra," my dad said. "I admit your last name sounds familiar, although I don't recall meeting your father. What does he do?"

Sam's neutral expression never changed. "He was a

police officer."

"Was?" Daddy asked. "He retired?"

"He passed."

"Oh, dear," Mom said, shaking her head and smacking Daddy's arm. "We're sorry to hear that."

"Thanks," Sam said, one shoulder lifting in a shy shrug. "It happened a while back."

Determined to get him out of this interrogation, I took the first noisy stair down, pulling Sam's eyes to mine. His gaze dropped, traveling over my outfit and back up.

Warmth seeped into my every pore and I smiled back at him as my family turned to see me descend the remaining stairs.

"You don't drink, do you Sam?" my dad said, turning back to Sam.

"Daddy!" I clomped down the stairs, trying not to break my neck in heels in my attempt to intervene.

"For a movie, Dad?" Ryan said. "Really?"

"Alcohol?" Sam said, breaking eye contact to turn to my dad. "No. I don't. She's safe with me."

"Good. Midnight then?" my dad said.

"That's one o'clock," Mom corrected him. "Our daughter is eighteen, if you'll recall."

Dad cleared his throat and gave her his stern expression that suggested they'd be talking about the issue later.

"Don't do anything crazy," Ryan said to me softly before drifting into the living room.

"Come on," I said to Sam, looping my fingers around his elbow and turning him to the walkway. I gave Mom a bug-eyed look behind his back.

"Stay out of trouble." Mom winked at me and closed the door.

Sam had texted me earlier and asked me to pick a movie. No guy had ever done that, so I'd taken my time and reviewed trailers until I found a movie a boy would like. Something with a lot of action, shootings, and people beatings.

Big mistake.

My stomach continued churning as we left the theater, and I promised myself never to make that sacrifice for a boy again. Drug cartels did horrible things to people. Disgusting, awful things.

Sam offered to drive us to Perks Express Cafe, the mall's best coffee shop, but I suggested we walk the colonnade instead, hoping he'd hold my hand. Clearly, I was getting desperate. The temperature had dropped and my three-quarter sleeve blazer did nothing to keep me warm as the wind blew against my bare legs.

"Did you like the movie?" I asked, walking with him.

"I'm not sure. I spent half of it wondering why you picked a movie you couldn't watch. You closed your eyes through most of it."

That meant he'd been watching me. "Sorry. Violent movies make me queasy. I have to close my eyes." I pressed my palm to my stomach. "The sounds of this one were…ugh, horrible." I tried to smile because I didn't want him to know I loathed violence. He might be into that fight club thing and I didn't want it to matter. Besides, I had no place to judge. If my project took off, I'd essentially be recruiting good students to threaten violent students with violence to put a stop to violence. Whenever I thought about my project's mission statement too long, it messed with my head. "Did I embarrass you?"

"No, but you didn't have to pick a movie you couldn't watch to get on my good side," he said, stuffing his hands into his pockets. "Trust me, you're already on it."

I smiled, wishing I could read him better. He'd said several sweet things tonight, yet he avoided touching me at every turn. Maybe he'd changed his mind. Maybe this chemistry was all one-sided and I didn't know it. Others I'd dated had tried groping me somewhere between *hello* and *do you like popcorn*. Nothing to wonder about there. Not that I wanted Sam groping me, although I'd feel a little better if he didn't treat me as though I had smallpox.

I stepped closer and looped my hand around his arm, noticing the definition of muscle under my fingertips, even with his arm extended and relaxed. "I felt bad for you spending the entire week saturated in Mansfield Park."

"You feel bad easily," he said.

"So…were you ever going to tell me you'd read the book?"

His gaze drifted to the pavement. "I hadn't planned on it. How did you know?"

"Your review went way beyond my notes. I just don't get why. I thought you wanted to pass it, not ace it. Which you did, by the way. Ms. Campbell is still in shock, I think."

A shy smile curled his mouth. "I just needed to clarify something. That's all."

"About what?"

He shrugged. "Just something."

I squeezed his bicep. *"What?"*

He paused. Glanced at me. "You."

"By reading Mansfield Park?"

"You said you could relate to the heroine." He shrugged. "So I was curious. Although I still don't see any similarities between you and Fanny Price."

I couldn't believe a boy would read an entire book to figure out a girl, especially a book he hated. It went beyond flattering. Maybe he liked me after all. "Fanny is pleasing," I said. "My mother says I'm pleasing."

He turned to me. *"Pleasing?"*

"It's a nicer way to say I conform to whatever setting I'm in and I don't make waves."

"That doesn't exactly sound like a compliment."

I sighed. "It's just that…someone has to be on my dad's side. You know? He cares what people think. Unlike my brother, who rocks the boat wherever he goes. My mother doesn't help by encouraging Ryan to question everything. She's quite the independent thinker and she can be rather extreme. Almost antiestablishment. My dad is logical. A rulebook kind of guy."

"And they're still married?"

I grinned. "Exactly. They argue more than they get along. I love them both and hate the constant tension. So I became the peacemaker. Fanny often plays the same role and I can relate."

"*Pleasing*," he repeated. "It's still not the word I'd use to describe you."

I'd have to be dead not to ask. "What word would you use?"

He grinned. "Let's save that one for another date."

"Did you just ask me out again?"

His arm flexed tight beneath my fingertips. "I think so, yeah."

I laughed at the surprise in his voice. "You may change your mind when you see the video someone made of us."

"Vanna and I saw it last night."

"You did?" I turned to see him smiling. I did, too. "I thought you'd be mad at me."

"Why would I be mad at you?"

"It was my fault. I stopped you that day."

"You really do guilt easily, don't you?" He frowned. "Actually, Vanna cracked up through the whole thing. Even her part. She especially got a kick out of my emphysema laugh."

The pervy laugh. "That's a relief." His eyebrow arched. "I mean, I needed you to watch the video so I could ask you a question, but I wasn't sure how to mention it. Now that you've already seen it, I guess I can ask." Only two blocks from the coffee shop, I could already smell freshly brewed coffee. "I'm creating a website and I'd like to use the title Student Body for Hire. I didn't like it at first, but the more I thought about it, the more it made sense for the nature of my website. I can set the tags so my website comes up whenever students do a browser search for that video. Makes for free advertising. And at least something good may come from the video."

"What's it for?"

"My Projects class. The gist is to match bullied kids with students willing to protect them. They pay a fee. Not to me but to the protector. It's like a dating site, but serious and nonprofit. If you don't mind me using the name and the list you started, I could publish the website in a few days."

"Wow, so you'd pay the website fees and do that much work just for a class?"

"Sure. I want a good grade obviously. But I'll be doing something for the greater good. You know? Bullied students who fear coming to school will finally have an option."

He stayed quiet.

"What?" I finally asked. "Bad idea?"

"No." He shrugged. "I've just…never met anyone like you."

"*Like me*. How should I take that?"

"Someone who does nice things for others without an agenda. It's so rare I almost don't believe you."

I shivered. "Says the guy who defended my brother without a single thing to gain."

"Actually, I was trying to get into your pants."

I giggled, too afraid to comment.

He grinned. "You do this website, and you may have to say goodbye to all your free time. Think of all the action movies you'll miss. All that blood and gore."

Sam acted like such a different person in private. Funny and sweet. I was beginning to adore him. "I'd *make* time for action movies," I said, turning from his curious gaze. "It's…important to me that the class does well. It's a seniors-only pilot. If they make it a regular class, it'll give the entrepreneurial types a step up. Maybe they can even skip the college experience."

"Is that what you want?"

"I've thought about it, yeah. I mean, who wants to start

life in massive debt? I love Mr. Smith's motto, too, although it's technically not *his*. He says to do what you love, and you won't have to work a day in your life. It's a novel idea…until you try to apply it to the assignment."

"What do you like doing?"

"Programming. Problem solving. Community work. My mom is the do-gooder in the family. She's a psychologist and social worker and big on everything community. She recruits Ryan and me into her cleanup and save projects."

"*Save* projects?"

"Save the beach, save the ozone, save the spotted owl, etcetera." We started walking again. "I wanted to do something constructive like that for my project. The assignment is to find an untapped market, find a way to deliver the product using technology, and advertise the product using social media."

"So you found a way to combine the two. Programming and…sort of community work. Within high school walls, at least."

"Thanks to you." I smiled. "We were getting desperate, too."

"We?"

"Adam and me. He was trying to help me come up with an idea. He's way more creative than I am and a better programmer. He's also the only person I can call at four in the morning when I can't sleep because a formula isn't working right."

"I'll bet. So why do you need my okay?"

"Linking the website with the video by using a similar title will give the website more exposure, but it could go the other way, too. The video is bound to get more hits. You're on it. Savanna is on it. I can get over the attention if you can, but it's only fair of me to ask you."

"Sure," he said, turning to me just outside the Perks' door. "You and I both know I owe you for those notes. You may have helped me make it to graduation. Finally."

Did he think I'd buy that? Others in his position would have picked up their GED and moved on. Anyone determined enough to go back to high school a fifth year, especially someone who clearly hated school, didn't need my help at all. "Then we're even," I said, watching three people leaving the coffee shop. "I helped you pass your review and you helped me with this."

"Because I agreed on a name? No one with a conscience would let you call that even." He grabbed the door and held it open, his hand brushing my back when I went first. "So yeah," he said, "I still owe you."

The brief contact created goose bumps across my skin. He'd only touched my back, but I couldn't stop thinking about it as we waited for our chai lattes, and later, after he drove me home and we talked until one in the morning.

He'd worked all day, looked exhausted, and we both had work tomorrow. But he continued asking me questions as if he didn't want the date to end. I didn't want it to end either, unless it meant he'd finally kiss me. When I delayed past one o'clock, the front porch light flickered, illuminating the driveway.

He glanced over my shoulder. "Not an electrical short, I take it?"

I looked at the front door. "No, it's my mom. She stays up late watching old movies. She has an emotionally stressful job and that's how she decompresses."

I turned to mention we didn't need to rush, but Sam had already hopped out of the car. One second he'd been sitting next to me, the next he opened my door.

I got out and pulled my purse strap over my shoulder, leaning against the Impala and shivering while trying to look like I wasn't. He ducked into the passenger side.

"Sam?"

He reemerged with the leather jacket and closed the door. "Hm?"

"Are you avoiding me?"

"Avoiding you? This is probably the longest

conversation I've ever had with a girl."

I dropped my gaze. "Not avoiding me, necessarily. Just not…touching me." I glanced at him. "Because it's noticeable. Like leprosy noticeable." I shivered from the cold night air and the intensity in those brown eyes.

He stepped forward and stretched the heavy jacket behind me and over my shoulders, engulfing me in the smell of warm leather. "I'm not avoiding you," he said, pulling the coat together before dropping his hands. "I'm giving you space."

The jacket was warm from his car, and I never wanted to give it back. "Space?"

"Something Cooper said made me think you'd need it."

"Adam?"

Sam dropped his forearm to the car, leaning casually next to me while his fingertips rested on the vehicle. "He said you don't do third dates. That you don't need the hassle. I figured someone might have gotten a little too hands-on in the past and thought I'd give you space. You know, *wait*."

I couldn't believe Adam told him that. "Wait for what?"

He stayed quiet, those fingertips lightly grazing my shoulder while his gaze followed, as though he were imagining skin under his fingertips instead of leather. I imagined it too, and a nervous tremble ran through me, causing those dark eyes to pivot to mine.

"I have a history," he finally said, "of messing up almost everything I touch."

I turned into him until our cloudy breaths merged in the cold air. If one of us moved even a little, we could be kissing. I'd never stood this close to him and couldn't stop myself from fixating on the thin scar splitting his lower lip at the corner. "*Almost* everything?"

"Yeah." The buzzing streetlight overhead made his tanned skin appear blue, his eyes black. I probably appeared the same. Ethereal, like a dream.

His thumb trailed a line against my cheek. "Why are you so nervous?"

"I'm not," I whispered, my voice trembling.

A smile tugged his mouth. "You're a terrible liar. Your voice changes."

Nervous shivering. Voice trembling. I had to be the most transparent person in the world. Heat crept up my neck to admit it. "I told you I wasn't good at lying."

"I remember," he said, his gaze dropping to my mouth. When his head started to lower, my heart jolted into a pay-attention rhythm. His eyes closed, mine did too, and then he was kissing me.

His lips felt warm and hesitant, which surprised me. I'd expected him to be rough like his reputation, but he kissed me softly, his fingers gentle as they brushed my jaw and tilted my face before he kissed me a second time.

This time I kissed him back.

Nothing about Sam felt cautious the second time as his hands pushed through my hair. He had strong lips. The knee-weakening kind. I pressed my palms flat to his abdomen, pulling back when the definition of muscle startled me. But I reached out again as his tongue grazed the space between my lips before he deepened the kiss.

I tasted the sweetness of cinnamon and ginger from our chai lattes. Breathed in the spicy scent of his aftershave and leather jacket. I loved the so-soft way he stroked my cheeks with his thumbs. He kissed me again, and again, until his hands slid down my sides and his hard body pressed me against the Impala.

My breath caught and he broke the kiss, pulling back.

I opened my eyes in a daze while working through the strangest sensation that I'd landed on the moon. The overhead streetlight hadn't stopped buzzing or turning everything within its reach a variety of blue hues. The street. My house. Sam. He leaned over me now, his forehead a few inches from mine as his gaze lingered on my mouth. I wanted him to kiss me once more but a harsh cold crept over my shoulders and forced a shiver through me. That's when I realized his coat had slipped behind me and now hung between my waist and the car.

"Your parents are expecting you," he said.

I blinked. Remembered my parents and dropped my hands from his waist to clasp them together. "You're right. I should go in."

He leaned behind me, grabbed the coat, and placed it over my shoulders, but this time when he pulled the jacket together, he gave a soft tug until we stood toe-to-toe. He dropped his hands, smiling slightly as he tilted his head. "Can I see you again?" he said. "Like this?"

I tried not to grin like a fool. "Yes."

"When?"

"School. Next weekend. Tomorrow." I stopped babbling and pulled in a nervous breath, hoping he planned to kiss me again. The porch light flickered, startling me into pulling away from him. "I have to go," I said, turning and hurrying across the street.

"Peyton."

I turned to him, knowing when I woke later that I wouldn't believe this had happened, that I'd wonder if it had all been an ethereal, blue dream.

"If I can work it out with my schedule, how about that dinner next Saturday?"

I smiled, my mouth still tingling from his lips. "Only if you kiss me like that again."

He slowly grinned. "Consider it worked out."

CHAPTER TEN

Sam

The plan had been simple; keep my hands off her until the third date. But when she'd looked up at me with those eyes the color of blue flame, I hadn't been able to stop myself. I should have left it at that. A soft kiss to end the date. Nice and safe. Nothing to freak her out.

Then she kissed me back.

This thing had already become way too complicated. The more I got to know her, the more I understood why Cooper and Ryan acted the way they did. Peyton was sweet and trusting in an endearing way that made me want to keep her that way. She brought out my better side, my protective side, which didn't work out in my favor because I still wanted to sleep with her.

Every time I'd watched her in seventh period, I had wondered what she'd be like to kiss or anything else. I'd wondered if her hair felt as soft as it looked, and it did. I'd assumed she'd have more flaws close up, and she didn't. I'd also known I'd get sick of her perky personality within minutes, and I hadn't. And like every other guy, I'd fantasized the sex would be a twelve on a scale of ten, but it no longer mattered. I liked her. That constant optimism and charitable nature. The way she kissed me. The way she looked at me.

God, the way she looked at me.

Most people stared at me as though I were a felony waiting to happen. Students at Ridgeview scattered like cockroaches whenever I approached.

Peyton never had, so it shouldn't have surprised me when she texted Sunday asking if we could do lunch this week to study for the Mansfield test.

Like she needed to ask.

Most nights I crashed at the gym, except on nights when *Mamá* worked a twelve-hour shift at the hospital, seven to seven. Vanna suffered from chronic nightmares and couldn't sleep alone at the house, so I made a point to drive home the nights when Ma couldn't be there. Even after an intense night of training, the lulling, forty-five minute drive would calm me enough to do homework, and after an hour or two of that, I could finally go to sleep.

But I had energy to burn Sunday night. My anxiety only increased when I pulled in to see Ma's white Corolla parked in the driveway.

God, not again.

I barely parked. Used one porch step out of six as I scrambled to the front door. Vanna had secured both dead bolts, which forced me to calm down long enough to get in the front door. I found my sister on the couch, looking up from her drawing pad as the TV's flickering light cast shadows across her worried expression. "I doubt she's asleep," she said. "It was a bad one."

Scowling hard enough to make my forehead ache, I pivoted without a word and headed down the dark hallway toward Ma's room.

I knocked softly.

"Samuel?"

She must have heard the Impala. "Yeah."

"Come in, *mijo.*"

Pushing the door open, I knew better than to flip the

light switch and navigated the dark instead. Once I reached the lamp in the farthest corner, I pushed the button, illuminating the room with enough soft light for me to see her stretched on top of the bed, forearm thrown over her eyes.

"*¿Qué hora es?*" she murmured.

"Almost midnight." She hadn't removed her scrubs or shoes. "This one must have hit fast."

"Why do you say that?"

"You didn't bother to change."

"Mhm." She moved her arm and the wet washcloth, and squinted at me with those unique hazel eyes, identical to my sister's. I got Ma's hair color, although the chocolate mass she usually wore in a knot no longer had the shine from several years ago. It didn't take more than a glance at her strained eyes and the tiny lines etched around her mouth to know her medication hadn't touched the pain. She smiled anyway. "Savanna said you had a date last night."

Apparently, my usually quiet sister couldn't keep her mouth shut. "*Sí.*"

"And you're going out again next weekend? The same girl?"

"*Sí, Mamá.*" Her curious grin made heat seep into my cheeks and I quickly grabbed the cloth out of her hand to rinse it in a bowl of cool water Vanna left on the nightstand. My old-fashioned *mamá* had wanted me to meet a nice girl since I'd turned sixteen. Folding and handing her the washcloth, I was determined to turn the subject back to her health. "*Usted necesita dejar de trabajar tanto.*"

She frowned. "I don't work any harder than the other nurses."

"Maybe. But you're working more than your usual three, twelve-hour shifts. You worked four extra days last month. Two this month. Just *stop*, Ma. *Please.* Why do you think I have two jobs?"

"That's the point. You shouldn't have to work so hard. A fulltime student holding down two jobs? That schedule will catch up with you, *mijo.*"

"I'm nineteen and have the stamina and energy of a professional fighter," I said. "You don't. You can't run yourself into the ground like you did in your twenties, Ma."

She rolled her eyes—her usual response to the truth about her health. "I'm fine, Samuel. You worry too much."

"At least quit skipping meals. The doctor said to get your body on a regular schedule with food and sleep. That the migraines would decrease." I was sick of repeating myself. "You're a nurse. I don't understand how you can ignore the symptoms of strain—" My voice disappeared, hoarse with emotion.

"Quite worrying, *mijo.*" She gave me one of her reassuring smiles. "Now tell me more about this girl. Savanna told me you helped her brother," she said, a renewed sparkle in her eyes. "Her name is Peyton?"

I wanted to be mad at Vanna for opening her trap about Peyton, but neither of us could stand to see Ma in pain. My sister would say anything to keep her distracted from it, and so would I. "*Sí.*"

"Such a pretty name. Did you know he was her brother when you helped him?"

I had no plans to relay *that* sordid story. "*Sí,* but that's not why I did it."

"*¿Por qué?*" she whispered.

I hadn't been sure myself until she asked. Ma was the one person I had difficulty lying to, especially now that it was just the three of us. "Because I couldn't just sit there and listen to it. I had to do something."

She smiled. Nodded. "Sometimes, Samuel…you're so much like him." Her chin trembled.

I stepped closer to the bed. "*Dios mío,* Ma. Don't start crying. *¿Qué pasa?*"

"I can't help it. Your *papá,*" she said, her voice shaking.

"He said the same thing…oh, countless times. You remember what kind of man he was. *Un buen hombre.*" We shared a smile. "I'm sure she was grateful. Did she thank you?"

"Something like that. She offered to help me pass a British Authors review."

"Your favorite class." She grinned. "And the romance began there?"

"No, that was pretty much it."

"Liar. You're dating her now. Admit it." She patted the bedcover next to her. "Come. Sit. *Háblame de ella.* We rarely get a chance to talk anymore, much less about a girl."

I sat next to her, willing to do anything to make her well. "What do you want to know?"

"*Mijo,* you've never brought a girl home for me to meet. I want to know everything, of course."

My face heated. "It's private."

"You think everything is private." She winced and pressed her fingers against her scalp. I forced myself not to overreact. "So she's pretty and popular," she said. "And you act awkward around her, which can only mean you like her."

Vanna. "I hadn't realized I was being awkward." Definitely time to change the subject. "Can I get you something else? Ibuprofen?"

"No, I'll be fine soon." Closing her eyes, she settled into the pillow a little easier and folded the cool cloth neatly over her eyes. "Mm. That's better. Now tell me more. She has red hair?"

"Copper." I sighed to think about it. "It…changes in the summer." I was talking too much. "But yeah. Red."

"She sounds *preciosa, mijo.*"

"She's okay."

"Mhm. You noticed all that detail about a girl's hair." She laughed and grabbed her scalp again. "You're already falling for her. I can hear it in your voice."

"*Ma.*"

"It's a sign."

"It's not a sign."

"Does she have green eyes?"

"Blue," I said, telling her too much. I sighed. "And yes, she's pretty and smart and nice to everyone. We have practically nothing in common."

"What are you talking about? You're handsome and smart. You used to get good grades when your *papá* was alive and things weren't…the way they are. You love your family and you have several good friends. How is she nothing like you?"

"For one, she hates fighting. Anything to do with it, actually."

Her smile faded. "I hated fighting, too, Samuel. But I still married your father, who was a retired boxer and a police officer. She'll overlook it if she grows to genuinely care about you."

"That's a big *if.*" My stomach growled audibly. The perfect cue to drop the subject. "I should check on Vanna. You know how worried she gets when you're sick."

She nodded. "I'm glad for you. It has a nice ring to it."

"What?"

"Sam and Peyton," she murmured. "Yes. I like it. And I want to hear more about her when it doesn't hurt so much to listen."

Frowning, I stood and pulled her shoes off her feet, dropping them next to the bed.

"Thank you," she whispered. "Goodnight, *mijo.*"

To see her this fragile made me miss *Papá* more than ever. He'd never have let this happen to her. It would have broken his heart to see her fall apart, emotionally and physically, without him. I guess that's what happened to childhood sweethearts when things didn't end happily ever after.

Love was such bullshit.

Leaning over, I kissed her forehead. "*Te quiero, Mamá,*" I whispered. "*Mejorate.*" I pulled the quilt to her elbows and turned off the light.

"I love you, too, *mijo*," she whispered. "And quit worrying about me. I'll see you in the morning."

Vanna didn't turn from the television as I passed her on my way to the kitchen.

"She better yet?" she asked, sounding like she had a cold.

"Not really. But she's well enough to talk. That's a plus." I'd busted my ass tonight and my stomach growled noisily again by the time I hit the refrigerator. After making a turkey sandwich and getting comfortable at the dining table, I noticed Vanna had a Kleenex shoved against her nose.

I noticed then her puffy, red eyes.

I stopped eating and swallowed the half-chewed bite that tore like sawdust down my throat. Vanna never cried, even when she worried about our *mamá*. My chest constricted as a panicky, protectiveness from years ago swelled inside me, and ignoring the adrenaline pounding through my limbs was like trying to ignore a gun pointed at my head. "What?"

She hit pause and waved a Kleenex at the TV. "It's this damn show."

I grunted in disbelief. "A *show*? You're crying over a *show*?" I didn't know why I was mad. She hadn't meant to scare the hell out of me.

"It's a bunch of DVDs Louisa gave me to watch."

Her best friend from the old neighborhood, Louisa, was a complete airhead. I couldn't believe the girl was into anything deep, much less something profound enough to make my hardass sister cry. "What show?"

She blew her nose into a tissue. "Naruto."

"What the hell is a Naruto?"

"A show."

I sighed. Curiosity would kill me if I didn't check it out. Picking up my sandwich and apple, I joined her on the couch. She'd stopped the frame on a blond, spiky-haired kid wearing a blue thing around his forehead. "I thought you outgrew cartoons."

"Do you have any idea how popular this anime is?"

"*Vanna*. It's a damn cartoon. You're crying over a cartoon."

"Oh kiss my ass," she said, glaring at me. "I'm not crying. I'm…misty-eyed."

Her swollen, bloodshot eyes and the red tip of her nose were proof she'd been bawling her fool head off. "Whatever you say, Rudolph."

Her eyes crossed to look at her nose. "I'll have you know I've been watching this show for two months." She wiped at the thick, black eye liner and mascara under her eyelashes. "If you didn't race to your room whenever you stayed here, you'd know that. And quit calling it a cartoon."

"I have classes to pass, Vanna, in case you forgot. Besides, working on homework puts me to sleep."

"I'll bet. Hey, can I get an online subscription? It's seven bucks a month or something. All the anime you can stand. I could watch it on the laptop in my room and you wouldn't have to see my face when you come home."

"Hallelujah."

"Really?" She grinned, not at all slighted. "I can get it?"

"Maybe." I shrugged. "Depends."

"On what?"

"If it's seven bucks a month, or *something*."

She grinned, a rare occurrence these days. Made me like the show already.

"I can't believe you're finally watching something other than news." I said. Vanna usually had her fingers glued to her laptop, perusing headlines and looking for the next big political issue to post on her blog. If she wasn't in the throes of some heated debate there, she drew caricatures for a political satire cartoon series she wrote for the same blog. She had a huge following, so she took it seriously as if it were a job. My sister was a pain in the ass, but anyone with eyes could see she'd do something mega important with her life someday.

Unlike her big brother.

She studied my half-smile. "It's not the sports channel, but if you don't have homework tonight, we could watch it. If you want. I wouldn't mind."

I'd started working two jobs at sixteen. Between those jobs, homework, and all the repairs that came with owning a piece-of-crap house, Vanna and I rarely ate together anymore, much less vegged out to watch a show. She missed the old neighborhood and the friends we left behind. Some days it felt like I was all she had, and my sister's eager expression made the guilt heavier. "I guess I could catch a couple episodes."

"Really?"

No mistaking it this time. She wanted me to hang out. "Sure, if you quit talking to Ma about Peyton. We went out *once*. It's no big deal. Don't get Ma all stirred up about it."

"I beg to differ, bro. It's a huge deal. And you went out *twice*. Skipping class and sushi, remember?"

Big mistake telling Vanna that. "So?"

"Oh, there's no *so* about this. Peyton Greene may go out with a lot of guys, but she doesn't *date* anyone. You must be blackmailing her."

"Just drop it."

"Tell me what dirt you have on her and I will."

"No dirt. I've told you before. You don't know her."

"And you do? Since when do you know girls beyond screwing them?"

I wished my sister wasn't such a tomboy and so blunt all the time. I pushed the last bite of sandwich into my mouth and examined the apple as if I hadn't heard her.

"Wow," she said. "Little Miss Cheerful must be as good as they say. Watch out though, I've heard she scratches and bites."

I grabbed a couch pillow and smacked her in the face with it, messing up her hair, which she hated. "Don't talk trash, Vanna. You'll turn into one of those bitches at school who make up shit just to have something to say. The same ones who talk about *you*."

She swiped her fingers through her hair, fixing it. "Are you saying you're *not* out to screw her like every other guy? Because that would be a flat lie. I saw how you looked at her that day on the lawn. And in the parking lot. And in sophomore hall. I've got eyes you know."

Tempted to hit her with the pillow again, I stuffed it behind my head instead, leaned back, and glared at the DVD picture, pretending her comment about every other guy wanting to screw Peyton hadn't hit a nerve. "I mean it. Shut up about her."

I hadn't been that abrupt with Vanna in a while, so when the silence stretched out along with her intense stare, I had a good idea why. "Please don't tell me you *like* her, Samuel."

Like didn't sum up whatever this was between me and Peyton, but I didn't want to jinx the whole thing by labeling it. What I wanted was to ask Vanna how a girl could have straight, silky hair one day and all those amazing curls the next. It couldn't be natural and I genuinely wanted to know. Still, I didn't ask because my sister would never answer a question like that, would likely ask what the fuck was wrong with me instead, and then proceed to call me a pansy and pussy-whipped for the next fifty years.

"Oh my god," she said, flipping sideways and giving me her full attention. "You *do* like her. H-holy cow. How much? When? *W-why?*" She rolled her eyes. "I mean. You know. Other than her body."

Christ, she'd become a babbling idiot within seconds. "Vanna—"

"I thought you stopped partying to stay more level-headed," she said, interrupting me. "Peyton Green is nice to *everybody*. You know that, right? She's even nice to me."

"So?"

"So I'd hate you to misinterpret good manners for real interest."

"Jesus, Vanna," I said, scowling, "why don't you tell me what you really think?"

"I didn't mean it that way." She looked down. Back up. "Do you think she is? Interested, I mean."

"Start the DVD."

She fell silent and studied me for a long moment. "Okay, but come clean with me first."

"About what?"

"You totally did her Saturday, didn't you? She blew your doors off and now you want the second course. You've heard she won't do the same guy twice, haven't you?"

Damn that sounded awful, especially coming from a sixteen-year-old girl. When and where the hell did my sister learn to talk like one of the neighborhood gangbangers? "*No.*"

"No, what?"

"No, I didn't *do* her."

"Hm. She must be an actual challenge, which means once you screw her—"

"Could you at least *try* to sound like a girl?" I turned to her. "I can't believe you kiss our *mamá* with that mouth."

"You'd prefer I talk like Little Miss Priss Peyton, who pretends she's innocent and sweet while working her way through the football team? Forget it. I live in the real world. Now what's the deal?"

"No deal." I shrugged. "She's…different. That's all."

"Different," she repeated, sounding doubtful. "Well that could mean a thousand things. Does she have any idea who you even are?"

Sometimes I wondered if Peyton saw part of me I didn't, because I still had no damn clue what she saw in me. Why she looked at me the way she did. "She knows me. I guess. I mean, what the hell is there to know?"

"You know exactly what I mean," she said, reaching

out and flicking my shoulder. "Hey. I'm talking to you."

Now *that* sounded like *Mamá* talking. I groaned and rolled my head to the side, shooting my sister my don't-fuck-with-me look. "*What?*"

Her eyebrows quirked. "Does she know you fight?"

"No."

"Then how the hell are you going to explain the next bruise?"

I shrugged.

"Ah, I get it," she said. "You're still working on the lie. Careful, stud, you're trying to nail a girl who hangs with the smart crowd."

Vanna knew I didn't date and why. "I'm not going to lie to her. I'll tell her someone hit me. I'll tell her the truth."

"Well that's never come up before. You planning to tell her *why* someone hit you? Because you love it? Because you make money doing it? You do know that would be a deal breaker. Jeez. The first girl you take a real interest in and you pick Peyton Greene. You're twisted. Seriously. There's no way this could work out, and since you're not the idiot you pretend to be, I know you have to know that. What are you thinking? Or is Father Bonner requesting self-torture as penance for a foul mouth now instead of the usual twenty Hail Mary's?"

"Can we watch this damn DVD before I graduate?" I took a bite of the apple, knowing exactly how Peyton would react if she found out I fought for *real*. Especially that I did it for the reasons Vanna said. For money and not a cause. Worse, because I loved doing it. No way would someone like her, a girl who couldn't keep her eyes open through an R-rated movie, understand how anyone could love fighting.

Vanna sighed loudly and flipped back to the TV screen. "Excusez-moi," she said, "but when your heart is on the floor and she doesn't even bother to step over it in her quick exit, don't say I didn't warn you. Peyton

Greene's the type whose parents have her life mapped out already, and I doubt they've included someone like you anywhere in it. Face it. She'll go to college next year, find some asshole frat boy to marry after graduation, and ten years down the road when you're still fighting tattooed beefcakes at fifty bucks a pop, she'll be dressing her three gorgeous kids in Gucci and doing the whole soccer mom…thing."

"Jesus." I glared at her. "Ease the hell up, would you? We've gone out *two* times."

She clucked her tongue. "And that's two more dates than you've been on with anyone else. Hells bells, I'd bet you can't even name *one* girl you've banged in the past."

I scowled to hear my little sister say the word *banged*. "Would you find a point?"

"Kristy," she said.

"What?"

"Your latest conquest."

Conquest? The memory was a blur at best and not because it happened at a party over a year ago. "Karla. It was Karla."

"Dude, it was Kristy. God, you're such an asshole."

"How could you possibly know who the hell I hook up with?"

"Because I'm the one they approach after you blow them off."

She was fucking with me now. "Seriously?"

"You don't believe me?"

"Why would they talk to you?"

"To get on my good side."

"What for?"

"*Du-uh.* To get on *your* good side, you moron."

News to me. "So tell them I don't have a good side."

"Because you do have a good side, when you're not being a jerk."

I shrugged, out of comebacks.

"Thank God Jonas got you out of that party scene.

You have a better moral code when you're sober. It's the only cool thing about living in this town," she said. "With all of the time you spent partying with your best *amigo*, Manny, and the rest of the Beaverton pack, the girls here don't know you. Oh, except Peyton. And check you out. On the hook and all ready to be reeled in. I'll bet you turn out exactly like *Papá*. All deep and sensitive. I'll bet when it happens to you, that'll be it."

"When *what* happens to me?"

"When you pull your head out of your ass and let somebody get to know the real you."

"Ah, the *real* me. As opposed to…"

"That unlikable, badass image you created by fighting every jerk at school when we first moved here."

I laughed. "Says my dear sister, Ridgeview's only *other* social pariah by choice."

"Come on," she said, her painted toe poking my leg until I pushed her bare foot away. "You can tell me. Peyton's it, isn't she? *The* one?"

I rolled my eyes and stared straight ahead.

She laughed at my irritated expression, until eventually her mocking giggle faded into a disgruntled snort. "Listen, Samuel, it's cool you like her and everything. But…"

"But what?"

"Don't get too into her, okay?"

I turned to her because she sounded genuinely worried. "Why?"

"Because she's not going to want a boyfriend who fights grown men. Men, by the way, who make Carter Delaney and his friends look like puny little wusses. Your idea of fun would freak her out." She frowned. "I mean, even *I* have difficulty watching you fight. The sounds of skin smacking skin and limbs twisting the wrong way…" She shuddered.

I couldn't bring myself to agree. Not aloud. If I did, then it would become too real. A situation I'd have to deal with. For now, I wanted to keep seeing Peyton. She made me feel different. Worth something. I wanted to date her as long as I could before this thing blew up in my face. "You're not going to say shit to her, right? About the fighting?"

She released another judgmental sigh and looked back to the TV. "Nope." Placing a Kleenex box next to me, she added, "It's your business if you want to set yourself up for an epic fall. Just remember telling her half-truths about the bruises is the same as lying."

Vanna could get scary psychic sometimes. "Debatable."

"And you'll only be delaying the inevitable anyway."

"I know."

"Not to mention, you have no consideration for the position you're putting me in."

"How did this suddenly become about you?"

"If she dumps you and breaks your heart, I have to kick her ass. It's my duty as your sister."

Despite all her swearing, piercings and tattoos, Vanna was as gentle as a kitten. I never took her threats seriously. Giving me another glance, she pushed the tissues toward me.

"I'm not going to cry over a stupid cartoon," I said.

She looked at me with pity. "Who said those are for the show?" Turning to the television, she hit play. "It's sad, really. You're about to get your ass handed to you, by a girl no less, and you don't even know it."

CHAPTER ELEVEN

Sam

I couldn't recall a time when I'd looked forward to school, but that was before I started spending every lunch hour with Peyton Greene, the hottest girl there. That she seemed oblivious of her appeal still fascinated the hell out of me. She ignored guys checking her out when she stopped by my locker in senior hall. She even pretended her girlfriends didn't stare and whisper in the commons while we studied.

She really got into literature, too. I'd never admit it to her, but the way she could ramble forever about character motivations was kind of cool. Occasionally she'd look up while talking and catch me studying her. But then she'd blush and smile that shy smile before looking away.

When my boss, Martin, texted me Thursday with an okay to leave the auto body shop early Saturday night, I hadn't been able to wait five minutes before calling Peyton to tell her we could do dinner. I'd been thinking about that kiss all week and couldn't wait to get her alone again.

But Saturday morning was busy as hell and when one of my co-workers had to go home sick, I ended up working my regular shift anyway, killing my plans with

Peyton.

At least this time I had the wherewithal to text Peyton, who agreed to meet me between shifts on Sunday. It sucked and I was disappointed as hell, but if she really wanted to know *me*, she might as well get good at disappointment. My schedule rarely let up.

I left Winchester Auto at five on Sunday, which gave me two and a half hours before my next shift started at the gym.

That left me thirty minutes to get home and clean up while Peyton drove directly from work—her aunt's bakery in Sandy where she decorated cakes. She'd suggested we meet at a small food joint in Ridgeview, *Rice Bowl XO*, and we both arrived fifteen minutes before the place closed. The stuffy little kitchen had four inside tables and no air conditioning. Most people got their food to go or sat at the wooden picnic tables outside. We both ordered the chicken and vegetable rice bowl and realized while talking that neither of us had an aptitude with chopsticks. She suggested we remedy the problem with practice.

We sat next to each other on the picnic table, propped our feet on the bench, and spent thirty minutes practicing getting food to our mouths without wearing it. I wouldn't have thought this the best suggestion for a third date, but it gave me a few opportunities to tease her, even touch her, since she had a worse time using the wooden utensils than I did and kept getting teriyaki sauce on her lip and chin.

On my most articulate day, I wouldn't know how to be romantic. But tonight the universe must have felt I needed a break, because I actually looked like I had a clue. We watched a beautiful sunset burn a section of the sky as we talked about trivial things we had going on at school. She smiled a lot, laughed just as much, and sitting next to her, so did I. For the first time in years, I stopped thinking about the bad shit in my past and focused on the present. Current-day clarity had never happened to me like that except in a fight.

"I'm wondering why you have that slight accent," she murmured, trying to talk and keep her lips closed as she ate. "Because I haven't heard you speak much Spanish before. Although you did call me a…a *chica guapa*."

"That's actually a compliment."

"Not the way you said it."

I frowned, wishing I could take that day back; I'd been such a dick to her. "I know, but it's still a compliment. You should take it that way, at least. Do you know what it means?"

That shy smile returned. "After sushi, my curiosity got the better of me. I looked it up using online translation software. So I have an idea."

Cool. That meant she'd been as curious about me after that near-kiss incident as I'd been about her. "Then you know I'm telling you the truth."

"Well, I know that *now*. But at the time, I assumed it was derogatory since I'd only heard you swear in Spanish."

I nearly choked to keep from laughing and spitting chicken bits across the grass. "When did I swear?"

"Oh sure." She smirked. "Like you don't remember."

I remembered plenty of times, but I couldn't imagine doing it around her. "I get that it had to be in class. Which one? We've had a few together."

She looked at her bowl and poked a chopstick at the cardboard bottom. "It was a couple of years ago. You really don't remember?"

"Accounting," I said, recalling the class where she'd sat in front of me, arranged alphabetically by our last names. She'd sat close enough to hear me, and I didn't doubt for a second that I'd sworn up a blue streak since I'd really hated Mr. Stephens.

She nodded. "You couldn't get your payroll to come out right," she said, taking a bite of sticky rice.

"Oh, sure. Make fun of a guy's payroll." She giggled into her napkin as I transferred a miniature carrot to my mouth in one smooth move.

"You'd messed up your company's taxes," she murmured, pulling her napkin away, "and I could sympathize because I had the same problem. My company had five out-of-state consultants. I don't recall ever getting that right."

"How do you remember details like that? It was three years ago."

"Because Mr. Stephens was such a jerk to everybody," she said, "and you made me laugh telling him off under your breath whenever he walked away. You made the class bearable. I may not have known exactly what you said, but I knew you were calling him *something*. I'm surprised you don't remember me giggling all the time. He made me stay after school because of it."

I remembered her giggling until her ears flushed pink, but I hadn't known she was giggling because of me or that he'd made her stay after class. "Stephens was a jackass."

"Especially to you."

"What did I call him?"

She finished chewing. "I told you. I don't speak Spanish."

"Come on. Give it a try."

She swallowed. Nervous. "Pendayho," she murmured. She brushed her tongue alongside her lip and caught a grain of rice. "I can't say it. And now you made me spit out my food."

"*Pendejo*," I said, watching her lick the sauce off her lips. "You're a natural. What else did I say?"

"You called him a…this one I can't say at all because it's always said too fast. Ca…cahberone?"

I laughed aloud to hear her say it like that.

"I said it wrong, didn't I?" She swallowed. "Sorry, I don't do the tongue roll right." She poked at food in her bowl, embarrassed.

"Nah, that was okay. *Cabrón*. See? You said it correctly. But hearing you say it as if it were a question, especially with that sweet voice, it sounds funny." I placed my empty carton behind us and took a drink of water.

"What does it mean?"

I debated telling her. "Let's just say it's pretty bad and you'd never say it like a question."

"You definitely didn't."

I felt my cheeks heat. "You have a good memory."

She shrugged. "Only with certain subjects. You're one of those people who stand out. I remember you. A lot."

Given the time reference, this was likely a very bad thing.

"I remember the first time I saw you," she added, avoiding my gaze while her dimples deepened. "You walked by me and did a double-take."

I looked down and away, my heart racing and not for doing the double take. I hated to think about those years and wished she hadn't seen me during any of it. I'd been a different person—a sophomore roaming the halls, lost in my dreary world of shit. Then this bright-eyed freshman girl with copper hair had passed me in the hallway. She'd had her books pulled to her chest and four friends in tow when her gaze had caught mine. I'd done a double take, and those blue eyes had stared back at me until we'd both turned to look at each other. Her friends had whispered and giggled, but Peyton had seemed oblivious, giving me a shy smile before turning back around.

Had I not been so absorbed in my own hell, I would have seen how different she was from other girls. Had I felt better about myself, I might have even worked up the nerve to ask her out. "Who would have guessed we'd be talking about it three years later," I said, trying to make light of a memory that bothered me more than she needed to know.

She placed her bowl next to mine. "So, how is it you have an accent when you rarely speak Spanish? Are you fluent?"

"*Sí.*"

"But you don't speak it."

"I speak it when I'm around people who understand it." Darkness had fallen and I had only a streetlight to see her. A cool wind blew her hair across her face and I reached out, pushing it behind her ear. "My mother has a strict rule not to speak Spanish in front of those who don't understand it. The same with English. We don't speak it around my grandmother and great aunt who have difficulty understanding it. It's rude." Her crooked smile made me wonder if she knew something that I didn't. "What?"

"So, you're saying if I came to your house, your mom wouldn't start going off in Spanish telling you to get rid of that red head? She'd tell me in plain English to stay away from her son."

I laughed. Knowing my *mamá*, I couldn't picture that scenario ever happening. "My mother would never say that. And we don't speak Spanish much at home either, unless we're alone or Vanna's out with friends."

Her doubtful expression could only mean she didn't believe me about the Spanish or didn't believe Vanna had friends.

"Are you saying Savanna doesn't speak Spanish?"

"Right. My parents spoke English *and* Spanish when I was little. They wanted us to know both languages. But when Vanna came along, she rarely spoke and none of us could understand why. Turns out mixing both languages became too confusing for her. My father suggested we only speak English at home. He didn't want her having problems at school."

"And it worked?"

"Yeah. With only one language to focus on, she started speaking more often. She knows a few words of Spanish you or anyone else would recognize, but that's it. Although she's taking French this year. Go figure."

"How did you keep speaking it if no one spoke it at home?"

"Mainly my dad. We spent a lot of time together, and

we spoke Spanish when no one else was around. He had an accent so…to answer your question, that's where I got it."

"Wow," she said, leaning forward and brushing her hands over her arms. "Your parents sound amazing. To give up teaching their daughter something so important to them, all to help her succeed in school."

Her sincerity made my chest tighten, and I suddenly became desperate to flip the topic back to her. "Why is it you *don't* speak Spanish? What foreign language did you choose?"

"You're assuming I took one."

I arched an eyebrow. "C'mon, brainiac. You know you did."

Her back straightened and she gave me a prim look. "Well, if you *must* know." I laughed. "I took Japanese. Rather, I'm *still* taking Japanese."

"Can you speak it?"

"After four years, I hope so."

"Four years?" I leaned back, impressed. "Wow. Prove it. Say something."

"Uh-uh. That would be rude, remember?"

I rolled my eyes. "Well, thankfully, my mother isn't here. You're safe."

"Fine." She paused before saying a quick mouthful of syllables, what ultimately sounded like a question. I assumed she'd spoken Japanese, but she could have spoken Mandarin for all I knew. Still, she'd spoken it well, what sounded like a million words that probably amounted to her asking where she might find the bathroom.

I grinned. "Now say something sexy."

Her eyes sparkled at my teasing tone, and I held my breath while a warm, sultry expression transformed her features. She said the next few words, whatever they were, slowly and an octave lower than her normal voice. I couldn't take my eyes off her and she eventually dropped her gaze to my hand gripping the picnic table.

"What did that mean?" I asked.

She chanced a quick glance at me and turned to the dark horizon, hugging herself in the cool air. "I can't tell you. I don't know you well enough."

Damn. Someday I'd ask her again. I wanted to know what she'd been thinking when she'd looked at me with that expression. "Sounded nice, whatever you said."

Her smile grew. "It was *very* nice," she said softly, gripping her arms tighter when another shiver ran through her.

I scooted closer to her and rubbed my hands over her arms to warm her up. "So, four years. That's serious. You're not planning to move to Japan, are you?"

She laughed. "No."

"Majoring in Japanese?"

"Um, no. I won't have time."

"Then why four years?"

She still wouldn't look at me. "That's way too personal a question for a third date."

My hands halted on her arms. "Wait, I just told you more detail about my life than most of my closest friends know. How is that question too personal?"

"Because it is," she said, tamping down a relentless grin. "Listen, Sam, there's no way I'm telling you. You can quit giving me your soulful pretty-please expression right now."

I couldn't stop smiling. "I didn't know I had a soulful pretty-please look."

"Well you do, and you can stop using it on me because it won't work." Her knees started bouncing when I kept smiling, and she pushed my leg with a halfhearted shove, giggled and looked away. "Stop it. You'll laugh."

God, I liked this girl. "I won't."

Her feet bobbed in triple time. "You'd have to swear you won't laugh. That you won't tell anyone else."

"I swear. Anything said between us stays between us." I actually felt strongly about this issue and maybe I needed to mention that later.

"And you swear not to laugh."

My focus dropped to her pale, exposed neck. I leaned down, kissing a soft spot under her ear. "I swear," I murmured.

She crooked her neck but didn't move away. "That tickles," she whispered.

"I can't help it," I said, dropping another kiss to her neck. "You smell so good."

She pulled back to look at me, still smiling. "Clearly, you have no sense of mercy, Sam Guerra. All right. I'll tell you." She blew out a nervous breath. "It's *anime*. That's my reason for taking Japanese. Now can we please change the subject?"

"Anime?"

"Let's drop the subject," she said.

"Um, no. *Hell* no. I definitely need to hear this. But first, let's get you in the car and warm you up." I brushed my hands over her cold arms. "Your skin is cold."

She looked to where she'd parked her Lexus next to the Impala before nodding and hopping off the table. After we tossed our paper bowls and empty water bottles into the trash, I threaded my fingers through hers as we walked across the parking lot, something I'd wanted to do during our last date.

She said she had to get something in her car so I focused on warming up the Impala.

When she opened the passenger door and plopped onto the seat engulfed in my leather coat, I paused for a reality check. The way she looked at me with those playful, blue eyes made my throat go dry. "So…anime," I said, determined to do this right. "You were going to explain."

Her dimples deepened. "You *want* to embarrass me, is that it?"

Damn, I was going to kiss her if she didn't start talking soon. "Come on. Just tell me."

"If it means we can move on to another topic." Her

grin faded and she turned to stare out the windshield. "Adam introduced me to anime in eighth grade and I totally fell in love with it." She huddled into the coat while dropping back against the seat. "But anime is Japanese, which meant I had to read subtitles or watch English versions. They didn't always translate well. That's why I wanted to learn the language. I wanted to watch the originals and understand what the writers intended."

"You like a cartoon enough to take another language for four years?" Saying it out loud didn't make it any more believable.

"Wait a second," she said, turning to me and holding up a finger. "Anime isn't a cartoon. Let's get that on the table right now." She shivered and folded her arms over her chest, her hands buried in the sleeves. "Besides, if you've never watched anime, an explanation won't do it justice."

"Maybe you should move closer. You're still shivering."

"I'm not cold anymore," she said, facing me and shifting to the middle of the seat where I met her halfway. "See?" She pushed her hands outside of the oversized sleeves. "Feel my hands. Warmer already."

I wrapped my fingers around both hands, warm and soft. "Then why are you shivering?"

"Um…" She looked down. "I shiver when I get nervous."

"You're nervous?"

She nodded.

"Don't be." I wanted her to trust me and wished we could skip to that part. Maybe if I kept her talking she'd relax. "Tell me about anime."

"What do you want to know?"

"I'm just wondering how a show could be so great it would inspire someone to learn another language just to understand it better."

She shifted and I put my arms around her, breathing in

her sweet scent. "The stories are amazing," she said as she leaned against me. "The fighting is internal as much as external. It's about personal demons. Personal growth. Empowerment. Living by a code. The importance of friends. Family. Honor and doing the right thing. Never giving up on what you believe." She turned to me with those dimples. "Never giving up, no matter how difficult things get. That's what I love the most." She stopped talking, an odd expression pulling her eyebrows together.

"What?"

"You're totally laughing at me."

"I'm *smiling*," I said.

"You think I'm lame, don't you? A geek even," she accused. I opened my mouth to deny it, but she pointed her finger at me. "Sam Guerra, I challenge you to watch twenty episodes of Naruto, look me in the eyes, and tell me you didn't cry at least once."

"Naruto?" No. Way. The same cartoon that made my hardass sister cry like a baby. Great. I hadn't smiled in seven years as much as I had in the last week, all because of this girl, who apparently wouldn't be satisfied now until she made me cry. "Peyton, I can tell you right now I won't cry over a cartoon."

She poked my chest, her finger unbending. "It's *not* a cartoon."

I pushed her finger to the side and inched forward. "Whatever."

A half-smile twisted her lips. "Sam, you're going to need to get your geek on a little better if you want to get to know me." Her eyes widened. "Do you want to know me, Sam? The real me?"

Great. Now I wished I'd stayed and watched that stupid show with Vanna instead of going to my room pissed because she wouldn't quit talking about my doomed relationship with Peyton. If I had, I could impress my hot date with the same nerd-speak that made her so tight with Cooper. "I wouldn't be here if I didn't want to know you."

"Well, if you really want to know what curls my toes, you should watch my favorite show. You can learn a lot about someone if you understand their interests, don't you think?"

The exact reason I'd kept the conversation focused on her.

"You have to watch it. Naruto is the ace of all anime," she said. "But you can't confuse it with Naruto Shippuden because that's the continuation. If you watch that one first you'll be totally lost."

Tired of the cartoon subject, I leaned in, close enough to kiss her. "There *are* other ways I could get to know you, *hermosa.*"

Her dimples appeared and she pulled back enough to place her finger against my lips. "*Try* to be good, Sam. This is serious stuff."

I liked this playful side of her. I liked every side of her. "You seriously want me to watch anime to get to know you?"

She giggled, clutching my shirt. "I do. It's one of those it's-important-to-your-girlfriend things. Would you watch it if I asked nicely?"

Girlfriend. The word lodged in my brain as I brushed her hair back. "I'll watch it, but you have to be there to translate."

"It has subtitles." Her widening eyes searched mine. "Did you just ask me to come to your house?"

I couldn't believe I had. "Yeah. I need to witness this toe-curling event myself." I brushed my finger along her ear, this time tracing her hair down her neck. She licked her lips and my focus dropped back to her mouth. I brushed my thumb along her lower lip.

"Sam?"

She had the softest mouth. "What?"

"I want to kiss you," she said, "but you should know it's five minutes after the time you said you had to go."

I turned to the small digital clock stuck on the dash and

frowned. "Give me ten seconds." I grabbed my phone, texted Jonas at lightning speed and hit Send before pivoting my attention back to her mouth.

"Who'd you text?"

"My boss at the gym. I told him I'd be fifteen minutes late."

"*Fifteen?* But you're only five—" The second my lips touched hers, the sweetest sound drifted up her throat and she reached out, clutching my shirt and pulling me closer. I shifted forward, causing a thudding sound—my phone hitting the floor—as I kissed her with zero intention of wasting one second of those ten minutes. Her bent leg between us kept me from getting closer, but I parted her mouth anyway, desperate to try. She brushed her tongue softly alongside mine, then my lip, as though tasting me. I remembered her doing that last night. A signature move. She shifted her leg and hooked it over mine. Pressed her hands to my chest, hesitating only a moment before her fingers drifted to my shoulders. I wanted to tell her to go for it, to do what she wanted with me, but it would have been too much too soon.

My hands moved everywhere, drifting down her sides and back. She kissed me repeatedly. Soft. Aggressive. The combination made me nuts. I pulled her against me, unable to get close enough as her knee slid across my thigh. I drew her closer, gripping her legs until she shifted over my lap a minute later and straddled me. I wasn't sure who was leading what, but I went with it anyway, pulling her hips flush with mine. She sucked in a breath, the sweetest sound against my lips, but she never even paused as she kissed me. I felt her fingers thread into my hair as she opened her mouth to mine. Cupping her jaw with one hand, I kissed her hard as I pushed my other hand under her shirt. The soft skin at her waist tempted me to try for more, but I didn't want to move too fast and screw this up. Besides, her sweet scent was making me crazy. I kissed her throat, finally recognizing the scent. "You smell like frosting. The really good kind."

"I do?" She sounded dazed as she dropped her head back.

"Yeah." I tasted her skin, expecting powdered-sugar sweet but getting soft instead.

Her fingers gripped my shoulders as I slipped my hands under the coat to drift along the narrow curve of her back. "Sam…"

Damn, she had a great body. "Hm?"

"That feels good."

Given our position, I imagined her saying the same words except with fewer clothes. My body's tense response reminded me to slow the hell down. "Peyton."

"We should probably stop," she whispered.

"I know." I kissed another soft spot on her neck.

"You have work," she added, curling her arms around my neck and getting closer. "And my parents are expecting me at home. But this is—" she sucked in a breath when I pulled her hips tight to mine, letting her feel how far I wanted to go, "—it's really nice."

"Mhm." I kissed her neck, her jaw, making my way to her mouth and starting everything all over again. Soon we weren't just kissing but moving together as if we were doing something else. Something more. Breathing hard, we barely finished one kiss before starting another. And if she didn't quit making those soft sounds with every breath…

I imagined all the things we could do together, just her and me in this car. Wondered even, if she was thinking the same thing. I grabbed the leather coat and pulled it off her shoulders, down to her elbows. She didn't act surprised, didn't even pause as she kissed me. I was beginning to think maybe…

"We really should stop," she whispered.

I leaned back against the seat, trying to put some space between us, but she followed me, her chest nearly in my hands as she started kissing me again. After another minute, I had one hand wrapped in her hair as my fingers brushed the side of her breast.

Damn, I was no good at making out sober. Way too aware of every move I made. Every move she made. When she didn't stop my hand, I tried for more the second time, realizing the second she moaned that if I didn't halt this now—

I gripped the jacket bunched around her elbows and pulled us apart, immediately wishing I hadn't. "If we're going to stop," I said, catching my breath, "we should do it now."

My voice had come out harsh and raspy, but she didn't seem to notice. Her hands remained pressed to my abdomen as she stared at me with wide eyes, looking like she'd woken from a dream. "You're right. I have homework," she explained in a whisper. "And tons to do on my website. We should…"

"Go," I finished for her. "We should definitely go."

Her lips were without lipstick now, and red and puffy after kissing ten minutes straight. She remained flush against me, apparently not wanting to go any more than I did. Maybe she didn't feel strongly about stopping. Maybe she wanted me to convince her.

"I don't normally do this," she said.

The tremble of vulnerability in her voice reminded me why I needed to stop and think a minute. Taking a deep breath, I leaned back and forced my body to relax. "I know."

"I haven't been with anyone, Sam," she said, biting her lip briefly and looking unsure. "So when I say I don't normally do this, I mean at all."

Any time she glanced down, her long, thick hair fell partially over her eyes. I reached out and pushed the soft tendrils back and her gaze lifted to mine. "I know," I said.

"But *how* do you know?"

She'd obviously heard the rumors about herself. What a downer subject. "I saw it in your eyes that day at your house. When you came down the stairs."

Her mouth twisted to one side. "You could tell?"

"You have expressive eyes."

She curled her fingers against my shirt. "Does that mean you're okay with waiting?"

She had to know I didn't *want* to wait, but her apocalyptic, relationship-ending expression kept me from mentioning it. My response had to be perfect or I might as well chuck the whole relationship right now. "I don't want you to have any doubts," I said, and meant it.

She gave me another uncertain smile. "Maybe we should go slower then."

I glanced at her hand on my left pectoral and those fingertips sliding back and forth over the ridge of a scar— an entirely different conversation I wanted to avoid. "Maybe you should define going slower," I said, "if you don't want me to cross a specific line. Because I think we've crossed a few lines already."

Her fingers halted. "Have we? I didn't notice. I mean, I've never...felt like this. It's really nice." She hesitated and leaned closer, kissing me again. Her mouth felt soft and uncertain.

Damn. The second her lips parted, I kissed her back, my fingers threading through her hair as I did. She felt better than nice. She felt perfect. I never wanted to stop.

Work. I could probably get out of it. Maybe Jonas or Bobby could take my four Sunday appointments this once. I was seriously considering it when my phone dinged on the floorboard, the sound of a text reply. Jonas was likely wondering what the hell had happened to me. I usually got to work with time to spare.

She moaned a sound of disappointment and pulled from the kiss. When I opened my eyes to look into those pretty blues, I could suddenly picture us together. As in, *together*. Like two people who did shit with each other all the time. Like trust and love, and all that crap I'd never wanted in my life. Apparently, I'd lost my ever-loving mind over this girl and needed to regroup. "That's probably my boss. I should go."

"I've made you way too late," she said. "Will you get in trouble?"

"No, Jonas is cool." Jonas might go nuclear on my sorry ass, but she didn't need to know that. Sunday night was his designated family night. He hated anything getting in the way of that. His wife, too, whose public freak-outs concerning family neglect could get loud and embarrassing.

Peyton slid off my lap and over to the passenger side, slipping one arm from the coat. "I meant to give this to you earlier."

I pushed the thick material back over her shoulder. "Wear it. I like it better on you."

She paused and pushed her arm back through the sleeve, wrapping the coat tightly around her. She sat a long moment, looking as sexually frustrated as I felt, which somehow made me feel better. Turning to me, she asked, "I'll see you tomorrow? Seventh period?"

"You'll see me before seventh period," I said. She smiled softly, still looking disappointed as she opened the door and got into her own vehicle. I waited until she drove out of the parking lot before leaving for work, hoping Jonas was in a forgiving mood.

CHAPTER TWELVE

Peyton

I had the *studentbodyforhire* website set to go live Monday after school. Adam and I loved turning mundane things into big events and planned a big go-live celebration in my room. He even planned to hijack a bottle of cheap champagne from his foster parents' pantry to add to our little carpet picnic. But none of that happened because Sam showed up late to school—seventh period late—sporting a black eye.

Everything took a downward spiral from there.

After he ignored my questioning stares during Ms. Campbell's Dickens review, he had the nerve to stop by my locker and say, "Hey," in that cute, flirty tone that made my knees weak.

I refused to look at him. "Hey," I said with a shaky voice, stuffing two books into my book bag.

"What?"

When I wouldn't meet his gaze, he placed a hand against the locker next to mine and shifted into my line of vision, making ignoring him impossible.

I looked down at the book bag I was holding. "Sam."

"I told you," he said, his voice dropping low so no one

else could hear. "I had to work. You got my texts. What's the problem?"

He'd been considerate enough to text me first thing, letting me know he'd be late. I had no idea how late until he texted to say he couldn't study at lunch and showed up later, just before the review.

As soon as Shelly Watson closed her locker next to mine and left us alone, my gaze pivoted to the bruise circling his eye. Imagining anyone hitting him made me want to lash out in an equally violent retaliation. I didn't know what to do with the horrid feeling, and since I expressed frustration, anger, and sadness the same way—through tears—I looked like an emotional spaz blinking rapidly to keep the tears back. "What happened to your eye?" I slammed my locker shut and dropped my book bag on the floor.

He shrugged. "A fist."

"*Whose* fist?"

He glanced over my head, and I followed his gaze to see Adam and Ryan approaching us. His gaze pivoted back to mine. "Can we talk later?"

"What if I want to talk now?"

"I have to work." He turned without so much as a goodbye then and headed toward the student parking lot.

I stood rooted to the tile, slack-jawed and staring at his back until he pushed through the outside doors.

"What happened?"

Ryan's voice snapped me out of my stunned silence and I noticed him and Adam standing next to me. "Nothing."

"Doesn't look like he took the news well," Ryan said.

"What news?" Adam asked.

I glared at Ryan. Daddy had been grilling me for a week about Sam's faded bruises and I had no explanation. For extra fun, the Guerra name had sounded familiar enough that he'd perused the local online papers and found out Sam had been the boy three years ago who'd hospitalized his own uncle. Due to Sam and Savanna's ages at the time, much of the case was inaccessible to the public, which left Daddy with just enough information to have a total freak out and ban me from seeing Sam again. My mother thankfully came to Sam's defense but an argument quickly ensued. When things went from bad to worse, Ryan pulled me upstairs where we listened for another thirty minutes until doors slammed and the house settled into a divorced quiet.

When Sam walked across the parking lot and out of sight, I turned to Adam. "My dad doesn't want me to date Sam."

"Tell him you study," Adam said with a shrug, surprising me by sounding reasonable. "You wouldn't be lying."

"I wish it were that easy," I said. "But I'm not supposed to see Sam at all. In any way. Until hell freezes over."

"It's the hospitalizing his relatives thing," Ryan elaborated.

Getting angrier, I handed Ryan my keys and slung my book bag over my shoulder. "Go ahead to the car. I'll catch up."

"*Pey-ton*," Ryan said, sounding exasperated, but I ignored him and headed for the parking lot.

Sam had the Impala running and the driver's window rolled down when I approached his car. The walk hadn't cooled me off even a little. I stopped abruptly by his door and dropped my bag, waiting for him to quit scowling at the Impala's hood and apologize, or at least notice me. When he didn't, I shifted a step and propped my hands on my hips. He responded by revving the car and frowning at a ticking sound coming from under the hood.

Several people watched us, and since I didn't want another video of me shared on social media any time soon, I waited for idle mode to avoid yelling. When he finished revving the engine, I asked, "Is that what you do to other girls when you don't like the conversation? You walk away?"

"I don't date *other* girls," he said, finally looking at me. "I date *you*."

"Oh, right," I said, clutching my elbows under his hard, untrusting stare. "I feel special, too. You walked away from me back there as if I'm just anybody."

"You're not just anybody," he said, "but I don't talk about my personal life with an audience, Peyton. Even for you. Now get in."

Did he just command me? I arched my eyebrows and he rolled his eyes, turning to look out the windshield. Did he really think I would follow orders? Seriously? Not in a million, trillion...

"Get in, *please*," he said, still staring out the windshield.

I guess he really hadn't dated much before, because even saying *please*, his statement sounded like he expected me to jump to attention. "Adam and I have plans. We're going to—"

"Peyton." He looked at me. "Get. In."

My mouth parted. He hadn't raised his voice or said anything mean. But something in those dark eyes and resolute tone told me if I didn't go with him *now*, this relationship would take ten steps back. It had taken me three years of debating and a dire situation to work up the courage to approach him the first time. I rubbed my elbows, still not moving in a pointless effort to prove something to one of us. A ridiculous gesture because I desperately wanted to go with him.

Dropping my gaze, I grabbed my book bag and walked to the back of the vehicle. Ryan and Adam waited by the Lexus, and I gave them a wave to indicate I'd see them at home. Ryan shook his head and opened the driver's door. When Adam hesitated, I showed him my phone so he could see I had it before turning and getting into Sam's car.

"Fine. I'm in," I said, looking at Sam. "Now tell me

who hit you."

He put his arm over the seat and turned as he backed the car out, then slammed it into drive and took off down the road. I snapped my seatbelt closed, giving him three full blocks to answer me.

"Why did you tell me to get in the car if you're not going to talk to me?" I asked.

"I'm *talking* to you," he said.

But beyond those four words, he didn't. "You told me you work nights at a gym," I said, prodding him to continue. "Doing maintenance stuff and closing for your boss, Jonas."

"That's right."

He sounded annoyed, which only made me mad. I shut my mouth and faced front, determined to stay mute until the end of time. I watched a mom-and-pop convenience store pass out of view. Several homes. A tree lot. The closed lumber mill. I'd never known anyone so private that he needed to leave the city any time we discussed something personal.

If only I could let things go. "You did go to work last night, right?"

"I said I did, didn't I?"

Wait. *He'd* been the one who'd insisted I go with him, so why was he being so evasive? I faced front again and folded my arms across my chest. After three more minutes of silence, I turned to stare at his profile. "Are you going to give me a real answer or not?"

His hand tightened on the steering wheel. "*Yes*, I worked last night."

"Then what aren't you telling me? Because none of this makes sense. How could you get a black eye between then and now? Did you really work at the auto shop today?"

"Yes." His gaze slid to mine, and for several seconds, I thought I saw guilt. But he turned away quickly and pulled into the Rice Bowl XO's empty parking lot, the exact spot where he'd parked last night.

He killed the engine without looking at me. "I need you to hear me out. Okay?"

This was so unfair. Why couldn't he be a normal boyfriend with a normal life? Given the constant bruises, his loner status, and the terrifying rumors about him, I doubted normal would ever come into play. "Are you in a fight club?"

He snorted. "*No.*"

"A gang?"

He shot me a get-serious look "*No.*"

"Is that the truth?"

"Listen, I may not have been forthcoming about what I do at the gym, but I'm definitely not lying to you about this."

"*Definitely* not lying?" I repeated. "What does that even mean? That you *sort of* lied before?"

"I didn't lie to you, Peyton. It's just…I didn't tell you everything either. I gave you a version of the truth."

A *version* of the truth? "Well what version did I get?"

"I close the gym six nights a week. That much is true. But it's not my primary job there."

"What's your primary job?"

"I assist with training."

"Training," I echoed, having prepared myself to hear he collected bad debts for Jonas by breaking kneecaps. In comparison, training didn't seem so bad. "Training people to do what? Body building?"

"Partly." He looked out the windshield and cleared his throat. "And fighting."

"I'm sorry." I cleared my throat, too. "Did you say *fighting?*"

He nodded, keeping his expression neutral, his body relaxed, except for his white-knuckle grip on the steering wheel that told me he wasn't. "My main is boxing. It's what I teach."

"Your main?"

"My strength. My specialty."

"So, you're telling me you're a...*boxer*?"

"I train people how," he said. "It's not a big deal."

He was nineteen and not even out of school. How could he be a boxer? "Sam, would you please be honest with me?"

"I *am* being honest," he said, turning to me.

"Then how does a person get a black eye training someone to box if you aren't actually boxing?"

"You don't know much about fighting, do you?"

I already felt duped; I didn't need remarks like that to make me feel stupid, too. "No, I don't," I said, "and I wanted to keep it that way."

He looked exhausted as he rubbed his forehead. "Please don't make this something it isn't."

"By *this*, do you mean *us*?"

"No, not *us*."

I turned my whole body to face him, took a deep breath and tried to appear calm. I'd keep an open mind. Give him a chance to explain. "Tell me how you assist someone with boxing."

"Oh, you know." He shrugged. "I show them how to throw the different punches. Watch their footwork. Wear the mitts. Catch the hits. Tell them what they're doing right or wrong. That sort of thing. My part is guidance, quick reflexes and observation. There's not much to it."

I couldn't grasp that anyone would voluntarily do this. "Do you owe Jonas money or something?"

"What?" One side of his mouth quirked upward as if I'd made a joke. "No. Jonas pays *me*."

I studied his face and bad eye, my stomach knotting at the thought of someone hitting him. Hurting him beyond a bruise. Hitting him hard and often enough, that he'd eventually have scars so horrid, the color would drain out of my brother's face one day while describing the sight of it to me. "If it's all quick reflexes and observation, then why do you have a black eye?"

His mouth pulled into that rare, full grin I adored.

"Every once in a while, one gets by me."

"One gets by you?" I waited for more. Some kind of enlightenment. A clarification beyond boxing that would explain how training at a gym could leave scars like that on his body. Scars I couldn't even ask him about because I wasn't supposed to know. "I've seen movies, you know. People wear protection. Headgear."

He looked out the window. "Not all the time."

"You're not telling me everything."

"Well why don't you just tell me what you want to hear?" he said, turning to me. "Then I can repeat it back to you since you're obviously not interested in the truth."

My eyes began to water and not because of his smartass tone. The truth was, he wasn't wrong. I'd thought I wanted the truth, but when images of gangs, initiation rituals, and fights that included knives and broken bottles passed through my head—much too often lately—I had to wonder if I was truly ready to hear it. I couldn't fathom him in danger or getting injured. Tears welled whenever I tried.

Like now.

"Peyton."

I turned to stare out the windshield and blinked rapidly, too late to stop the tears slipping over my eyelashes. "I'm sorry," I whispered, mortified as I choked back a sob and pushed my face into my hands.

"Goddammit," he said under his breath.

Hearing him swear, I attempted to muffle all sounds of crying until my shoulders shook. Images of horrendous scars I'd never seen kept materializing in my imagination. The more I tried to be cool, the more emotional I got. Some days I hated my hypersensitivity to harsh realities. I wanted to be tough, like his sister. Someone he could respect. A strong, streetwise chick who didn't cry if her boyfriend took a beating. A girlfriend who thought it a turn-on to make out with a badass who had battle scars. Instead, I'd become a bawling spaz, overcome with emotion at the sight of her boyfriend's black eye.

What a loser.

"Stop," he said softly, sliding across the seat before I could apologize again for being ridiculous. His arms wrapped around me and I buried my face against his collarbone, humiliated. "I'm sorry. I was being a dick."

I shook my head. "It's not you," I whispered before making a sniffling, gurgling sound that only made me cringe and cry more.

"*Mi amor*...stop." He pulled me closer. "Then what? Why are you crying?"

"Because I'm a stupid girl," I mumbled into my hands, but the words came out garbled and incoherent. I shook my head, loathed at how weak I must have looked.

"I'll need you to repeat that," he said with a barely suppressed laugh. "But not in Urdu this time."

I smiled, despite feeling childish and stupid. "You wouldn't understand."

"At least give me a shot at it."

I wiped under my eyes and pulled back to look at him. "I really care about you, Sam."

His thumb brushed my chin that wouldn't stop trembling. "I care about you, too."

"I can't pretend this doesn't bother me." I stared at the blue mark circling the corner of his eye. "You have a new bruise every week and you don't care. How can you not care what happens to you?"

"It's not every week."

"Last week you had two bruises."

"That was two weeks ago. You make it sound dramatic."

If he'd seen how Daddy went off the deep end any time Mom defended Sam, he wouldn't say that. He'd understand why I needed him to be normal. "Well your eye *looks* dramatic." I brushed two fingers over the swelling. "It has to hurt."

"It doesn't."

He didn't flinch but I knew he had to be lying. I turned to the window, watching drops of rain pelting the glass. We'd only been dating a week. I had no right to make demands. Still, I couldn't stop myself from asking, "Sam, would you quit if I asked?"

"No."

Of course not. He barely knew me. He didn't owe me anything. My chin wobbled and I looked away. "Okay." I sniffled. Wiped under my nose. Noticed the rain coming down harder now. Everything outside was soaked and small puddles were growing. "We have to...we have to think about this."

"Think about what?"

Clearly, Sam and I wouldn't find a middle ground on this, and as I fought the urge to bolt, I realized Adam had been right about me. I had control issues. My life felt tied to Sam's now. Inexplicably tied to him and this weird, violent life he led that made me want to run.

"Peyton?"

"I don't think I can do this," I blurted, looking down from his dark, intense eyes. "It's not your fault. I knew you did something violent...and I thought I could handle it. But I...I can't. I shouldn't have said yes when you asked me out. It's not your fault. It's mine." I shoved my fingers over my mouth, knowing I'd likely continue rambling apologies for another thirty minutes if he let me.

The sounds of rain coming down heavy against the car filled the silence. Panic tightened my stomach. I thought back to what I'd said, what sounded like a break-up. Did I just break up with him?

God, I had.

Seconds ticked by and I had to fight my peacemaking instinct to smooth things over by taking everything back.

"Let me get this straight," he said. "You're seriously talking about breaking this off because I have a job that sometimes causes a bruise or two? Did I hear that right?"

"When you put it that way, it sounds unreasonable."

"It *is* unreasonable."

I scrubbed my face, overwhelmed. Whatever this was between us, it was way too much. Too much passion. Too much intensity. Too much everything. I couldn't handle it. I needed the sanctuary and solitude of my bedroom. I needed time away from him so I could think.

Twisting out of his hold, I reached for the door handle and his hand circled my wrist. "Peyton, stop. Just…stop. You'd get soaked. Besides, I'm not letting you get out in the middle of nowhere."

"This isn't nowhere."

"It's hell and gone from your house."

"I'll call Adam. Or Ryan."

"No, you won't. I brought you out here. I'll take you home. Quit overreacting and talk to me."

Tears blurred my vision.

"Dammit, Peyton," he said. "This isn't a big deal."

"To *you*." I sucked in a breath, imagining red lines radiating from white, raised scar tissue. Lines that extended six to ten inches across his chest and stomach, that looked hideous and painful. "You could get seriously injured, Sam. How can you be so blasé about this?"

"I'm not going to get hurt." His thumb brushed my wet cheek.

"It's not that I don't care," I said, needing to keep explaining. "I do. Too much. I don't want to stop seeing you." I noticed our fingers entwined between us. "I really don't, but—"

"Then don't," he whispered, his fingers threading into my hair as he kissed the corner of my mouth. "Don't stop seeing me."

The moment he said those words, the second he kissed me, my convictions cracked. I wanted him to quit this thing that left marks on him. He wasn't offering to do that. He wanted me to look the other way, to pretend I didn't care. "Sam, you forget I've seen you walking into school like this for years. Black eyes. Splits in your lip. I think you even had a broken hand once. It bothered me then and I didn't know you. Imagine how I feel now. Would you want to see me hurt every week?"

"Those were from street fights." He cupped my jaw. "I don't do that anymore."

"Wait, you were in street fi—"

He kissed me once, so quickly and firmly, that it startled me into shutting up. "You," he said, his breath mingling with mine, "are being crazy." He kissed my cheek softly and I closed my eyes. "Nothing has changed, Peyton. Don't make everything so complicated all the time. Focus on you. Do your thing." His fingers threaded through mine as he kissed me again. "You're going to be busy working on this website project, keeping up with your classes, and decorating cakes for your aunt. You won't have time to think about me. Don't think about what I do if it bothers you."

"But what you do—"

"I train," he said, pulling back to look at me. "That's all. And believe me when I say there's a huge difference between training and the real thing." The stark regret in his voice made me want to interrupt him to ask. "I'm not working two jobs for fun. I do it to help support my family. I can't quit because you have a problem with it. I'm not asking your permission, Peyton. But you do matter to me. A great deal." His hand brushed my cheek. "I don't want to stop seeing you and I don't want to see you upset. Just…ignore the occasional bruise. That's all I'm asking. See? Simple. Not complicated at all."

How did this happen to me? Logically, I shouldn't feel drawn to him as much as I did. We barely knew each other. "I do want this to be simple," I whispered. "Instead, it feels complicated and awful."

His mouth tilted in that half-smile. "That's because you're thinking too much."

"God, you sound like my dad."

"Wow, really?" His eyebrow quirked. "I've never been

compared to a man who has six years of higher education."

"He's a total chauvinist, Sam. It's not a compliment."

He frowned. "That's a little harsh, don't you think? I'm hardly sexist. I just don't worry about things like you do. It's not a crime, you know." His thumb brushed my cheek again. "So…are we good?"

I looked down. Eventually nodded. I wanted to believe him so badly that part of me did, and when his head lowered and his mouth closed over mine, I kissed him back.

I had no idea how long we kissed until I felt his hand slide under my shirt to the clasp of my bra. I pulled back to look at the clock. "We've been kissing over an hour. Shouldn't we go? You have things to do before work, right?"

His gaze shifted from the clock to me. "Yeah. But I like this better. Do you want me to take you home?"

"No." I'd answered him without thought, not at all certain I wanted to stop. Goose bumps shivered across my skin wherever his fingertips still touched. "But what are we doing?" I whispered.

"Whatever you want." His hand moved slowly over my bra clasp, tickling my skin. "Do you want me to stop?"

It was dark and gray outside and the rain showed no signs of letting up. No one was around, not that it would matter with the fogged up windows. "Not yet," I whispered and his mouth covered mine in that demanding way that made my insides liquefy. The clasp released.

Everything got warm and blurry after that.

CHAPTER THIRTEEN

Peyton

I published the website Tuesday and sent out a few mentions on free forums. Adam and I set up our little carpet picnic of cheese, crackers and soda, even though we didn't have much to celebrate. Nothing happened as we talked for over an hour, weighing the pros and cons of my next idea. Once we had a few students in the database, I wanted to add more fields and a revised Terms and Agreements page, allowing me to collect confidential student information from each of them. To monitor the students' lives, well-being, and grades in an environment where bullies no longer had the opportunity to tear them down was the only way to measure the success of the database. This was all under the assumption that someone would eventually use my website.

After I took Adam home and worked on several hours of homework, I spotted a new email with a subject line that read, Bullied.

I opened it and looked at the student's information that appeared to be legit. Within thirty minutes, I had three more. Two Bullied. One Bodyguard.

Even though I recognized the names, I knew I had to

brace myself because the sudden flurry of submissions couldn't be real. Maybe Ryan or Adam had called a few friends. Maybe the emails were nothing more than quick mock ups to appear valid.

Although, I couldn't imagine either would do this to me, even as a joke.

The next email had a subject line that read, You've Got Money. I opened it. Stared at the amount of two hundred. Checked the header information and confirmed it was the real deal.

Holy cow.

Of course, I should have known people wouldn't read the guidelines. No one was supposed to send money without a matchup confirmation from me first.

Within an hour, I was deep in a mixture of emails and money transfers. I finally texted Adam, freaked that I hadn't considered how much money I might be handling if the project actually took off. I was a high school student. This didn't seem legal, although I'd talked to Daddy and knew that it was.

Adam advised creating a separate savings account if this thing was really going to happen.

I texted again a few minutes later when I needed advice on how to handle the online bullying, which was nearly as bad as the physical threats.

This time he called.

"You realize that's a whole different set of friends," he said with a sigh. "Want me to rally up a few who might be interested?"

"Like who?"

"Michelle. Terra. Jacob. Hell, Troy blew all of last Sunday trying to outmaneuver a computer virus in real time because he was bored. He'd probably love tackling something like this."

I had the strangest feeling this was about to get crazy. "Okay. Gather up the usual suspects, I guess. Tell them they'd be doing me a huge favor."

"Not to mention, a cool hundred or two never hurts."

I smiled, even though I felt bitter that it always seemed to take money to motivate anybody. Anybody, that is, but Sam. "If you think of anyone else techie enough who might be interested—"

"I'll call 'em," he said. "Quit worrying."

"Adam," I sighed. "What would I do without you?"

"Are you kidding?" he said, a grin in his voice. "You'll never be without me."

*****

By Wednesday morning, twenty-two bullied students had submitted matchup information and wired two-hundred each. I knew all of the students but three, only because those three attended Ridgeview *Jr.* High, which violated the Terms and Agreements they obviously hadn't read on my home page.

By Thursday night, I had forty-eight bodyguards and forty-one students under protection or waiting for a matchup. I'd received more Ridgeview Jr. High applications and emails from their parents willing to send the money. When I managed to find matches for most of them, I realized I'd violated my own Terms and Agreements page, so I rewrote the page.

Wiring money that wasn't technically mine freaked me out to no end. So far, I'd wired close to four thousand dollars to thirty-three guards, quite a few who had taken more than one student.

Most applicants weren't eighteen and couldn't send electronic funds. In the end, it didn't matter. The amount of friends, siblings, and parents stepping forward to help these bullied kids shocked me. Payments and thank-you notes poured in.

When I woke Friday morning, I had three anonymous donations, twelve more bullied students, and twice as many bodyguards. Nine new applicants attended other schools, and six of those schools weren't even in Oregon.

That's when I had my first panic attack.

I was hyperventilating over the bathroom sink when Mom found me. She suggested I call my aunt to cut down my hours at the bakery, which I did, reducing my time to working Sundays only. Scaling down my hours helped, but it wasn't enough, and whenever I wasn't busy with homework or spending a couple of hours with Sam after school, I was transferring money, comparing class schedules, and emailing applicants potential bodyguard names. The erratic flurry of work kept me from finding a routine, which left my life and peace of mind in a constant state of flux. The entire ordeal gave me a new appreciation for Sam, who held down two jobs and somehow kept up with his homework while still finding time to see me.

Three weeks into the project, Adam showed up one Friday night and coerced me into going out to dinner with him. A forced break, he called it, which turned out to be a mistake because apparently I could think of nothing else now but the project. Eventually he broached the entire reason for the dinner. He was worried about me, so was Ryan, and he suggested I narrow my clients to Ridgeview High only, as originally intended. But I couldn't consider it. I didn't know how to say no.

Even when I started getting threats.

*****

I'd been half-asleep, standing at my locker between first and second period the following morning, when a boy barreled through a group of students and slammed into me, knocking us both to the ground. The hit winded me, but I gathered my senses in time to see my friend, Maru, grab Tim Nash by the shirt and smack him into a locker. Tim immediately pushed back, Maru came back even harder, and before I knew what was happening, they'd dropped to the floor, fists flying.

Maru was the stronger fighter, but Tim stupidly kept hitting back, which only made things worse and last forever. I yelled for them to stop, a moot effort since I could barely hear myself above the crowd of cheering students. Within seconds, the shouting had garnered the attention of numerous teachers, who bolted out of their classrooms to see the commotion. It took three of them to pull Maru and Tim apart.

From my spot on the floor, I watched the teachers haul both students down to the office. My entire body trembled. Getting the wind knocked out of me didn't help, but I knew the real reason for the shakes. Violence scared me to death.

The blond-haired boy who knocked me down stood and held out his hand to me. "S-sorry," he said.

I grabbed his hand, feeling as though I'd been in the brawl myself. "Thanks," I said, recognizing him. "Wait a second…you're Scott. Maru is your—" I paused, thinking twice.

"Bodyguard." He pulled me to a standing position. "Go ahead. You can say it."

I managed a weak smile. "I take it Tim shoved you."

"That's putting it mildly." He nodded, his eyebrows crinkling together. "You okay? You're shaking."

I pulled my hand from his. "I'll be okay. I just hate violence. It freaks me out."

"Tell me about it. I'm going to go explain what happened," he said with a nod toward the office. "I don't want Maru getting in trouble for me."

I knew it wouldn't matter what Scott told the powers that be. School policy dictated both parties fighting would get suspension. I needed to call Maru later and apologize, even though he signed on for this thing long before I'd implemented the website.

I turned back to my locker to get my notebook when something hit me from behind, so hard that I had to catch myself against the door. I grabbed my shoulder as pain radiated down my arm, but when I turned to see who'd hit me, not one of the students behind me looked guilty.

My eyes watered as I rubbed where a knot was growing on my shoulder blade. Now at least I could say I knew what a sucker punch felt like.

*****

I stared at a note in British Authors, unable to grasp what I was reading, even though I'd read it over twenty times. My hands shook as I scanned the typed words again while Ms. Campbell's voice drifted around me.

P,

Big surprise planned if you don't kill the website. Hoping you still like to play hard.

When it registered that Ms. Campbell had stopped talking, I looked up to see how long I'd drifted off and frowned to see Vice Principal Tanner standing at the front of the class whispering with Ms. Campbell. He finished and turned, pointing in my direction and crooking his finger.

I froze.

All heads pivoted to me and I turned to Molly Graham behind me, who glared back at me as though I'd just fingered her in a murder. I whipped back around. "Who?" I asked. No way did he want me. "Which one of us?"

"Grab your things and come with me, Ms. Greene," he said. "You won't return today."

I stared, feeling shell-shocked as I closed my book. Eventually, I picked up my things, folding all of it against my chest like a shield. Disbelief kept me seated a few more seconds. I wanted to pretend the note in my hand didn't exist. I also wanted to give Mr. Tanner time to figure out he'd made a huge mistake. No one had ever called me to the office. I was an honor roll student, did community service on a regular basis, and had a part-time job. What more did they want?

I stood and forced my trembling legs to move forward. This had to be about skipping class with Sam. It had only been the one time, but I still felt like a delinquent as I followed Mr. Tanner to the door. I glanced at Sam, whose scowl made me look away before I closed the door behind me.

157

"Don't worry your pretty head over this," Mr. Tanner said, leading me to his office. He waved a hand to the faux leather chair across from his desk. "I told Mr. Smith I had no doubt you'd be agreeable to the idea."

I sat, tempted to comment about the sexist *pretty-head* remark when my brain shifted into a different gear. What did Mr. Smith, my Projects teacher, have to do with this? "Could you explain why I'm here? I think that would help."

He closed the door and sat behind his desk. "My apologies," he said, scratching his head until he'd made a dent in his springy, black hair. "I thought you understood. Several people have directed my attention to a certain bodyguard website you created."

"You make it sound like it's a secret. Is that what this is about? My website?"

"Yes, we need you to shut it down."

I'd felt less stunned after that earlier sucker punch. "What?"

"Admittedly, your idea was creative, Ms. Greene. But it's causing the school problems."

I realized my mouth was open and closed it. "You can't ask me to shut down my website."

"You didn't create this for your Projects class?"

"I did."

A polite smile pulled his mouth into an unattractive grin. "Then your project is school business and we have every right to tell you to shut it down."

I shook my head. "I'm providing a needed service. How can that be a problem?"

"We're getting complaints from parents. A large number actually."

"*Parents?* What parent wouldn't want their student to feel safe at school? Who are these people?"

"You're encouraging violence, Ms. Greene." His pasted grin faded. "The conflict with school policy is clear."

"Well it's not clear to me." I shifted, uncomfortable

under his stare. "How am I encouraging violence?"

"We suspended four students last week. Two this morning. That's six students who would be in class today if you had not encouraged them to fight."

"I didn't encourage anyone to fight."

"Three of those students, as I understand it, are your bodyguards. Do you mean to tell me you don't pay people to fight?"

I shook my head. "I don't pay anyone anything. The student pays. All I do is hold the money and make the transfers. It's not my money to spend. Even the donations."

"Donations?" He blinked rapidly, his glasses sliding to the end of his nose. "Donations from who exactly?"

"Citizens supporting the cause."

"The *cause*?" His tone suggested my website had become a doorway to the occult.

"The cause of protecting the student body," I explained. "The donations are for students who can't pay for protection."

"You're telling me you don't make a dime?"

I shook my head. "It's nonprofit. All overhead is strictly voluntary."

He picked up a pen and leaned back. "You understand it's my job to protect the student body, Ms. Greene. Not yours."

"I know," I said. "It *is* your job."

The silence grew heavier. "Then I should get back to it, don't you think?" he said. "The good news is that Mr. Smith has agreed to give you an A for your project."

"Why? We have weeks left in the semester. I have to compile and analyze results. I have to write a paper to present my findings."

"The website has proven successful enough, and Mr. Smith is happy to give you an A. No paper necessary. Although, we require you to discontinue the project first."

I couldn't decide if this was a bribe or an ultimatum.

"And if I don't shut it down?"

"You fail."

Ultimatum. Wow. I couldn't believe the school's VP just threatened me. "In other words, Mr. Tanner, you're bullying me to shut down a project because parents are bullying you."

"I wouldn't use the term *bullying*."

"What term would you use?"

He cleared his throat. "Not bullying."

"What you're doing right now is the definition of bullying," I said. "You're in a position of authority over me physically and otherwise. You told me to do something, and when I refused to do it—"

"*Are* you refusing to do it?"

"Yes, I am." His eyes narrowed and I shifted again. "And when I refused to do what you asked, you threatened me."

"That's another inappropriate term. I didn't threaten you."

"I'm curious." I felt my temper rising. "How do people stay confused as to why students bully other students, when the adults are acting the example of the problem? Kids are killing themselves, Mr. Tanner. Every day. Because the school environment you think you have under control has become so toxic for some students, that it's a fate worse than death. *Death*. Yet no one seems concerned about this. And now—"

"Ms. Greene."

"*And now*," I said, refusing to let him interrupt me, "when a student steps forward with an idea, a *good* idea, for a mashup website to alleviate the problem, your plan is to threaten me by tarnishing my grade point average if I don't shut it down. Sorry, that's bullying by anyone's standards."

"I said your idea was creative, Ms. Greene," he said. "Not *good*."

"I happen to think it's a good idea. Mr. Smith agreed."

"Well, I don't agree, and I stand by what I said. You

can't label me, or the parents who contacted me with their concerns, as bullies. It's not the correct term here."

"Fine. I'll explain your offer to my mother tonight. Maybe she can explain how the VP overriding my teacher's opinion by failing me when my website meets all the criteria for this project isn't bullying."

He'd paled a fraction. "I didn't mean you'd fail the class, Ms. Greene. Just this project."

"The project *is* the class. Didn't Mr. Smith explain that?"

"Listen," he said, sliding forward and placing both hands flat on his desk. "I think we got off on the wrong foot here. I'm capable of being reasonable. I'll ask Mr. Smith to give you an extension. A chance to do another project. How does that sound?"

I couldn't fathom finding the time to do another project. "Fine, I'll take the extension."

"You'll do another project?"

"I will," I said, wondering how I'd come up with another idea, much less the time to complete it.

"I think you'll see this works out better for everyone," he said.

"What'll work out better?"

"Removing the website."

"I'm not removing it," I said. "I'm agreeing to submit another project. That's all."

He sighed and ran a palm down his face. "I don't think you want to push me on this matter, Peyton."

I didn't appreciate his sudden use of my first name. "Beyond this class, my website has nothing to do with this school except that most of my customers happen to attend here. You have no jurisdiction over the website, or me. I've withdrawn my project and I've agreed to submit another one. That's the best I can do."

"Then you give me no choice," he said, rubbing his jaw. "I'll have to call your parents. I hate to do this. You've been an excellent student. It's a horrible way to end your time here."

I clutched my books. "My mother supports this project. Believe me when I say the last thing you want to do is try to bully her, too."

"*Quit* using the term *bullying*, Ms. Greene, or you'll find yourself in detention. Perhaps worse."

My eyes watered. Detention freaked me out and I couldn't comprehend suspension or expulsion on my record. The release bell rang and I stood, determined not to cry. I wanted to show him his threats hadn't worked. I could be tougher than that. "May I use your copier?"

He looked startled by the request. "We don't normally allow students to—" He paused, staring at my watery gaze. "All right. Follow me." He stood and walked to an adjacent office where the staff and I watched him punch a code into the copier.

I unfolded the threatening note, placed it carefully against the glass, and made a copy.

"What is that?" he asked.

"It's for you," I said, pulling the original from the glass and handing it to him. I grabbed the copy. He read the original, his eyes widening before I turned and stalked back into his office to stand by the door.

"Where did you get this?" he asked, following me.

"My locker. Before seventh period." My legs shook, weak as a newborn lamb. I had no idea what Mr. Tanner knew about my rumored reputation here. Did faculty get wind of that sordid stuff? My stomach churned to know he'd read the playing hard comment. "Consider this my official complaint that someone at this school is threatening me. I need your protection, Mr. Tanner. Can you help me?"

"Do you have something more…concrete than a typed note?" he said, sitting in his chair again. "Maybe something in handwriting?"

I stared at him, took a deep breath, and turned to lower my shirt down my shoulder blade enough to uncover the growing bruise from that morning. "Only this."

His eyes rounded. "How did you get that?"

"Someone." I looked down. "I don't know who. Someone punched me from behind earlier today. I turned around but there were too many students." I released my shirt and turned to him. "Can you help me?"

"Of course." He sounded confident but looked uncomfortable. "We'll do what we can."

"Like what?"

He stared at me in silence.

So no, he couldn't help me. "I see."

"You know," he said, "in looking up your website, I found an interesting video of you and your friends. I recognized your brother, too. Have you seen it?"

I nodded as heat crept into my cheeks to recall the lewd dialogue. A shiver ran through me to imagine Mr. Tanner hearing those things while watching me.

"Do you think this—" he waved the note, "has anything to do with that?"

"They want me to take down the website. It states it clearly on the note."

"Interesting," he said. "I wouldn't agree. Perception is everything, Ms. Greene."

Was he saying I deserved this treatment because of a stupid video? The air suddenly felt too hot and I opened the door to see Sam leaning against the wall. He straightened when he saw me, his scowl shifting over my shoulder to the VP behind me.

"Ms. Greene?"

I pulled my books tightly to my chest and turned to see him still seated.

"Have your parents seen the video?"

I shook my head. "Not that I'm aware."

"Interesting," he said.

I sensed Sam's simmering presence behind me before his hand brushed my back. "Is it interesting?" I said. "Most would probably find it disturbing. I mean, the person who created the video is obviously a student here since he or she made the video in the school parking lot. I wonder what the media's spin might be on a school that churns out kids who produce videos with that type of content. On school property, no less. With the added audio, the video is practically child pornography. And as you said, perception is everything."

He lost his superior smile somewhere between the words *media* and *child pornography*. "You can close the door, Ms. Greene. I wouldn't want to keep you after school hours. We'll talk again soon."

I closed the door, my hands shaking the entire time. Turning, I bumped into Sam and dropped everything. Our heads nearly collided when we both bent to retrieve the items.

"Sorry," I said, snatching the note and stuffing it in my pocket as I simultaneously grabbed my A Tale of Two Cities paperback. My hands wouldn't stop shaking.

He gave me the notebook and grabbed my trembling hand, holding it firmly. "What did he want?"

"He—" I stood and shook my head, letting my explanation die a quiet death while I blinked hard and tried not to cry. Sam took one look at my watery gaze and pulled me into a hug.

I wanted to be tough but melted against him instead, not caring that anyone stared or whispered. Students milled around us on their way to the buses, gawking as they passed. I doubted anyone had a clue Sam and I had become a couple. At least they hadn't until now.

His arms tightened. "You're shaking. Tell me what he said to you."

I took a deep breath and backed away from his hold, determined not to fall apart at my first real challenge. "I'm overreacting. He…he gave me an ultimatum. That's all."

He dropped his hand to hold mine and we headed toward senior hall. "*What* ultimatum?"

"He threatened to fail me if I didn't pull the website."

"*What?*" He sounded as shocked as I felt. "You told him to go to hell, right?"

"No. Of course not. But I did tell him I'm keeping the website, which means I have to submit a different project."

"That's bullshit."

We stopped at his locker first. "Well, he didn't exactly give me a choice."

"I don't know. After what you said back there, I'd say he's the one who walked away with the nosebleed. Child pornography? Jeez, Sunshine. You don't pull any punches."

Daddy would be livid if Mr. Tanner told him what I said today. "I panicked when he threatened to fail me. All I could think was how my mother would have handled him. Whenever she's on a crusade for the underdog, she finds her opponent's weak spot and *squeezes*. At least that's what she calls it. When she's really trying to scare someone, she mentions the media. I might have overshot a little."

He grabbed his last book and closed his locker, grinning. "Must be where you get your tenacity."

I dragged myself in stunned silence to my locker with him next to me. "Mr. Tanner was bullying me into pulling down a site I created to prevent bullying," I said, pushing in my combination. "I'd laugh if I wasn't so shocked."

"He's just pissed a high school senior is making progress on an issue this country can't find consensus on, much less resolve. You kicked the shit out of him back there. Call me twisted, but it totally made my day."

"Yeah. Tough words from me, a person who has no idea for a second project. But I'm motivated more than ever now for the bodyguard project. I just decided to go national. Maybe he can put that in his pipe and smoke it."

Sam frowned. "Peyton, you can barely keep up as it is. You'll drop."

"If the website is really working," I reasoned, stuffing two more books in my bag and closing my locker, "I have to help everyone I can, don't I? Maybe what I'm doing will prompt someone else to start a similar project." His doubtful smirk told me what he really thought. "Okay, I'll admit the weeks ahead feel endless. But this is what I've always wanted. An idea that forces change. A good change. Do you know what it means to me to have already found that? I don't even have a degree, and already I'm making a difference."

"Yeah, and your schedule is about to become worse than mine."

"I know. Ryan already thinks I'm working too many hours."

He leaned back against someone's closed locker. "You do, but I'll bet Naruto Uzumaki would have done the same thing. He'd have stuck with it like you are."

I looked up at him, unable to tamp down a massive smile. "You watched it! You watched Naruto!"

His smirk became a half-grin. "I traded sleep to catch the first twenty episodes. It helped that they're short."

I stepped between his legs and kissed him right there. "Well? What did you think?"

"The show is totally you. And you're right," he said. "It's addictive."

"Did you cry?"

He grinned and I couldn't stop myself from kissing him again. "Like I'd tell you if I did. But do that one more time..." I leaned in, stopping just a half-inch from his mouth, "and I might admit to getting a little misty-eyed."

CHAPTER FOURTEEN

Peyton

I didn't talk to my parents that night because I had no idea how to start that conversation. Huge mistake. Mr. Tanner called them the next morning, giving my dad all day to stew about it. He launched into me about it over the dinner table—his favorite place of attack.

"You'll do as you're told and pull it," he said, his hard gaze promising a hardcore interrogation if I didn't comply. My brother's worried gaze swung to mine.

"How can you say that?" I asked. "You helped me write the terms and conditions. I thought you supported me."

"I did. But now it's a problem. Don't shake your head at me, Peyton. Shut it down."

"No."

He looked stunned—my own reaction after the word left my mouth. Thinking back, I couldn't recall ever telling Daddy *no*. "What did you say?" he asked.

He'd never been a violent man, yet he could still scare the bejeebers out of me when his voice rose to a vibrating level or dropped to that menacingly calm manner, like it just did. "I said *no*." I cleared my throat. "I'm not pulling the website."

He braced his wrists against the table. "Tanner told me what you said. Challenging him the way you did. You're making a bad reputation for yourself, Peyton. Is that what you want?"

"She already has a bad reputation," Ryan muttered. "And challenging Tanner isn't how she got it."

Daddy locked eyes with my brother. "What's that supposed to mean?"

Ryan glared back. "What do you think it means?"

"*Ry-an*," I whispered. He turned to me and shut his mouth when he recognized my pleading eyes.

Daddy's attention pivoted from me to my mother. "This is what happens when you encourage them, Maggie. She's on her way to becoming an insubordinate like Ryan. First that Guerra boy and now this. It's as though I'm not even here. I no longer have any say in my own home."

"Insubordinate?" I echoed.

"You know I expect more, Peyton. This sudden defiance is due to that Guerra boy's influence. I'm sure of it."

"Sam has nothing to do with this," I said. "And you can't deny my point to Mr. Tanner was a valid one. If the current system worked, students wouldn't need to rent a bodyguard. Do you realize how much two hundred dollars is to someone my age? Yet they're paying it. Their parents are paying it. Their parents' friends are paying it. What does that tell you?"

Daddy eyed me critically. "You act as if your generation is the first to have bullies. It gets better after high school."

"And in the meantime, we do what?" I said. "High school is difficult enough without having to look over your shoulder all the time."

"I was harassed," Daddy said, as though I hadn't said a word. "*I* lived. Believe it or not, the experiences motivated me to succeed. No one wants to live in the wrong section of town."

"That's a disgusting thing to say, Paul," Mom muttered under her breath.

"I hope that's not the new measurement of a successful childhood," I said. "To live through it? As opposed to what? Not live through it?"

Mom looked up. "She's making perfect sense to me, Paul. And I'm proud of what she's doing."

He stopped chewing. "Of course you are."

"Take your jabs at me if you want, but your daughter is right," she said. "Something needs to happen and the current establishment isn't doing it."

"Which means you'll be parading behind her with banners and horns, I'm sure," he said.

Ryan and I exchanged nervous glances at Daddy's sarcastic tone. The usual pre-empt to a massive blow-up.

"I support her in keeping the website," Mom said. "If that means I go toe-to-toe with the school administration when they decide to threaten her again, then that's what I'll do."

My dad started chewing vigorously this time. The beginning of the end. "You want her to fail a class, is that it?"

"They *can't* fail me," I said, pulling his baleful attention back to me. "Not legally."

He glared at me over his glasses. "You have a degree in law I don't know about?"

"It's a simple deduction," I said, ignoring his condescension. "They can't fail me for a project I won't submit. I told you I'm submitting something else. Everything I do with the website is outside the school's jurisdiction. Why are we still talking about this?"

"Now see? That makes this worse," he said. "You don't have to submit it, which means you're continuing the project out of spite."

"I'm continuing the project because it's the right thing to do, Daddy. I'm not exactly having fun, you know. This is taking up all of my personal time. I barely see Adam anymore."

"Yet you see enough of the other one," he added.

I wouldn't let Daddy pull me into another argument about Sam, which was likely his real agenda. Sometimes I wondered if he thought more about Sam than I did. "Do you think I like the threats I'm getting? Or when people punch me in the hallway?"

Ryan stiffened, his gaze swinging to me. "Who the hell punched you? When?"

"Yesterday in the hallway." I shook my head. "Someone hit me in the back. I didn't see who."

"It's a horrific bruise," Mom muttered, who had seen me in my pajama tank top this morning.

"*What?*" Ryan asked, looking between us. "Where was I?"

"It was…nothing," I said. "I didn't mention it because I didn't want you to get upset."

"Upset?" he said, scowling. "Try pissed. Did you report it?"

"I told Mr. Tanner."

"And?" Ryan's nostrils flared. "What's he planning to do about it?"

I shrugged. "What *can* he do?"

"But we should—" Ryan stopped, hitting the same conclusion I had after it happened.

"Honestly, I'll take a punch over the threats," I said. "First the lewd emails with way too much personal information. Then this note in my locker. It's obvious some of these people know me. I'm starting to get paranoid."

"I want you to print those emails for me," Mom said. "Right after dinner. I intend to show them to Mr. Tanner personally."

Daddy's gaze shifted from Mom to me. "If you'd just follow the rules and not cause waves, people would leave you alone."

"That's a crock," Ryan said.

"Mhm. And I suppose because you're eighteen now," Daddy said, still looking at me, "my opinion means nothing. You are still living under my roof. I could take the Lexus off your hands. Maybe you'd change your attitude if you and Ryan had to ride the bus again."

"Perfect," I said, getting angrier. "Stick us on the bus where the bullying is the worst."

"The car is mine," Mom said.

Daddy gripped the table, looking at her. "Your point?"

"You can't take it, is my point." Her eyes pivoted to me. "I'm giving it to her as an early graduation gift."

"Ah, I guess we're back to assuming she'll graduate," he said, picking up his fork and stuffing another bite of chicken into his mouth.

"You know me well enough, Daddy, to know I loathe conflict. That upsetting people *really* bothers me."

"I'm not so sure," he said. "In fact, I'm beginning to think this is just a way for you to get back at me because I don't want you to see that boy."

"His name is Sam." I leaned back and forced my shoulders to relax. "Why can't you see why I'm doing this? People have given bullies amnesty for decades simply because they're under eighteen. It's reverse ageism. Could someone at the firm do these things to you without dire consequences? Stalking. Harassment. Assault and battery. Theft. Sexual—"

Daddy's eyes bugged. "What?"

"She has a valid point, Paul," Mom said, scooping a small bite of mashed potatoes into her mouth. "Explain to me why someone her age can't get the same protection as you or I, simply because she's a student. If you can give me a logical explanation, then I'll pull the website immediately."

My mouth dropped open.

"*You'll* pull the website?" Daddy said, looking uncertain. "How will you manage that?"

"Because it's mine," she said.

"Mom," I interrupted. "Wait."

She held her palm up to me. "The website is mine, Paul. It's registered in my name and I'm paying for it."

Ryan's eyes rounded and pivoted to mine. He'd watched me buy the domain and certificate using my own debit card.

"Wait." My dad waved his fork at her. "You used *my* money for this project?"

"Our money," she corrected. "Which means your problem is with me. Not our daughter."

"Are you *insane*, Maggie?" he asked, dropping his fork to his plate. "The negative attention alone…do you want our daughter subjected to that?"

"I've already received dozens of phone calls from parents commending Peyton for implementing this idea. You heard your daughter. Who do you think pays these bodyguard fees?" He hunched over his plate, refusing to acknowledge the question. "Oh, relax Paul. When this is over, we'll all take a nice vacation. Meanwhile, we hunker down and stick it out together."

Ryan swallowed audibly next to me.

Daddy stared at her a long, uncomfortable moment. "I hope you enjoy your vacation. I won't be going," Daddy said, pushing his chair back loudly and leaving the table.

Ryan and I watched him go, heard the front door slam and his car start. I turned to Mom through tears. "Why did you lie to him?"

"Because he should be on your side." A tear slipped down her cheek. "You're already under enough pressure, honey. Adding another project to your schedule. There's nothing I can do about your workload or what's to come, but *this* I can do something about."

"What's to come?" Ryan said.

"Your father is right," she said. "This is about to get uglier. Bullying has been a hot topic for a long time. One people feel strongly about. Both sides." Her voice shook and she placed her fork down to wipe her watering eyes.

My brother stood and quickly moved to Daddy's chair, putting his hand over hers. "He's wrong, Mom. Please don't cry," he said, getting teary himself.

She clutched his hand. "It's a good idea, Peyton," she said, turning to me. "No matter what happens, try to stay focused on the students you're helping. Or the parents who donated money to keep their children safe. Know that I'll back you up every step of the way." Her jaw set sternly. "Promise me you won't quit this. It's too important."

"I promise. I won't quit," I said, unable to focus on much beyond Daddy walking out. My parents had problems like everybody else. They argued more than they got along. Still, Daddy had never walked out and I felt responsible. "He's coming back, isn't he?"

She never replied, forcing a smile instead as she stood to clear her plate.

Later, I heard Daddy's car pull into the driveway as I worked in my room. I figured everything would be okay, until I found a pillow and blankets on the couch the next morning, and several mornings after that. Clearly, this situation wouldn't resolve itself.

Especially if no one was talking.

Spending more time with Sam kept me sane. He'd guessed for a while things weren't great at home, even though I wouldn't talk about it. To keep me distracted, we started setting up homework dates after school where we could get dinner so I wouldn't have to go home. It quickly became our routine, and if we finished and still had time before his shift at the gym, we'd talk and kiss in the Impala, sometimes ending up in the backseat as we pushed those lines we said we wouldn't cross. Making out with Sam was the only time I forgot everything else.

It helped that he was an incredible kisser.

Then one day when I was near tears and too emotional to talk, he held me in the front seat and started talking about his family, I think to get my mind off my own. I nearly stopped breathing, snuggled against him and afraid to break the spell. He'd dodged most of my personal questions in the past, giving me only tidbits of information at a time to keep me happy. But something happened that day in his car, and soon I longed for afternoons, sitting in his arms while he talked about his dad, his mom, and family moments when Savanna was little.

Sam had grown up middle class in Beaverton and couldn't remember a time when the Impala hadn't been part of his life. He could recall back to age four how he and his dad spent every Sunday restoring the car. How his dad taught him about the older models and the value of holding onto things long past. They'd spent weekends and nights at the gym, where his dad had taught him boxing, as his grandfather had taught his dad, and his great grandfather had taught him.

I smiled every time he referred to his dad as *Papá*, the term he used whenever engrossed in a story. He said the endearment with that accent and such affection that I envied his dad for taking up such a large space of Sam's heart.

His father had been an attentive family man. Much more than mine. I wished I could have met the man. I think the Sam I knew—the side he kept hidden from most everyone else—would have been Sam all the time had his dad not died. But seven years ago, Officer Luis Guerra went to work and never came back—shot and killed while issuing a traffic ticket. Sam wouldn't talk about much that had happened since then. Most of the time, he'd change the subject if I asked, usually by kissing me.

And because I loved the way he kissed, I pretended not to notice.

CHAPTER FIFTEEN

Peyton

Adam and I had just finished studying for an economics test one afternoon when a second project idea finally hit me. If I duplicated my bodyguard database and matched students willing to pay other students to tutor them, I could avoid half the work required to set up a tutoring website. The school already had free tutoring available, so I didn't have to worry about an explosion of submissions once it went live. But personal experience told me not everybody could teach, including the tutoring volunteers. Could there be an untapped market there? A small one?

For the first time in my life, I was willing to accept a C if there wasn't.

When I told Sam about it later, he insisted I'd be taking on too much work, but he supported me anyway because he always did. My competition was a free service at the school, so Sam suggested I set up the website to allow students to name their own tutoring prices. I could only hope maintaining records on varied pricing wouldn't make me crazy by the end of the semester.

The frontend setup took little time. I implemented the idea by replicating my database, purging the fields, and producing a second website. I resented the extra money a second domain cost me, not to mention the upkeep once the responses started coming in several days after I published the site, but whatever. I was willing to do anything to keep the *studentbodyforehire* website up and running.

Two weeks into this insane schedule, my bedroom desk became an uncomfortable headrest. I started falling asleep while working on a regular basis, and that's where Adam found me Friday night before Halloween. He coaxed me awake with a tall mocha and convinced me to go to a movie with him.

He told me I needed the brain rest, and I proved him right by falling asleep twice in the theater.

"You're hitting burnout, Peyton," he said, as we left the movie, "and if you don't let someone help you soon, you'll end up no good to anyone. Why don't you let me take over the database for a while?"

"You're sweet and I love you for offering," I said, turning to hug him by the concession stand. "But you have too many tough classes this semester."

He shrugged. "I can handle it."

"Absolutely not," I said, opening my eyes mid-hug to see Savanna across the theater, staring at me with her mouth twisted in a snarl. A pretty, olive-skinned woman stood next to her.

I released Adam abruptly. "Oh my God. That's Sam's mom," I whispered as the older woman followed Savanna's gaze to me.

Adam glanced over his shoulder. "So?"

"I haven't met her. This is awkward."

"Only one way to fix that."

Sam had never offered to introduce me to his mother, and I didn't want to encroach on an area of his life he wasn't ready to share with me. The strained moment drew out until I finally waved to them. Savanna's cold gaze made me want to turn the other direction.

"This is bordering on rude," Adam said. "We either go over there now or leave."

My brain fast-forwarded to meeting Mrs. Guerra officially one day and having the embarrassing experience of explaining to her why I turned and walked out at the movie theater without introducing myself. "Right." I grabbed Adam's sleeve and moved my feet forward, quickly pinching my coat closed when I remembered I wore my brother's t-shirt with a printed exclamation I didn't need Sam's mother to see. Dread made my breaths shorter the closer we got. "Hey, Savanna," I said.

"Hey," she said, curt as ever.

"Savanna?" the woman said, smiling at me with a glance. "Introduce me to your friend."

I smiled in return, searching for any resemblance between the woman and Sam. Definitely the color of her chocolate brown hair and that mischievous smile. She also had an alert wariness that made me think of him.

"Um, she's Sam's friend." Savanna took a deep breath and nodded to me. "*Mamá*, this is Peyton Greene. Peyton, my mother, Isabel."

"And my friend Adam," I said, clutching his sleeve tighter.

Isabel Guerra's face brightened and she extended her hand, shaking mine, then Adam's. "*Peyton*. It's wonderful to meet you. Finally. Samuel has talked about you several times. I'm certain he wished to introduce us one day himself, but he couldn't miss work tonight. Would it be wrong if I invited you to a late dinner next Saturday without his permission? I'd like an opportunity to get to know you better."

She had a contagious grin. "I'd love to, if Sam doesn't mind." She seemed warm and wonderful, as Sam had often described her. She was genuine and easy to like. I wished I could say the same about Savanna.

"He mentioned you hate violence," Isabel said. "Is that why you're not cheering for him tonight?"

"Cheering for him?" I arched my eyebrows and looked to Savanna, whose eyes had widened to huge proportions.

"Actually," Savanna chirped in a high voice, "Samuel is on a…date. Um, with someone else. Ob-obviously."

"What?" I blinked.

Isabel Guerra's gaze jerked to her daughter and she pinched her arm. "Don't you dare say that about your brother."

Savanna stepped back and rubbed her arm. "It's true."

"He did no such thing." Isabel turned to me. "Peyton, don't listen to my daughter. My son would never—"

Her lips moved but I didn't hear another word. Adam must have recognized my duck-and-run expression because his fingers entwined with mine.

Sam dating other people while dating me? It had never occurred to me. All that time together, everything he'd said and done. That our entire relationship might have been some kind of ruse to string me along until he got…what? Sex with the nympho? Did he believe the rumors about me after all?

God, no. That couldn't be. He wouldn't have, would he?

Staring at Vanna's please-don't-shoot-the-messenger expression, I realized Sam had duped me again with more versions of the truth.

"It was nice…" My chin trembled as my voice shook. I stepped back, unable to keep it together. "It was nice to meet you, Mrs. Guerra." Yanking my hand from Adam's grip, I whipped around and hurried toward the door.

"Peyton!"

Savanna's shout registered but I refused to stop. I swiped a tear and hit the silver bar to the exit door.

When Sam's sister yelled my name a second time, I pushed my way through a crowd of people in hopes to get to my car before she got to me. I couldn't take more remarks. I needed to disappear. Needed quiet. A moment to think. A bush I could hide behind to vomit.

The sound of pounding feet registered just before Adam's shout behind me. I felt a hard grip on my elbow, a sudden jerk, and fell back into someone as a car whizzed by me, practically brushing my clothes in a fast exit from the parking lot.

I stared open-mouthed at the back of the blue car, imagining myself crushed under four wheels or flipping over the hood. Nausea turned my stomach and I squeezed my eyes together as Adam turned me to him.

I hadn't realized I was shaking until he folded his arms around me and crushed me against him. "You scared the hell out of me!" he said, his breath hard on my shoulder as he held me tighter. "Don't you ever fucking do that again, got it?"

Adam never swore, at least around me, unless he couldn't help himself. The only time I could remember him sounding this upset had been three years ago after Ryan relayed what Jason had tried to do to me. "I'm sorry," I said, sniffling. "I...I wanted to..." Disappear. I still did.

The sound of someone rushing up to us made him turn.

"What the hell, Peyton?" Savanna said, breathing hard. "You trying to kill yourself?"

"Get away from her," Adam said coldly, releasing me to get between us. "You've done enough."

"I know. I shouldn't have said that," she said, sounding sincere. "I'm sorry." She looked at me. "I lied. Samuel isn't on a date."

"What the hell is wrong with you?" Adam said. "Do you *enjoy* hurting people?"

She looked down. "No, I always cover for him. I'm just...bad at it."

"Covering for him?" Adam said.

I recalled Sam mentioning it over sushi. *Vanna covers for me whenever anyone asks questions.* "She's telling the truth," I said, stepping next to Adam. "Sam told me as much weeks ago."

"Your face," she said. "Almost the second I said it…I realized the lie was worse than the truth."

"What are you talking about?" Adam asked.

"When my mother mentioned cheering for Samuel," she said, turning to Adam. "I didn't know what to do. She wasn't supposed to know yet." She looked at me again. "But that's where he is. He's got a fight. That's what she meant by the cheering comment."

"You mean he's *training* someone to fight," I corrected.

Sweat had formed on her brow and she twisted to see her mother through the glass door, frowning at us. Savanna swung back around, looking more stressed. "He *does* train fighters, but part of that training is fighting. The real kind. No headgear or padding. Just fighting."

"What?" My voice sounded a million miles away.

"Maybe it's time you see what he does when he isn't with you," she said. "Go to *MMA Northwest*. It's in Beaverton. That's where he's at."

I could only assume that was the name of the gym, but I couldn't go. I'd purposely avoided seeing him in that place, doing what he did that left all of those marks. I couldn't take it. "He won't like me showing up when he's working."

"You need to see him, Peyton," she said. "Trust me on this."

I didn't trust her for anything, but the urgency in her voice made me think maybe I needed to go. I turned to Adam. "You know Beaverton, right?"

"That doesn't mean I know where it is." His eyes widened and he looked at Savanna. "He fights MMA? Seriously?"

She nodded. "It's training, but yeah. He fights."

"Holy shit," he said.

Adam's expression only reinforced my decision never to visit Sam where he worked. I had a sick feeling that was all about to change.

Savanna glanced between us. "There was a tire place that burned down last year. It was on the news. Do you know where it is?"

"I know where it *used* to be," he said.

"Two blocks south there's a large building. Looks like an old warehouse. Bars on the windows. No big sign or anything to tell you what it is. Looks like Alcatraz from the outside. You can't miss it. Take her there. If you get there by ten, you'll make it in time."

"Time?" I asked.

"To see the fight. They always leave his fights for last." Isabel called out to Savanna then and she turned to her mom and back at me. "Ask for Bobby. Tell him Sam's expecting you or he won't let you in." Her mouth curled up at the corner, reminding me of Sam's reluctant smile when he didn't quite believe me. "I can tell you care about him, Peyton. I guess we'll soon see how much." She turned and sprinted back where her mom waited for her.

Adam stared at me. "Well, obviously you should go. Right?"

"I should," I said, nodding. "Probably."

"Let me drive you." He grabbed my keys from me. "In this state you're likely to get yourself killed."

*****

"Want me to come with you for moral support?" Adam asked, turning to me.

I hadn't said a word to Adam on the drive there, having no idea what to say. Everyone had warned me. Sam had denied belonging to a fight club or a gang, but this building hadn't a single sign that I could see.

Seemed underground to me.

"No," I said, grabbing the passenger door handle. "This is between Sam and me. I should do it alone. Just...wait. No matter what. Okay?"

He took a deep breath and nodded.

I stepped from the car and headed toward the front of the slum-like warehouse building. Showing up without a word of warning felt dishonest, but if Sam was truly fighting tonight, then honesty shouldn't be high on my priority list. A light glowed next to a battered door and bar-covered window with a small sign behind it that read *MMA Northwest*.

From what I could see, the inside looked normal, almost welcoming. I opened the door and a rush of warmth blew past me as loud cheers sounded somewhere else in the building. Two men perched on stools behind a tall counter stared at a computer screen.

"Yes!" The younger one with a shaved head smacked the counter with an open hand. "And that's a takedown."

"Excuse me," I said, voice shaking.

The boy jerked his head in my direction, his green eyes widening. He hit the other man's arm. The thirty-something guy finished watching whatever on the screen and turned to me, the bridge of his nose so crooked that my attention immediately fixated on it. A beige woolen cap and a toothpick protruding from his mouth made his dockworker look more unpleasant as he gave me a not-so-subtle once-over. "Can I interest you in a membership, darlin'?" he asked.

Exhaustion caused the darling comment to squash my last nerve, but I shook my head and sucked it up. "I'm supposed to ask for Bobby."

"You found him," he said, grinning and sliding off the stool.

The man stood maybe five feet, four inches, an inch shorter than I did. He seriously didn't need height to intimidate. Between his barrel chest and those arms resembling chiseled stone, I threw out Sam's name just to feel safe again. "I came to see Sam Guerra fight tonight."

"You're just in time," he said, nodding to the flat screen and jabbing a thumb over his shoulder. "He's in the cage."

I blinked. "The cage?"

He frowned. "Want me to show you where it's at?

Can't say I recall seeing you here before. I'd remember if I had."

"This is my first time here, so yes. If you wouldn't mind."

His eyes narrowed. "You're a friend of Sam's?"

"Yes." I swallowed hard as he studied me. *"Girlfriend."*

He shoved his hands into his gym pants pockets. "Figures." He nodded his head toward the back. "Follow me. I'll show you where everybody's at."

He hadn't exaggerated. The place seemed practically deserted while I followed him through the building, taking several twists and turns. Despite the building's iffy exterior, the inside was huge, practically new in appearance with its well-lit rooms and white walls. Wall-length mirrors made some rooms seem doubled in size. Mats covered floors and lined walls. Spaced apart throughout some areas and crowded in others, all the equipment appeared well used but in good shape. Heavy, hanging bags littered one area, leaving little walking space between, and several more rooms held rows of cardio and strength-training gear.

The dampness and familiar locker room odors drifted past me as he led me into the largest area, what looked like a gymnasium. Two empty boxing rings filled one side, and an octagon, elevated cage filled the other, along with sixty or so people cheering loudly. The thing had steel wire, what appeared to be a chain-linked fence, re-enforced with panels and padding.

The acronym. MMA. I finally remembered it. Mixed martial arts. A sport so extreme and violent it remained under constant scrutiny to ban.

I hopped twice to peer over the men and women blocking my view, only to see a blur of movement inside the cage. Stumbling forward, I tried to get a better view. Someone yelled Sam's name. My eyes pivoted to the cage's corner. A bald, burly man with arms so large they wouldn't quite drop to his sides yelled Sam's name again, along with instructions. Blood rushed in my ears, along with the loud shouts from people surrounding me, keeping me from hearing what he said. I followed the man's gaze to Sam in the center of the cage. He moved fast, a blur of speed and muscle wearing nothing except long, black shorts as he dodged a kick to the face, only to catch a quick follow-up kick to the jaw that knocked him hard to the platform.

"You meet Jonas yet?" Bobby asked casually.

I shook my head. Sam had taken a smack to the face by a man clearly intent on breaking his jaw. I couldn't care less about Jonas right now.

"He's the cornerman yelling at your boyfriend."

Dammit, I couldn't see anything. Taking several more steps forward, I watched Sam work his way out of a hold. He flipped the other man onto his back and hit him with fists wrapped in black, fingerless mitts. The things seemed thin as gardening gloves. No way did they spare his hands from the impact. Or his opponent's face, which snapped grotesquely to the side after a third hit. Sam stood. His massive opponent, wearing yellow shorts, pivoted and used his legs to grab Sam and twist him back to the ground.

I stood on my tiptoes but couldn't get close enough to see anything. Noticing an arm, then two legs and feet, I moved to see Sam pop off the ground, as did his opponent, who plowed into him and pinned him to the cage. Cheers sounded.

Sam held the man in a bent-over position and slammed his knee into his face three times. A referee walked around them, observing and backing up when Sam's opponent pulled out of the hold. Sam slammed him to the side of the cage and started punching his side, violent and relentless.

I shut my eyes tightly until a horn sounded.

"Jonas tries to hold a cage match once a month," Bobby said. I blinked my eyes open to see Sam making his way to the opposite side where Jonas had a stool waiting. "We get a larger crowd when Sam's fighting."

I had to ask. "Why?"

"It's his boxing background. His matches tend to be less floor work and a lot of action up top. Lots of punches. Not a boring second with that kid in the cage. You watch. Somewhere during the second round, he'll get serious. He uses the first round like a second warm up. Know what I mean?"

Sam breathed hard, taking small sips of water, his focus on Jonas' face as he nodded to everything his cornerman instructed.

I turned to Bobby. "I can't see his expression from here but he looks pretty serious to me."

Bobby grinned. "You'd know if Sam got serious, darlin'. Trust me. Right now, he's getting a feel for the differences in Javier's technique. He's testing him. Forcing him to stay off the platform and work those punches that he helped him hone the last five weeks. But once he's had enough fooling around, your sweetie pie is gonna turn into a killer."

A minute couldn't have passed when Sam and his opponent stood while both cornermen grabbed their stools, kits, and left the cage. The ref yelled a few words and the two fighters went at each other again. Javier landed a kick to Sam's face and his head snapped back from the blow. He didn't drop this time but shrugged off the kick and bounced backward, taunting Javier then with a wave. His opponent snarled and rushed him, hitting him in the stomach and taking him all the way back to the cage wall. Sam moved to his right and placed the man in a hold, quickly flipping his opponent into the air. Javier landed on one foot and brought his other leg across Sam's torso, clamping down on his body and pulling Sam to the platform. Javier moved like a gymnast, and even from the back, I could hear the thud.

I shut my eyes tightly while Bobby mumbled, "Javier has a mean scissors takedown."

I opened my eyes to see Javier holding Sam's leg twisted in what looked like a painful hold. Sam pulled out of it easily and popped from the floor. Javier followed, hitting Sam several times in the back and grabbing him around the ribs to lift him off the platform.

Sam's feet left the ground only seconds when he pulled up his elbow and viciously hit Javier's face with the back of it, until he freed himself from the hold.

"Oh, yes indeedy," Bobby said. "This is getting serious."

It nauseated me to watch, yet I couldn't turn away. Sam pivoted and bounced back on his feet in time to avoid another kick to the face.

My vision framed black as I focused completely on Sam.

He looked so…alive. Focused. Breathing deeply yet not out of breath. For the first time since I'd walked in, I was able to block out the violence long enough to absorb the small details I could see from the back. The definition of muscle was visible only by his smooth, solid moves. I could see the blur of dark tattoos winding along his upper arms. Another tattoo on his back took up the lower left quarter, making it impossible to miss. His body went beyond athletic. Sam was perfect.

"You're quiet over there," Bobby said. "I take it you haven't seen this side of him."

If he meant half-naked, then yeah, this was all very new to me. I watched Sam and Javier trade body blows while Sam backed him into a corner. "This doesn't look like training to me."

"*Training?*" Bobby let out a blunt laugh. "You could call it that. Jonas puts Sam in with anyone needing to beef up his boxing game. One serious right hook from the kid and you can forget it. Next thing you know you're staring at the ceiling and he's on you like a dog with a bone. Game over."

Sam pulled from a hold and twisted, putting Javier into a headlock. The man struggled to release himself while everyone cheered. He hit Sam twice in the ribs to get him to release. Sam only adjusted his hold.

Javier's face turned purple. "Shouldn't someone stop this?" I asked. "He's going to black out."

Bobby laughed, clapped and whistled loudly.

I wished Sam would win. It would be over then. But Javier continued to struggle, his movements futile until he brought his hand up to place it behind Sam's neck, his other hand moving around Sam's leg. In one lift, he threw Sam's entire body through the air and onto his back, hard enough to rumble the platform.

I cringed, tears blurring my vision as I moved forward with the crowd to see if Javier had broken Sam's neck. People shifted and moved forward. Shouted. Cheered.

I grabbed my stomach and hoped I wouldn't throw up.

Bobby's hand touched my elbow. "Don't worry. I told you, he's not serious. You can see how mad Jonas is about it, too."

My gaze flew to Jonas's red face, the only indicator from back here that the man was ready to kill someone.

"He wants your boyfriend in the cage, and not for these little matches," Bobby said. "Sam's got what it takes to go UFC. Anybody can throw a punch, but Sammy has a killer combo you wouldn't believe. Great instincts. Quick reflexes, too. The best I've seen in a long time, given his training."

Please get serious. The words passed through my head like a mantra. Sam and Javier grappled but I couldn't see squat due to the beefcakes standing in my way. Periodically, I spotted arms and flailing legs. I jumped several times, looking over shoulders and moving forward, pushing past people as Bobby followed me. "How long has he been doing this?" I asked, trying to distract myself.

"Sam started boxing at six. Maybe five. I can't remember. His old man taught him."

"No, I meant *this*. The mixed martial…stuff."

His grin twisted. "Jonas says he knew the kid had it the second he saw him in a real match. I think he was eight?"

"Had *it?*"

"The gift. Fighting is the kid's calling." He laughed once. "His old man said he was born hitting. Sam's confident but not stupid. A quick learner. He watches a move once and picks it up. A real natural. And damn, the kid is fast. Jonas and his dad were longtime friends. It didn't take more than a suggestion to get Luis on board with training seriously. Sam started jiu-jitsu and kickboxing right after. Jonas taught him personally. That's high praise, believe me."

Sam stood, bouncing backward, and Javier went after him.

"Javier's jiu-jitsu is good," Bobby said. "Real good. He's a bit of a brawler though. Jonas and Sam have been working with him for several weeks now."

"Working with him?"

"Yep. To get his boxing skills up to par."

"Why would Sam help train the man he's fighting?"

"Javier's got a real match in a couple months. The other fighter's technique is similar to Sam's. Notice Javier is consistently trying to take Sam to the ground. That's *his* area. If he can get a good hold on Sam, he might get him to tap."

"Tap?"

He nodded. "You tap." He patted my shoulder to demonstrate. "You know, to yield or surrender. Although, I doubt Sam would ever do it, even if it meant a broken arm or leg."

Things blurred and my head got woozy.

When the next kick came at Sam, he smacked it away and jumped back three steps. His head dipped to the side as Javier studied him. I sensed a change in Sam and I couldn't have said why. Was it in the set of his shoulders? Or the sudden stillness in his stance?

Suddenly, I felt scared for Javier.

"There it is," Bobby muttered. "We're too far back to see, but he has a murderous expression when he gets down to business."

"He's serious now?" I took a step forward.

"I'll say," he said, moving with me as he shifted his toothpick to the other side of his mouth. "Say goodnight, Javier."

Sam lunged, releasing a swift kick to Javier's side, who tried deflecting the blow by tightening his midsection and dropping his hand. The few unguarded seconds gave Sam all the time he needed to burst forward and land two punches to Javier's face—a crushing upper cut, followed by a right hook, delivered so hard and fast that Javier fell to his back in a blink. The crowd erupted in cheers and Sam jumped over him, straddling Javier's waist to pummel him relentlessly. I cupped my hands, covering my mouth, too shocked to scream as the ref slipped between both fighters and shoved Sam away.

"Yep," Bobby said next to me. "Told you. Man, he's exciting to watch, ain't he?"

Bile rose. Javier hadn't moved yet.

"Well, obviously Javier has more training to do," Bobby added thoughtfully.

At Javier's side, Sam dropped to his knees opposite the ref, saying something while helping the other bleary-eyed man to his feet. Javier had been wide-eyed only seconds ago and now looked as though someone had hit him over the head with a concrete block. They bumped gloves and Sam said a few words while patting him on the shoulder.

Jonas met Sam at the cage door and handed him his shirt and water.

Still cupping my mouth, I watched them descend the stairs. People moved around me, their voices distant as my pulse sounded in my ears. Sam handed the water back to Jonas and pulled out his mouthpiece, walking into the crowd and disappearing from my view. Bobby gabbed about a back injury next to me that ended his own fighting career. When I spotted Sam again, he was closer, too close, and walking in my direction while pulling the black t-shirt over his head.

There under the bright lights, I glimpsed two jagged scars stretched across Sam's abdomen, just before he finished covering his sweaty torso with the material.

He stared at the floor, looking intense as he listened to Jonas.

Nausea had me pushing my fingers over my mouth as I glanced toward the door and the crowd disbursing back into the gym that bottlenecked my way out. I backed up another step, planning to run through them if I had to.

That's when Sam turned, looked up, and saw me.

CHAPTER SIXTEEN

Sam

I jerked to a stop and someone slammed into me, muttered a quick apology, and walked around.

Jonas turned, still talking and oblivious to my holy-shit moment. He smacked my arm. "You listening to me, boy? Your pops would kick your ass right now. You're gonna get your fool head knocked off one of these days going into a match with that lackadaisical attitude. Just 'cause you're no longer fighting for a belt, doesn't mean you can screw around. You do that once more and you can forget the cage. I'm about pissed enough that I may pull you out of rotation altogether." He gave my jaw a soft slap. "Hey. Look at me."

"I heard you," I muttered, my gaze remaining glued on those round, blue eyes.

A lie. The truth. Not a single sentence came to mind that would explain what she'd just witnessed. She'd seen the last part of the fight, which meant she'd seen a side of me that terrified my own mother. Regret pulled me back to so many moments I could have told Peyton the truth. If I had, she wouldn't be looking at me now as if she didn't know me.

Guilt made me want to turn away but I couldn't. Not while those watering eyes burned with questions, accusations, and the knowledge that I'd purposely kept all this from her. It didn't take a genius to guess why I hadn't told her.

She never would have agreed to go out with me.

Jonas followed my gaze. "You know that girl?"

Peyton's gaze darted from me to Jonas and she took a step back.

"Ah, wait now," he said, a grin in his voice. "Beautiful *and* a redhead. That's the girl you've been spending so much time with, isn't it? Now I get why you're late all the time. What's her name? Paige?"

The second her gaze swung to the exit, I knew what she planned to do.

"Peyton!" I shouted, but she'd already made a beeline for the door. I bolted after her. "Wait!"

She'd disappeared into the small, lingering group blocking the exit and I followed, pushing my way through them. Her fast stride had taken her halfway down the hallway by the time I came out the other side. I shouted again for her to wait. Sprinted after her when she didn't. When I caught up with her and she quickened her pace, I grabbed her elbow before she could bolt again. "Dammit, *stop.*"

She pulled her arm out of my hold so abruptly that she fell against the wall. "I have nothing to say to you!"

I didn't know who looked more shocked by the uncharacteristic outburst, her or me. She lowered her gaze, her cheeks flushing pink at the people glancing over at us. "I'm sorry," she said softly, politely, before turning and walking away. "I...I need to think. Just leave me alone, Sam."

"Just wait a second," I said, but she ignored me and walked into the bag room. Since I knew she didn't plan to work a bag any time soon, I followed her. "How did you know to find me here?"

"Your sister," she said over her shoulder, stopping to look around.

"Vanna?"

"Do you have another sister?" She perched her hands on her hips and turned to me. "Oh, wait. It's possible you do and I didn't get that version of the truth."

I had no idea how to respond to her. Sarcasm had never been her thing.

"Of course, I meant Savanna," she said, rolling her eyes and walking past me, back into the corridor.

I followed her across the hall, this time through the door leading to the gear and vending machine area. "When did you talk to my sister?"

She propped her hands on her hips, staring at the vending machines. "Tonight. At the movie theater."

"Movie theater?"

She glanced at me. "You know, the place we had our first date."

After spending time together for weeks, nearly every day, I was finally seeing a side of Peyton I didn't like. At all. I'd grown accustomed to her raw honesty and bright outlook. Maybe if I ignored her sarcasm long enough, she'd turn back into her sweet self and finally talk to me. "Actually, that was our second date."

She frowned. "Want to know what she said?"

"Not really."

"She said you were on a date tonight."

My mouth fell open. "A *what?*"

"You know. Out with someone else. Another girl," she said, as if I needed the clarification. "She told me this in front of your mother, no less. I've never been so humiliated."

"My *mother* was there?"

"Yes, and it was horrible. She was upset. She even pinched Savanna's arm."

"That's because she knew my sister was full of it," I told her, certain I was right. "My mother knows how I feel

193

about you. She'd never believe that."

A line crinkled between her eyebrows. "Well, she'd said you'd mentioned me. But I thought she was being—"

"Polite?" I said. "No, she wouldn't say something like that just to be polite. And I didn't *just* mention you. We've talked numerous times about you. She's been after me to have you over. You know, to introduce you. Dinner. The whole shebang. And Vanna knows how I feel, too. In her own distorted way, she probably thought she was…hell, I don't know. I've never understood how her brain works. Look, it doesn't matter. Nothing excuses what she said. For what it's worth…I'm sorry."

Her eyes clouded with uncertainty and she folded her arms awkwardly over her chest. "To Vanna's credit, she eventually took it back. She mentioned covering for you. Being nice must not have set well with her though, because she sent me *here* to watch you nearly beat someone to death."

"Did she say why?"

"*Why?*"

"Why she sent you."

"She said she believes I care about you. I guess this was a test to see if I'd still want to know you after watching you practically kill someone." She looked down, her frown growing until she abruptly stalked past me and into the corridor.

I followed her. "Do you?"

"Do I what? Still want to know you?" Her dark eyes kept flicking over me as if gauging the distance between us.

"Yeah."

She increased her pace, ignoring the question.

"God, you believed her, didn't you?" I asked.

"I don't know what you mean." She zoomed past Joey and Finn, friends of mine who turned to stare at her backside until they caught my glare.

I blew by them, still scowling when I caught up to her.

"When she said I'd gone out with someone else," I said. "You believed her, didn't you?"

"She was very convincing."

Well, fuck. No wonder I couldn't get her to talk to me. "Peyton." I touched her shoulder. "Would you please just talk to me?"

She jerked away without breaking stride. "I have to go," she said, walking into the free weights room. I halted at the door and leaned against the frame, watching her move around the equipment. Even when mad and lost she looked beautiful to me. She'd pulled her hair into a ponytail since earlier over dinner, and long curls now framed her face. Between those sexy low-rise jeans with a hole in the knee and an oversized and wrinkled white t-shirt with black lettering that spelled, *Screw you, too*—her brother's, obviously—she looked like home to me.

She turned, her usually full lips thinned into a stubborn line. "Where is the damn exit in this place?"

I told myself she hadn't been crying. That her red-rimmed eyes were the result of her chronic insomnia. "I'll show you."

Folding her arms over her chest, she walked toward me, her angry expression changing with every cautious step, until her gaze dropped to my shirt, lingering on my arms. It finally occurred to me she'd never seen me like this. Not the tats. Not any of it. Hell, I hadn't even had time to put on shoes.

"You should have told me," she said, her gaze dropping to the floor.

For someone who could form a lie in his sleep, I couldn't come up with a single word, true or false, to get myself out of this. "I know."

Those blue eyes shifted to mine. "But it still doesn't explain the scars."

The question-like comment had come out of nowhere, what felt like a sucker punch. She couldn't have seen me. Not from the back. Although I hadn't put the shirt on until…Christ, had she seen me? "Scars?"

"Y-your lip," she said. "And eyebrow."

Relief flooded me that she hadn't seen the worst of it. I hadn't prepared for that talk. I doubted I'd ever be ready for that talk. "You want to talk about scars now?"

She tightened her grip on her elbows. Nothing in the way she licked her lips just then indicated it, but I got the feeling she knew I'd purposefully dodged the question. "I need to go anyway," she said, her watery gaze lifting to mine again. "Will you please get me out of here?"

I'd agree to anything if she'd quit looking at me as if I'd broken her heart. "Come on."

She followed as I turned and led the way down the corridor. My mind scrambled for options. Three more friends passed us, their glances curious because I'd never brought a girl here—a place that had essentially become my second home. It only took one glance at my face to know I'd fucked up big time. "Good fight, Sam," was all they said, hurrying past us.

Most members parked in the back and left out the side door, so the front area remained empty and quiet when we passed through it.

I stopped at the door to say something, anything, but she passed me, heading toward her car without so much as a go-fuck-yourself. Like a damn loyal puppy, I followed her, wearing nothing but shorts, a thin t-shirt, and my gloves. When she continued walking without a backward glance, desperation took over and the unthinkable flew out of my mouth.

"Do you really want to know how I got the scars, Peyton?" My throat threatened to close but I kept talking, pushing past the sensation. "Because I don't think you do."

That she stopped at all told me she hadn't completely written me off. I held my breath until she turned, giving me one last chance to fix the mess I'd made. Instinct had me grasping for any morsel of bullshit I could think of. I had to find a way to spin this. Weeks ago, I could have done that easily, but now…

Nausea twisted my stomach into a knot. Her blue eyes begged me for the truth. She'd gutted me with the same look only weeks ago—the day she'd told me she cared about me and cried in my arms over nothing more than a small bruise.

No matter how much I wanted to, I couldn't erase the hurt I'd caused tonight. I wanted to deflect the truth. Turn the issue back onto her. But blaming her unique ability to make everything complex as I had that day in the car had been a dickhead move the first time. I couldn't do it to her again. She needed to hear the truth, even if it killed me to give it to her.

"My uncle—" I swallowed, unable to produce a modicum of spit to finish the sentence.

Her look was thoughtful as she stepped closer, her shoulders tense as she focused through the overhead light to study my face. Her gaze paused on my eyebrow and dropped to my lip. She'd done the same thing too many times to count, always with the same unspoken question in her eyes. The once good memory pained me to think about now—those curious eyes in the darkness of the car and her soft touch as her fingertip pressed the mark on my lip before she'd kiss me.

"Your uncle," she repeated. "The one you said came around after your dad died?"

"He didn't…come around." I had to force each word. "He moved in."

"Because your mom got sick."

"Right."

"I don't think I'm following. What does that have to do with—"

"Peyton," I interrupted her, tasting bile because I couldn't wait for her to figure out what I'd meant. I had to say it now. Quickly. Before I talked myself out of it. "He was a recovering alcoholic who fell out of…recovery. He was a mean drunk. He was also…left-handed."

Silence stretched between us, making seconds seem like hours. Then her breath hitched, and I knew she finally understood my vague explanation. To show her that part of my life, even without the details, made me nauseous enough I might have puked had she not been standing there. Our relationship, if it survived this night, would forever be different. She'd see me differently now. Look at me differently. God, I wanted to take it all back. To tell her the truth had been a lie.

Her eyes watered as she pressed her palms together in a prayer position against her mouth. "Is that what happened to cause—" Emotion cracked her voice and her gaze dropped to the ground.

"Don't you dare fucking pity me," I said. "You wanted to know. I told you. End of story."

"I don't pity you," she whispered and turned away. "I just…don't know the right thing to say. I have to think. I should go."

She looked back once more, her expression uncertain, before turning and walking across the parking lot.

That I desperately wanted out of this conversation made watching her walk away bearable. But habit forced my gaze to scan her Lexus parked under the streetlight, and when I realized the car was running, I did a double take, narrowed my eyes and noticed someone in the driver's side. Adam Cooper.

Watching us.

That one of the most private, painful moments of my life had taken place in front of her best friend caused something inside me to snap. Humiliation. Resentment. Anger. I didn't recognize the rage as jealousy until I took off after her. My bare feet cut against asphalt for fifteen feet, but I didn't care. I grabbed her shoulder and turned her to face me. "What the hell do you have to think about all the time? Just say what you feel."

Tears had pooled in her eyes and I wanted to look

away. I couldn't see her like this. Hurt. Disillusioned. Exhausted. All because of me. "I don't function that way and you know it," she said. "I plan. I prepare. List the pros and cons. Qualify. Quantify. It's how my brain works, Sam. I have the next ten years of my life mapped out in spreadsheets, for petesake. How many people do you know who do that? Everything I've ever wanted and how I plan to get it. Everything…except you." She pressed a shaky hand to her mouth. "God, it's all so messed up. I'm too tired for this. I can't sort it out."

She couldn't sort it out because she wanted to break up with me and couldn't do it to my face. She had too soft a heart. But I couldn't let her leave until she did. I'd lose my mind if I let her walk away without hearing her decision. I had to hear her say the words. "Then let's keep it simple."

She looked up at me.

I took a deep breath. Braced myself. "Do you want to end this?"

"That's not a simple question."

"Yes it is." I shrugged. "Yes or no. True or false. Simple."

"This isn't a Boolean expression, Sam." Tears slid down her cheeks. "Quit making fun of me." She pivoted away from me and pushed her hands over her eyes, crying silently until her shoulders shook.

What just happened? "Dammit, I wouldn't make fun of you. I don't even know what a Boolean expression is." I swear the girl could talk circles around me sometimes. "Peyton." I took a step forward. "Stop crying." If she didn't pull it together in the next ten seconds, I was totally going to go to her. Like a dumbass without pride, I'd wrap my arms around her while jerkoff watched from her car.

"*No,*" she whispered. "There's your answer."

I stiffened at her response, hopeful until I realized I'd forgotten how I'd worded the question. "No," I repeated. "No…what?"

"I don't know," she said, sniffling. "I'm beyond

keeping up. I told you, I'm tired and I can't think."

"Peyton. Look at me."

She wiped her eyes and turned.

All the defensiveness drained out of me. She looked an emotional wreck. I did that. "Is it that I fight, or that I didn't tell you?"

Her watery eyes searched mine. "Both."

Great. "Look, I get it. Mixed martial arts can seem a little harsh."

"A little harsh? It's brutal."

"I realize that's what outsiders think."

"*Outsiders*? Is that what I am to you? An outsider?"

"N-no." I fumbled to untwist my words. "I meant someone who doesn't fight."

"What happened to you? Why is it you enjoy hurting people?"

A rigged question if ever I'd heard one. "Why do I *what*?"

"Enjoy hurting people."

"Is that a perverse way of asking me if I like fighting?"

"Yes," she said, lifting her chin and moving forward to stand in front of me, "that's what I'm asking you."

"Yeah, I *do*." I shrugged. "So?"

"You enjoy bashing someone's face in with your fist. Really? That's fun for you?"

This wasn't going to end well. I knew that now. "I'm not dragging those guys into the cage, Peyton. They're trained fighters. It's a competitive thing. The same as any other sport. Football or hockey. If you can't get that, I don't know how else to explain it. I mean…fuck. You sought me out for exactly this. Isn't my reputation the entire reason we met? Or have you conveniently forgotten you offered me money to threaten Delaney and put him down if he didn't back off your brother?"

"I never expected you to…put him down. What is this, euthanasia?" She took another step, close enough to touch. "I told you that at the time, too. I told you just to threaten him."

"And I recall telling you only a fool threatens a group of four, especially that size, thinking something as vague as his reputation will keep him from having to throw a punch."

Her mouth parted. "You never called me a *fool.*"

"I was thinking it."

She stuck her chin out. "Well, I was right though, wasn't I? Delaney and his friends backed off. You never had to throw a punch."

I had no comeback.

"But what I saw in there," she said, pointing to the building, "is different. Everything I'm doing, all of this work, is for others. Someone else. Anyone else. Can you appreciate how much pressure I have on me right now? Have you read what people are saying about me online? People are trying to discredit why I'm doing this. They want the website to fail. A reporter with one of the top national news magazines called the house today wanting to interview me. That's the third reporter this week. I've received twelve blogger invites for interviews. Rabid political commenters are challenging me to debates. How long do you think I can put these people off for you?"

"Wait. For *me?* Look, I know you're under a lot of stress but—"

"Yes, I'm totally stressed out." She pulled a stray curl from her eyes. "This entire thing is blowing up bigger than I can handle. People I don't know and don't trust are starting to research me. Six weeks ago, Sam, I would have told you there isn't anything to research. But now I'm dating a guy who works in a gym and trains people to fight. Then to see how you do it." She shook her head and held her stomach. "I've been worried for weeks that someone might figure out what you do. Why do you think I haven't asked you the name of the gym or tried popping in for a visit like most girlfriends would have? I don't want one of these people linking us together and turning my website into something it isn't."

That pissed me off. "People know we're going out."

"I'm not talking about kids at school."

I rubbed a hand over the back of my neck, getting more pissed. "Well I don't give a damn if every fucking reporter in the country knows we're dating. You shouldn't either. So why do you?"

"Do you *really* have to ask? It looks like a massive conflict of interest. Here I am busting my hump trying to *stop* violence, and you're somewhere in a cage knocking somebody's brain loose. I'm dating a guy who likes to beat the snot out of people. And why? I don't have a reason. I wouldn't know what to say. For…for…"

"Money…is that the word you're searching for? Because we discussed this already. Jonas pays me to do this. It's part of my job. I have to keep this job, Peyton."

"Fine. I get it. But do you have to be so happy about it? I've never seen you so…alive. You were in your element, as if you enjoyed hurting Javier." Her gaze lifted to mine, eyes wide. "Did you?"

I might as well try to explain color to a blind person. "Why do you keep asking me that? And looking at me like that?"

She shook her head, looking confused. "How am I looking at you?"

"Like you're scared of me now."

"*Scared* of you? After watching that in there, I don't even know who you are."

I took a step closer and brushed my fingers against her cold cheek. "You know me," I said, my voice going soft, as it always did when I touched her. I reached out my other taped hand to frame her face. "You know me better than anyone else, Peyton. I don't talk to other people the way I do you." Those blue eyes turned glassy from tears again. She tried to look down but I wouldn't let her. "God, tell me you know how special you are to me."

Her chin trembled and she took a small step forward,

reaching for my waist. Her fingertips felt cold through my already wet shirt as she curled them against my sides. Closing her eyes, she pressed her forehead to my chest. I wanted to push my fingers through her hair and kiss her. To forget the whole damn thing. "Is there any way you can get past this?" I asked.

She stood, quiet and unmoving. Just breathing.

I kissed the top of her head, my fingertips lingering along her jaw as I closed my eyes. "Can you?"

She nodded and I felt a glimmer of hope. "If you plan to stop," she murmured, turning her face up to me. "Tell me you plan to stop. Someday. *Any* day. Maybe after graduation. Or when Savanna finishes school and your family doesn't need you like this. Tell me you plan to stop someday and I'll…I'll…"

Stay. She'd practically said it. She'd placed the solution in my hands. Given me the easiest out I could have asked for. I could tell her exactly what she wanted to hear. Buy myself a few more months. Maybe a few years if things worked out. Maybe by then, it wouldn't matter.

It was the perfect plan, but one I couldn't consider. After tonight, I'd hit my limit on lying about myself. About what I wanted. I dropped my hands to my sides. "I'm a fighter, Peyton. It's who I am. What I do. I'll never stop."

Her hopeful expression crumpled and she took a step back, dropping her gaze to the asphalt. "Bobby was right. You're going to let Jonas train you. To fight USC."

"UFC," I said, correcting her because Javier had slammed the good sense out of me, apparently. "Ultimate Fighting Championship."

"Sorry." She nodded. "UFC. He told me Jonas wants you to fight professionally."

Bobby might get his teeth kicked in if he didn't shut his mouth. "It's true. Jonas does want me to train," I said, wishing she'd look at me. "But it's not in the cards for me. I'll never fight professionally."

The question was there in her eyes as her gaze lifted to

mine.

I shrugged. "I was too many credits short last year to graduate. Jonas wanted me to get my GED and start training. When I told my mother what I planned to do, she fell apart. Begged me not to do it. I told you she hasn't been right since my father died. I couldn't be the cause of more stress and pain. So I gave her my word I wouldn't train professionally and I meant it."

Her eyes searched my face. "Would you fight professionally if you could?"

"What does it matter?"

"It matters to me. I want to know."

"If my mother wasn't sick and I hadn't made that promise to her, then yeah, I would. If I thought I was good enough, that I had a legitimate chance, you bet. I'd do it in a heartbeat." I took a step closer so she'd see my face and know I meant every word. "I'd walk around with cauliflower ear, the same as every other guy in this fucking place, and I'd live the next thirty years without a dime to my name. I'd do *anything* if it meant I could get another shot at it."

"Another shot at what? A gold belt?"

"No, at being the best at something again."

"The best at something? At *fighting*?" She shook her head. "I don't understand why. You're smart, Sam. You could do anything."

"God, whatever you do, don't sound like everybody else," I said, unable to take the save-Sam-from-himself speech from her, too. "You said it yourself. I'm happy in there. Fighting is the only thing that ever came natural to me. That I felt good doing. I'm fast, I have decent instincts, and my dad taught me almost everything I know. In there, Peyton…it's the only place I can still hear his voice. Like he's right there with me. *Still* here. And I need him to be."

Those blue eyes widened, and it occurred to me what I'd said aloud. Something I'd never told anyone else. Shit. I turned and began to pace.

"Sam—" she whispered.

I stopped moving. Hearing her behind me, her voice wavering, her tears right there, I bit down until my jaw hurt. I was *this* close to coming apart and it was anybody's guess what would fly out of my mouth if I did. "Forget it," I said over my shoulder, unable to look at her. "I shouldn't have said it."

"But you did." Her small footsteps crunched across the gritty asphalt. Her fingertips brushed softly against my back. "You hear your dad? You hear his voice?"

There was no judgment or question of my sanity in her tone. "Every time," I said, pulling away. "To not hear him would be impossible. We practiced every night. Trained every weekend since I can remember. Until the day he died. He sacrificed everything, Peyton. He had opportunities to advance his career, but he stayed a traffic cop to keep a regular shift. So he could put more time into his family. Into *me*. It was supposed to be…a safer choice." My eyes watered and I immediately turned to pace again so she couldn't see. "Whether I'm in the ring or the cage, it's not Jonas I hear. Or the ref. Or even the crowd. I hear *him*. It's his voice telling me what to do next. Telling me if I'm getting it right or doing it wrong. Don't you get it yet?" I stopped. Looked at her. "Anything that's good in me, in *there*, is him. I'll never give it up entirely. Not for you. Not for anyone."

She stayed silent, her palms clasped in prayer position over her mouth again. "Okay," she whispered.

"And *don't* cry," I added, because she was doing that rapid blinking thing and I really couldn't fucking take more tears right now.

She turned to the Lexus. "I should go."

Of course, she had to go. Her boyfriend had way too much baggage. She couldn't get away fast enough. "That's it then?" I said. "We're done?"

She shivered and it occurred to me how cold I was

wearing nothing but shorts and a t-shirt in the freezing night air. "Right," I said when she remained silent. "So the never-giving-up-no-matter-what thing. That was all bullshit, right?"

She stiffened and eventually looked over her shoulder, her gaze never reaching mine. "I thought I meant something to you, Sam. But there are too many versions of the truth floating around. I don't know what to believe anymore, except…I don't think I do."

How could she think that? She'd become my whole damn world since that first day on my lawn. "Look, I know I fucked up." My voice sounded strange. Raspy and rough. Emotional. It was embarrassing but I took a step forward anyway. "Just…don't go."

"You waited too long," she said, her voice clogged with tears. "I can't undo this. I can't forget." She lowered her head into her hands and scrubbed her face. "I'm too tired to think. I…I have to go. I'm sorry."

Before I could stop her, she ran across the parking lot and jumped into the passenger side of her car, shutting the door. Her voice sounded muffled as her head dipped behind the seat. Cooper, her good fucking friend, leaned over and put his arms around her.

I clenched my fists and turned, my temper sliding into the red as I stalked toward the building and headed straight to Jonas' office to get my things. First things first. I had to get Bobby or Jonas to close for me tonight. Then I planned to find my sister and kick her sorry, meddling ass.

CHAPTER SEVENTEEN

Sam

"Savanna!"

I slammed the front door, barely taking three steps before *Mamá* ran from the kitchen to block my path, her hands wrapped in a dishtowel between us. "Calm down, Samuel. I mean it."

I looked past her to see Savanna on the couch, wide-eyed and poised to bolt. Too bad the little shit had nowhere to go without getting past me first. Ignoring Ma's warning, I took another step.

"Samuel, calm *down!*" Ma shoved me back with her hand flat against my chest. *"Control de sí mismo!"*

I hesitated only a second and stepped around her while Vanna dove over the sofa's back. Ma gripped and yanked my bicep, pulling me back briefly. "Samuel! You will not go near your sister with this temper! Do you hear me?"

Vanna poked her head up behind the couch. "I'm sorry, Samuel!" she shouted. "I swear it! Let me explain!"

No explanation existed that would matter to me. But Vanna was a *girl.* She was *family.* Two solid reasons I couldn't and wouldn't knock her to the floor, even if I wanted to. Scaring the hell out of her with empty threats was all I had left.

"Quit hiding," I said, "you jealous, conniving little bi—"

Ma's hand cracked me across the face before the expletive left my mouth, and the startling sting snapped me out of my single-mindedness long enough to take a stunned breath and look down at her.

"What would your father say seeing you act like this toward your little sister?" she asked, pointing a long, narrow finger at me. "Or using that language in my house? You're supposed to protect your family. Not terrorize them to tears."

Ma's eyes watered the entire time she spoke—her usual reaction whenever she'd had to strike one of her children. On top of that, her pallor had worsened, making the hollowness in her cheeks more prominent. Not knowing if another migraine had caused her frail appearance or if I had, I took a full breath, focusing on the lasting burn in my cheek as perspective crept back in.

"Well?" she asked. "Are you finally calm?"

"Calm?" I glared at the sofa, knowing the little *mocosa* was back there. "Vanna'll be lucky if I calm down by next April." I looked to Ma. "Do you have *any* idea what happened tonight?"

"Yes, *mijo*." She glanced to the floor. "Savanna said Peyton went to the gym. She knows the truth now."

"Did either of you realize I had a *cage* match tonight?"

I heard Vanna sniffle behind the couch as Ma's lips pressed together. She looked paler now than she had only a minute ago. She shook her head.

"Well, according to Bobby," I said, "she saw most of it." I rubbed my forehead, physically ill to remember the horrified expression on her face. Peyton had never looked at me that way, even when she thought I belonged to a stupid fight club.

"I'm sorry, *mijo*. And I understand why you're upset." She turned to the huge hazel eyes peering over the sofa back. "Savanna shouldn't have interfered." Her gaze swung back to mine. "But you must blame yourself for Peyton's ignorance regarding the fighting, Samuel. Not your sister."

My adrenaline dissipated a little more with every word, and as sanity crawled back in, a dull ache crept into my body. The blows I'd taken during the fight had begun to take hold. I had to take a hot shower soon or I'd feel this tomorrow in the worst way. I rested my fingers against my neck, forcing the cramp to relax. "It isn't *that* she found out. I would have told her eventually. It was *how* she found out. She had no idea what she was walking into tonight." My voice sounded thin. Ready to break. "You didn't see the way she looked at me."

"I really am sorry!" Vanna said tearfully.

I rolled my eyes, trying to remember how much I loved my sister. Trying to remember what we'd both endured together not too long ago. "Just come out, Vanna. I'm not going to kill you."

Her head came up slowly, those hazel eyes bright with tears and smeared mascara. "You swear? You don't plan to murder me even a little?"

I sighed and turned to our *mamá*, who pointed that finger a second time. "I have your word you won't touch your sister in anger?"

"Of course, I won't. Jeez, Ma. When did I hit Vanna last? I had to be seven."

"*You* were ten," Vanna said, crawling back onto the cushions. "*I* was seven. And it hurt."

"So did the smack *Papá* gave me." I looked at them both and shook my head, without hope as I turned for my room.

Ma watched me walk past her. "What are you going to do?"

I stalked toward my bedroom. "I'm taking a shower and going to bed."

"I meant about Peyton," she said, following me down

the hallway. "I met her tonight. She was so pretty and polite. A lovely girl."

Yeah. Lovely and gone. "Nothing." I grabbed my still damp shirt and pulled it off, disappearing into the darkness of my room. "It's over."

She stopped to linger in the doorway, watching me move around in the dark as I rifled through the top dresser drawer. "She'll get past the shock," she said. "The violence of it, I mean. Give her the night to think on it. You can talk to her tomorrow."

I shook my head, figuring out too late that I had no clean t-shirts. Fucking wonderful. I'd have to wash clothes tonight before I could crash. "You didn't see the way she looked at me, Ma. You didn't hear what she said."

"What did she say?"

"I don't want to talk about it."

My curt tone probably hurt her feelings, but I was holding on by a thread and trying not to say something I couldn't take back. It was all I could do to be curt. Grabbing a pair of dark sweat shorts and a white undershirt, I headed for the bathroom, pretending not to notice her recoil at the sight of my torso when I walked by her.

"I'm here if you want to talk," she said softly.

"I don't."

"Goodnight then, *mijo*."

I could barely manage a simple, "Mm," as I shut myself in the bathroom.

Dropping my forehead against the wall, I stilled and let it all sink in. Fuck. I hung my fingers on my neck again, pulling at the bunching muscles. I'd let Javier beat on me a little too long tonight. It had felt good at the time. Like I was in a serious fight and not pretending to be someone's opponent. I'd been pretending to be someone like Javier for months now. Someone who had bigger and better fights ahead of him. An actual path.

My neck hurt more than usual. I couldn't recall if Javier

had hit me or if I'd landed wrong. It was difficult to say on nights like tonight, when I didn't feel much of anything until afterward. I needed an ice soak but heat would have to do. Turning the faucet as hot as I could tolerate, I let the water pound against my skin. For fifteen minutes, I stood under the spray, waiting for tonight's events to settle into another bad memory. I closed my eyes and let the water run over my head. Damn, I'd never wanted to cry more in my life. Wished I could. Something to get rid of this painful lump in my throat that felt as big as a grapefruit. *You waited too long,* she'd said. *I can't forget.*

That meant she couldn't forgive me or get past what I'd done. She wouldn't come back.

After the night I'd had, trying to relax was pointless. I finished the shower, took several ibuprofen, and put clothes into the washer. I stalked wordlessly through the living room to the kitchen, unable to look at Vanna as the faint sound of Naruto Uzumaki's voice drifted from the TV. Swearing under my breath, I opened the freezer and grabbed an ice pack. My sister knew I'd gotten hooked on the damn show while trying to get closer to Peyton. She had to be a prize sadist playing that shit right now.

Back in my room, I paced in the dark, holding the ice pack against my neck. I saw my old leather jacket sprawled on the corner chair and thought of the numerous times Peyton had worn it before leaving it in the Impala last week. She'd even worn it to school twice, as if she wanted everyone to know she was mine.

Mine. What a joke. How did I ever think Peyton Greene could be mine? She'd taken four years of Japanese just to understand anime better, when I couldn't even manage to graduate high school in four years like everybody else. I glared at the coat until I couldn't bear it any longer. Crossing the room, I grabbed it, lifted the thing to my nose and breathed in deeply to catch the faintest scent of her on the collar. The sweet smell glided over me like warm water and I closed my eyes. Definitely not my imagination. Definitely her.

Tossing it onto the chair, I doubted I could hate myself more. Would I have done things differently if I could go back? Possibly. Probably.

And she never would have gone out with me.

Pacing again, I tried recalling everything we'd said. To find a loophole. Something to fix this. Instead, the image of Cooper putting his arms around her materialized, and jealousy like nothing I'd ever felt burned in my gut, so potent, that I had to release the toxic energy or throw up. Without thought, I pivoted, pulled back, and punched the wall. A painful, nearly crippling vibration traveled up my arm, and I closed my eyes to feel every second of it.

The cracking sound should have been a bigger concern. I could have broken my hand but couldn't bring myself to care. I turned and walked to the bed, moving my fingers and shaking my hand out as it pulsed with a warm, new pain. Dropping onto the mattress, I slumped forward and wedged my elbows against my thighs, contemplating never fighting again just for her.

I never thought I'd consider quitting for anyone, but for her, I tried.

My sister's light, quick steps sounded outside the door before she knocked and poked her head in without an invitation. She didn't flip the light switch as she peered through the darkness lit only by the one working streetlight on the block. Her gaze rested on the bed where I sat holding the ice pack against my stupid hand. "What the hell did I just hear?" she said.

I had difficulty replying. Everything seemed utterly pointless. So goddamn endless. "I punched the wall."

"Damn. You okay?"

"No."

"Did you hurt your hand?"

"No." Not really. Not how she meant.

She flipped the light switch and I squinted like a vampire at dawn, following her gaze to the large crack in the wall. "Well, you didn't punch a hole through," she said. "That's good. Did you hit a beam or something?"

"Yeah. Or something." I could barely comprehend my stupidity in punching a wall, and ultimately the stud behind it, with my bare hand. It's not as if we needed another doctor bill. And Jonas would have killed me had I broken my hand. "Just chalk it up to yet another reason to move you and Ma out of this fucking house, and *town,* as soon as possible. Europe, at this point, wouldn't be far enough."

She blinked and stared at me as though we hadn't yet met.

I shrugged, feeling impulsive and dumb as hell. "I'll pick up some sheetrock, plaster or whatever tomorrow," I said. "We still have paint in the shed. Ma doesn't need to know."

"Um, not that you care right now," she said, "but I've decided not to lie for you anymore. Well, maybe at school when you have to work, but that's where I draw the line. You're on your own with everything else. Especially girlfriends."

"I know." After today, I really did. "I'm not asking you to lie. I'm asking you not to point it out to Ma if you don't have to. That's all."

"That's doable."

"Thanks."

She watched me a few seconds longer. "I'm sorry, Samuel. I really am."

"Whatever."

"Can I say one thing in my defense?"

"No."

"I saw Peyton at the movies tonight hugging her friend," she said, ignoring what I'd said. "It…it kind of set me off."

I dropped my head, not needing to picture them together again. "Let me guess. Cooper?"

"Right."

The thought of him with her now, consoling her,

pissed me off more than I wanted to admit, even to myself. Probably because it was unfair as hell. They'd been friends longer than I'd been in the picture. "They're friends," I said. "Friends hug." At least Peyton's friends did, and it didn't take an intelligence analyst to figure out why.

"Well, it made me mad. I must have gotten used to seeing you both together. I don't know. It threw me. Then when Ma made me introduce her and she asked Peyton why she wasn't cheering for you tonight, I went into a panic spiral. I knew you weren't ready to tell her yet. That's when I said you were on a date. It just came out. Since you've made sure you don't have any friends in Ridgeview, I didn't have many options. I'm sorry. I panicked."

"No shit." I rubbed my forehead, imagining what Peyton must have felt. If the tables had been turned, if someone had told me Peyton was seein' another guy…I didn't want to think about what I would have done. "You really suck at pep talks, Vanna. I'm only getting more pissed."

"Then a car almost hit her," she added.

"What?"

"It was kind of my fault. After that, I don't think Adam Cooper could hate me more," she said. "He wanted to kill me tonight. Ma was mad, too. It was awful. I had no way out except to tell the truth."

I looked at my red knuckles. The floor. Knew I could have prevented all of it. "I know."

"You do?"

"Yeah."

She paused. "Want me to talk to her? I could tell her what a misunderstood hard case you are. I wouldn't be lying."

If only Peyton and I had actually had a misunderstanding. "No."

"I could make you sound more…more…"

"No." I looked at her. "It's over. She asked me to quit

fighting. It has to be over."

Her eyes rounded. "She actually asked you?"

"In so many words."

"Could you? I mean, is she worth it?"

To stop fighting would take such a large piece of me away, I knew I'd disappear forever. Ironically, after knowing Peyton, I knew I'd never disappear for anyone ever again. "She's worth it. But no, I'm not quitting."

Maybe Vanna cared; she looked sad as hell. "I'm sorry, Samuel. Are you mad at me?"

I shook my head. "No. Just…stay out of my private life from now on."

"Deal."

*****

The constant rain began after Halloween like clockwork. We wouldn't have more than a sun break or two between now and June, which made the next Monday the grayest fucking day of my life. Even the rain resembled my mood—a depressing gray drizzle one second, a torrential downpour the next.

Seeing Peyton everywhere would kill me. To be around her and not be with her, especially the way I still felt, made me give serious thought to getting my GED just to get the hell away from her.

I had good reasons for not connecting with anybody when that bastard moved us to Ridgeview five years ago. I hadn't needed more bullshit hassles than I already had. Well, now I had one.

A big one.

For extra fun, Peyton didn't show up Monday. This should have been a good thing. Instead, the not knowing why wore me down by third period. Peyton never got sick, by her own admission. Then where the hell was she?

I considered driving to her house to find out, but I think that would officially make me a stalker. So I waited for sixth period to talk to her brother. The kid needed serious pointers in building muscle anyway or he'd end up the only student to fail Weight Lifting. After warming up, I ambled to where he rested on a bench press away from the others—his usual. I leaned over the weight bar. "If you want to bulk up," I said, smiling when he jumped in surprise, "you need to add a strength training cycle."

"Dammit, Sam," he said, clutching his chest as though staving off a heart attack. "I said quit sneaking up on me. *Fuck.* You're worse than Peyton."

"Sorry. Thought you could use the tip."

"I have no damn clue what you're even talking about. A strength training cycle? What the hell do you think I'm doing over here, churning butter?"

"You'd probably bulk up faster if you were. Look, adding more weight and reps each week is a start, but if you want an A in the coach's classes, he needs to see you push yourself until guts start coming out of your pores."

"Who says I'm not getting an A?"

I couldn't stop the smirk. "Peyton told me your dad went ballistic when your parents got a letter that you slipped below a C."

He rolled his eyes. "It's just one of his many issues with me," he said under his breath. "Failing this class has an upside though. It finally got him off Peyton's case for a while. He can't go a day without coming down on her."

I frowned. I knew her parents had been arguing about her website project, but she'd never mentioned that her dad slammed her daily about it. No wonder she stayed out so late at night.

"So how do I make my guts ooze?"

"Add another twenty or forty pounds to what you have here and do four sets of three, maybe five, repetitions." I looked at his scrawny biceps. "Maybe start by doing three reps and work your way up."

"Sam, I appreciate your attempt at whatever this is…some kind of Wuss Outreach Program. But I need a spot and no one in this group is about to volunteer for that job." His eyes followed me as I added an extra twenty pounds to each side. "Dude, did you hear me? That's way too much weight. I want to keep my trachea intact, thanks."

"I'll spot you."

"What?"

"I'll spot you," I repeated, letting out a blunt laugh at his raised eyebrows. Regardless of where Peyton and I stood with each other, the kid's blunt honesty had started to grow on me.

"Are you serious?" He flipped onto his side. "Why?"

"Because I'm tired of all the bullshit," I said, fixing the weight.

His sudden, broad smile with dimples, similar to his sister's, depressed the shit out of me. "Does this have something to do with Peyton?" he asked. "Did she put you up to this?"

"Yes and no." I nodded at the bench. "Let's get started." Ryan adjusted quickly, flipping onto his back and grabbing the bar.

"What the hell does that mean, anyway?" he asked. "Yes and no?"

"Yes it has to do with Peyton, and no she didn't ask me to do this."

"Vague as ever," he said, inhaling and lifting the bar off the rack.

I grabbed it just before it would have dropped and snapped his neck. "You're doing it wrong," I said, lifting the thing back onto the rack. "Why don't you wait for me to actually spot you next time."

"Thanks. I figured that out." He sat up. "What does this have to do with my sister?"

"Nothing. Jeez, man. Stay focused. Quit thinking I'm talking to you because of your sister. I'm talking to you because I want to talk to you." He looked past me and I followed his gaze to see Delaney and his cronies watching us as they talked trash. "Is she okay?" I asked casually.

"Is who okay?"

"Peyton." I turned to him. "I noticed she's not here today, and she's never sick."

"She didn't text you?"

Great. He didn't know about the breakup. This was about to get uncomfortable. "I don't think we're seeing each other anymore."

His eyebrows arched. "How's that?"

"She said everything's messed up right now and she needed time to think. Whatever that meant."

"That's her trademark, Sam. You better get used to it. She overthinks everything. Whatever is going on, you shouldn't let her think too long on it. Call her." He frowned. "Or…is this because of my dad?"

I stilled. "What about him?"

He looked down. Back up. "Never mind."

"Hey, you're the one who brought it up."

He sighed. "He's been on her case since you picked her up at the house. She asked me to catch you outside before you knocked. I didn't make it, obviously. Dad noticed the bruises but waited until the next morning before asking Peyton to explain them. When she didn't have an explanation, he did some searches because he was certain he recognized your last name, and not in a good way. Made a few calls. The next thing I know, he's going off on her about never going out with you again. And I do mean going *off*."

She hadn't said a word. "Did he say why? What he heard about me?"

"He found out about your family. About your uncle going to prison. I dunno. That domestic violence stuff…he doesn't want Peyton around that. There's more to it but you'd have to ask her. It's not my place to say."

"It was the hospital thing, wasn't it?"

"Maybe. Giving Dad a little information is worse than giving him the whole story. He learned just enough to have a complete flip-out. It didn't help matters when Peyton told him to stay out of your family's business," Ryan said.

"Peyton can get pretty uppity. Our mom is the same way. But you don't have to worry. She can keep a secret. Whatever you told her, she's never said a word. Even to me."

"You're saying the entire time Peyton and I dated, that your parents were against it?"

"No, Mom liked you. Let's just say you've become one more point of contention between them. Then the website thing happened and, well, they haven't stopped arguing ever since. Peyton's been under a lot of strain. She's not used to being the problem child. That's generally my area."

"Why didn't she say anything?"

He pushed his hair out of his eyes. "Why would she? She never intended to stop seeing you. You know how she is when she sets her mind to something." He shrugged. "Still, the stress finally caught up with her. It definitely contributed to her getting sick."

Crap. "So she *is* sick?"

"She hit burnout Saturday night. It happens every time. She holes up in her room all day without a break and after a few days, she passes out from exhaustion. I found her at her desk Saturday night and helped her to bed. Sunday morning she could barely move. Could barely even wake. Looked pale as a ghost, too. Mom made her stay in bed and called our aunt to tell her she wouldn't be working her shift. She finally woke this morning."

"She's okay though?"

He nodded. "She seemed coherent this morning, but Mom made her stay home and rest. Peyton's like our mom that way. She throws herself into something a hundred and fifty percent, all driven with purpose until she makes herself sick. It usually takes one of us to strong arm her into slowing down."

Like I needed to feel worse about pushing her Friday night to talk to me.

He positioned himself on the bench. "Okay. What am I doing wrong?"

It took a second to shift back. "For one, you're not breathing right. You don't want to exhale until you're pushing the bar away from you. Start pulling air into your lungs and expanding your chest." He did. "Then when you don't think you can inhale another breath, try two more inhales. Expanding your lungs straightens your spine and gets you into perfect position. Right," I said, nodding. "Like that." I put my hand on the bar. "Now lift and take it to your chest slowly." He did it as I continued talking, my hand resting on the bar as I guided it down. "Up. Again. Don't exhale all your air. One burst, then slow." He followed instructions verbatim. A great listener. The perfect student. "Now two more."

Once finished, he placed the bar on the rack, looking supremely satisfied. "Thanks. But I'm still wondering what this does for you," he said, his gaze sliding to mine but upside down.

"What's with you thinking everyone has an angle all the time?"

"Because everyone has an angle all the time. Everyone wants something. What I want to know is what do *you* want?" He slid a hand under his head. "What are you getting from this?"

"Nothing."

"Why aren't you seeing each other?"

"I told you. She said she needed to think."

He flipped onto his stomach. "Yeah, but think about what?"

"Me. She found out something she didn't like," I said. "What are you doing? Taking a break? Do three more."

He grinned, rolling to his back and doing three more presses. I shifted the conversation to the proper diet that would help add muscle and energy without adding fat. He did another three.

"Don't you have to bail?" he asked, resting the bar on the rack.

I checked the clock on the wall and realized I had only

eight minutes before everyone else hit the shower. "Yeah." I grabbed the bar and leaned over him, talking low so no one else could hear. "Do you remember that day with Delaney? In the locker room?"

"Ah, here it comes," he said. "You want me to talk to her, don't you? Because I owe you one for saving my ass. Right?"

"No. In fact, I don't want you talking to her about me at all. Including this. Today."

"Really?" He sounded genuinely surprised. "Then why'd you bring up Delaney?"

"Remember what you saw?"

"Yeah. I saw the locker door. A lot and up close. We've become intimate since dick wad has a habit of bashing my face into it."

"No, I meant the marks."

He frowned, looking confused.

"Mine," I finally said.

His gaze dropped and he swallowed. "Yeah. I remember."

"Don't ever tell her, okay?"

He sat up and ran a hand through his hair, eyeing me curiously. "Why?"

"It would upset her." I swallowed, imagining it. "You know how sensitive she is. It would hurt her unnecessarily, you know? There's no point."

His mouth hung open as though he wanted to say something.

"We're cool then?" I asked, checking the clock one more time.

"Sure." He nodded. "We're cool."

CHAPTER EIGHTEEN

Sam

I saw her standing by her locker first thing Tuesday morning. I would have tried talking to her, but Tanner got to her first, looking disgruntled as ever. He curled a finger at her, and she closed her locker to follow him to the office.

I spotted her again in junior hall after second period. Her eyes rounded as she approached and when she didn't immediately look away, I thought seriously about stopping and talking to her. I wanted to.

She smiled slightly, until several of her friends swept by, laughing and pulling her into the fold. She looked back once more, her curious expression taking me back to when we first saw each other three years ago.

I turned away, wishing for the first time in weeks I could go back to being the person I was before we'd dated. Wishing I could blow her off without thinking twice. Because other than those brief seconds of eye contact, the remainder of the week became a blur of awkward, tense moments pretending we didn't know each other. Each time our gazes met, she'd quickly turn away, killing me a little each time.

After two weeks, I had to stop looking at her altogether. It was the only way to get through it. Several weeks into that hell, and Jonas and Bobby got involved.

I'd been kneeling on a mat Friday night, wearing the mitts and guiding the punches and footwork of an eight-year-old boxing prodigy when Bobby called out my name, waving me over to Jonas's office.

Sighing, I left Max with his dad to take ten minutes, and followed Bobby to Jonas's office, then my small bedroom.

My boss looked too comfortable sitting on my bed and staring at the television he'd purchased for me over a year ago.

"What couldn't wait until after my session?" I said, leaning against the doorframe.

"Put a sock in it and watch," Bobby said, sitting next to Jonas and grabbing a carton of Chinese food and a plastic fork before turning up the volume.

I tuned in as a loudmouthed woman went off on a tangent about the Ridgeview High administration, explaining how they'd unfairly suspended her daughter twice for fighting, and finally kicked her off the cheerleading team. Her angel daughter couldn't be a bully, she claimed, but I recognized the last name. It was a flat lie. "The school's policy to punish both students is unfair," she said. "Especially when one student is only trying to defend herself. Something's got to be done."

The news team segued to another location and another reporter, who stood off the Ridgeview High School parking lot next to Peyton.

"That *is* her," Jonas said, plopping a pot sticker into his mouth and turning to me. "Right? Your girlfriend?"

I nodded, having no intentions to update them on my love life.

"You didn't tell me she was a celeb," Bobby said, grinning. "Look at that red hair. She's gorgeous, Sammy. Good going."

I wished Bobby would shut the hell up. She'd worn her hair straight today, which gave it a soft shine that made me want to run my fingers through it and pile it in my hands.

Reporter Mark McAvey introduced the segment by describing Peyton's website, how it began as a class project and quickly morphed into a national debate of using violence to stop violence, all thanks to social media. I'd already seen her brief interview with a female reporter earlier in the week. The station had asked for viewer questions and promised a longer interview to answer them.

"Did you have any idea when you started the project it would turn into this?" McAvey asked her.

The wind blew those copper strands against her face and she pushed the silky lock behind her ear. "No," she said, turning to the students at her left, specifically two girls who kept bumping her forward and waving at the camera. She turned back to McAvey. "And for numerous reasons, I wish I hadn't. But dozens have asked me to keep the website and I promised them I would."

"You wished you hadn't created the website?"

"Right."

"Why?"

What an idiot. Anyone could guess looking at the shadows under her eyes.

"The work is more than I'd anticipated," she said. "I hadn't considered the project would be this successful."

"How many hours do you work on the project each week?"

I shifted restlessly to watch her, missing our conversations over homework or in the car. I missed holding her. "About four hours a day," she said. "Sixteen to twenty on weekends."

"That's almost a fulltime job," McAvey said. "And this is nonprofit?"

"Yes. I'm volunteering my time."

"This next question is from a viewer," he said. "Do you have anything in place to determine if a bully is applying to be a bodyguard, simply to get easy money?"

"Students know who the bullies are," she said. "Since the student paying for protection has to approve the person I assign them, I eventually figure out who the bad guys are. That's what occupies most of my time. The constant communication. Both parties have to be willing to work together."

"Interesting. Another viewer wants to know how you came up with the idea."

She smiled until dimples formed. "The concept of paying one student to protect another came from an old eighties movie. Fiction, obviously, but I was desperate and willing to try anything."

"Desperate for a project or a bodyguard?"

Her face turned pink. "Both." She licked her lips, nervous. "But it didn't turn out as I'd planned."

"Why?"

"Um…he wouldn't take the money."

I smiled, remembering all of it as I watched the familiar blush seep into her cheeks.

"You tried to hire someone as a bodyguard? Did you need one?"

She looked down and bit her lip softly. "Yes." She shifted. "No. I don't know."

"She got a date instead of a bodyguard!" someone yelled in the background.

"Is that true?" McAvey said with an unattractive leer. "This was actually my next question because dozens of viewers have asked."

"About what?"

"The video of you and another student that went viral. The one with over one hundred thousand hits and growing? Were you asking him to be your bodyguard?"

Several students whistled and Peyton lowered her face into her palms, turning redder as catcalls ensued. "No," she finally said with a laugh, pulling her hands down her face. "We had no idea someone had filmed us."

"Were you asking him out?" the reporter asked. "As the video suggests?"

"We were just talking." She fanned her face. "Oh my God. My parents might be watching this. I should go."

He laughed and grabbed her arm when she turned. "I promise not to embarrass you if you answer a few more questions."

She grabbed her elbows and braced herself, looking nervous now.

"You explained in a previous interview that this started out as a class project," he said, "but the school administration received complaints and asked you to submit a different project because they believed you were encouraging violence."

A fine line formed on her forehead. "Correct. They asked me to submit a different project, which I agreed to do. The website is a project I'm doing on my own."

"No grade and no money," he said. "Why do all of that work when so many are against you keeping it online?"

"For every demand I receive to take down the site, I receive ten more requests asking me to keep it. I'm doing this for those people. I'll be their voice as long as they need me to be."

"Well, you've made many sit up and take notice. Your brother told us you've received interest from two companies who want to hire you, along with scholarship offers from several universities. Do you plan to attend college or get to work right away?"

"I haven't decided. Maybe both."

"Another viewer wants to know if you think the need for your website only proves that School Resource Officers are ineffective. It's my understanding Ridgeview has one on the payroll."

"Resource Officers are around for more than that. And I wouldn't say he's ineffective. He's limited in what he can do if he doesn't see the fight. Bullies notoriously find their victims when they're alone. That's the whole point of hiring students to protect students. It's the only way students can ensure their own safety."

"Speaking of safety," McAvey said. "Your brother also said you've received numerous threats for keeping the website online. He wanted it known that your more technical friends are trying to track those people down through social media and other online areas. Do you find it interesting that you're getting bullied as well, all because you're trying to stop it from happening to others?"

"I don't find it interesting," she said. "But it doesn't shock me either."

I shoved my fists into my gym pants pockets, glaring at the screen as Jonas and Bobby both turned to me. "Anything serious?" Jonas asked.

I shook my head because I had no idea. This was the first I'd heard of it.

"Some might be surprised to find your family still supports you despite the threats," McAvey went on to say. "What would you say to those who call your parents irresponsible for allowing you to continue this?"

Peyton gave a questioning glance over the reporter's shoulder to where I assumed Ryan or Cooper stood. "Certain people make sure I'm never alone. Nobody's worried."

"Even you?" he asked. "Because you have an entire database of bodyguards to choose from if you like."

More catcalls, along with offers of personal protection, erupted.

She smiled, turning pink again. "No, I'm not worried."

"Smart *and* courageous," McAvey said, turning to the camera as he concluded the interview with a closing statement.

Bobby stood. "I don't agree. That's a stupid brave if you ask me," he muttered on his way to the door. "People can be crazy. Better keep a closer eye on her, Sammy boy."

Jonas waited to speak until Bobby left. "You look ready to kill someone."

When my jaw ached, I realized I'd been clenching my teeth. "She's scared."

He looked to the television. Back to me. "How do you know?"

"That tremble in her voice," I said, reaching for my phone on the table. "It's telltale that she's lying."

"Who you calling?"

I paused on my way out the door. "Someone I can count on for brutal truth."

CHAPTER NINETEEN

Peyton

I jolted awake, my whole body tingling as the dream faded to blunt typing sounds. Moaning, I curled up tighter, keeping my eyes closed. I wanted to get back to Sam and me in the backseat of the Impala, but the click-clack of fingertips against the keyboard and the periodic mouse tapping forced me back to my room and the endlessness that had become my reality.

There wasn't a Sam and me.

I opened my eyes to see Adam still at my desk, his hair sticking out everywhere from running his hands through it. "It's like a record," he said, clicking the mouse. "A whole seventeen minutes since you fell asleep."

"Only seventeen minutes?"

"Hey. It's better than sixteen."

I clutched my pillow, watching him raise his arms and stretch his back before standing. He'd been so sweet, helping me enter data for my second project while I dreamt about my ex-boyfriend. "I feel strange," I said. "Things look weird. I keep seeing floating black smudges."

"I think optometrists call those floaters," he said, still stretching. "Do I have three eyes?"

"No."

He walked over and sat on the bed. "Then we don't have to worry about you having a psychotic episode yet. You realize that's what's going to happen if you don't relax and get some sleep."

"I'm trying."

"You can't *try* to sleep. That's a sure way to stay awake. Just clear your mind. Let it come naturally."

"I can't clear my mind," I said. "If I could clear my mind, I wouldn't slip into a dream the second I fall asleep."

"Did you have another nightmare? You weren't moaning this time so I couldn't tell."

Moaning? I had to quit falling asleep with people around. "No nightmare. I'm fine."

"Then why do you keep waking up? Scoot over." I inched back on the bed and he sprawled out next to me, propping up on an elbow. "I'll bet you could sleep if you felt safe with me here."

I swatted his shoulder and closed my eyes, sinking further into the pillows. "I feel fine with you here. It's…taking me a while, I guess, to adjust to this craziness."

"People are sending you detailed threats," he said. "Some on your life. I'd be seriously worried if you ever adjusted to that."

"Hm." I closed my eyes, too exhausted for rebuttal.

"Can I ask you something?"

I wanted sleep badly but knew it was pointless to try. When his fingertips brushed my cheek the same way Sam would touch me, my eyes snapped open. "What?"

His blue eyes shone brightly. "Can I kiss you?"

"Adaaaam," I said, pulling back from his touch. "We've discussed this. You know I don't—"

"Want to ruin our friendship," he said. "I get it. I want to kiss you anyway. Just to see."

"To see what?"

"To see what it's like. Not only are you single again, but you're weakened from your own crazy plotting." He arched his eyebrows suggestively, which only made me giggle.

"Doesn't it matter to you that I care about someone else?"

"Um…no." He quickly shook his head. "See? I'm not putting anything into it. No investment in the outcome. It's a kiss just to see. And no tongue. I promise."

Any other day, I would have sat up and smacked his arm for saying that. But I had no fight left in me. I felt hollowed out. "Just this once?"

His smile faded when he realized I was serious. "Just this once." Slowly he leaned down and I closed my eyes, pretending he was someone else as his lips molded to mine. It didn't work. Even the way he breathed, nervous and quick, felt different from Sam.

I blinked my eyes open when it was over, missing Sam. "Well?" I asked. "Not so hot after all, right?"

He smiled. "No. Actually, it was pretty nice. If I'd thought you *wanted* me to kiss you, it would have been nicer."

"Pretty nice isn't even worth closing your eyes for, Adam. One day, you're going to kiss the right girl in the right moment and you'll wake up on the moon. Then you can tell me again how much *pretty nice* did it for you."

His eyebrows crinkled. "Wake up on the moon? Where did that come from?"

I couldn't stop smiling. "When you open your eyes after the best kiss with the one person you want to be kissing, you'll feel like you've been transported to the moon." His expression looked doubtful. "Or something."

He rested his chin against his palm. "Were you *transported* the first time Guerra kissed you?"

I grinned. "Yes."

"He kissed you under that freaky, blue streetlight outside, didn't he?"

"Yeees," I giggled and wiggled at the memory, wanting to look away but hugging a decorative pillow instead.

"Jeez. Just look at you," he said, brushing his fingers over my cheek again. "You transform at the mere mention of him. Your entire face changes. You're glowing, Peyton."

My cheeks overheated. "Get real."

"I'm being totally real." He studied my face. "In fact, I think I finally get it."

"What?"

"The back and forth thing in the parking lot. Every time you walked away, he'd say something and you'd go back to him or he'd come after you. I seriously began to wonder if you'd ever make it to the car. But I get it now. Because barefoot or not, if you ever looked at me like that, I'd run across a parking lot, too. I'd cross a damn desert for that look."

"Adam, you're embarrassing me." Even my ears felt hot.

"I saw it in your eyes that first day at his house, you know." His solemn gaze shifted across my face. "You liked him even then. And now you totally love him, don't you?"

I'd watched the silent version of our viral video at least fifty times in four weeks, just to relive the beginning of Sam and me.

"Tears would be a yes?" he asked, his thumb swiping under my eye even though I hadn't cried. "I didn't mean to make you cry."

"I'm not crying."

"No, but you're doing that watery-eyed, blinking thing you do when you're pretending you're tougher than you are."

"Adam, I'm okay. You know I have a different type of cry to go with almost every emotion." I pulled his hand from my face. "Part of me knows it'll be easier this way. To stay away from him. I'm not stressed someone will find out about him. But...I miss him like we've been apart a hundred years. I keep thinking time will make it better, and then I see him by his locker, in class or the parking lot, and…it doesn't get better. It gets worse." My cheeks heated. "I miss everything, Adam. Talking over homework. Or in his car. Kissing and…stuff. More than I can say without making a fool out of myself."

"I get how it feels to make a fool of myself for someone." He hesitated. "That's how I know…that we have to stop hanging out together."

It took a few seconds for what he said to sink in. "*What?*" I tried sitting up but he pressed my shoulder to the bed.

"Don't freak. It's no big deal," he said, a reassuring smile forming. "I mean, it *is*, but it really isn't. Not in the large scheme of things."

"Of course, this is a big deal. In the short term, long term, small or large scheme…are you crazy? What did I do?"

"Nothing." He shook his head. "You didn't do anything. I've just been sitting in the friend zone too long, waiting for you to see me differently when it's never going to happen. I knew the instant I met you how I felt. What you'd mean to me."

"Like the moment I met Sam."

He looked down. "Yeah."

"Adam—"

"You can't help it. I get it." He pushed his hair away from his eyes. "I also know your feelings won't change for me, even if you never get back with him. So. If I'm going to get over you, it's not going to happen while I'm with you." He shrugged. "Just look at it as putting me out of my misery."

I laughed while tears formed. His honesty. His humor. I didn't want to imagine life without him, but asking him to stay in this with me wasn't fair either. "You're doing this because of the reporters, aren't you? Because they printed that horrible stuff about your real parents to try to smear my reputation for knowing you. Guilt by association, and all that."

"It's exactly what I said, Peyton. Do you want me to say it? Because I will if it'll make it easier."

I shook my head. "You don't have to say anything."

"I'm in love with you," he said anyway. "And I can't be."

A huge lump formed in my throat. "You know I love you, too."

"Yeah. Differently than what I'm talking about though."

He became a blur through tears. "I'm sorry I couldn't respond differently when you kissed me," I whispered, threading my fingers through his.

"I know." He looked at our fingers entwined and didn't pull away. "It's not your fault. It's also not forever and I'm not saying I want to avoid each other. I just need to get past this. It's getting painful."

"I know." This was miserable.

"You're gonna be okay."

How was he comforting me in all this? "No I won't." My lower lip trembled but I was determined to keep it together. "I've just lost a boyfriend and my best friend in the same month. I'm pretty far from okay."

"You didn't lose me. I'm stepping back for a while. And I don't think you lost Guerra. I'd bet money you could resolve the entire thing with a phone call."

"Sam hasn't looked at me for two weeks, Adam. He's obviously over it."

"If he was over it, he could look at you. Why don't you talk to him? I mean, I've never liked the guy. But if *you* love him, there's got to be someone decent underneath that crappy attitude of his."

My fingers tightened around his. "There is, Adam. What he shows everyone…it isn't Sam. He's such a sweetie. If you saw the way he treated me, you'd know he—"

My bedroom door jerked open and we jolted apart.

Ryan stood in the doorway, scowling at us.

"Dude," Adam sighed, irritated. "You scared the hell out of us. I thought it was your mom or dad."

"Really?" Ryan said, sounding annoyed. "Well I thought you were supposed to be working."

Adam and I glanced at each other, quickly untangling our hands as he pushed himself into a sitting position. "We *were* working," he said. "And then we were talking."

"Looked like something else," Ryan said.

Adam's mouth dropped open a little. So did mine. I'd never seen Ryan act like this toward Adam, and they'd been friends over ten years.

"Nope," I said, forcing myself not to sit up and straighten my clothes, knowing how it would have looked. I shouldn't have let Adam kiss me. I hadn't even wanted him to, and now I felt guilty, as though I'd cheated on Sam. If I could just sleep a few hours, maybe I'd start thinking rationally again.

"I should go." Adam looked down at me. "The foster fuckup is no doubt waiting for his car so he can get to the tavern. Probably some toenail-eating contest going on tonight that he doesn't want to miss. You know how he gets when I'm late."

His foster parents had proven themselves violent sociopaths on several occasions, and I worried about him, especially when he said things like that. "Thanks for the help," I said. "Text me later?"

He frowned.

"I mean," I said, remembering we were taking a step back, "have a good weekend."

He winked and gave me his easy grin, grabbed his work cap and book bag, and slipped past Ryan on his way out. "Later, man."

"See ya," Ryan said as they exchanged nods.

When the top stair squeaked and I knew Adam could no longer hear us, I rolled onto my side. "You should have knocked. You scared the bejesus out of me. Adam, too."

My brother stared at me hard until the front door clicked closed. "Did I interrupt what I think I interrupted? Did he just kiss you?"

One would think I'd robbed a bank, given his livid expression. I frowned and threw myself back onto the bed, my forearm over my eyes. "Yes. I let him kiss me. Better have me arrested."

He shut the door hard, making me jump as I pulled my forearm from my eyes to watch him stalk around the bed. "Why the hell would you kiss him?"

"Why wouldn't I? Isn't that what everyone wants? Me with Adam?"

He threw himself into my desk chair with a loud sigh and turned to me. "Lose the damn attitude, Peyton, and talk to me."

I didn't want to talk, or cry, or explain myself anymore, except maybe to the one person who would no longer look at me. "You want to know how I feel? Truly?"

"Yeah."

A lump formed in my throat.

"Well?" he said.

"Well," I huffed. "I'm mad. I'm…I'm *pissed*, even, if you must know. I've spent weeks telling the right person *no*, when I wanted to say *yes*. Then tonight I said *yes* to the wrong person. It didn't amount to anything more than a harmless kiss, but I feel so guilty I could kill myself. I've lost my two best friends within a few weeks of each other, and now you're mad at me, too. Everything is messed up and I don't know how to fix it."

He stared at me with an expression I didn't recognize. "*You* don't get to sound like this," he said. "Ever. Got it?"

The anger in his voice startled me. "Like what?"

"*Beaten*," he said. "I mean it, stop talking like that. You're freaking me out. What the hell has gotten into you, anyway?"

I rubbed my temples as another lack-of-sleep headache started to pound "I told you. My life is a mess. One jumbled complication after another. I can't think."

He glanced at my laptop screen. "You can't think because all you do is work. You can't keep doing this, sis. It's unhealthy. You're going to lose your mind, holing up here every night and weekend."

"Reporters are harassing me when I leave and I have more work than I can ever finish. What else can I do?"

"When you dated Sam, you saw him every day, finished all your homework *and* the database upkeep, and you were happier than I've ever seen you, even with Dad constantly on your case. I could hear you through the bedroom wall, singing all the time. What happened between you two anyway? And don't tell me it was because you found out he trains MMA fighters by actually fighting."

My eyes widened.

"Adam told me weeks ago," he said with a shrug. "Still, with the way you felt about him, that wouldn't have been enough to make you walk away from him. I know you too well."

I pulled myself into a tight sitting position and clutched a pillow. "I can't tell you."

"Well that's a first," he said, leaning my desk chair back on two legs, which I hated. "You've always told me everything before."

"This is different." I hugged the pillow tighter. "It's between me and Sam."

"Really? That's funny, because *he* told *me* you found out something about him you didn't like."

"You talked to him?" I scooted forward. "He said that?"

"I talk to him every day, Peyton. We have sixth period together, remember?"

"Yes, but you've never been talking buddies before. Am I supposed to believe you're good friends now? Because only a little while ago, you couldn't stand that I was dating him."

He shrugged. "Apparently, someone told him I'd

dropped below a C in Weight Lifting. He took pity on me and started helping me put a little bulk on these bones." He held up his arm and flexed it, showing a line of definition. "What'dya think?"

"Impressive."

He dropped his arm and leaned back. "To a hamster maybe."

I inched forward again. "So what else did he say?"

"This and that." He wouldn't look in my direction. "Honestly, he rarely mentions you."

Was he toying with me? "On those rare occasions he does mention me, what does he say?"

"Just what I told you, and he only said that because I asked repeatedly."

"That was *all* he said?"

"Well, that and he made a point to ask me not to tell you about his scars."

My heart skipped a beat because Ryan's next response might turn out to be a game-changer. "Did you tell him you'd already told me?"

He dropped his gaze to mine. "Are you insane? I want to see my eighteenth birthday, thank you very much. Oh, and he asked me not to tell you he's helping me in Weight Lifting." He smirked. Grunted. "Wow, I just realized I can't keep a promise for shit."

"But why the scars? Why is it a topic *now*...after we broke up?"

He shrugged. "He said it would upset you unnecessarily."

I'd already glimpsed Sam's midsection and those two jagged marks—a sight I still couldn't get out of my head, along with those defined abs. I tossed the pillow aside. "Quit toying with me, Ryan, and talk to me before I lose my mind."

"But this is so fun."

I looked at him seriously. "Can I tell you something without you telling Sam?"

"How sweet and trusting you are after I just rolled on Sam without conscience."

"If you swear it to me, I know you'll take it to the grave."

"Fine." He rolled his eyes. "I promise. Now tell me."

"The last time Sam and I spoke, I asked him about the scars on his face. He told me his uncle was left-handed and a mean drunk. I haven't been able to put it from my mind. Do you think that's what happened? The other scars I mean?"

He released the chair, dropping the front legs and his feet to the floor. "He told you that?" The horrible things people did to each other rarely surprised Ryan, but he looked shaken by what I'd told him. Maybe because he'd seen the scars and I hadn't. "I wouldn't begin to know how to make scars like those, but if his uncle did that to him…I say good riddance to the bastard. Seriously. I hope the psycho rots in jail."

Nausea churned my stomach. "I handled it so badly, Ryan."

"What?"

"The breakup."

"There's no such thing as a good breakup."

"That's my point. I didn't want to break it off. It just…happened." I shoved my face into my hands, feeling hot. "One thing led to another. He kept pushing me." I looked up to see his eyes rounding. "To *talk*," I clarified. "I was exhausted and still trying to process what I'd seen. That he hadn't told me about the fighting. I couldn't think straight, much less talk and straighten things out. When he finally came clean about that part of his past, I rewarded him by leaving. Nice, right?"

"Quit being hard on yourself. You don't have a mean bone in your body."

"Apparently, I do. And every time I think about it, I get sick. After I finally collapsed into sleep for two days, it occurred to me I'd been angry with Sam for not telling me about the fighting, when I'd been lying to him all along. I've known about the scars and didn't say a word."

"That's because you want me to see my eighteenth birthday, right?"

I shook my head. "I mean, yes. It started out that way. I waited and waited for him to mention it, but he never did. After a while, knowing this about him and not saying anything became a bigger issue. Eventually it became a lie. Then the website thing blew up, the threats started, and everything morphed into crazy. When I finally got some perspective, I wanted to apologize to him. As early as that first day back at school. You know, for walking away. But I realized if we talked and worked things out, I'd need to tell him what I've known all along. I honestly can't fathom how to do that. And if I don't tell him, how can I ask him to be straight with me if I won't be straight with him?"

"You think way too much."

"It's only fair."

"I'm a dead man then, aren't I?"

"No." I looked down, feeling miserable. "Every time I imagine that conversation, I realize I can't broach the subject. There's no way to do it. In fact, I can completely see why he hasn't told me. How do you bring something like that up?"

"Which means you should be the one to do it."

"But now I can't." I wiped my nose. "If we got back together…Ryan, this project has ballooned out of my control. The reporters are so intrusive. They already printed that stuff about Adam's family. And Sam…that video was bad enough. I don't want to draw any more attention to him. People are waiting…no, *hoping*, for me to fall off the pedestal the media put me on when all of this started. What if they try talking to Sam, as they did you and Adam?" I pressed my palms to my cheeks, horrified to imagine it. "Wow, what if they did already? Maybe that's why he won't look at me."

"So go talk to him. See him in secret if you have to, but

go talk to him."

"And get past that reporter following me around everywhere? How? The media is bent on discrediting my intentions, and they're going after my friends and family to do it. If Sam and I start talking again, they'll know he's more than just a face in a funny video. They'd find out about his background in fighting, the trouble he's been in, or worse, his past with his uncle."

"You're that worried about him?"

"Sam is private in an epic way, Ryan. He's had so much violence in his life. *Real* violence. The kind that's only touched my life *once*. And look how I handled it. For two months, only three people knew. I witnessed everyone at school *gleefully* jump on the bandwagon to believe the worst about me. I don't want that to happen to Sam. He's already got such a reputation. The media…they'd write the details of his life as though it were entertainment, all to make me look like a hypocrite with a corrupt agenda. Everything I've done would blow up, and I can't do that to the people I'm helping. Or to Sam. Especially to Sam."

"Like I said…you could see each other in secret. I mean, Jane Austen *wishes* she wrote something as romantic."

"This is *so* not romantic."

"Well, you either tell him you love him or I will," he said. "It's as simple as that. I'm not giving you a choice."

My heart fluttered like a hummingbird to hear someone say it aloud. "Is it that obvious?"

"It is to me. And tell him I told you about the scars if you feel you need to. I've lived a full life."

I rolled my eyes at his flair for drama. "I should wait until everything dies down."

"Face it. You've waited a month, and if anything, things have ramped up. It's like Jon said. People are as violent about bullying as they are abortion. They're violent about violence. This is never going to die down. You have to talk to Sam now. Don't wait until you feel better about it."

"Now?" I stared at him. "You mean right this minute?"

"Why not?"

"Because he works Fridays."

"He works every day. Surprise him. Go see him before you can talk yourself out of it."

A flicker of life pulsed through me to consider it. "What about the reporter outside?"

"I have a plan for him."

"Like?"

"Just leave him to me. Meanwhile, get in the shower and wake up. Use some eye drops for petesake. He's going to think you've been crying."

I rolled my eyes. "I have been crying."

"Well try not to look like it." He smirked, pulling me off the bed. "Go and let me handle the rest."

CHAPTER TWENTY

Peyton

The rain had settled into an annoying drizzle by the time we arrived at the gym parking lot. I stood next to the side door where others had exited and now clenched my parka hood tightly after the strong wind had blown it off my head three times. Only two cars remained. The Impala and a white Ford Explorer. I had no idea who owned the Explorer. Could be a new girlfriend. Someone who could take care of herself and didn't need *three* people and *two* cars to get her to Sam. Did girls fight mixed martial arts? Maybe he was seeing someone he could relate to better. Someone who could throw a punch. Someone who didn't need a barf bag to watch a cage match.

I turned for one of Ryan's encouraging nods.

Feeling less than glamorous in my faux fur-lined, navy-colored coat, I shifted my foot to scratch my calf muscle. I'd worn a gold-colored sweater, jeans, and my black Durangos that looked like boots with thick heels. Ryan had said I looked great.

I felt like a loser.

The doorknob squeaked, and I pivoted to see Bobby's face emerge from behind the door. Relief and disappointment made my shoulders sag as he spotted me.

"Hey, there!" he said.

"Hi, Bobby."

"I didn't know Sam was taking his girl to the party."

His girl? Oh, No. Maybe Sam *was* seeing someone else and just hadn't bothered to tell Bobby I was no longer that somebody. And a party? God, this had been a big fat mistake. I glanced at Ryan, who grinned, having no idea the humiliation I'd walked into.

"Well, come on in." He grinned and waved me toward him. "Sammy'd kill me if I left you standing out here, especially with the worst of the storm still comin'." The knowledge that Ryan would be waiting for me helped propel me forward. Once inside, I dropped my hood back and followed Bobby through a dark corridor. I'd forgotten what a maze this place was, never mind the heebie-jeebies that came with navigating it in the dark. "Sam was still showerin' last I checked," Bobby said, "but you can wait here."

He led me into a bright office where I stood holding my elbows and feeling stupid. I should have texted Sam.

"Got to head home myself," he said. "Can I get you a Coke or water or something before I go?"

I shook my head. "Thanks. Have a good night."

His head dipped. "You too. Be safe in this weather. It's supposed to be hell on earth tonight."

The wind picked up after Bobby left, making the building creak. To keep my mind off the creep factor of this place, I drifted around the office, glancing at pictures until I walked into an adjacent room with a narrow, full-sized bed and large chest. Also a table, television, microwave and laptop—Jonas's home away from home.

My dad slept at work, too. A lot lately.

I pushed the gloomy thought away and walked back into the office, examining the numerous pictures on the walls. I passed the same faces and smiles, watching five young boys age in each picture. Jonas' boys, I gathered.

Sam had mentioned the man had a brood. Some pictures had a blonde woman, presumably his wife. Most captured matches—ring and cage. My eyes stopped on one in particular. Sam. I'd recognize his eyes anywhere, even on a young boy holding a large gold belt and wearing a huge grin. His hero-worshipping gaze wasn't for the camera though, but the man next to him—an older Sam, who stared at his son with adoration. His dad's hair was black, similar to Savanna's, and his smile had a slant to it that reminded me of her devious grin. Otherwise, I was looking at Sam. Isabel Guerra likely found herself staring at her son on a regular basis.

"Peyton?"

I swung around to see Sam standing in the doorway. "Sam." I struggled for something important or intelligent to say. "Hi."

A line formed between his eyebrows. Not a great sign. "What are you doing here?"

"Bobby let me in."

"I figured out that part."

His hair looked combed and damp, almost black. He wore faded jeans and a black t-shirt, only this time he wore nothing to cover his upper arms. The shirt pulled across his defined chest and biceps, showing muscles so taut it became difficult to focus on anything else. Tattoos stretched past his shirt to his elbows. I longed to see what images he'd liked enough to etch permanently onto his body. "It feels warmer in here than when I first walked in. Did you turn up the heat?"

"No."

Just me overheating then. "Is this your dad with you?" I pointed to the wall behind me to change the subject.

His eyes shifted to the picture. "Yeah. How did you know that was me?"

I turned to the picture. "I could recognize your eyes anywhere. Besides, you're the image of him now. How old were you in this?"

"Nine."

How impressive that he'd won matches even then. "I can't believe how lean you were. Muscles like that on a…what would you have been? A fourth grader? You looked so happy."

"I was."

My heart squeezed to hear the distant sadness in his voice, but I was determined not to get emotional. "You were cute," I said, clearing my throat. "If I'd been a third grader at your school, I would have been completely smitten. You know…assuming you didn't want to arm wrestle or punch me."

When he didn't say anything, I turned to see a wariness in him I hadn't seen in weeks. "Peyton, you didn't drive all the way out here for small talk," he said. "What are you doing here?"

"Um—" I bit my lip, waiting for my courage to kick in. "I came to talk to you. But Bobby mentioned you planned to go to a party tonight. If you can show me out, I'll talk to you later. School maybe. Or somewhere. Another time. Never mind, I'll just text you."

"You're already here. Just say whatever you came to say." He put his overnight bag on Jonas' desk and leaned back against the metal slab, bracing his hands along the edges.

I'd never known anyone else who could look tense in a relaxed position like Sam could, and after no eye contact for two weeks, having his full, intense attention again made saying this more difficult. "I wanted to apologize."

Genuine surprise rounded his eyes. "For what?"

"Getting upset with you. About fighting in the cage. That you lied about it. Or didn't mention it. Whatever. It was hypocritical of me, considering."

He looked confused. After that horrible, fragmented apology, I felt confused, too. "If this is about your dad, Peyton, I already know."

"My dad?"

"Ryan said your dad has been after you to stop seeing me since the first night. Looks like something good came out of our breakup. You won't have to deal with that hassle anymore."

I couldn't believe Ryan had told him that. "Seems he's just full of information lately."

"I'm glad at least someone told me."

I frowned at the deserved and pointed jab. "I don't talk to Daddy about you. He doesn't know about us...not seeing each other."

"I'd think you would have said something. You know, to get him off your case."

I shook my head. "With my dad...it's complicated."

"You don't have to explain. Believe me, I get that family can screw with your life," he said, practically saying Savanna's name. "What I don't get is why you didn't tell me. You'd always been so...forthcoming, I guess. It threw me to find out you'd kept so many secrets from me."

"Secrets?"

"Yeah. Your dad was one thing, but *threats*, Peyton? You can't compromise your safety by keeping everyone in the dark about what you're going through. It's not brave. It's stupid."

"Stupid?" Well, that stung. "I can't believe he said something to you about that. He promised me weeks ago that he wouldn't."

"He didn't. I saw the interview today."

I stiffened. "Oh."

He looked smug that I didn't have a comeback. "I called your brother after. I guess when it comes to your safety, his word to keep a promise means jack because he told me the threats have gotten so detailed, so...graphic, that your parents went to the police last week and then to the school. How could you keep something so important from me?"

He sounded angry. "Wait, are you *mad* at me?"

"Yeah. I guess I am."

"You have no right to be mad at me. You and I weren't even talking."

"You were getting threats when we dated." He folded his arms across his chest. "Go ahead and deny it. I dare you."

Ryan must have told him everything. "You'd have demanded I take down the website like everyone else has," I said. "Even my mother caved after the last threat, and she doesn't cave for anyone."

"She obviously made you an exception."

I stared at him. "I didn't want to fight with you about it. You know that we would have."

"Maybe," he said. "And then I'd remember how important the website is to you. How much you want to make a difference in people's lives. How much you love what you're doing. I would have backed off. Eventually."

The liar. He was way too overprotective. "Why don't I believe you?"

That half-smile appeared. "Well...I didn't say I'd let you out of my sight after that. But I'd have been cool about the website."

"Sam—" My voice came out a whisper, clogged with emotion, and I looked down so he couldn't see. "I just...I can't be expected to check in with everybody whenever a person threatens or punches me."

"Punches you? *What?* When the hell—"

"Can we please not fight?" I scrubbed my face, exhausted. "It's not why I came."

"We're not fighting." He stood as if I meant to leave. "We're talking."

"Then let's talk about something else."

"Like what?" He shrugged. "You said you came to apologize. You did that."

"My dad and the threats...it's not why I'm here. I wanted to apologize for something else. Something so much worse."

He shoved his hands into his pockets, looking braced.

"What?"

"You were right. What you told me. I thought I could handle it and I couldn't. Or I didn't. At least not very well. I should have stayed. I should have talked to you. I'm sorry for the way I reacted."

He shook his head once. "I have no clue what you just said."

"Your *scars*, Sam. On your chest. Your stomach." I took a shaky breath. "You asked Ryan not to tell me about what he saw that day, and he would have kept his promise, except that he had already told me weeks ago. I knew about the marks before our first date."

A tiny but deep line formed between his eyebrows—the only change in an otherwise chiseled expression.

I forced myself to keep talking. "I didn't want you to think less of my brother, which meant I couldn't tell you I knew. I couldn't ask you how or why. I blamed the fighting. It's why I reacted the way I did to your black eye. Then you told me about your uncle and now I think I may have been wrong. That it wasn't someone who used a broken bottle on you during a street fight. That maybe your uncle did that to you. But you never talk about your life after your dad passed away. You stare at me whenever I've asked questions, expressionless….like you are now."

As if to prove me wrong, his mouth clamped tight. After another long pause, he turned and walked to the office door, bracing a hand against the doorframe to stare into the dark corridor.

The air suddenly felt thinner to breathe. "Please don't be mad at him," I said, taking a step forward. "Ryan knows me better than anyone. Better than Adam. Better than you. He knew I was genuinely interested in you. Between your reputation for violence, and the scars, the idea of me dating you completely freaked him out. He thought telling me about what he saw would scare me off from wanting to know you. But I didn't care. I still don't."

He leaned against the doorframe as though he needed a

building to keep him standing.

"A while ago," I rambled on, "you said you understood why Ryan didn't want me to see you. You said if you and I had been friends, even *you* would have told me to stay away. Do you remember?"

"Of course I remember." He still didn't turn to look at me. "You'll never stop going to the mat for him, will you?" he said.

I looked to the floor. "No, I guess not."

He finally turned but I didn't have the nerve to look at him. "I envy him."

"My brother?" My gaze lifted to his. "Does that mean you're not mad at him?"

He shook his head. "I'm someone's brother, Peyton. I get what he did."

The tension in my shoulders drained, leaving me shaking with relief. "He's actually the one who pushed me to tell you tonight instead of waiting. I wanted to tell you weeks ago, but…anyway. It no longer matters why I didn't. I should probably go. Ryan is outside waiting for me."

"He's outside? Right now?"

I nodded. "He thought I should talk to you sooner than later. He came with to help me avoid a reporter camped down the street from our house. Jon and Cindy helped, too. It took three cars to give him the slip."

His gaze dropped to the floor briefly. "Can you stay? A while longer, I mean. You can tell your brother I'll take you home."

"What about your party?"

"My friends aren't going anywhere."

I debated the wisdom of staying another minute. He seemed restless and uneasy, which was so unlike him. But I wanted to stay. To spend more time with him. I pulled my phone from my pocket and sent Ryan the text. "Are you certain you don't mind taking me home?" I asked as my phone vibrated with Ryan's instant answer of, "good," along with a smiley face. "Because in thirty seconds, I won't have a ride," I said.

His wary gaze slid over me. "I don't mind."

"All right." I stuffed my hands into my coat pockets, having no idea what to say. He once said we couldn't be friends. What were we now?

He glanced past me to the picture taken with his dad, smiling briefly. "That was the first belt I'd won outside of local competition."

I turned to study the picture, unable to hide my affection for the way he talked about his childhood. He and his dad looked adorable. So close. The perfect picture. "Your dad didn't worry about you competing at that age?"

"No. They modify the rules for kids. Three one-minute rounds. They can stop the match if a fighter takes too hard a hit, and you can always throw in the towel. My dad never would have let a fight continue if it looked like I'd seriously injured another kid, or vice versa."

I looked at him. "You said local. Did you travel out of state?"

"Constantly. At that age, the better a fighter, the more difficult it is to get a sparring partner. We had to travel just to train seriously. When I turned nine, we started competing in different states. It was fairly exciting to a nine-year-old."

"For him, too." I examined the picture again. Their smiles. "It's an amazing picture, Sam. Captures perfectly how you've described him to me. How I imagined your relationship to be. I've never seen a parent look prouder."

"My mother said he was proud." The catch in his voice made me turn to him. "I hope he was."

We stared at each other. No one had ever affected me the way Sam had. He was so deeply sensitive about his dad's memory that I reached the verge of tears every time we discussed the man. Like now.

I blinked and looked away, focusing on anything else. "Why does Jonas have a bed back here?"

"Uh, that's actually—"

"For the injured?" I turned, giving him a teasing grin. "The poor souls who don't walk out of the cage? Perhaps Javier had to crash here a few hours after your fight?"

"The bed is mine." He jammed his hands into his pockets and cleared his throat. Looked to the floor. "I stay here several days a week. This is where I lived when Tanner expelled me senior year for fighting. I've been here ever since."

"You lived *here* last year? The gym?" There went the juvie theory. "Is that even legal?"

"On paper I stayed with my Aunt Rosa. Everyone worked together to make it happen. Jonas basically became my surrogate father after my dad died, and when I had to find another school, it made sense to come back. I'd spent most of my life here. I still had friends here, partied here, and I spent most of my time at the gym anyway."

"Your mother didn't care?"

"Yes and no. Jonas approached her first. Convinced her I needed the space. He'd been looking for someone he could trust to close. He'd also been busting my chops to get out of the party scene. To train seriously. I told him I would if he'd give me a job and let me stay here. He didn't want me sleeping fulltime on his office couch, so that's when he bought the bed and the other things."

"You went to school though."

He nodded.

"Your Aunt Rosa didn't mind you staying here?"

"Well, at eighteen I could technically stay where I wanted. And my Aunt Rosa is my dad's sister. She wanted me to stay here if that's what I wanted." He looked to the picture. "But as much as I needed the space, my mother's health deteriorated after I left, which is why I returned to Ridgeview to finish my last credits. I stay at the house several nights now to keep an eye on her and my sister. Vanna doesn't do well by herself, especially at night, and my mom's gone three nights or more a week."

It was difficult to fathom living in this place. "How can

you take the quiet here?"

"I need it, actually. The job takes a toll on me," he said, "and not why you might think. It's very…social. After four hours of putting myself out there every night, I need the quiet to center. I'm used to being alone. I prefer it."

Perhaps that was my cue. "I don't think the storm's going to let up any time soon. Maybe you should take me home before it gets any worse," I said, rubbing my arms. The relentless wind and rain still slammed the gym's walls. "We can talk on the way. I hate that I make you late for everything whenever we're together."

He didn't say anything as he nodded and walked past me to gather a few things from his room, along with his jacket and keys. "Let's go."

CHAPTER TWENTY-ONE

Peyton

He led me through two corridors, navigating the dark like a bat until we approached the glowing exit sign that helped me see him better. Stopping by the door, he turned and opened what looked like an alarm panel.

"What did your uncle do?" I asked, finding my courage in the half-light. His hand stopped on the panel as his dark gaze slid to mine. "I mean, what did he do that made you want to hospitalize him?"

Silence stretched between us until I wished I hadn't asked. "He hurt my family and I couldn't let it go. Why? Still wondering if I'm that psychotic you saw fighting in the cage?"

"I never said you're psychotic."

"You didn't have to. Your expression that night..." He swallowed. "It was enough."

It wasn't the first time I'd wished I could rewind back to that night. "I was...surprised," I whispered. "I'd never seen that side of you. I don't know who that is. Then to picture you like that outside of the cage. In a life situation. I guess it's difficult for me to imagine you angry enough to hurt someone like that."

He stared at me, still suspicious. "Why do you want to know?"

I hadn't been sure until he asked. "I…I want to know that side of you."

He sighed, looking suddenly tired. "I guess if I were to tell someone about it," he said, "it should be you. You've taken more crap from your family and friends about my past than anyone else. I probably owe you an explanation."

"We're friends, Sam. You don't owe me anything."

"Friends?" He shut the panel door and turned to lean his shoulder against it. "Okay, friend. How real do you want to get?"

"I want the truth." I wasn't at all sure of that statement. "I know…that he hurt you. You said as much."

"Right."

"But you said he also hurt your family. Was it your mother?"

"No. He was in love with my mother."

I was so stunned, my mouth fell open as an unexpected protectiveness for his dad swelled in me. It must have shown on my face because he almost smiled. "Don't worry," he said. "She has tunnel vision where my father is concerned. It would never occur to her, even now, that his brother saw her romantically. But in hindsight I remember signs I didn't understand at the time."

"Well, yuck. Just…yuck." It was all I could think to say.

This time he smiled. "He may have been sincere in the beginning. To help, I mean. His presence did help my mother, I think. For a while, she got better. But after a short time, her health took another nosedive and so did our finances. Then my uncle lost his job and tried to sell the Impala. That's when things got worse. My mother found out about the Impala and had a meltdown. She told my uncle he wasn't to touch it again. That my dad wanted me to have the car and that's how it was going to be."

"Good for her."

"Yeah, except he looked at me differently after that.

Then ultimately blamed me when they had to sell the house."

"That's when you moved to Ridgeview?"

"*His* idea, not my mother's. He'd been trying to move her away from the family. Her friends. The gym. Anything that reminded her of my dad. Claimed it was best. I hated Ridgeview from the first. The school. The house. Where we lived. The first kid in my neighborhood who challenged me got his ass handed to him. After that, they came several at a time. Never fewer than three. Sometimes I did okay. Other times I didn't."

"Were you still boxing?"

He nodded. "Jonas continued training me, even after my mother could no longer pay for it. He'd drive all the way from Beaverton to pick me up, at least three days a week. Sometimes more. On the days he didn't, I had to deal with the neighborhood kids. Petty gangbangers trying to prove themselves. I'd come home messed up, which only stressed out my mother more. She got sicker. Times got tougher. When my uncle could no longer find small jobs to help us get by, he used it as an excuse to fall off the wagon. That's when he started belting me around."

I couldn't allow myself to picture someone hitting him. If I did, I'd start crying, and I'd promised myself I'd stop getting emotional in front of Sam. "Your mother didn't do anything?"

"She didn't know. The mornings after, he'd blame the bruises on street fights. Half the time he wasn't lying."

"And you never told her."

He shook his head. "I worried she'd get sick again, the way she'd been before my uncle moved in. The idea of losing my dad *and* her was worse than taking a beating every other week. When the poundings became more frequent, more…severe, I learned to disappear. Spent less time at the house. Avoided him when I could. That's when he went after Vanna."

"Savanna?"

His mouth slanted down. "I'd left one night, out walking, when he found Vanna's flat iron plugged in. He accused her of leaving it on all day. I'd seen him go ballistic over less, but that night he was in rare form. He hit her twice, close fisted. She almost lost consciousness. Then he dragged her into the bathroom where he held the flat iron to her throat. You know, to teach her a lesson."

"He *burned* her?" I put my hands to my throat, trying to process the information when my mind refused to accept it. I imagined the large flower design tattooed on her neck, understanding now the reason behind it.

"She'd been covering for me with our mom," he said. "About my uncle's violent side. So when he hurt her, she didn't call our mom. She called me. It must have taken me less than a minute to run twelve blocks but it wasn't fast enough. He was gone when I got there. All I could think about was how often I'd left her alone, vulnerable to that psycho's mood swings. How I'd fucked up and couldn't take it back. I didn't leave her alone for a long time after that."

"You couldn't have known."

"Don't go easy on me, Peyton. The sociopath once heated a zippo lighter and held it to my arm for leaving the kitchen light on. I should have known he was capable of doing something just as demented to my sister."

I'd burned my finger playing with a metal flip-top lighter as a child. I knew how hot those things could get. My watery gaze shifted to the tattoo on his left arm, then his right, wondering which one.

"I found her doubled-over in the bathroom," he said. "Her right eye had already swollen shut and her throat...I'd never seen anything like it. I cried just to look at it. She was so little at the time, smaller than other eleven-year-olds. I'd never seen anyone in that much pain. She was looking to me to help her, and all I could do was cry."

"You were young, too."

His unflinching scowl told me he didn't care about excuses. "Eventually, I pulled myself together and called two of my dad's friends from the old neighborhood—both police officers. They arrived within minutes, bringing the local police and an ambulance. They picked up my mom and drove her to the hospital where they'd taken Savanna and me. I finally had to explain what my uncle had been doing. Smacking me around, I mean. They put out a warrant for his arrest, but he was an out-of-work construction worker. It's easy to drop off the grid when you answer to no one."

"So he got away with it."

He nodded. "Someone in the family was always with us after that. For the first few months anyway, until they thought it was safe to leave us alone. We thought he was gone for good. Then one day he showed up after my mother had gone to work. He'd already talked himself into a drunken rage. Demanded I let him in. Said he wanted to get his things. Threatened to kill me if I didn't open the door.

"God, you didn't."

"No way was I letting him near Vanna. I told her to lock herself in my mom's room and call the police. Which she did while I tried to keep him out. But the lock didn't hold. He broke the doorknob on the third kick. The next thing I knew, I was face down on the driveway, trying to get up as he kept kicking me back down."

I held my hand to my mouth, knowing I didn't want to hear this.

"Eventually I blacked out and…" he shifted uneasily, "when I woke, the pain had been…more than I could stand. I could hardly breathe. I didn't know it at the time, but he'd taken the broken end of a car antenna and struck it across—"

I sagged against the wall, unable to hide my difficulty with this. Had I not locked my knees, I would have slid right to the floor.

He ran a hand through his thick hair. "Sorry. You get the picture now."

"It's okay." I held my stomach, steadying the queasiness before speaking again. "I want you to finish. I have to know."

"There's no pretty way to say it."

"I don't need pretty. I need the truth, even if it's difficult to hear."

His mouth compressed into a doubtful line. "I hadn't been wearing a shirt at the time. My skin had no protection when he hit me. The first strike happened when I was unconscious. I was still half out of it when he struck me a second time. I'd been awake enough to watch. To feel it cut through but I couldn't—"

I clutched my midsection, trying not to get sick. I seriously needed to sit but didn't want him to see me so weak. "I'm okay," I said, looking to the floor and focusing on a piece of lint. "Please finish."

He sighed. "I rolled and the third strike hit my shoulder, cutting through my upper arm," he said, speaking faster. "I managed to get to my feet, but I had three broken ribs and collapsed after a few feet. This time he shoved his boot against my neck to hold me down while hitting me six more times across the back. I guess he was finally satisfied when it looked as though I might bleed out right there on the pavement."

"Okay…stop." Intense nausea made me cover my mouth and I sagged a little further against the wall, unable to forget the image of that smiling nine-year-old. "I can't take anymore."

"Sorry."

I swallowed bile and took several deep breaths. "I…I don't know what to say."

He shrugged. "There isn't anything to say."

"I'm sorry," I said into my hand. "I keep telling you I won't get emotional and then I do. You must think I'm a weakling."

"Or very compassionate," he said. "Which you are. Besides, I know how it feels. It's worse to see it happening to someone else. Going through Vanna's ordeal had been far worse than spending several days in the hospital after what he'd done to me. I can't imagine what my mother must have felt. I know her guilt was tremendous. Her feelings of helplessness. And when my uncle continued to elude the police, she lost all sense of safety. She could barely eat or sleep, much less work. Worrying about us made the migraines more frequent. Her panic attacks worsened. Family and friends helped us when they could. It took months to get her somewhat right again, only to suffer another setback when the bastard showed up two years later, claiming sobriety and wanting forgiveness."

"But you didn't believe him."

"Hell no, I didn't believe him. I wouldn't let him through the door. When he shoved his way past me and I caught a whiff of alcohol on him, I...lost it. Vanna said I hit him from behind."

"That was when you were sixteen."

He nodded.

"You hospitalized him and you don't remember doing it?"

"Not well. Little pieces. I remember the surprise on his face after he went down. I remember the point I'd broken my hand hitting him and had to switch to my left. I remember hearing my mother shouting into her phone. My sister screaming. The neighbor who pulled me off him...his shirt smelled of a wood fire. Like he'd returned from camping. I remember useless things like that."

"You had to have been scared. No one would blame you."

"That's just it." He shook his head. "I wasn't scared, even though my mother later told the police that. I think something snapped in me that first time with Vanna. When I saw what he did to her. It's why I can't remember much. All I could picture the entire time was the bastard holding her head to the counter as he shoved the iron against her throat. Exactly how she'd described it to me. Nothing could have stopped me that night. Not until he stopped moving. And even then, I wouldn't stop. It wasn't fear or revenge, Peyton. It was rage."

"Sam…" I whispered.

"But don't tell Vanna. She doesn't need to know that. She thinks I was protecting them."

"You were."

"But now *you* know it wasn't just about protecting them. Look…Peyton. I don't want anyone else knowing, okay? Vanna already lives with enough guilt. She doesn't need this added to it." His gaze dropped to the floor. "I only told you because I don't want any more misunderstandings between us. I did what I did. I can't go back and undo it. I wouldn't even if I could. I have no regrets about that night." His gaze lifted to mine. "Does that make me a terrible person to you? A monster?"

I shook my head, thinking of Sam's dad. What he would have felt to know his children endured that horror at the hands of his own brother. "When I think about what he did to you, I want him to suffer. I hope he hurt for weeks afterward. I hope he stays in prison until the end of time."

"Don't."

The softly worded command startled me and I looked at him. "What?"

"Don't sound like the rest of us," he said. He smiled and reached out, brushing his thumb across my cheek. "It's not you. You inspire."

I blinked back tears. "A wall is the only thing holding me up right now. I'm hardly inspiring."

The storm thrashed the door as he stepped closer to me. "You asked me once what word I'd use to describe you," he said. "It's that. *Inspiring.* You inspire every person you meet. Even me, and I didn't think I could be inspired again. Not after what happened."

I shook my head when words wouldn't form.

"It's not very romantic, I know."

I sniffled. "Actually, it's the nicest thing anyone has ever said to me."

"Peyton." His gaze searched mine. "I have to know…is it just the fighting? Is that the only thing keeping us apart? Because right now—"

"I don't care about the fighting."

His eyebrows arched. "You don't?"

I shook my head once. "I get it now. Why it's so important to you. Why you can't give it up. The memory of your dad. Making a success out of something you love to do. It's the entire reason I'm still laboring over this project night and day when *everyone*, including my mom now, is pressuring me to quit. After what you told me that night, and tonight, I think I finally understand you. I get that you need this in your life to be happy, and I want that for you. I want you to be happy."

"I'm confused," he said, that intense gaze holding mine. "Did we break up?"

I looked down. "I don't know."

He shifted, pressing his hand to the wall and brushing his fingertips over my cheek. "You don't?"

"I know I should stay away from you. That I shouldn't be here." Goose bumps traveled down my neck where he touched. "But I want to be with you. I'm selfish."

"Selfish?" His thumb stroked my cheekbone. "You're the least selfish person I know. How long have you felt like this?"

"Since that night I walked away. I just didn't know how to get around the fighting thing."

"What fighting thing? I thought we just settled that."

"*We* did, but everyone else who wants to crucify me over this website hasn't had a chance to weigh in yet. And they will. *Happily*. I can't think about just me. I have to consider the people who email me every day asking me to be careful. To keep doing what I'm doing. Sam, the people who are against what I'm doing…they can't know about you."

His mouth flattened into a line. "So you're saying you want to see me, but not in public?"

"*In secret* sounds so much better. That's the way Ryan said it. The way you worded it sounds like…like…"

"Like shit?"

"Yeah."

"That's because it is. Listen, Peyton. If we want to be together, then we will. I'm not going to hide from the world because a bunch of parents are losing their damn minds over a website, alright?"

"You say this now and then one day a camera crew will follow you here. They'll make a camp outside and ask your friends questions until they know enough to print a twisted version of you and it'll be my fault. When I think of what they might find out, what they might make public…I couldn't do that to you."

His thumb brushed my lower lip. "But you want to be with me."

"Sam, people are writing horrible things about me online. They're prying into my personal life. They're crazy enough to threaten me. To threaten my brother and my parents. They'll do those things to you, too. Are you listening to me?"

He leaned closer, slowly, and kissed my cheek, soft and lingering. "I'm listening to you. And it only proves what I already know." He pulled back. "You belong with me. The sooner everyone knows you *are* with me, the safer you'll be. People will think twice before threatening you."

"What about your privacy? Those things that happened to your family…"

"Peyton. Quit protecting me. I'm not a student in your database. I can handle myself. Besides, *I'm* supposed to protect *you*."

"Oh wow. Sexist alert."

A smile curled his mouth as it hovered above mine.

"Yeah, and maybe this once you can just deal with it."

"Okay." His hand lowered to my hip, pulling me against him. "Maybe I will."

And then he kissed me.

CHAPTER TWENTY-TWO

Peyton

The storm thrashed the building with loud wind gusts and relentless waves of rain. We kissed and kissed, until my purse dropped to the floor and he yanked the coat from my shoulders, pulling me to the wall again.

His mouth dropped to my neck as he wrapped me in his arms. His breath felt warm, his lips hot, and I clung to him, my hands brushing over the raised scarring of tattoos along his biceps. "Where should we go?"

"You feel good right here," he said, kissing my throat.

"No, I mean—" I couldn't say it aloud. "My parents think I'm staying somewhere else tonight. We could stay here. Or drive somewhere private."

He stiffened and lifted his head to look at me. "You want to stay here?"

I nodded. "You'd have to miss your party."

A slow smile curved his mouth. "Screw the party."

It hadn't occurred to me we'd be doing this. I had nothing for birth control and my nerves tightened at the notion of bringing it up. But someone had to. "Do you have something? Protection?"

He nodded and pressed me to the wall, his mouth

lowering to mine, except this time he kissed me slow. Gentle.

We eventually landed back in Jonas' office, still kissing as we made our way to Sam's room. When he turned to lock the door, I stepped out of my shoes and pulled off my sweater, letting it drop behind me just as he turned to me. "There's not much furniture," I explained.

His gaze dropped to my bra and all that skin it didn't cover. He'd never seen this much of me, although he'd *felt* plenty when we'd made out. "Sorry," he said, a sheepish smile curling his mouth as he crossed the small room. "It also smells like a gym. This isn't the best place for this."

"That's okay." I became oddly aware of my dangling, gold earrings, knowing that within the hour I wouldn't be wearing much else. "Have you…been here with anyone else?"

He shook his head and brushed my hair back. "No, and you're about to ruin this place for me forever. I'll never sleep in this bed again without wanting you here."

"I thought you preferred being alone."

"Not now. When I'm with you." He took his time kissing me, no longer experiencing the same anxiety, apparently, that made my hands shake when I pressed them over his chest. His fingertips threaded through my hair and it fell across my left shoulder in a mass of curls.

"Have you always been safe?" I whispered, plagued by practicality and logic when I didn't want to be.

He smiled against my lips. "Yes." He didn't pause as he undid the top button of my jeans and slid his hands inside to push them down my hips. His touch wasn't new to me, but my stomach cramped with nerves as his fingers brushed my skin. Probably because I knew for sure we wouldn't be stopping this time.

I stepped from the material, feeling much too naked compared to him. He suddenly seemed so tall and massive. I hadn't felt this nervous since we first met, and it took all of my courage to reach out and pull the hem of his shirt from his jeans.

"*Wait,*" he said, grabbing my wrist.

I froze at the panic in his voice. "What?"

Glancing at my startled expression, he lowered his gaze and slid his hand gently over mine, pulling in a breath. "Sorry. Habit."

"Sam...other girls have seen you," I whispered, hyper aware of his thumb stroking my hand. "Why am I different?"

"Because you are," he said, kissing me once. "And they haven't seen me. It was never...personal. Nothing like this. I can't explain."

He didn't need to. I'd gone to parties. Knew what he meant. I'd seen couples meander into a bathroom or bedroom together, only to return to the party again five or ten minutes later for more drinking, their clothes slightly rumpled. The notion of it seemed sordid. Not personal at all, as Sam had said. I'd always thought everyone's first time was special. Clearly, that wasn't the case, at least for Sam. "Oh."

His gaze drifted down. "Yeah."

I didn't want to focus on his past. "You fight without a shirt."

"It's required." His eyes lifted to mine. "Jonas and Bobby are the only two who know the truth. Everyone else thinks a car accident caused...this. What I don't want you to see. I don't think you get how bad it is, Peyton. My own mother cringes to see me without a shirt."

"That's just the pain of knowing what happened to you." His raw apprehension made me ache for him. I pressed my hand to his jaw. Kissed him. "I want to be with you, Sam. Do you have any idea how important this is to me?"

"Sorry." He swallowed hard. "I'm totally killing the mood."

"No, you're not. I'm self-conscious, too. I've never done this before. I don't know what you expect from me.

And I'm about to be completely naked in front of you."

"Yeah, completely naked and perfect."

"I have at least a hundred flaws I could point out to you," I said, knowing he had to have felt the tremble in my hands. "Nothing like what you're worried about, but it's still important to me. We have to trust each other, Sam."

He let out a breath and gripped his shirt, hesitating and looking as though he might get physically sick. When he finally pulled the material over his head, my gaze immediately shifted to his torso and the two, pale lines of scar tissue that traveled mid-chest through his abdomen and faded under his jeans. I touched one, trailing a finger across it. Uniformed dots lined the scars in various spots. Sutures. My fingertip passed over a mangled section of skin. I pictured metal ripping one line through another. Stitches hadn't been able to fix the damage. Not completely. The marks looked painful and wrong on such a perfect body. Still, they were such a secondary vision to his muscular physique. Everything faded against his dark skin, those nice shoulders and sculpted abdomen. He was sinewy and lean, with definition showing more muscles than I knew existed. He was breathtaking.

I couldn't stop a growing smile.

"What?" he asked.

I lifted my gaze to see his Adam's apple bob as he waited for an answer. "I don't know how to word what I'm feeling."

The worry line deepened across his brow.

"Let's just say you don't look like a high school student," I explained, my voice shaking as I lifted my cold fingertips to brush his sculpted pectoral and the scar that ran through it. The muscle flexed and I smiled again, thinking tons of things I shouldn't be thinking. I suppressed nervous laughter by clearing my throat. "You're beautiful, Sam. Really."

He made a sound in his throat—a combination of laughter and doubt that yanked my attention from his body. "Seriously?" he said. Those intense eyes searched mine as heat flooded my face. He started to smile. "You're blushing."

I pushed my hands to my cheeks. My face had to be blotchy red to feel this hot. "Oh, wow. I am. Don't look at me."

I tried to step back from his arms but bumped my heel against the wall instead, nearly losing my balance. He stepped into my space, a hand going to the wall behind me as he grinned broadly. "Why? I like looking at you. You're gorgeous."

"Because this is embarrassing," I said, ducking under his arm then and diving onto the bed. I pulled the blankets over my head. "I'm all blotchy. Don't look at me!"

That contagious laugh of his made me grin as the bed dipped under his weight. He attempted to pry my grip from the covers. "We've practically done this how many times? You can't possibly be shy. Even if you're all blotchy."

"I *am* shy, so don't laugh." I brought the blankets down to my chin to see him sitting on the bed wearing nothing but jeans. My gaze slid down those shoulders and a large symbol tattooed across his bicep. For the first time, I noticed the raised scar running a line from shoulder to elbow under the ink. "I'm kind of terrified."

"You want to back out?"

Ah, my last chance to stay a virgin forever. "No. I want this with you. I just…can't believe we're finally doing this."

His smile faded. "Me, too." Leaning down, he pushed the blankets aside and kissed me. The narrow bed gave us little room, and I snuggled closer when he shifted next to me and propped up on his elbow.

"You're shivering."

"Sorry," I said, gripping my elbows. Only an idiot would hold herself when she had a body like Sam's to hold against her. "I can't help it."

"Don't be nervous." He kissed me. "I want this to be

perfect for you."

My mind raced to a million little things that could make this experience anything but perfect. "I noticed you locked the door. Jonas doesn't come back at night, does he?"

He shook his head, kissing my throat while he undid the front clasp of my bra. "I thought it would make you feel more secure if I locked the door. So you know no one will interrupt us." The clasp loosened, unsnapped and I looked at the ceiling, trying to keep my breaths from turning into short, nervous pants as he peeled back the material. The slight tremor in his hand told me he was nervous, too.

He continued to kiss me, and eventually my underwear followed my bra to the floor. "*Linda*," he murmured between kisses.

I could barely think. "Who?"

"Not who. You. You're beautiful," he said, gliding his hand over my skin and creating a trail of goose bumps across my abdomen and down my hip. He kissed me as his fingers went lower. When he finally touched me as he hadn't before, I inhaled sharply.

He stopped.

I refused to let my nerves ruin this for both of us, so I purposely shifted a little and dropped my hip, waiting for him to touch me again.

When he did, I tried focusing on his lips and the similar way we kissed. No matter how hard I tried, my attention kept shifting back to his hand and fingers. Those sensations. After a while, I forgot to be embarrassed and turned my body completely into his.

"Perfect," he whispered, kissing me and pulling my thigh higher. We'd done this with our clothes on several times already. This felt better.

"Why aren't you undressing?" I whispered.

"I will," he said, lowering his mouth to my throat as his hand continued to create sensations I couldn't ignore. He pulled me flush against him. Told me I was beautiful. That he wanted me to close my eyes and relax.

I closed my eyes but couldn't relax. Everything felt too intense. Too fast. My heart rate. My thoughts. How did I end up in a gym with Sam Guerra? Was I truly ready for this? Did he love me?

I held tightly to his shoulders. My body felt too hot, too coiled, and way too tense.

"Trust me, *hermosa*," he whispered again.

It was too much and I sucked in a breath, grabbing his wrist. "Sam—" The sensation hit before I could ask him to stop, and then I didn't want him to stop. I gasped as a bone-weary fatigue that had plagued me for weeks slipped away in waves. I buried my face in his shoulder, holding myself against him until everything stopped and all I could hear was our breathing.

Reality crept back and I became aware of Sam's smooth arm still under my head, his lips kissing my shoulder. The entire experience had left me feeling akin to a deflated balloon. A deliriously sated, deflated balloon. Embarrassed, I met his gaze, unable to stop a shy smile. I didn't know what to say. "I can't believe that just happened."

"What?"

"*That.*"

He smiled. "I want to hear you say it."

My cheeks heated. "No." His growing grin told me he was trying to make me blush more. My face felt beyond flushed. I felt on fire with embarrassment. It was everything I could do not to press my face to his shoulder. "I mean, most of my friends don't even know if they've...if they've..."

"Come?" His gaze slid over me and I felt my cheeks burn hotter.

"Yeah. That was..." Amazing, I wanted to say. Instead, I just swallowed hard and blushed longer. I doubted I'd ever be able to talk as candidly about sex as Cindy did. "I don't think guys usually do that. Just how much experience do you have?"

"Enough," he said. "And none. Does that make sense?"

"No."

"All I know," he said, a smile curling his mouth as he pressed me back on the bed to hover over me, "is that I want to be the only one you ever look at like that."

"Like what?"

"Like I'm it for you. Because…I want to be."

"You *are* it for me," I whispered, pressing my hand to his chest to feel his heart beating rapidly. "I told you, I've never felt like this."

He studied me, still looking unsure.

My hand drifted along his side. "Can I touch you wherever I want?" I asked.

"Anywhere."

I let my hands slide down his stomach and ribs, eventually reaching his back. He stiffened slightly, but he didn't stop me as I brushed my fingertips across the hard ridges of welted skin.

He watched my reaction, which was impossible to hide as I blinked rapidly. "I'm sorry," I said, brushing a tear back before it fell. "I'm doing that teary thing again."

"It's okay."

"It's worse than I imagined," I said softly.

"I know."

The scarring was tremendous. It bothered me, but not in the way he probably thought. I reached up and kissed his neck as another tear fell and slipped into my hairline. The yummy, soapy scent of his skin surrounded me, and then his hand moved under my hips, sliding me under him.

When I let my legs glide along his, he moaned and pushed his hands into my hair, kissing me as only Sam could before he reached over the side of the bed for his wallet.

Making love with Sam turned out to be a series of starts and stops that I'd never imagined when fantasizing about this moment. That he was gentle didn't matter. It hurt more than I'd expected and even after I got used to it, I couldn't stop my mind from racing a million miles an hour.

I'd thought the entire episode would be intense and over in a minute. It's how my girlfriends had described their experiences. But Sam went slowly, as though it were our last time together. It all would have been intensely romantic, too, had my addled brain stopped thought hopping for two seconds to enjoy it. I couldn't grasp I was *doing it*, my first time, with the school's biggest badass, Sam Guerra. How did I even get here? What would people think if they knew? What would Ryan think? Or Adam?

Holy cow, my parents…Daddy would have had a stroke.

"*Hermosa*—" He pulled me back to the moment with the soft whisper in my ear. He always spoke in a mix of Spanish and English whenever we made out. I often wondered why, but I didn't want to ask for fear he'd stop. I loved to hear it, even when I didn't understand it. I closed my eyes, feeling everything. Being here with him. What we were doing. My skin against his. It was almost too much. I couldn't help the tears that blurred everything around me. I was so in love with him. Every touch between us felt special and filled with meaning. I wanted him to feel the same. Sometimes, I thought maybe he did. And when he called me his love—*mi amore*—I imagined he'd said he loved me instead.

He hadn't, but I pretended he did, and when he kissed me again, everything felt infinitely better.

CHAPTER TWENTY-THREE

Sam

I returned later, holding everything we'd dropped by the exit door plus two bottled waters. She was asleep under the blankets, with one of those sculpted arms wrapped around my pillow. I could only stare at her. She'd come back. What the hell had just happened? The whole experience had been unreal.

Fantastic and unreal.

Crossing the floor, I sat on the bed, feeling like an inexperienced kid again. When her eyes fluttered open, she smiled until a dimple poked into her cheek. "I didn't mean to fall asleep." She quickly propped up on her elbow, her dangling, gold earrings shining in the light as she reached for a bottle. I'd already downed one and dropped the other bottle I held to the floor. She unscrewed the cap and took a sip, her gaze sliding from mine to halt briefly on my bare back. Ignoring my first impulse to shift and remove the worst from her view, I forced myself to stay still. To let her look as long as she needed. The small indent between her eyebrows deepened as her mouth curled down. Her gaze returned to mine and she forced a small smile. "Did you want to take me home right away?" She twisted the bottle cap, tightening it before dropping it onto the floor.

"Do you want me to?"

She stretched out on the bed looking content to stay forever. "What I want is sleep. And you next to me." I smiled because I felt the same way. "Can I sleep here with you? Or do you have trouble sleeping with someone else?"

"I don't know. I've never slept with someone else."

Her dimples deepened. "Is that a yes?"

"Yeah, that's a yes." Like she had to ask.

"How long until we have to get up?"

"Five hours before Jonas gets here to open. We can go at five-thirty to avoid running into him, if you're worried about it."

"I vote early, but only because Jonas is important to you and I probably won't sleep much anyway," she said.

"Because Jonas is important to me?"

"I don't want him to think the worst of me."

"He wouldn't."

She scooted back, leaving enough room for me to lie next to her. I discarded my jeans and slid under the blankets to wrap my arms around that warm, amazing body.

"Lately I sleep in ten-minute intervals," she whispered, yawning. "Although I think we found a cure for my insomnia. Five minutes ago, every cell in my body was buzzing, and now I can barely stay awake."

"Good," I said, grinning.

She gave my chest a soft slap, sighing and sounding sated as she curled into me. "It's like jetlag."

"Sex and jetlag? Seriously?"

"*After* sex," she mumbled, closing her eyes. "Silly."

I brushed my hand down her arm, too awake and freaked out to let her sleep. "Now that we've crossed that line, I'm going to want you like this all the time. You know that, don't you?"

"Mhm." She kept her eyes closed, smiling. "Our schedules are insane though. We'll have to do some serious maneuvering to find a way to be together. I can get out on Friday night. And you have Saturday off. That's two nights."

I liked where this was going.

"I wonder," she murmured, sounding sleepy, "what the Ridgeview rumor mill would say about this. I heard from several people that I dumped you. Ryan said guys were talking in the locker room, saying you dumped me. Given our reputations, they'll think we got back together because we like to tear each other apart."

She wasn't wrong about the rumor part. Reaching behind me, I grabbed my phone to check I had the alarm set for the right time. "I know how I got my reputation," I said. "Hell, I helped create it. But yours? I still don't get it."

"It's a long story." She rubbed the shadows under her eyes. "I don't want to talk about it. Let me be happy, Sam."

I dropped my phone to the floor and flipped back around, kissing her forehead. "You're happy?"

"Mhm."

A warm satisfaction burned through me. "You know I don't give a damn what people say, but that particular rumor pisses me off. Especially given the reality. I would have asked you weeks ago, but I didn't want you to take my curiosity the wrong way."

"The wrong way?"

"Like I was expecting…I don't know. Someone wilder."

She opened her eyes and pulled her head off the pillow, rising onto her elbow. "Did it bother you? That this was my first time?" Her gaze dropped to the bed shyly. "I know it's probably better for the guy if the girl has more experience."

"No it isn't." Was she trying to change the subject? "That's not why I asked."

She searched my eyes, a lazy smile curling her mouth.

"Mm." She kissed me once and dropped her head to the pillow again. "I'm tired. It feels like you drugged me. You're a drug, Sam Guerra."

She looked rumpled and cute, and she was trying to change the subject. "Give me the short version and I'll let you sleep."

"Promises, promises." She rolled onto her back. "Okay. But no questions or I'll stop talking."

"Fine. No questions."

"Short version. It was the end of Freshman year, my dad asked me to attend the Spring Fling dance with a boy, who happened to be his supervisor's son. I told my dad I didn't want to go. He said it was important." She shrugged. "So I went. Later in his truck, the boy tried to kiss me and I didn't let him. He got mad. That's when he tried to force…things."

"Wait." I stiffened. "He what?"

"No questions, remember?"

I pulled back to look at her. "You're going to hold me to that? Seriously?"

She put her hand on my chest. "Sam, don't."

"What do you mean *don't?* Don't get mad? How about pissed?" I rose on my elbow and looked down at her. "Who the hell did this?"

She threaded her fingers with mine and said, "He *tried* to force me, but I scratched him and bit clear through the hand he had over my mouth. He let me go and I slid from the truck while he bled all over his precious leather seat. I ran to the nearest store and called a friend—Jon, actually—to pick me up. Then the first Monday back at school, the…boy…told everyone who would listen that I liked it rough to explain the scratch marks on his neck. Nobody bothered to ask him about the hospital bandage on his hand. He must have had at least twenty stitches." She frowned and I noticed the tremble in her chin. "And that's the short version of how I went from a bookworm nobody to a hellcat hot mess overnight."

Why did she think she had to act so calm about this with me? I sure as hell wasn't. "Peyton, tell me *who*—"

She put three fingertips to my mouth, stopping me cold. "A month later he graduated, and two weeks after, he died in a car accident. Drinking and driving."

The memory of his cocky grin materialized in my head. It must have shown on my face because she slowly removed her hand from my mouth.

"Jason Thompson," I said on an exhale, depressed now because I couldn't kill him. The son of a bitch was already dead. Damn, he had to have outweighed her by seventy pounds, most of that muscle. And where the hell had I been?

"What?" she said. "Why that face? He didn't hurt me, Sam. It never got that far."

The first time I'd seen her had been the same year. She'd looked so innocent. She looked innocent still. Those large, blue eyes. That shy smile. Jason fucking Thompson might have taken it all away had she not reacted as quickly as she had. "I should have asked you out that first time."

"You mean that day in freshman hall?"

It was insane to consider and pointless to mention, but I nodded. "My life was royally screwed at the time. But I wanted to talk to you. To know you. I just wasn't ready for you to know me."

"I wished you *had* asked me out," she said softly, "but not for the reason you're thinking."

"You never would have gone out with him."

"No. But would we be here? Like this? Because I wouldn't trade this, Sam. Even to erase that moment with Jason."

I let out a slow breath to see the honesty in her eyes. "Probably not," I said softly. "I was so pissed back then. At everything. I had a bad temper and zero patience. I *might* have been a gentleman for a couple of weeks, max. But I would have pressured you. Until you gave in or you got rid of me. We wouldn't have lasted a month."

"I would not have gotten *rid* of you," she said, eyes wide and appalled. "Besides, I can't imagine you as anything but sweet to me." She brushed her fingertips through the hair at my temple. "You would have waited until I was ready. I know it. I know *you*, Sam. You would have waited."

She did know me. She probably would have had me wrapped around her finger even then. "Maybe. But I'm glad you didn't know me. Especially that year."

She pressed her hand against mine, the contrast of our skin stark under the light. "Your uncle came back only a week or two before that happened with Jason. You hadn't come to school for a while after." Her face softened. "That's why you didn't hear about it when it was the hot news. The football scholarship. His potential. The tragedy of it all."

"Complete bullshit." I scowled. "I want to beat the crap out of him. Actually, I want to kill him, but now he's dead and I can't do shit."

She considered what I'd said with thoughtful eyes. "Jon never left my side that last month before graduation. But watching over me wasn't enough for him. A few days after it happened, he and Adam jumped Jason from behind and pounded him as a warning to stay away and keep his mouth shut. Does that make you feel better?"

I looked at her. "Did they hospitalize him?"

"No."

"Then I don't feel better. Although I like your friends more."

"I didn't know about it until last year, actually," she said, frowning. "Adam finally fessed up after he drank too much at a party and got into confession mode. My guess is that Jason never retaliated because he hadn't wanted the truth to come out." Her gaze lifted to mine. "Can you imagine that? An eighth-grader and freshman getting the jump on a senior? Jason Thompson, no less? I can't even picture it."

I dropped down next to her. "Why didn't you deny the rumor? Just tell everyone the truth?"

"Because it seemed worse…anyone finding out the truth. I can't explain why. And when I didn't deny it, my rep just grew from there. Any guy I went out with…let's just say by the time I'd make it to a second date, it would get back to me what they were saying…" Her voice drifted off and she rested her cheek against my bicep to close her heavy eyelids. "I hate this subject, Sam. It was horrible, but it happened three years ago. Now we have this. I just want to focus on being happy."

I looked at those long lashes and the soft angles of her face. "Is that why your dad melted down about the bruises on my face?"

She nodded, gazing up. "After Jason did that, I was so humiliated that I didn't tell my parents. When he died, they insisted I go to the funeral. I wouldn't. I couldn't. That's when Ryan told them everything. I'd never heard my dad cry before that day. He completely broke down in the foyer. On his knees and everything. He's never stopped blaming himself." She closed her eyes, her chin trembling. "Please be patient with him, Sam. He'll see how well you treat me and he'll get past this. Right now we have to give him time."

I settled my head on the pillow. "There you go inspiring me again."

"Mmm," she hummed happily, another smile forming. "Inspiring. I like it. I still need to find a word for you."

"You already did, remember? Except you said it in Japanese and wouldn't tell me what it was."

She opened her eyes and ran her finger along my chest. "No, you're thinking of when you told me to say something *sexy* in Japanese. Then I wouldn't tell you what I said because I didn't know you well enough."

"Does tonight qualify for knowing me better?"

She pressed her forehead to my chest. "Yeees. But I don't know anything sexy in Japanese." She pulled back.

"That night, I said the first thing that popped into my head."

I arched my eyebrows. "Do I have to coerce it out of you?"

"You have to promise not to laugh."

"Were you picked on as a child or something? You always think I'm going to laugh at you."

She grabbed a long lock of her hair. "Red, remember? Of course, the kids teased me. Endlessly."

I couldn't imagine anyone teasing her, especially for her hair. "You're totally not going to tell me what you said, are you? You're stalling."

She grinned and pressed her fingertip softly to my lip, saying the phrase, a plethora of syllables, "*Anata ga suki ni natteiru.*"

She'd said it in the same soft voice, exactly as she'd said it that night. I recognized most of it and narrowed my eyes at her delayed translation. Dimples poked into her pink cheeks and she looked to my chest. "It means, *I'm beginning to love you.*"

My heart thumped heavy as a gong. I studied her face for any sign that she might be joking. Watched the crimson travel from her ears to her forehead while those blue eyes shifted back to mine. "You're not laughing," she whispered.

"That's because it wasn't funny."

Her gaze lowered as her fingers pressed softly over my chest. "But is it okay?"

She had to have felt the change in my heartbeat now pounding against her palm. "Yeah. It's okay."

She smiled and closed her eyes, snuggling into my arms. "Good. Because I do. I love you, Sam."

I held my breath as those words turned over in my head, too stunned to say anything back. A minute later, her warm, patterned breath fanned my neck and I knew she'd fallen asleep.

I wanted to stay like this. Keep her with me, here

where we were perfect and she was safe. But daylight would make our lives crazy again. I couldn't change our insane schedules or do anything about her website controversy. I couldn't even stop the threats on her life. But I could try to fix this problem with her dad.

I only hoped she'd agree with the direct approach.

CHAPTER TWENTY-FOUR

Sam

I hardly slept. She barely moved until my alarm sounded.

Twisting over the side of the bed, I dreaded that we only had thirty minutes to get our shit together before reality dawned.

The bed bounced when she jolted upright. "What time is it?"

I shut off the alarm and looked over my shoulder. She'd pulled an entire blanket to her chest and now pushed her hair from her eyes, her gaze widening at the sight of my back.

Awkward silence drew out. "You'll never get used to it. I see it all the time and I still haven't."

She tried smiling. "It's not the scars," she said, pressing the blanket tighter against her chest. "It's the why and how. I don't think I'll ever get my arms around it. Although this tattoo is a trip." Her finger traced the scars in a loop shape, which meant she was tracing the snake tattoo wrapped around the welted lines on my lower back.

"I may do the entire thing eventually," I said. "Front and back. To cover all of it. Make it look…different, at least."

"I like how you look *now*." Her finger continued to trace my skin. "Although…whoever did this one was brilliant. He covered some of the scar tissue, yet somehow drew attention to it, too, but with attitude. How apropos for an MMA fighter."

I snorted. "Retired MMA fighter."

"The artwork is beautiful," she whispered.

I agreed. "He's very good. And expensive."

She shifted next to me and examined my left arm. "Did he do these, too?"

"Yeah."

"Does it mean something?" Her gentle touch glided along the pattern.

I loved it when she touched me. "It's Celtic. A peace symbol."

"Interesting. With that temper of yours, I wouldn't have guessed."

I smirked. "Exactly why I need the reminder permanently etched into my skin."

She grinned and switched to the other side, her eyes sparkling in fascination. "And this one? Part of it looks like a tree."

"The Tree of Life," I said. "The symbol is for Balance."

She bent and kissed my arm softly where the tree line blended with a scar line. When I looked at her, she dropped her gaze. "I hate what he did to you."

And I hated this topic. I grabbed her elbow and pulled her down next to me. "Five-thirty," I said, pushing her onto her back and nuzzling her neck until she laughed.

"Five-thirty?"

She smelled sweet, even in the morning. "You asked for the time. And it's probably five-forty now."

"Wow." She turned her head on the pillow and I continued kissing her neck, wishing we didn't have to go. "I can't believe I slept straight through. It's been weeks since I've done that. Even when I got sick, I kept waking from weird nightmares. Five hours of sleep and I feel like I could run a marathon."

I pulled back. "Or you could spend the day with me."

She shifted her head, leaving that mass of beautiful copper hair strewn across the pillow. "Don't you work today?"

"Nope. One of my oldest friends, Manuel—Manny—is leaving for boot camp. That's why the party last night. Actually, it's continuing through today and Sunday. His parents have a gorgeous house on Lake Oswego and let him have it to destroy himself for a weekend."

"Are you saying you want to introduce me to your friends?"

"Why wouldn't I?"

"You never suggested it before."

"That's because I don't want to share you. We barely get one or two hours at a time."

"When would we go?"

I shrugged. "We could pop in this morning and shake his hung-over ass awake." I grinned. "He'll love that."

She rolled her eyes. "Oh nice. Great first impression of me."

"Manny'll be the one offering you a Bloody Mary at nine a.m. Trust me. You'll have him beat on first impressions."

She rolled to her side, her hair falling over her eyes. "You do know I'm not a morning drinker, right?"

"Me, too." I kissed her once and sat up. "In fact, I don't drink at all anymore. Promised Jonas I wouldn't. Look, we'll stay a couple hours, then you're mine for the rest of the day."

She grinned. "I like this plan."

"It's kind of last-minute. You sure?"

"I'll get way behind in my work," she said, sliding from under the blankets to get dressed. "But I'm not passing up an entire day with you. We've never had that." She blushed as I watched her retrieve her clothes and slip into her jeans. I smiled, wanting her again. She grinned as if reading my thoughts and yanked on her shirt before throwing my jeans at me. "I have to text Ryan. I need a shower but I don't want you dropping me off. The Impala has a distinct sound and it'll only set off my dad. I don't want anything negative getting in the way of today."

My stomach churned as she pulled out her phone. "Are we already back to that? You're going to lie about seeing me?"

"Not really a lie. It's adapting," she said, a sly grin forming as she typed. "I'm going to tell my dad a version of the truth."

She wore deviousness like a little black dress. I was totally attracted. But I didn't want her lying to her parents or anyone else about me. I wanted everyone in the world to know she was mine and I was hers.

I had to talk to her dad, sooner than later.

An hour later, we sat outside Perks Express Coffee, our butts wet from the curb as we checked out the broken branches and destruction from the storm last night.

When Ryan pulled into the lot, he was shaking his head as he parked next to where we sat.

"What?" Peyton asked as he lowered the window.

"Guess who followed me?" he said, nodding to the lot entrance.

She looked past the car to the other side of the lot. I followed her gaze, noticing seven cars, with another pulling in next to them. When she stiffened, I knew she'd recognized it. Her eyes welled as she turned to me. "Do you see what I mean? Why people can't know about us? This was a bad idea. I shouldn't go with you today."

"Bullshit," I said, scanning the cars. "It's the beige sedan, right?" The question became moot the second I saw the man sitting behind his steering wheel lower his camera. "Never mind."

"Nice, right?" Ryan said.

"Stay here," I said, setting my coffee down.

Peyton's hands looped around my bicep, keeping me from standing. "Don't," she said, the fear in her voice stopping me. "Sam…just don't."

"I'm not gonna do anything," I said, brushing my finger over her cheek to let her know I was calm. "Just talking. I swear."

She reluctantly let go of my arm. I reached into my pocket for my phone and stood, making my way toward him. The driver had already started his car and pulled out when I stopped ten feet away, took careful aim at his license plate before snapping a picture. When he realized what I'd done, he stopped the car. I quickly zoomed on his face and took another picture. Grinning and lowering my phone, I made my way over, motioning for him to lower his window.

The haggard, blond-haired man looked leery but he opened his window anyway, leaving his car running.

I braced my hands against the door. "Why are you following my girlfriend?"

He shook his head. "Following?"

The high-tech camera he'd set on the passenger seat persuaded me I was right about him, and I reached in, grabbing his coat collar as I remembered my promise to Peyton. "Yeah, *following*. And taking pictures. Which are you? A reporter or an obsessed parent trying to prove a stupid point?"

"Neither." He shook his head. "It's not what you think. They're paying me to find out what she does outside of school. That's all."

"Christ, you're a private investigator?"

He nodded.

Apparently, new to the profession, too, because he probably shouldn't be telling me this. Peyton hadn't been wrong. Her project had hit insane levels of interest and paranoia. "Who's paying you?"

"I can't tell you that."

I leaned forward. "Fine, then I'll make this simple.

There's only a handful of people I care about in this world, and you've made one of them cry for the last time. People are threatening her online and off, while dumbasses like you are stalking her all over town. If you don't leave her alone, I'm going to upload this picture, along with your license plate number. Then I'm going to ask my sister, a prolific blogger, to explain to her loyal followers how you accepted money to follow a pretty high school girl around town. I'm thinking your name will become national headlines inside a week, if not sooner. Get my meaning?"

His bloodshot eyes against his pale, sweaty skin made him look drunk. "It's not a subtle point you're making. My assignment ends today anyway and I've already got what I need."

I let go of him and stepped back. "If any negative, made-up shit gets out and I pin it back to you, I swear to God you'll hear from me again because—" I held up my phone, "—I've already got what I need, too."

He stared ahead as his automatic window closed.

I watched him drive away and headed back to the car where Peyton waited for me, looking totally freaked. "Who was he?"

"A PI."

"*What?*" she asked, eyes darting. "Who would—"

"He wouldn't say."

"Jesus," Ryan muttered. "This is getting ridiculous."

"Tell me you didn't threaten him," she said.

"Not exactly." I shrugged, my gaze dropping to Ryan still hanging half out of the Lexus. "Let's say I found his pressure points, mentioned the media, and squeezed. Either way, you shouldn't see him again."

"I don't care how you did it," Ryan said with a grin. "I'm just glad he's gone."

✳✳✳✳✳

Peyton met me at the mall two hours later. We drove together, and once we got past the introductions and my old life finally merged with the new, we had a good time.

My friends liked her immediately, she liked them, but I still wasn't ready to share my first entire day with her. After a few hours, we said our goodbyes and took a walk together along a brick pathway by the water.

The day's second sun break ended and the gray had rolled back in when she turned to me and slipped her arms around my waist, dropping her forehead against my collarbone. She'd worn her hair curly today—its natural state, she said—and it fell around her shoulders in a tangle of waves. I couldn't resist scooping handfuls of it before turning her face up to mine. "What? You seem sad...suddenly."

"I'm not. I'm happy. But I'm constantly worried someone will see us, Sam. I can't pretend I'm not. The wrong person, like that PI. That everything you've told me in confidence will somehow come out and what we have will become this horrible thing you'll regret. I couldn't take that. I couldn't take you resenting or hating me. I don't want you to regret last night."

"You're overthinking again, Peyton. Have a little faith in me. I could never regret you, much less last night."

She shook her head, unconvinced. "My website started as a good thing and now people have made it into this awful...snowballing...horrible...."

"Listen to me," I said, cupping her face. "It's still a good thing."

Her mouth curled down as she tried getting her emotions under control. "Maybe, but I have to fight every day to keep it that way. I'm just so tired of fighting...the world. It sounds dramatic but that's how it feels." The wind blew a curly lock of hair across her eyes and she flicked it away.

"My dad used to say the harder the fight, the sweeter the victory," I said. "You'll fight like hell, Peyton, and you'll win. I know it."

"You always support me. How can you have so much confidence in me? Nobody else does."

"That's crap. Your brother does. Your mom does. Besides, I recognize a good fighter when I see one."

Her cheeks flushed pink and she crossed her arms over her chest, turning to look out past the glistening water. "Now you're embarrassing me."

"That's because you embarrass easily."

"Oh sure. Blame me."

I curled my arms around her waist. "While we're on the subject…"

"Of what? Embarrassing me?"

"Fighting."

She looked over her shoulder. "Yeees?"

"Would you let me teach you a few moves?"

The hint of a smile tugged her mouth. "I thought that's what you did last night," she said softly, relaxing against me.

I tightened my hold around her, molding her body to mine as I nuzzled her neck and inhaled her sweet scent. Waiting for Friday night would prove excruciating if she kept saying things like that. She felt so good. Fit me perfectly. "I meant self-defense moves," I whispered. "But if you had something else in mind, I'm listening."

Thunder rumbled in the distance as she leaned up and kissed me. When she pulled back, she looked hesitant. "Did Ryan ask you to do this?" she asked. "Teach me self-defense moves? He rarely leaves my side anymore and has me carrying pepper spray in my pocket. Adam was just as bad when we were still—" she paused, her eyes shifting. "Do you really think someone would hurt me over this?"

"I don't put anything past anyone," I said, serious. "I know you handled Thompson, but I'd like to teach you a move or two that doesn't require you biting your way out of it. A way to protect yourself without that kind of close proximity. Or if you have to be that close, I want you controlling the situation."

She sighed. "What would you teach me? Because I'm telling you right now I'm not getting into the cage with you."

I couldn't keep my hands off her and slipped my fingertips under her shirt. The skin at her waist felt so soft. "I don't know. Could be fun."

She giggled and closed her eyes, letting me kiss her neck. I ran my fingers through her hair and stared at her pretty profile, pretending this might last beyond high school.

"Okay," she whispered.

When another rainstorm rolled in, we headed back to Ridgeview and spent the afternoon at Pauli's Pizza, sharing a veggie and tofu pizza—her choice—while talking by a roaring fire.

Even I thought it was romantic.

Trying to keep the afternoon positive, I didn't share my plan to talk to her dad, and later, when she noticed I'd followed her home, she had walked to the end of her driveway by the time I stepped from the Impala. "I know you said you're worried," she said, folding her arms over her chest, "but you don't have to follow me. I told you I don't want my dad to hear your car."

"That's why I'm here." I shut the door. "To talk to your dad."

Panic rounded her eyes and she stepped forward, trying to push me back into the car. "No. Wait. See, that's…that's not a good idea."

I walked past her and up the sidewalk. "It's not a big deal," I said, my stomach knotting with nerves. "Your dad and I need to get a few things straight. That's all."

"Sam!" She sprinted around me and blocked my path again, grabbing my arm to keep me from knocking. "I appreciate what you're doing. I do. But it's not a good idea."

She wouldn't release my arm. "Peyton—"

"Sam. I *mean* it." She pressed her other hand against my chest and tried pushing me back. "I have no idea what he'll say. He's been extremely upset lately, and—"

The door yanked open behind her and she turned with me to stare at her dad. His frown grew as his gaze shifted to her hand still clinging to my arm while the other pressed against my chest.

By the time his homicidal gaze reached mine, I tried to remember he couldn't see me anymore. He saw Jason Thompson.

Ryan had been making his way down the stairs, when he jerked to a sudden stop at his dad's murderous profile.

"What the hell is going on?" Mr. Greene said. "You do something to upset my daughter?"

"Daddy, I—"

"I'm not talking to you," he said quickly, looking down at her. "Wait, I *am* talking to you. Where have you been, young lady? Or do I need to ask?"

"I told you. I went out."

"You told me you went out *shopping*," he said. "I thought you were going to the mall. Then I hear *his* car pulling up."

"I did go to the mall, and that's where Sam met me. We went to see his friends in Lake Oswego." Dropping the name of one of Portland's nicest, richest cities hadn't been a coincidence. Peyton tended to ramble when nervous and didn't stop there, telling him more details about my friends than I even knew. When she began to ramble about America's duties to those suffering in the wars overseas, her dad interrupted.

"Peyton, I thought I was clear—"

"Sir," I said before this whole thing blew up any bigger, "if you're not too busy, I'd like a minute of your time."

"Daddy—"

He put his palm up, shushing Peyton as his gaze centered on me. "You would, would you?"

Ryan slid down several stairs. "I need a minute, too, Dad—"

"Wait, Daddy. I—" Peyton sounded stressed as she fumbled for an explanation, "Sam came by to…to…"

My gaze swung back to Mr. Greene and I thought of what *Papá* would have said in this situation. The *truth*. He would have said the truth. "I didn't know until recently you disapproved of Peyton seeing me," I said, interrupting her stammer as her mother approached from the living room. "I wanted to discuss that. Maybe clear up any misunderstandings about my background and…my intentions."

I couldn't see Peyton's expression, but she had a death grip on my arm that almost hurt.

"I have something to say," Ryan blurted.

"Not now, honey," Peyton's mother interrupted him. "Let Sam talk to your father first."

"Dad," Ryan said, taking a deep breath and a step forward. "I'm gay."

All heads swung to Ryan, who wavered under his dad's piercing stare as though he might pass out. For a tension-filled moment, I seriously thought he would.

"You choose *now* to tell me this?" his dad asked, not sounding surprised by the news as much as the timing of it.

"Um…" Ryan shifted his weight from one leg to the other. "It's not the ideal time but—"

"It certainly isn't," Mr. Greene said, turning back to me. "Come in, Sam. We can talk back in my office." He turned and pointed to Ryan. "*You* I'll talk to later."

Her dad disappeared down the hall as Peyton twisted to look at me, her face pale. She mouthed my name.

"Come, Sam." Her mother curled her finger at me and smiled, even though she looked as worried as Peyton did. "I appreciate you stopping by tonight. A little more understanding in this house could go a long way."

I stepped past Peyton and followed her mother to a small office with an impressive, oak desk holding stacks of books and manila folders. Taking a seat in an uncomfortable chair across from Peyton's dad, I swallowed hard, waiting for Mrs. Greene to close the door before I started talking. She smiled one last time and the clicking of the door sounded like a death knell.

I stared at him, not even knowing where to begin.

"How about you start with your uncle," he suggested.

I shook my head. "To know anything about me...I need to start with my dad."

CHAPTER TWENTY-FIVE

Sam

I should have known I'd manage to screw things up in less than forty-eight hours.

Once I'd spilled everything to Peyton's dad, he thanked me for my honesty, mentioned something about courage, and shook my hand. By the time I left, I had Mr. Greene's blessing to date his daughter.

I hadn't expected anything good to come from doing the right thing—nothing ever had in my past—so the entire outcome had shocked the hell out of me.

Peyton wouldn't stop grinning when I saw her Sunday between jobs. Getting her father's approval had obviously taken a huge burden off her. That smile and those dimples had been worth the grueling thirty minutes it had taken me to answer his questions.

For twenty-four hours afterward, I'd arrogantly thought nothing could touch me.

Then Monday happened.

I'd been running a few minutes late and hadn't made it to the locker room early enough. The second I opened the door, I recognized Ryan's voice swearing up a blue streak. Two more steps in, and I saw Delaney fall over a bench and onto his back. Ryan looked crazed as he jumped over the bench to mount Delaney like a professional fighter. The ensuing ground and pound he unleashed on the guy would have made any mixed martial arts instructor sit up and take notice. I certainly did, and once I quit gaping, I sprinted to Ryan's side and yanked him off Delaney. Even after I shoved his skinny ass several feet to the locker, he kept swinging, nearly hitting my jaw. That's when I smacked him against the locker and subdued him with a forearm hard over his chest. "It's me! Calm down!"

He recognized me then, looking out of his mind. I'd never seen him like this. Whatever Delaney said, it had to have been about Peyton. Nothing got the kid this pissed except bad shit said about his sister.

"Jesus," Delaney said, shoving himself from the floor to wipe the blood off his lip and nose. "You little faggot. What the hell—"

"Tell him what you said, ass wipe!" Ryan said, pushing at my arm to jab a finger toward him. "He's right here. Tell him what you said!"

"Whatever it was, it's not worth suspension," I said. "You don't need that shit on your record. Get a fucking grip already." The kid had an actual future ahead of him. I didn't want him throwing it all away for this piece of shit.

"Tell him!" Ryan shouted.

Delaney, who outweighed Ryan by at least seventy pounds, looked to me and back to the kid, smirking as he wiped his lip and thought twice before opening his mouth.

"Gutless prick," Ryan huffed. "Why don't you tell him what you're planning to do to his sister while he's *doing* mine?" He swung at Delaney again, still several hours away from calm. "Tell him you fucking jerk! Tell him exactly what you planned the next time you saw her alone, with or *without* her consent."

I hadn't fully digested what had happened to Peyton three years ago. Imagining Delaney doing the same thing to Vanna, yet one more person trying to hurt my sister, and it took the last remnants of my control not to react. My gaze slid to Delaney. "Is that right?" I said under my breath, releasing Ryan abruptly as I turned to look at the waste of space about to lose. "What did you plan to do to my sister, *cabrón*?"

"We speak English in this country, spick," Delaney said, spitting blood on the floor between us and not saying another word. He glanced behind him to see Maru and another guy sitting on a bench only ten feet away, watching this go down.

"*English*, you idiot," Ryan said, "is only one of a few hundred languages in this country."

"I asked what you said about my sister," I said, my gaze never leaving Delaney's.

"*What* is going on in here?" We all turned to see Coach Reynolds walking down the ramp toward us. Vice Principal Tanner followed him, apparently on a quest for mold because I'd never seen him in the locker room before today.

"I didn't do shit," Delaney spoke first, pointing to Ryan. "Princess here attacked me for no good reason."

The coach halted in his tracks, looking too stunned to comment.

My gaze followed everyone else's. Ryan stood wild-eyed now at the prospect of suspension.

"That's total bullshit," I said, turning to the coach, who I'd trusted enough to tell about my scars—the price I had to pay for earlier dress-downs in a class I could easily pass. "He was giving Ryan shit and I knocked him on his ass. Ask anyone. He's had it coming all semester."

Ryan made a confused, incoherent mumbling sound but he didn't deny it.

"No way, man," Delaney said, shaking his head vehemently and pointing to Ryan. "*He's* the one you need to suspend. Guerra pulled him off me."

Coach and Tanner's doubtful faces were almost comical. Nothing Delaney was saying sounded believable, yet he was telling the truth. For once, my reputation for fighting might actually pay off. "The kid's got arms like bat wings and your story is that *he* attacked *you*?"

Coach tried tamping down a smile as a few other guys piled into the locker room, including Delaney's buddies.

Tanner crooked his finger. "How 'bout I take all of you down to the office until you can get your stories straight?"

"No need to. Ask *them*," I said, nodding to Maru. "Hey, man. Who threw the punches? Me or Ryan?"

Maru grinned. "That shrimp? No way." He looked to Coach. "Delaney's been in the kid's face all semester. Guerra here finally put him in his place."

I looked at Tanner. "You've seen the video. I'm the kid's bodyguard and everybody in school knows it."

"Yeah," Delaney said, "and we all know how she's paying you, too."

"That's enough," Tanner snapped, grabbing Delaney's attention long enough for me to cross the few feet between us.

"Guerra!" Coach said, obviously recognizing my intent.

I had a left hook ready when Delaney turned back, and the second my fist slammed into his jaw, I thought of Peyton and the disappointment she'd feel when she realized I'd become yet another reason for her website.

Delaney spun and dropped to the ground while Coach rushed me from behind, grabbing me by the elbows as if I had planned to do more. If I'd wanted to hurt Delaney— seriously hurt him—I would have used my right, and I wouldn't have pulled the heat off it.

"See?" I said, nodding to Delaney. "It happened like that."

Tanner peeled Delaney off the floor to sit up. "That does it. I've had it. You're both out of here," he said.

I looked to Ryan's huge eyes as he shook his head. "Tell her I'm sorry," I said, letting Coach pull me down the corridor and out the door.

*****

Tanner sat in his chair, turning to Delaney first. "I just talked to your dad, Carter, and guess what? He's sick of getting bad news about you. You're suspended. A week. Your dad is on his way here. Wait outside my office. I want to meet with both of you, together. I also want to be clear that expulsion is in your direct path should you get in one more fight." He looked at me. "And you. You were already on probation from your last expulsion, Sam. I'm sorry. You're out."

Keeping my face expressionless, I watched Tanner, remembering the last time I sat in this chair, hearing the same news. Remembering how he'd treated my girlfriend only a month ago.

"If you want to deny culpability, you have the right," he added. "But I can tell you right now that's not going to fly. You threw a punch in front of two faculty and numerous student witnesses."

When I stayed quiet, Delaney stood. "Couldn't have happened to a nicer guy."

"Dickhead," I muttered.

"Psychotic," he said.

"That's enough!" Tanner stood, opposite Delaney. "Why are you still here, Carter? Get the hell out of my office!"

After Delaney had gone, Tanner sat again, looking disgruntled when he turned to me. "I apologize. That particular student tends to bring out my colors."

I shifted my chin in my palm, waiting for my official dismissal. I recalled having to sign something last time.

"Look," he said, "we have two weeks left of the semester—"

"So?"

"So," he said, exhaling loudly, "I'm willing to make some concessions. I'll tell you what I told your mother just now. I'll talk to your teachers today and tomorrow morning. If any are willing to give you a grade for what you've completed, I'll allow it. If it means you come back and take a final exam to get it, I'll allow that, too. Just not during school hours."

I wanted to be pissed, but the guy was being decent. "Why would you do that?"

"Because not everyone has the guts and intelligence to come back a fifth year, Sam. That's why." He rubbed his jaw thoughtfully. "You understand my hands are tied *here*, but I want to do what I can for you." He grabbed a pencil and scrawled on a Post-It pad, pulled off a sheet and handed it to me. "Call this woman—Camilla Brown. She's a friend of mine. She can help you out."

I looked at the paper and back to him. "Help me with what?"

He shook his head. "Just give her a call. You want to graduate, don't you? She'll have more options than I can provide."

I blinked.

"Your mother is one difficult woman to understand once she gets upset," he added. "And I speak Spanish."

My expulsion would hit her hard. I imagined more panic attacks. Less time between migraines. Failed attempts to get her to eat. My own stomach felt like a vat of acid. "She'll be okay," I said, more to myself than to him.

"I'll call your mother tomorrow regarding the outcome of your classes," he said.

"Thanks." I stood and made a move to leave.

"Um, Mr. Guerra," he said when I was almost out the door. I poked my head back in. "You're not to hang out on school property. Not for your girlfriend or any other reason. Got it?"

I nodded, knowing I might not have a girlfriend after today. God, I dreaded that conversation.

Grabbing my coat and bag from my locker, I stopped by Campbell's classroom to take one last look at Peyton. I thought of each horrible instance in my life that had guided me to this school, and eventually to her. Had *Papá* never died…had my mother never gotten sick…had my uncle never moved us here, I never would have met her.

Looking at my past from that perspective, I felt several kinds of fucked up. How had anything good come from those horrible events? Yet something had, and she tapped her pencil now, looking worried as she watched Campbell lecture. How would she explain my getting kicked out of school to her parents? How the hell would I explain it to her?

Did the why even matter when a person permanently screwed up his life?

*****

Peyton pulled the Lexus into the closed lumber mill parking lot—the midpoint between our houses. I'd been shocked at first when she'd agreed to see me, then dreaded how pissed she'd be. If my actions made her cry even one more time…

She opened the door and jumped inside, launching herself across the seat to kiss me. After falling into my lap, she giggled and curled between me and the door, exactly where I wanted her. She hugged me hard before kissing me long and slow.

Eventually she pulled back, frowning. "Why did you do that today?"

"I thought you said Ryan told you."

"He told me what happened but I want to know why."

"Why?" I shrugged. "First, the asshole threatened my sister. I don't care if he was just taunting Ryan. He couldn't have hit a rawer nerve on your brother. Not after what Thompson did to you. Was I supposed to let Tanner suspend him for defending my sister's honor? Because he would have, you know."

"I know. But this is exactly what you were avoiding the day we met. You've worked too hard to graduate."

"I'll figure something out."

"Did you really hit him? Carter Delaney?"

"Kind of."

Her eyebrows furrowed. "Kind of?"

I looked down. "I used my left. I also held back…a lot. Let's just say I didn't hit him half as hard as I wanted."

"Thank goodness," she said, hugging me tightly again. "I've seen your right hook. You would have put him into a coma and then we'd have more problems than we already do."

"We?" I pulled her away and brushed her hair back. "*Hermosa*, this is *my* problem. Not yours."

She looked ready to cry. "What are you going to do?"

"I've made an appointment with an advisor at MHCC. A friend of Tanner's, believe it or not. She told me over the phone I could get my high school diploma through the college."

"Does that mean you'll start classes in January?"

"I won't know until I talk to her again. Martin has more work at the shop than I can stand and I'm adding extra lessons onto my schedule at the gym. It works out better for my family."

"I'll bet your mother doesn't see it that way."

"No, she doesn't."

Her face crumpled. "Well, I can tell you *my* life is about to suck lemons. Ridgeview will be an abyss of despair without you."

I cocked an eyebrow. "An abyss of despair?"

Her lower lip trembled. "Worse than that, but there aren't words to adequately describe it."

I kissed her. "I'll miss you, too."

She hugged me. "Thank you for helping Ryan," she whispered. "Again."

"Are you kidding? We're not even close to even. The guy outted himself trying to save me from your dad's wrath. Then he pulled that ground and pound on Delaney for—"

"Ground and pound?" She blinked.

"It's exactly what it sounds like. And trust me, it's an impressive sight when it's executed well. Not everyone his size would try to smack the shit out of Carter Delaney. I still don't get why he did it. I knew Delaney hit a raw nerve, but he wasn't talking about you. He was talking about Vanna. Ryan doesn't know Vanna."

"But you're his friend," she said. "Sam, I don't think you realize what you have in Ryan. He's the most loyal person you could know. I want to be mad at him because he shouldn't have lost it like that today. But he did it for you. I can't be mad at him for that, even though it's cost you so much."

"The bitch of it all is that I can't be on school property. How can I make sure Delaney will stay away from Vanna if I can't be there? I'm sure he was just bullshitting to get under Ryan's skin, but if he wasn't…"

"Trust me when I say Carter Delaney won't get near Savanna. We'll all make sure of that. She can even join the carpool if she wants."

Where did this girl come from? I kissed her once, twice, and things quickly escalated. I couldn't get close enough. "Can you come by the gym later?" I whispered, pulling her against me to kiss her neck.

"I have way too much work tonight," she said. "My database has practically become a dating site. Some of my bodyguards are even hooking up. It takes forever to get through the junk mail now. I think it's that video. My own fault."

It occurred to me what she meant and I stopped kissing her. "Wait, are guys asking you out through your website?"

Her gaze lowered to my chest. Even at twilight, I could see her cheeks turn pink in the darkness of the car. "Yes and it's embarrassing. I don't have time to read that junk. I just want to do the work."

"Tell those *pendejos* your boyfriend is the guy in the video," I said, peeling her coat off her shoulders, "and I'll kick their asses if they don't leave you alone."

"I don't think that would go over well coming from the

administrator of an anti-bullying website." She looked down as I undid the top two buttons of her blouse. "Sam," she whispered. "What are you doing?"

"Undressing you."

With a devious sparkle in her eyes, she looked past my shoulder and out the window to the desolate parking lot surrounded by trees. "What if someone catches us?"

"They won't." Her third button caught on a thread. Impatient, I slipped my hand under the material at her waist. "I want you so much."

"Me, too," she whispered, kissing me.

"After what happened today, I didn't think you'd talk to me."

She halted the kiss and pulled back. "Why wouldn't I talk to you?"

I shook my head. "The violence thing. I figured you'd walk again."

"You thought I'd…walk again? *Sam*—" She shifted over my lap, straddling me and giving me that hurt look that killed me. "How can you say that? I thought the other night meant something to you."

"You know it did."

"I told you I love you, Sam." Her eyes drifted down to her hands as she played with my shirt collar. "And I meant it." She looked at me. "I love you so much it sometimes scares me. What do I have to do to make you believe me?"

I studied those blue eyes and thought seriously about saying it back to her. *I love you.* What was so easy to do should have been easy to say, but it wasn't. Peyton used the word *love* like most people used *please* and *thank you*. I barely used it with my closest family members, and even then, it was usually only in my head. "I believe you," I said, pulling her mouth to mine. A half-truth if ever there was one, but she didn't question it as she kissed me back.

*****

Mamá looked at the dinner table, perching her hands on her waist in satisfaction before giving Peyton a wink. "I think we're ready."

Peyton grinned and quickly moved the sweetcorn gratin to the other side of a plate next to the avocado salad, checking me then for approval.

With a shoulder resting against the kitchen doorframe, I hadn't stopped smiling all day, watching them giggle and whisper while fixing Christmas dinner. Ma was showing Peyton how to make her amazing *pollo con piña*—a family recipe she'd only shared with Vanna, who still appeared to be irked that Ma had brought Peyton into the recipe-sharing fold. I'd only mentioned it to Peyton for her love of pineapple.

Any time I tried to eavesdrop by offering to look for a spice or reach for something, one of them would shove me out of the kitchen.

Ma turned now to the living room where Vanna sat glued to the news. "*Mija*, turn off that infernal news. Don't make me ground you on Christmas Eve."

"Fine." Vanna grunted and shut it off. "Coming."

Peyton sat next to my mother, whispering in conspiring tones. My attention shifted to Vanna, who had been acting weird all day.

"So," Vanna said after everyone started eating, "I heard a podcast this morning. An interview with you."

I followed my sister's gaze to Peyton, who'd stopped chewing and looked a little pale. "Oh."

"Another interview?" Ma asked.

My sister smiled. "I'll say."

"Let her tell it, *mija*," Ma said. "If she wants to."

Peyton chewed a couple of times, her eyes pivoting to Ma. "There isn't much to say."

"Well, if Peyton isn't talking then I'll have to," Vanna said. "An eighth grade girl killed herself in Illinois two days ago, they say due to online bullying. KSMR radio interviewed Peyton yesterday. Apparently, they'd done their homework." She nodded toward me. "Especially on you, Samuel."

I grabbed another scoop of the sweetcorn, my gaze shifting from Vanna to Peyton. "How much homework?"

"I'd planned to tell you later tonight," Peyton said softly before plowing her fork through her rice several times, her eyes darting between my plate and hers. We'd already had this discussion, so I didn't know why she looked nervous. I'd never blame her if my past came out. She knew that.

"There, you see?" Ma said. "This is none of our business, Savanna. Let's talk about something else."

"It was that bad?" I asked, unable to wait until later.

Peyton took a small drink of tea. "Define bad."

Shit.

"Your boyfriend has won numerous boxing and MMA belts," Vanna said, trying to sound like a DJ doing an interview. "*Mixed martial arts*—a sport—blah, blah, blah, that's left numerous fighters paralyzed, blah, blah, and some *dead,* blah, blah, blah, due to the brutality of the sport."

Peyton's frown grew as Vanna continued the recap, which told me my sister wasn't embellishing the interview.

"He asked Peyton to explain," Vanna said, looking to Ma, "how she could be against violence when her boyfriend participates in one of the most violent sports out there."

"I told him he might as well compare apples and oranges," Peyton told Ma, her cheeks turning pink with remembered anger. "I told him MMA is no different than football or hockey, and that all physical sports have an element of risk."

I smiled as she practically repeated my own words to my mother. Peyton hadn't always felt like this.

Vanna nodded at me. "He also made the mistake of asking Peyton if she supported you participating in such a violent sport."

"Great," I murmured.

All eyes jerked to me.

"That's when Peyton excused herself from the interview," Vanna said. "It was very dramatic."

"This rice is especially good, Peyton," Ma said cheerfully, trying to change the subject. "Did you add something extra?"

Peyton stared at her plate. "No."

"My blog readers are curious," Vanna said, folding her arms next to her plate. "Half say you can't be *for* violence to stop violence."

"Then your blog readers are either twelve," I said, "or stupid."

Ma nearly dropped her fork. "*Samuel.*"

"Sorry," I said. "But the people threatening Peyton are supposedly civilized, claiming to be against violence."

"What do you think, Peyton?" Vanna said.

Peyton looked fierce now. "I think everyone wants a one-size-fits-all answer to society's problems and there's no such thing," she said. "I think there's gray area. Lots of it. And I think we can't continue to throw out lazy, catchall responses to every problem we have. It's arrogant and ignorant."

I winked at Peyton. "What she said."

"I love it," my sister said. "Can I quote you on that?"

I kicked Vanna's leg under the table.

"Ow!"

"Yes," Peyton said, leaning forward. "In fact, you can also quote me on this. The reason I know there's gray area, is because I care about someone very much who wants to be, who *should* be, a professional fighter. The idea of him getting hurt makes my stomach drop to my shoes, but I'd support him a hundred percent if he took that path. Why? Because mixed martial arts is a professional competition. It has nothing to do with bullying. I don't want it brought up when I'm talking about bullying. And I'll smack the next person who references MMA, my boyfriend, and my website in the same sentence."

Ma's eyebrows shot up.

Peyton straightened and grabbed her fork. "Strike the last phrase. I wouldn't smack anyone."

I swallowed. Watched her eat her first bite of the chicken she helped make. She moaned and turned to Ma. "Oh my gosh. That is so good, Mrs. Guerra."

"Thank you." Ma blushed. "It's been through generations of revisions. I don't think I'd change it now. What do you think?"

"No." Peyton looked like she was in pineapple chicken heaven. "I wouldn't change a thing. It's perfect."

"I have another chicken recipe made with mandarin oranges, toasted almonds and Madeira wine. If you think you'd like that as well."

Peyton moaned. "Of course. Sounds heavenly."

I was still in shock. "Are you serious?"

Both of them turned to me. "Don't you like it?" Peyton asked.

"I meant what you said to Vanna. About the fighting."

She looked back to her plate. "Yes, except the smacking part."

Vanna dropped her fork loudly and immediately scooped it up.

Mamá tried to smile. "So, Peyton. What does your family do Christmas Day? I want to know what my son will be up to while Savanna and I eat all these delicious leftovers."

"Brace yourself, Vanna," I said.

Peyton smiled, knowing Vanna's allergic reaction to nice people. "My mom takes a few days off to make twenty homemade pies each year for the mission downtown. Different stores donate the ingredients. My brother and I help her deliver. Sometimes we stay and serve. So basically, Sam will be a delivery boy tomorrow and quite possibly a food server." She grinned at me with those dimples. "After that, it's home and more eating."

"Don't let her lie to you," I told Ma. "She works just as hard. Peyton peeled apples half the day yesterday."

Vanna rolled her eyes.

We hadn't gotten far into a Christmas movie later, something about second chances, when Peyton sank against my shoulder. I looked down to see her asleep. She passed out early more often than not lately.

"She works too hard," Ma whispered, a smile brightening her face as she watched Peyton from her chair. "Your father was like that. He never knew when to quit. She has so many of his qualities. It doesn't surprise me you love her."

"What?" Vanna's head snapped up, almost asleep herself from eating too much. "Love who?"

"*Ma*," I whispered, checking Peyton's face.

Mamá rolled her eyes. "Admit it, *mijo*. You love her and she loves you."

If I hadn't been so curious, myself, I would have changed the subject. "How do you know?"

"It's obvious every time you look at her."

"I meant *her*," I said. "I'm an open book, clearly, but she loves everyone, Ma. She throws the word around on a daily basis. To her friends. Her brother. Her parents. *I love you* were probably her first three words. How do you know she means it…you know, like the rest of us mean it?"

"How do I know she's *in love* with you, you mean? Because she said the idea of you fighting makes her physically sick. She even has nightmares about it. Yet it's all she wants for you. She wants you to have a chance to fight professionally because it's what you want. What she thinks will make you happy. That's love, is it not?"

I swallowed, surprised to see Ma still smiling, given the topic. "She said that?"

Ma nodded. "What do you think we talked about all afternoon? *You.* She loves you very much."

I looked down at Peyton's serene face.

"Go," Ma said. "Take her home. She needs her rest. You can talk about it when you see her tomorrow."

Vanna's gaze slid to Peyton. "What are we talking

about?"

"How Samuel's life will change when he starts training again."

Vanna did a double take. "What?"

I blinked. "When I start *what?*"

"Training," she repeated. "Because Peyton is right." She looked at my girlfriend with affection. "Your father would have wanted you to be happy. To do what you feel you need to do."

"Peyton said that?" Vanna said, echoing my thoughts.

Ma nodded. "Perhaps I can let go a little bit now, knowing I'm not the only one worrying about you." She pointed at me and squinted. "But you're still taking those two classes this spring and getting your diploma. I don't care how hard Jonas works you."

"Yes, ma'am."

"Tell Peyton goodnight for us and that we loved having her. Come on, Savanna." She waved to my sister. "Bedtime."

Vanna scowled. "It's only nine."

"And it's bedtime," Ma said over her shoulder.

Vanna flicked off the movie and stuck her tongue out at me as she followed Ma to the back bedrooms where I knew she'd dive into work on her laptop.

I kissed Peyton awake, and she stayed groggy and apologetic the entire time it took to get her from the sofa to the Impala. The second I covered her with my leather coat, she fell back asleep. My mind raced as I tried to think of what I'd say, how I'd approach the subject tomorrow, after Christmas with her parents.

Christmas. Great timing, but I couldn't wait. I had to find out if she'd meant what she said tonight. The rest of my life couldn't start until I did.

CHAPTER TWENTY-SIX

Peyton

"I still can't believe you're making me hit you on Christmas," I said. Blowing a loose curl out of my eyes, I watched him in one of the gym's wall-length mirrors as he approached me from behind.

"Well, you're not hitting *me*. You're hitting an attacker." He looped his arms around me, locking my elbows to my sides. "I'm five seconds from assaulting you. What are you going to do about it?"

His arms flexed around mine like steel bands and my gaze met his in the mirror. He was such a handsome attacker. I wanted to do other things with him that didn't include practicing eye gouges.

"Why are you thinking?" he said, looking irked. "Do you know how many things I could have done to you already while you stand there thinking? Speed is essential, Peyton, especially for someone your size."

"I know."

"Then don't think. *React*. The point of all this practice is for muscle memory to take over. You shouldn't have to think about what you're going to do. Now defend yourself and attack me." He dragged me backward then, holding me tight to him.

I lifted my right foot, using his leg to aim my heel against the joint where his foot met his shin. I was determined to make him happy, to execute the move perfectly this time, but when I brought my foot down, my overzealousness kept my adrenalin pumping and I didn't pull back fast enough. I kicked him hard and he released me abruptly.

Stumbling out of his arms, I pivoted to watch him limp backward as I cupped my hands over my mouth. *"¡Hay, Dios mío!* Sam!"

His limp was profound as he walked in a circle, looking pained even as he smiled proudly, the way he often did whenever I spoke Spanish in the right context. He'd been teaching me a little and I didn't always get it right.

"I'm so sorry," I said, the words muffled into my palms before I pulled my hands from my mouth. "Are you okay?"

He shook his head. "No."

"Really?" My boyfriend was made of steel. Surely, he wasn't serious.

"It hurts like hell," he said, "which was the entire point of the exercise. Imagine what you could have done to me had you used full force. Believe me, I wouldn't be chasing after you. That was good, Peyton. Seriously."

I kept a hand over my mouth as he walked toward me, still favoring a leg. "Can we stop now?" I dropped my hands. "We've been doing this for two hours."

"You have to admit all this practice is paying off. Look how quickly you incapacitated me," he said with a grin as he pulled me to him. "It makes me feel better knowing you can."

"Knowing I can incapacitate you?" He lowered his head and nuzzled my neck until I giggled. "That's really twisted, Sam." I curled my hands against his sides, thankful we had the gym to ourselves tonight. "Sparring is one thing. Practically disabling you is another. We need to work on your romancing skills."

He backed me up to the mirror, his hands smoothing down my tank top to slide over my sweats and down my hips. "That comes next," he whispered, kissing my neck.

Goose bumps traveled across my back and I closed my eyes. He had a good handle on those moves already. "Does that mean I get to take a shower? We only have a few more hours before my parents expect us back."

"Soon. Just a few more questions," he said, stepping back enough to lean both palms behind me, trapping me between his arms.

"You are not quizzing me on Christmas, Sam." I moaned. "For petesake. You're relentless."

"Consider it your Christmas present to me."

"I already bought that."

"Please? For me? It'll make me feel better."

I could never say no to him. "Okay."

"Name two of the most vulnerable areas you should consider in a close quarter attack?"

"The eyes and windpipe."

"Two effective ways to hit the windpipe?"

I slow punched my fist to his throat, touching his Adam's apple. Then pulled back and opened my hand, bringing it back to his throat slowly in a side strike.

He nodded. "Other vulnerable areas on the head?"

"Temple and base of the nose because of the—" I swallowed my revulsion, "—potential vibrations to the brain."

He started to smile. "Strongest body points to use when in a close-quarter attack?"

"Elbow or knee. Depends on the situation."

"Things to remember when attacking the knee."

"Four striking angles, down, up and the sides. Or five if I kick directly into the knee. My foot position depends on the striking angle. Extend my leg. Break the knee."

"Did you mean what you said last night?"

I blinked. "What?"

Looking tense and vulnerable, he framed my face with his hands. "Did you. Mean. What you said last night? At dinner. That if I could train and fight professionally, you'd be supportive?"

"Um…" I searched his eyes. "Yes. Why?"

"Last night, my mother gave me her blessing to train. To really do this. She said you talked to her. That you convinced her."

"I did?" I swallowed hard. "She doesn't care if you finish school?"

"Well, there's that caveat. But my other teachers gave me passing grades, so I only need two classes to meet Oregon graduation requirements. It's doable."

"But—" At first, I had no idea how I truly felt, "—you already have two jobs. Two classes. How would you find time to train?"

"I'll make the time. Work harder. Are you kidding? I'd work my ass off twenty-four hours a day for a shot at this."

I lifted my hands to my cheeks. "Um, okay. Let me think." What did this mean exactly?

He studied my expression and dropped his hands from my face. Stared another long moment before pivoting away. "You can't do this after all, can you?"

I crossed my arms over my chest and dropped my gaze, staring at my shoes as I voiced the one thing that bothered me the most about it. "I know it's selfish to say, but how will you find time to see me?"

He turned to me from pacing, incredulous. "How could you ask me that? I'm already so damn crazy in love with you I can barely go twenty-four hours without seeing you. Seriously? Was that a real question? Or are you just checking to see if I'm listening?"

My eyes watered. I uncrossed my arms and folded my hands behind my back. Shifted my weight side to side. Tried to pretend I wasn't about to cry. "You're in love with me?"

"Peyton." He stared at me, his hands moving to his hips. "Come on. I know I never said it in so many words, but you *had* to know."

I shrugged, unable to get past the lump in my throat to say anything. When tears formed, I wiped under my eyes and looked down, embarrassed.

"Peyton." Within seconds, he'd moved in front of me, his fingertips brushing along my cheek before he leaned down and kissed me. "*Hermosa*, don't. I know I should have said something before, but I'm a—"

"Big, tough fighter who won't say things like *I love you* to his girlfriend?" I said, gripping his wrists as he cupped my face. "I get it, Sam. No need to explain."

"No, I was going to say I'm an idiot. Because I do love you. And I can say it. And I will. As many times as you want me to."

"It sounds really nice," I said, wiping my eyes and giggling when he hugged me to him. "So you might be saying it all the time."

He hugged me harder, as if it was a relief for him to say as much as it was for me to hear. "*Sam*," I whispered, as it all sank in slowly. "I can't believe you can finally do this. I wasn't certain your mother was listening to me. I'm…I'm kind of stunned."

He pulled from the hug. "Imagine how I felt."

"Does Jonas know?"

"I wanted to talk to you first."

I searched his eyes. "Why?"

"Because I want your support. I need it. And I'm worried once I start this that—" His gaze drifted over my face. "You know I'm going to get hurt, right? It's a certainty. I'll *lose* fights." His hands gripped my shoulders tighter. "There'll be times when you'll wonder what the hell I'm doing in that cage. But I can't talk about quitting once I commit to this. I have to give it a hundred and fifty percent. Can you do that? Can you see me broken and banged up, and still support me instead of asking me to quit?"

I'd been biting my lip. "Depends."

A smile pulled at his sexy mouth. "On?"

"I want you to promise me something first."

"What?"

"Three things, actually."

His eyebrows arched. "*Three?* Wow, Ryan was right. I shouldn't let you think too long. Even seconds, apparently."

"Ryan said *what?*" My mouth parted with several retorts ready on my tongue. Instead, I tried to look superior. "Well, if you can't manage three teensy-weensy promises to the girlfriend you *supposedly* love then you should just say so."

He grinned and pulled me to him, lifting me against him and kissing me. I wrapped my legs around his waist until he slid me onto a table full of towels and leaned over me, trapping me between his arms. "Alright. What do you want?"

I lost my smile and got serious, brushing my fingertips through the hair at his temple. "I can't watch you fight. I couldn't take seeing you get hurt. I think it would kill me to watch someone hitting you."

His immediate frown told me his real feelings. "You know more than anything I'd want you there. All of this is happening because of you. But I get it's hard to watch. I can live with it."

"You can?"

"I'll learn to," he said. "What else?"

I poked his chest. "No goofing off in the first round. You have to get serious immediately."

"Have you been talking to Bobby and Jonas?"

"I'm serious," I said, my ferocious stare negated the second he grabbed my hips and pulled me against his waist. "Quit kidding around, Sam. Look what happened to Anderson Silva against Chris Weidman. He lost a championship belt horsing around."

He let go of a huge, incredulous grin. "Are you watching MMA now?"

I rolled my eyes. "Don't go getting all revved up. Headlines only. Well, usually. This was an older clip."

"Silva didn't lose the fight goofing around," he said.

"That seems to be the big debate. You have to admit, he wasn't taking Weidman seriously. He let his guard down."

"You totally watched that fight, didn't you?"

"A small portion only."

His smile broadened. "Silva's antics were part of his strategy. He gets into his opponents' heads. He also knows what pleases a crowd. Fighting is entertainment, you know."

I gripped his shirt and pulled his face close to mine. "But *you* won't be entertaining. You'll be fighting. Promise me you'll be serious!"

He laughed. "I promise."

I pressed my forehead to his and closed my eyes, chin trembling to think he might be humoring me. "I mean it, Sam. Really."

He pulled back and lost the smile. "No more joking around. Got it. What else? Your last demand of me, Princess Peyton."

"Don't be so cocky. You might have trouble with this last one."

"Whatever it is," he murmured, kissing me. "I'll do it. For you."

"Promise?"

"Yeah. For you. *Anything.*" His hand moved under my shirt. "What is it?"

"Simple." I smiled. "You have to win."

EPILOGUE

Peyton

I pushed my way past people as I headed down the aisle toward the ominous octagon-shaped cage. Thankfully, I hadn't arrived too late. Spotting Sam's second biggest fan in the front row, I eased between two men arguing and plopped into the empty seat next to Ryan. Savanna's seat.

He turned to me, eyes popping. "Holy shit! Sis! What the hell are you doing here? I thought Vanna was running late."

For Sam's first fight, Ryan and Savanna had found themselves sitting next to each other. By the second round, the two most negative people alive had quickly become friends. They hadn't missed one of Sam's local fights since.

"I couldn't do it," I confessed, setting my laptop case between us. "I had to be here." He stared at me. "All right, if you must know. I begged her for her ticket. Cost me a hundred bucks."

"Sounds like Vanna."

I rolled my eyes. "Yes, she loves to be smug and superior, just like you."

"Too bad you didn't tell me your plans," he said. "We could have driven together. I don't want you driving by yourself on such a long day trip."

"I was up all night with the database and had a test first thing this morning, so I wasn't sure I'd make it. Plus, my supervisor wouldn't let me take the day off. Two other people have been out sick," I explained. "But he had a change of heart and approved the time off this morning."

"You're working way too hard," he said. "Even Sam says so. When are you going to give up the website?"

"Never."

"Then when are you going to recruit someone to help you?"

"If that's an offer, you're hired."

He smirked. "It wasn't an offer. But if you think it would help, I guess I could start pitching in a bit. It is still my school, after all."

"Good," I said, grinning as my stomach knotted with nerves. "Then we're partners."

People settled into their seats while several announcements played overhead. Ryan kept checking me, as if I had some medical condition. "Does he know you're here? He'd flip, you know."

I shook my head. "I didn't want to jinx it." Sam hadn't lost a fight, although he assured me it would still happen. I wasn't the superstitious type, but I didn't want Sam losing his first championship fight because I couldn't stay away.

"You gonna be okay?"

"I have to get through five rounds without throwing up," I said. "So no."

They announced Sam's name and all heads turned to where he came out. Jonas, his main cornerman who shouted instructions, and Bobby, his second chief who took care of Sam's cuts and bruises during the breaks, both followed him.

Samuel "Stonefish" Guerra—a nickname the media had given him due to the mysterious scars marring his torso and his reputation for quick and merciless knockouts in the first round—was the challenger and underdog.

Some referred to Sam as the Sleeper Fighter, not because the audience found him boring to watch—he'd often proven the opposite—but due to his tendency to take out his opponents with a rear naked choke, a sleeper hold, when forced to the platform by a better jiu-jitsu fighter.

The champion tonight happened to be brown belt instructor in jiu-jitsu and an accomplished boxer. Jonas and Bobby had assured me not to worry, that Sam was one of those rare fighters who often performed better when he started to lose.

Did that mean I needed to watch him lose first?

Once Jonas had learned Sam could train, he'd hired him fulltime as a boxing coach, which forced Sam to quit his other job. True to his word, Sam had taken the two junior college classes and received his high school diploma while honing his boxing, kickboxing, and Brazilian jiu-jitsu skills. Still, Jonas had thought something still lacking and quickly added Taekwondo to Sam's repertoire, hoping to discipline his mind, spirit and body to work better together.

When Sam's training began, I thought Jonas and Bobby had no idea what they were doing. The grueling regimen pushed Sam to his limits. I worried it might kill him, until I talked to several other fighters at the gym and learned this was the norm for anyone serious about a fighting career. Sam's mother's health had improved some, and beyond those three nights he stayed with Vanna when his mother had to work, Sam lived at the gym. He came to me some nights, but most nights I went to him.

In eight months' time, Sam had gone from a lean one hundred seventy-five pounds to the top of his middleweight class at one-eighty-five. Between the defined muscle and scars, he looked more like a killing machine than a twenty-year-old mixed martial arts prodigy.

I watched Sam, deeply focused as he moved closer and removed his shirt. He went through a quick inspection by the officials before they allowed him into the cage. Still flush after his warm-up, he held up his hand and gave a brief wave to the crowd as they cheered. I wondered if he was thinking about his late *papá*. No doubt, his father would have had several things to say to his son about a fight that could potentially launch him toward sponsors and a UFC career.

The announcer sounded overhead, and everybody turned to see the champion and his corner team strolling down the aisle to the center of the auditorium. The man had tattoos from neck to wrist and he'd streaked his blond hair with red lines, which resembled bloody claw marks along the sides of his head.

"Hey," Ryan said, glancing at me. "It's okay. Sam can take this guy."

I nodded, knowing he had to be right.

The ref talked to them while I measured Sam against the champion. A head taller, Sam looked lean and serious. His opponent looked bulkier and meaner.

The round began and the two immediately collided, trading blow for blow. Each vicious and brutal hit made the crowd nuts, cheering to a nearly deafening level. When Sam's head snapped a little too far to the left, I covered my eyes, unable to take it. Ryan yelled for him to "get out of there" and "move back," followed by several whoops and cheers. Time passed in slow motion, but eventually the horn blew and I opened my eyes to watch Sam walking to his corner.

Jonas and Bobby had one minute to clear the cobwebs, fix Sam, and come up with a strategy.

I was able to watch more of the second round because it looked like Sam had him beat. Then the champ slammed his knee into Sam's side three times, lifted him, and tossed him back first onto the platform. I covered my face with my hands, nauseated and wanting to cry. I heard the repetitive pounding against the platform and Jonas yelling the same instructions, repeatedly, which told me Sam had to be stuck.

I glanced up long enough to see him slammed flat to the platform again. Closed my eyes and heard another slam.

The horn blasted.

Both fighters had walked back to their corners when I looked up. Bobby held an ice pack to the back of Sam's neck while Jonas made him spit bloody water into a bucket as he talked to him. The ice would cool him quicker. Sam had red welts on his body, he was breathing hard, but he wasn't bleeding. Not externally anyway. He looked focused and nodded as he listened to everything Jonas said while taking small sips of water.

"What do you think?" I asked. "Is he winning?"

Ryan didn't blink while staring into the cage. "Um…"

Great. I started panicking as the fighters began.

The champ wasted no time and pinned Sam to the cage wall before flipping him through the air and to the platform. He was on Sam in a second, putting him in a hold that suggested he might break Sam's arm. I wanted to look away but couldn't while waiting and hoping for Sam to tap, something that Bobby told me he'd never do.

Veins bulged in Sam's neck from the pain while his fingers ground against the platform. Jonas yelled out several words I couldn't understand, no doubt a countermove, and Sam contorted himself to roll into the hold, finally breaking away. He moved his legs above his opponent's shoulders and grabbed him in a scissor-like grip, bringing the champ down to the platform. Sam jumped him, landing numerous blows to his face and shoulder. The champ flipped around, tried to get away, but Sam pulled him back and the wrestling ensued. I wanted Sam off the floor because I could never decipher who had who.

The horn took eons to sound.

When it did, I noticed Sam bleeding at the corner of his eye. He blinked rapidly and sat on the stool, pulling out his mouthpiece while Bobby took something from the ice bucket and placed it against the cut. Sam breathed hard and deep, holding his shoulder in such a way, I worried he might be injured. Jonas shook his head, making him spit out more water as he talked nonstop.

"Sam!" Ryan yelled.

"He can't hear you," I said, looking to the champ whose right eye had started to swell shut.

"Sam!" Ryan jumped. "Sam!"

I turned to Ryan. "What are you doing?"

Ryan lifted two fingers to his mouth and let out one of his ear splitting whistles. "*Sam!*" he yelled louder.

We stood close enough to Sam's corner that he heard Ryan's whistle and last shout and looked over. My brother grinned and Sam's gaze pivoted to me, his eyes rounding.

For five seconds, only Sam and I existed. He smiled but I recognized the worry in his eyes. He knew this was difficult for me to watch.

"*Acaba con él!*" I shouted, pumping both fists into the air as I bounced on the balls of my feet.

He smiled at my shout to finish off his opponent. I'd learned so many Spanish variations for punch and jab and hit while watching Jonas and Bobby train Sam. Words like *chingadazo* and *madrazo*.

Jonas smacked Sam's cheek and pointed at his eyes, telling him to pay attention.

When Sam stood again, I turned to Ryan. "Why'd you do that? You broke his concentration. Now he might lose."

"I swear it's got to be obvious to everyone but you," Ryan said, cheering and clapping loudly. "He had to know you're here. No way will he lose in front of you."

The two fighters went at each other as though it were the final round. I remembered Bobby's words about the crowd's preference for pummeling over floor work, because the second both fighters started trading kicks, punches and knee jabs, the crowd roared, sounding like an uncontainable mob.

Sam began to hit relentlessly, a series of right-handed blows. After six hits, the champ could barely jab back before taking another hit. When his hands dropped a fraction, Samuel "Stonefish" Guerra made his move. In two fluid hits, he landed a killing left uppercut, followed by his decimating right hook that spun the champ and dropped him on the platform in an unconscious heap.

The crowd roared as I grabbed onto Ryan, screaming and jumping while a blur of waves and cheers sounded around us. When I looked back to the cage, the ref lifted the new champ's arm.

I kissed Ryan's cheek, hugging him while he pulled out his phone to take a picture of Sam with his arm up. Savanna and Isabel would want the good news as soon as possible.

Sam pulled his mouthpiece out and turned to us.

"You did it, baby," I mouthed, bouncing on my toes so he'd see me.

That half-grin I loved so much formed as he pointed at me. "For you," he said.

ABOUT THE AUTHOR

Callie spent the first three decades of her life in Portland, Oregon before picking up everything and moving to the South for much needed sunshine and a change of pace. When she's not reading or penning contemporary romance and young adult novels, she's absorbed in all things supernatural, fantasy, sci-fi, anime, and of course, romance. She's also very devoted to her numerous adopted animals.

Discover other titles by Callie James:
https://calliejamesauthor.com

Please connect with me online:

Twitter: https://twitter.com/CallieJames
Facebook: https://www.facebook.com/CallieJames
Goodreads: https://www.goodreads.com/CallieJames

STUDENT BODYGUARD FOR HIRE

www.ingramcontent.com/pod-product-compliance
Lightning Source LLC
Chambersburg PA
CBHW031149120726
47905CB00006B/1870